HOOD

An Abaddon Books™ Publication
www.abaddonbooks.com
abaddon@rebellion.co.uk

First published in 2017 by Abaddon Books™,
Rebellion Intellectual Property Limited,
Riverside House, Osney Mead, Oxford, OX2 0ES, UK.

10 9 8 7 6 5 4 3 2 1

Editors: Jonathan Oliver & David Moore
Cover Art: Chris Payton
Design: Sam Gretton & Oz Osborne
Marketing and PR: Rob Power
Publishing Manager: Ben Smith
Creative Director and CEO: Jason Kingsley
Chief Technical Officer: Chris Kingsley
Hunter of Sherwood™ created by David Moore
and Toby Venables

ISBN: 978-1-78108-516-5

Printed in the UK

HUNTER of SHERWOOD
HOOD

A GUY OF GISBURNE NOVEL
TOBY VENABLES

ABADDON
BOOKS

WWW.ABADDONBOOKS.COM

For David Moore,
who was with it from the beginning.

PROLOGUE

Kyrklees Priory
November, 1161

THERE HAD BEEN two distinct screams. The first—that of a woman in agony—had jolted Prioress Elizabeth from a sleep troubled by anxious, convoluted dreams. In them, she had been lost in a desert, and she had encountered a column of cascading water in the shape of an angel. The shimmering vision had drawn attention to the Prioress's nakedness and, as the bemused woman had struggled to cover herself, began to laugh in contempt at her fumbling efforts. Scorn weirdly transformed the divine being's face: limpid water became opaque flesh. Its eyes turned pink and watery, its pale skin puffy and blotched—finally culminating in a bristled, wet snout.

A pig's face.

And the laugh... The laugh had grown in volume, ringing in her ears, its music changing from a liquid babbling to a masculine boom, and to something far worse—something less than human. It was no longer merely mocking, but mindless and chaotic; a hoarse, croaking squeal thrust in her face.

As the Prioress shuddered awake, its fading memory merged with the woman's scream.

She guessed it had been going on for some time. Beneath the cry, somewhere beyond the thick door of her cell, she already heard hissed whispers—sisters awoken by the commotion, descending from the upper dormitory. But even in her distracted state, she knew to whom that scream belonged. She had known it before her feet hit

7

the cold floor—had recognised those familiar, mewling tones even through the distortions of pain.

Mary, lately of Hoppewood. Admitted to the order just six months past. And now... what? Dying? The Prioress was briefly thrilled at the thought, but suppressed the feeling.

The girl's shriek pierced the air while Elizabeth gathered herself; the harsh tones echoed about the cold stone walls as she hurried out into the cloister.

The darkness was deep, the arches of the cloister barely visible, and the air had the bone-aching chill of night. Still several hours until the matins bell.

A glowing apparition jolted unevenly towards her along the cloister and in the direction of the cries, both hands held aloft in the misty air, one curled about a thick candle. Beyond, the Prioress could see nothing but an indistinct white shape and glowing, foggy breaths. It stopped at the sight of her, and hovered hesitantly in the dark. Several pale, ghost-like figures flitted in the background— more sisters spilling from the entrance to the day-stairs.

Another cry split the night air, then broke off into sudden silence.

"You!" snapped Prioress Elizabeth. "Don't just stand there! Light my way!"

The figure scampered forward—the young novitiate Adela, her coif half awry. A clever girl, practical, but still with much to learn. For a moment the girl dithered, unsure whether or not to walk ahead of the Prioress. Elizabeth shoved her on impatiently. "Go! Go!"

Then came the second scream, one to which the walls of the Priory were less accustomed: the thin, fragile cry of a newborn babe. At last, full realisation dawned.

"Hold the candle up, girl," snapped Elizabeth. "*Up!* I can't see where I'm going!"

The journey to the source of the screaming must have taken only moments, yet it felt like an age. Her panicked senses twisted the world into vivid but weird impressions: the looming, dancing shadows; the pulse of her heart, like a bird battering at her breastbone; that awful, impossible sound.

Sister Adela stopped dead at the door to the cell. It was not her place to enter here—and judging by her expression, she had a horror of what she thought must lie beyond. The Prioress did not hesitate, flinging open the door and pushing past into the cramped cell.

There were three within.

One was supine upon the pallet, her pale, puffy face sweaty and streaked with strands of hair. Her dull cow-eyes glinted like wet pebbles in the candlelight, and widened in terror at the sight of the Prioress. Mary of Hoppewood, sister of the Cistercian order. Now also revealed as fornicator. Somewhere beyond her fury, Elizabeth felt that warm thrill again—she had finally been handed the stick with which to beat this wretch.

The second figure quelled her mood. Crouched by her patient, momentarily frozen in the act of passing an armful of stained rags to the exhausted Mary, her long face strangely austere in the dim light, was Briga. At forty, Briga had a half-dozen years on Elizabeth— was, in truth, senior in every respect but her station. There were those said Briga could have been Prioress herself a dozen times over had she not felt her mission to be elsewhere. Elizabeth had a vivid memory from the very first week of their acquaintance when she had overheard Briga telling a younger nun: "I ask only to use these two hands to serve God" (here, she clasped her hands together) "and to help His people" (here, she spread them apart).

The admiration this humility inspired among her sisters could easily have spawned resentment, but the Prioress could not bring herself to feel it. Briga was a soul entirely free of malice, whose wisdom and support had been material in making Elizabeth's tenure the success it was.

Now, however, the older sister turned and met the Prioress's gaze with such stony resolve that it chilled her to the marrow.

A thin cry broke the spell.

The third figure present had only just come into being. As Briga completed the transfer of the wriggling bundle, Elizabeth spied its tiny hand—splayed like a starfish, grey and glistening—quiver above the crumpled cloth.

"How could you keep this from me?" she hissed, advancing.

"You, of all people!"

Briga stood, her hands raised in a gesture of defence—not of herself, but of the stricken girl upon the pallet.

"She came to me for help." Her voice was calm, matter-of-fact. "In truth, I had already guessed. Her flushed face, the swell of her breasts... When you've seen the signs as often as I..." She glanced back at the pathetic creature upon the bed and the babe now suckling upon her, her face one of pure compassion. She sighed and turned back, her expression hard once more. "She needed aid. So aid was given."

The words stung like a subtle rebuke, yet it was not this that dumbfounded Elizabeth. In every nunnery in the land there were women whom God had seen fit to bless—or test—with beauty. There were even those whose beauty and bearing seemed somehow amplified by the plain dress of the sisterhood. Sister Adela was such a one. The fact the girl herself seemed blissfully unaware of her own attributes only made it worse; the Prioress, who had known life before the priory, knew that such innocence was as likely to inflame lust as quench it. She kept a close eye on those girls.

Such was not the case with Sister Mary of Hoppewood. She was plain and dumpy, her hair red yet lacking fire, her skin pale but with an unpleasant sheen, like uncooked pastry. In fact, her whole being had the air of something *unfinished*.

Others, like Briga, did not see her this way. They spoke of her energy, her fervour. They found her hard-working and honest and full of promise, if a little lacking in character. Elizabeth, however, had always found the girl strangely disconnected. She said all the right things, to be sure, and did her duties better than most. Yet something about her gnawed at the Prioress. The mere sight of the girl turned her stomach. Several times she had snapped at her, quite unreasonably. Then she had determined to keep her at a distance, and the fruit of that strategy was plain to see.

The Prioress's revulsion had been hard to fathom. There seemed to be no cause—and this was what troubled her the most. At first, Elizabeth had done what any decent Christian would do: she had blamed herself, and had meditated hard on her own failings, striven to improve. But the feeling that there was something wrong with the girl—a profound defect that only she, the Prioress, had discovered—grew to become a certainty. As time went on, she became further convinced that the bland being that went by the name of Mary was a disguise—a puppet, skilfully animated to obscure whatever thing it was lay behind.

Quite what any man had seen in her—even in the throes of drunken lust—was utterly beyond the Prioress. A challenge, perhaps. The challenge of completing what was incomplete. Of fixing what was broken. She had found many men who were slaves to that vain urge—had, at times, seen it override all others. It originated, she supposed, from a noble impulse somewhere in the soul, and therein lay its danger. The world had less to fear from men who knew full well they were acting on base instinct than those who had convinced themselves they were doing good.

"I want her out of here," she said, her voice determinedly flat.

Briga shook her head. "She cannot go anywhere. Not tonight." There was no other who would dare defy her Prioress this way—no other to whose protests Elizabeth would listen. "She must rest and nurse the babe, or both will be at risk."

Mary, meanwhile, shot a panicked glance at the Prioress and gave a kind of whimper. From any other creature, it might have stirred Elizabeth to mercy. But with this... this... The burning fury rose in her again. She wanted to beat the girl's head against the flagstones.

"One day," she said, "then I want her gone. And this cell scrubbed clean." She turned to leave.

Before she could reach the doorway, now filled with staring faces, Briga had darted past her and slammed it shut. "Wait..."

The Prioress glared at her. "If you are going to come to her defence..."

"She has been with us just six months, and was with child before she even came to us..."

"And that *excuses* it?"

"If she were a fallen woman—"

"She *is* a fallen woman!"

"If she were a fallen woman, one who had come to us now, heavy with child and in distress, you would afford her every protection, every aid."

"She is no mere woman. She is a bride of Christ! This cannot go unpunished."

"Nor should it," said Briga. "But if there's any punishment to be meted out, then it must also be meted out to me. I brought her here. I protected her."

The Prioress clenched her jaw. Even Briga could go too far. "It is not merely a question of punishment," she said. "The girl cannot stay. Surely you must see that? This brings shame on us all."

"Of course you are right. But there are other, wider matters here..." Briga came in close, so the others might not hear. "I understand that shame, I do. As does King Henry. He is not the most pious of kings, but his mind is sharp and his eye roves everywhere, ever open to opportunity. Sadly, these facts do not work in our favour. He ever looks for reasons to reduce the power of the church in his realm. Monasteries have been closed for less, and even if that came to nought, there are benefactors upon whom we depend who would likely abandon us at the hint of scandal. And who do we help then? How do we heal? What souls do we save? We may minister to matters of the spirit, but the good Lord made us of flesh and blood, and we cannot help anyone if we do not protect our own."

Briga's arguments were always near-impossible to counter. It was her irrepressible pragmatism—her determination to serve body and soul with equal vigour. She'd left the Prioress's mind a whirl. Before she could respond, Briga stepped in closer still.

"We have known each other many years, Elizabeth. I know I have no right to speak in this way, but I do so because I know you will listen. Come what may for me, this I counsel: punish her as you see fit. Make her do her penance, for the rest of her days, if necessary—God knows, she is not likely to ever forget this. And if and when she understands and repents her sins, forgive her. Christ forgave her namesake the Magdalene, whose sins were the greater. But, above all, let her stay."

Elizabeth opened her mouth to protest, but Briga raised her palms.

"It is all she wishes from life. Keep her shame and ours safe within these walls. That way, our work can continue, and all here keep a roof over their heads."

It was a sly trick of Briga's, invoking the saint, and one with which Elizabeth could not easily argue. She stared at Briga for what seemed an age; but Briga, fearless, held her gaze.

She sighed, cast a glance at the snuffling, sweaty creature upon the pallet, and bit back her distaste. "The babe..."

"There is a couple I know past Skipton, in service of William le Gros. Their baby son died not a week ago. They have lost two before, but this one hit them hard. I am certain they will take the child as their own, and thank God for it."

"For *that?*"

"It's just a child! A boy, come to us just days after theirs was lost—and the grieving mother still with milk. I will not hide the truth from them; why should I? Sister Mary made one mistake, but she is otherwise a virtuous, hard-working girl. If we do this, both they and we are the better for it—in the world, and in here." She clutched at her breast. "What the Lord saw fit to take from them, He also, in His wisdom, has given us the means to restore."

A veteran of the pilgrimage to Santiago de Compostela, Prioress Elizabeth was not afraid to tread the difficult path. But there was no denying that the solution proposed by Briga seemed to serve the greatest good. Certainly, the alternative would be hard indeed.

The Prioress nodded. Briga exhaled in relief and grasped Elizabeth's hand. The Prioress indulged her for a moment before withdrawing it. "I will consider her punishment. And yours."

Suddenly aware that the sobbing of Mary had ceased, and sensing that she was listening intently to their conversation, Prioress Elizabeth cast a glance at her. What she saw in those fleeting seconds made her hand go to her mouth in horror. They were the eyes of a dead animal. All trace of emotion had fallen away, but it was not the expressionless mask that shocked the Prioress—it was the dark thing which, in that brief moment, seemed to flicker and uncoil behind it. What Elizabeth glimpsed behind those dead eyes was not fear, not hostility, not even dull confusion. It was no human thing at all, but a great, yawning vacancy—a limitless abyss whose formless oblivion seemed to threaten all light, all life, all meaning.

Elizabeth felt her face flush hot, and her heart thump in her breast like a bird thrashing to escape its cage. Then, as swiftly as the vision came, it went. The girl's face screwed up like the pink, bristled snout of a pig, and she snorted and wailed once more. "Oh, thank you! Thank you, Mother Elizabeth! God's grace be upon you—now and for ever!"

Prioress Elizabeth shuddered and turned back to Briga. The older woman, ever sensitive to the needs of others, was frowning at her quizzically. "Do what you must," the Prioress snapped. Her throat felt tight, her mouth dry, and she turned and fled along the dark passage without waiting for the candle to light her way.

SISTER MARY WATCHED as the Prioress departed, the nervous young novitiate flying in pursuit. As the door slammed shut, she turned back to regard the strange, alien creature upon her breast, its lips glistening with her milk.

"You understand, girl, what is to happen?" said Briga, hovering over her. Mary nodded.

"We need some mark or token. Something he may carry with him."

"Why?"

"Why...?" Briga laughed. "So you may know him, of course."

"But I am a sister of the priory."

"And so I hope you shall remain," said Briga, smoothing Mary's matted hair. "But I could not live with myself if I let this child out into the world without some means of establishing his provenance, his true blood. It doesn't mean you have to seek him out again; just that you *can*. It puts the choice in your hands—and yours alone. Choices, and the ability to make them, are blessings from God; like this poor babe, they must be nurtured and cherished."

Why not? thought Mary. Connect the progeny to the sin, and the sin to the sinner. To the man. There could be value in that...

She opened her palm to reveal a small disc of dark metal, her flesh marked red from where she had gripped it. Briga frowned as Mary held the greenish-brown thing out to her. She took it, turned it over and over. Somewhat larger than a penny and deeply tarnished, it had a crude symmetrical pattern hammered into one side. Towards the edge, a hole had been drilled, where it could be worn on a thong—and now, she supposed, would be again.

"What is it?" said Briga.

"I don't know. I found it in the forest." That was a lie. It was what the man had tossed at her afterwards. He had promised silver or gold, but by the time she had scrabbled after it and discovered no more than a worthless piece of copper, he had gone. He thought he had cheated her, no doubt, but he knew nothing of her real intentions. Though clearly of little worth to him, it also carried his lordship's emblem. A foolish oversight on his part.

And so she had kept it, perhaps to use against him; if it stayed with the bastard child perhaps she still could. She had taken him inside her because she sought his power, the power of a lord. The means of harvesting it revolted her—but that was the nature of sacrifice. It had to *matter*. And the strength was in her now.

For a while it seemed that the wild act had only delivered disaster—disaster in the shape of the child who was never meant to be, who came out of nothing, whose existence was to bring only chaos. But now, with that problem solved, she sensed a new pattern emerging, other possibilities unfolding. It seemed, perhaps, that the desired outcome may yet be achieved, albeit by an unexpected route. Such were the mysteries of the universe. It would take time, but she had found a strong ally within these walls—forged a bond with the strongest possible fighter for her cause.

She watched as Briga, ever practical, cut a length of thong from the cross about her neck, and with it tied the copper token about the child's ankle before scooping him up into her arms. "I shall tell his new parents to keep it upon him always," she said. "Remember it, Mary of Hoppewood."

There was no doubt in her mind that she would do that. Mary nodded, and squeezed a tear from her puffy eyes.

Briga rose, clutching the bundle. "I must get him away. You cannot care for him here. Tomorrow you will feel like the Devil himself has turned you inside out, but by the next day you will be feeling strong again. And all this will be as a dream." A look of great sadness fell on the elder nun. "You are sure this is what you want, child? I have fought your cause, but the Prioress would not stop you going with him."

Of course she wouldn't, she'd be glad to see the back of her. But that wasn't how this was to unfold. Mary gave a sob, made her lower lip tremble, bit it, and nodded. Briga bowed her head, and left without further word.

Mary fell back on the pallet and sighed heavily. In truth, she was grateful to Briga for taking the squalling brat. It saved her drowning it.

I

FAMINE

I

Thynghow, Sherwood
6 February, 1194

SIR RICHARD DE Percy turned his horse about, his eyes scanning the mounted men surrounding him in the dark of the icy glade. "Then we are all in agreement?" Some cried a hearty "Aye!" Others merely gave a curt nod. It did not matter. The question itself was superfluous—simply by turning up here they had shown accord—but de Percy wanted to have them declare it, all the same. And if some had come merely out of curiosity, or to see him fail, what of it? They had come.

He stopped at the top of the large, low mound and drew himself up in his saddle. "This is a historic place of gathering," he said. "Used by men since centuries past. Now it is witness to a new union, no less historic. All the lords of the North, together, for the first time. We have had our differences, God knows"—there were a few chuckles at that—"but tonight those are put aside. We stand united against the common enemy."

He held out a gloved hand, and at the signal a squire darted forward and pressed into it a leather flask. De Percy raised it high in the freezing air, his breath misting about him in a moonlit halo. "I drink to you, my lords—to unity, to God and to our certain success..." There came a gruff chorus of approval. The wine hit his throat like ice; a stray drop coursed down his chin and made him shudder. He heard the clap of one leather-clad hand against the back of another: his liegeman Thomas of Ferham, right on cue.

As others took up the applause, de Percy tipped the flask and gave a splash of wine back to the cold earth upon which they stood. An old superstition. It meant nothing to him, but much to some of those here. They would see good fortune in it.

The sound of gauntleted hands clapping against palms, thighs, and saddle pommels now filled the glade like rain. De Percy turned about again, surveying the sea of faces suspended in the glowing fog that rose from the horses. Even the naysayers, now, were with him. Grudgingly or not, he did not care; it was not their love he was after.

A rain began to spit down, but in spite of the numbing cold, he felt a smile of satisfaction spread across his face. He, Richard de Percy, still only twenty-four years old, had done this—had done what others thought impossible, and by sheer force of will. It had taken weeks of persuasion, a lifetime of talk, but he had shown them, friends and rivals alike, that he was now a force to be reckoned with. Every one of them, not so long ago, had believed the house of de Percy spent. Since the death of his father, all eyes had been on his brother Henry, the Fourth Baron—but Henry was weak in mind and body, and more often in France than England these days, patronising some shrine or other. He would not find what he needed there, and it did not help his standing, absenting himself whilst crops failed and tenants starved. Strong leadership was needed now, and Richard would supply it. Soon his brother's health would fail entirely. When it did, he would be ready. Even if it did not, he meant to show that he alone knew what was best for the house of de Percy. What was best for England.

All that remained tonight was for him to introduce the agent of his plan. Then, his standing would be assured. At the thought of it—at the unwelcome, niggling doubt that it raised—he lifted himself up in his saddle again and gazed towards the north. The position he commanded upon the top of the ancient mound—carefully calculated to place him head-and-shoulders higher than even the nearest of the surrounding barons—gave him a clear view beyond to the impenetrable black of the forest. Nothing stirred.

"When is he coming, this man of yours?" called a voice.

"He'll be here," said de Percy.

"May we not at least know who it is?" said another. "I like to know what my gold is paying for."

De Percy recognised the gruff, cynical tones of Roger de Montgard and grinned. "Believe me, Sir Roger, you will not be disappointed."

They were politician's answers—speaking without saying anything. But they were delivered with such conviction he knew none could possibly doubt him. This was something he had learned from his father in the ten short years he had known him; another of the many lessons his brother had never quite grasped. People do not need answers. They need only to *believe* you have them—that you will do what is needed on their behalf. *They say faith will move mountains,* his father had once said, shaking his head. *It will not. But it will move men. And if enough men will follow you, you may do anything. Anything at all.* Richard had always taken that as a sign that he, and not his brother, would one day lead the family. And was it not he who had brought them to this hill?

Even with the agreement of the Northern lords, however, this night had not been without its challenges. In order to preserve the secrecy of the gathering, each had been required to set out at a different time— even on different days. All were heading to a variety of destinations for perfectly plausible reasons, their journeys nonetheless carefully timed to converge on this place, at this time. Many had muttered at the wisdom of it, gathering in the forest past the witching hour, in a place said to be haunted by shucks and draugs—never mind outlaws whose arrow-points thirsted for noble blood. Then there were the unresolved disputes, the unsettled scores, the predatory opportunities—all the more keenly felt during the hardships of recent months. Since arriving, many had looked askance at old rivals, for the moment less concerned about ghosts and outlaws than a neighbour's dagger in the back.

But none of that mattered now. Provided this damned, never-ending rain finally lifted and—God forbid—his final guest didn't fail him. Already a muttering was filling the awkward silence of the glade, the barons' thoughts drifting to their beds. It was, de Percy judged, time to remind them of their purpose.

"My lords!" he called out. All eyes turned back to him. "Hood has become a problem for us all. There's not a man here has not suffered some loss because of him. It was not always so. In the past, some of us profited from his presence—standing by whilst the outlaw humiliated the Prince and his lackeys..." He let his eyes rest on those few in the gathered party who remained loyal to John. They would go with the prevailing wind when there was nothing left to cling to. Their mere presence here said as much.

"I have even heard of those who thieved their own revenues and blamed it on Hood so they might keep it for themselves and deny the Prince his due." There was laughter at that—some, de Percy knew, more out of nervousness than amusement. He wanted them to know he knew their secrets. Urging his horse forward, he wheeled before his guests, meeting the eyes of each. "Now, with the King's return imminent, our Prince is fled to France, and the game has changed. Hood's influence has grown. It is no longer a question of the damage he inflicts, the coin he thieves. He mocks us." There was a mutter of agreement. "He undermines our authority daily, sets himself up as a king in the forest. The common folk flock to his cause. They hunger, and not just for food. How long before he moves to wrest our own lands from us?" As his voice grew in volume the mutter became a rumble.

"Our King returns, but he is not here yet. His justiciars listen not to our entreaties. The Prince—a protector to some—has left these shores. Now our crops fail, and famine stalks the land. Discontent spreads like a sickness. And it is a long, long way to London..." He turned his horse and brought it to an abrupt halt. "These are difficult times. It falls to us to take action—to end Hood's rule before he exploits the weakness of the land—aye, and of us too, to his own ends. For this task I have no doubt that the King, when he comes, will show his gratitude. For let us be under no illusion—it is no longer a question of mere robbery or humble poaching. It is a question of treason!"

Some cheered. Their horses stamped. Such was the din that de Percy barely heard the whistle from the trees. He looked past the assembled throng to the branches of the forked oak, and saw the watchman perched there uncover his lantern three times. De Percy raised his hand.

"My lords! He approaches!"

II

ALL FELL SILENT. One by one, they drew their horses back from the path.

De Percy peered into the gloom. At first he could see only the barest movement in the low, swirling mist—the shimmer of moonlight on black. Bit by bit, it resolved into the shape of a man upon a horse—a stallion, as black as its night-clad rider. The figure itself was faceless, hooded and cloaked in rough black leather. It seemed otherworldly, even demonic. Some shrank back as it passed. De Percy recalled a passage in the Apocalypse of John—the one regarding the Four Horsemen. Was it Famine who came on a black horse, or Death?

For others gathered there, the strange garb was all-too familiar. As de Percy's champion neared, passing between the parted ranks of nobles, the muttering returned, here and there breaking out into grunts of protest, even cries of outrage.

This, de Percy knew, would be his most difficult moment. There was hardly a man here who had not at some time wished Sir Guy of Gisburne dead, who considered him as much an outcast as they did Hood.

Gisburne stopped his horse at the top of the gentle slope and drew back his hood. All fell into a sudden, expectant silence. It was the first time de Percy had seen him up close; he was rough and unshaven, his gear and clothing a mish-mash of unmatched parts—

more like a Flemish mercenary than a knight. More like an outlaw. The rough-clad warrior peered about with narrowed eyes.

"Whose stupid idea was this?" he said.

A chorus of protests erupted. De Percy could barely make out the words, but the anger behind them was plain enough, and some of it was now clearly directed at him. Smiling pleasantly, he rode forward and called out against the din. "Welcome, Sir Guy. Welcome indeed..."

"*This* is your proposed solution, de Percy?" growled Roger de Montgard.

"Gisburne is Prince John's scullion!" called William de Mowbray.

"No more than a common pay-sword!" shouted another. Many grunted in sympathy.

"He is also Hood's sworn enemy," shouted de Percy with sudden force. The crowd quietened. What else did they need but a pay-sword? What else had they expected for their gold? But de Percy knew this was not what offended them. It was that *this* mercenary was also a knight. One of *them*. If he could only appeal to their pragmatism... "Just one man has proved himself the outlaw's equal, and he stands before you now."

Gisburne rode four steps closer to his host and stopped. The noisy dissent ebbed into silence; all were agog to hear what Gisburne would say next.

He regarded de Percy for an age, his expression unreadable. "I was surprised to see you extending the hand of friendship, Sir Richard, considering it was from your family that Prince John wrested the land on which I now reside."

De Percy smiled as if completely at ease. "But you came, nonetheless..." he said. Then, seeing Gisburne was not going to respond further, he shrugged. "It was a small piece of land. Hardly a loss to our estates."

"Indeed. Trace its ownership further back and you will see it belonged to my father before King Richard took it and sold it to yours."

De Percy laughed. "Follow that line of reasoning, and there'd not be a man here with more than a barn in Normandy. Some not even that." There were chuckles at this. De Percy let his smile drop. "Rest assured I have no designs on your land. What every man here now owns, and can pledge to you in return for your service—*that* is the point." He gestured. "Look about you. What do you see?"

"Every noble in the North together, in Sherwood, in the open? I see a target."

De Percy leaned towards him. "You see us *united*."

Gisburne snorted. "Because your crops fail, your people starve and your revenues dwindle. It's amazing how hardship focuses the mind."

"What difference does it make where the spark came from?" shot back de Percy. "What matters is the fire. These are men who in the past have regarded each other only as enemies, now standing together. Does this not convince you of our purpose?"

He saw something in Gisburne's otherwise implacable demeanour shift and pressed on.

"Kings, princes... They are of little import in these times. Together, we lords gathered here hold sway over the whole of the North of England."

"All but Sherwood," said Gisburne.

De Percy smiled wryly. "And so you begin to divine our purpose... Well, perhaps that is not so hard. It is he who is not present, who rules over Sherwood with his rabble, who we would now see ourselves rid of."

Gisburne sighed, his breath rising in a plume of fog. "Two things, Sir Richard," he said. "First, if you think Hood is not here—that he does not know exactly what takes place in his own domain, and is not now poised in the shadows, watching this comedy unfold—then you are a fool."

There was a grumbling at that. Several eyed the darkness between the trees.

Sir Richard de Percy, however, was unperturbed. "What of it?" he snapped. Raising his voice, he turned to address the surrounding shadows. "This gathering is our message. Let him listen and know our intent. For what can he do against us all? What *dare* he do?"

Gisburne nodded as a rumble of defiance came and went. "At last count, he had more than three hundred fighting men, most of them archers," Gisburne said. "What he could do—and, yes, he *would* dare—is have arrows aimed at the hearts of every one of us at this very moment. A man in such a position could destroy all the lords of the North by the raising of his finger."

The gathered crowd ruffled like leaves in a wind. Those who had been eyeing the trees now sank deeper into their saddles.

De Percy was not yet done, however. He merely drew himself up further. "It is not whether a man *can*, Sir Guy, but whether he will. You know Hood better than anyone under heaven. So, will he, Sir Guy?"

Gisburne paused before replying. "No," he said, and there was another rumble of consternation. This time de Percy allowed himself a smile of satisfaction. "You have made it too easy for him. That's not the game he plays."

"Then help us defeat him," said de Percy, raising a clenched fist. "You understand his game. That is why I brought you here, why I present myself to you now, why we have buried our differences and gathered here." Another pregnant silence followed, broken only by the snort of horses and the distant screech of an owl.

"I said there were two things," continued Gisburne. "The second is more pertinent."

"And it is?"

"It cannot be done." A murmur of protest. "An army could not do it. You know this, or you would have done it already. Any force sent into that"—he gestured towards the thick, dense oaks, which extended unbroken for miles—"would be harried, dispersed, starved and picked off one by one. They would be game for Hood's arrows. It is *their* domain—the domain of hunters and foragers, not knights. They understand it. You do not."

"You're right," said de Percy, raising his hand for quiet. "We could not do it. But *you* could. You know this forest. You hunted here as a boy, alongside the old King..."

"The same could be said of Prince John. Perhaps you should send him."

Several guffawed at that. "You also *know* the man," continued de Percy. "His ways. His foibles..."

"And it is with that authority I say it cannot be done."

But de Percy sensed something evasive in Gisburne's demeanour. There was something about which he was not being truthful.

"But you yourself proved that it can."

"It was different before," said Gisburne. "I drew him out. He will not make that mistake twice."

"But you did catch him..."

"Aye, and let him go again!" called a wag from the crowd.

De Percy drew closer. "I know what energies you have spent in Hood's pursuit. What his capture and his escape meant to you. We wish only that you, with our aid, see this task to its ultimate end, in whatever way you see fit. In pursuit of it, we can put as much wealth and resources at your disposal as any king can muster. A deal *more* than some, I dare say."

Gisburne frowned. "Do you begin to see yourself as king now, Sir Richard?"

De Percy tensed. His horse stamped in response. "We have a king," he snapped. "And his return is assured. Until then, we do what we must." He leaned towards the dark figure. "I am loyal to King Richard, but loyalty is not enough, in these troubled times. We must also show strength. If we reveal ourselves, the guardians of the North, unable to deal with one common outlaw, well..."

Gisburne nodded slowly. "Be careful you do not appear so strong the King takes *you* as a threat, Sir Richard. The Lionheart has spent a lifetime crushing those he did."

"And doubtless he will return to that task. *In France.* He has made his feelings about our damp island plain. But we... We remain to make the best of it. These are *our* lands. And we will not let our hard-earned birthright go." He leaned forward again, his hands pressed on the pommel of his saddle. "Let me put this to you another way, one I know you will appreciate. Hood's army is growing. The people already sing of him as their champion. One clear victory, and every empty-bellied peasant who feels himself wronged will flock to his cause. And then the trickling dam will break. We would face open rebellion. Civil war. The whole of this fragile, leaderless kingdom would fall into chaos." Gisburne's expression shifted again, and he pushed home his advantage. "Fight him. Your own way. As only you know how. Defeat him at last, as you did Tancred de Mercheval in the northern islands..."

Gisburne's brow furrowed at the mention of the name. "How do you know of that?"

"I know many things, Guy of Gisburne. I know that you care for the order of this realm. That you alone can prise this grub from his tree. And that you are not a coward..."

Gisburne stared at him for a long time, and de Percy knew, finally, that he had him—that in this moment, he had won over the barons, too. "Do it, Sir Guy," said de Percy. "If not for us, then for the kingdom. For justice. For order." It did not matter that he and Gisburne were enemies. It did not matter that de Percy himself only half-believed what he had said. What mattered was that he was asking Gisburne to do the one thing the man desired above all else. As de Percy's father had been fond of saying during the Lenten fast: "Most men find it easy to resist anything—except the things they want."

"Justice!" came a scoffing voice. Roger de Montgard urged his horse forward. "I hear you have turned your hand to protecting common peasants, Gisburne. That you helped a murderer escape the noose out by Farleton not two weeks past. Is that what you call 'justice'?" His eyes flicked at de Percy and away again. "Perhaps the trouble is, you yourself are a little too much like Hood."

A group at de Montgard's back muttered agreement. De Percy fumed—but it was Gisburne who beat him to the response.

"The man was not a murderer," he said. "I spoke for him, not because he was a peasant, but because he was innocent."

"Innocent?" said de Montgard. "He shot an arrow through the heart of a tax collector from the upper window of his cottage. In broad daylight, no less! And now he's free. Free to run and join the other troublemakers in Sherwood, who make outrages like this a daily occurrence!" There were cheers this time.

"If there's one thing that proliferates during a famine, it's enemies of tax collectors," said Gisburne, then shook his head. "That man shot no arrow."

"Two men witnessed him at the window," insisted de Montgard. "One saw him draw and shoot with his own eyes. And there was a longbow found in the house."

Gisburne turned fully to face him. "Damn near every house in England holds a bow. And the arrow entered the body not from a high angle, but straight. It was shot by someone standing upon the ground, not the window."

"And the man who saw him draw?"

"A liar. One who had been in dispute with the accused man in the past; very likely himself the murderer."

"By what authority do you assert such a thing?"

"By the authority of common sense. Have you ever tried to shoot a longbow from a cottage window, Sir Roger? Have you even set foot in such a place? If you had, you would know what his judges plainly did not—that such an act is impossible. That damned bow was six feet long. The ceiling by that window was barely five-feet-and-a-half high and the dormer no more than three wide. These are not castles with high ceilings and arrow slits; one could no more shoot a longbow from that window than send a horse down a rabbit hole."

"Fa-doodle!" sneered a voice in the crowd. De Percy recognised the mannered tones of Simon de Shirburn. "Are these the same jongleur's tricks you employed in London when Hood led you a merry dance and gave you the slip?" The speaker—and several around him—snorted at the jibe.

"You of all people should know I speak the truth, Sir Simon," said Gisburne. He did not even bother to look in the knight's direction. "It is by the same trickery that I know you grew up in just such a cottage. The castle in your own demesne has high lintels, yet when I saw you last in Nottingham I noticed you duck your head each time you pass through a door. You have done well to hide your humble origins, but some habits are hard to break. Good of your late father to acknowledge his bastard, though." One or two laughed at Sir Simon's expense, but there were rumbles as well.

"Enough!" roared de Percy, shocking the assembled men into silence. "This bickering is pointless. We know why we are here.

What we want." He eyed Gisburne. "What we *all* want... We await only Gisburne's word for the deal to be struck. Then we can all be free. Well, Gisburne, what do you say?"

Then the one thing happened for which de Percy was not prepared.

"I say no."

For a moment, de Percy did not grasp his meaning. "No?"

"I am done with Hood." Looking around, the rain pattering more heavily against his horsehide coat, he added: "And you could have asked me this in a tavern."

De Percy stared, dumbfounded, as Gisburne started to turn his horse around.

The lords began to mutter, all eyes once more on de Percy. He felt his head throb. His neck grew hot. Suddenly, it seemed this meeting, this night, everything he had planned—his entire future—was slipping away from him. His mind racing, De Percy rode forward, blocking Gisburne's path. "Done with him?" he said, with a dry, humourless laugh. "How can you be done with him? How can you not see this to its end?"

"Because it's what he wants," said Gisburne. "I am done doing my enemy's bidding." And he began to manoeuvre his horse around de Percy's.

"You'll not leave here, Gisburne!" called de Montgard. De Percy turned and saw the old man advancing, sword drawn. "If we can't deal with one pest tonight, we might as well rid the world of another!"

Others now drew their swords as de Montgard, just yards from Gisburne, raised his blade... then suddenly stopped.

It was a sound that had stayed his hand, that made them all stop dead, in frozen silence.

It was, of itself, unremarkable: the sound of one leather-clad hand clapping against another. Slowly, languidly. What marked it out was that it came not from the gathered company, but beyond, from the trees.

III

"EXCELLENT!" CALLED A reedy voice. "A fine night's entertainment!"

De Percy saw Gisburne's face register the shock of recognition. All eyes now turned towards the distant speaker—and from the shadows at the edge of the forest walked a dozen or more horses. As de Percy clapped eyes on the rider in the midst of them, his jaw fell slack.

Prince John, circled by twelve Norman mercenaries, dressed for war.

"Not fled to France, as you see. Well, not just yet, anyway." There was a buzz of consternation among the assembled nobles. The Prince looked drawn and tired, but nonetheless managed to muster his customary smirk. "You must pardon the intrusion, but I thought it the opportune moment to announce myself. Do please put that sword away, Sir Roger, before someone gets hurt."

De Montgard gaped, his blade drooping. William de Mowbray flapped, as if he was trying to speak. John waved a dismissive hand. "No, Sir William, before you say it, I was not invited. But you cannot imagine I take no interest in what goes on in my own lands—especially when my brother's Great Council seeks to boot me off them."

"This is Gisburne's doing!" hissed de Montgard, finally finding his voice.

"No, it was not Gisburne who told me," said John. "Formidable as his talents are, they are no longer put to work for me." He looked momentarily pained. "All the better for him, things being what they are. But you may thank me later for saving your life, Sir Roger."

"Thank *you*?"

"Had I not interceded, and had you made your attack on Sir Guy, you would undoubtedly already be dead."

De Montgard glared at Gisburne. "Other blades would have followed mine. But for you, he would not have left this glade alive."

The Prince narrowed his eyes. "I wouldn't bet on it, Sir Roger. And I am quite the betting man." He broke his horse away from the escort and rode forward through the assembled barons, eyeing their swords, still drawn against each other. "It would seem your alliance is more fragile than you thought, Sir Richard. That's the trouble when loyalty is freely given. Even my trusted Sheriff, William de Ferrers, has seen which way the wind is blowing and defected to the other side. That is why, on the whole, I prefer to *pay* for loyalty— although there have been one or two exceptions..." He drew close to Gisburne. "You are well I hope, Sir Guy?"

"I could be worse. And you?"

De Percy marvelled at the familiar manner with which this dishevelled figure addressed his Prince, as if the two were equals.

Prince John gave a weak smile. "I could be better," he replied. "Well, anyway... Here we all are. I confess I've always wanted to know what my loyal barons get up to at night." He turned his horse about, as if surveying them, then looked back at Gisburne. "I also wanted to know what your answer would be."

"You came all the way out here just for that?" said Gisburne.

John smiled. "I'm often hearing stories that my pleasures are perverse. But it's enlightening to know how one is regarded, is it not Sir Guy?" He turned back to the barons. "I also wished to look upon your happy faces one last time before departing for France—to know better what lay behind them. And that, I believe, I have done. Something to bear in mind for when I return, which I shall." He narrowed his eyes, then broke into a smile again. "Anyway... Since it is such a bitter night, and since Gisburne is not taking up your offer, perhaps we can all now return to the comfort of our beds?"

"My lord," pleaded de Percy, "we need him..."

"You have his answer. I have no say in the matter."

De Montgard snorted dismissively and muttered something about having "no stomach for a fight."

As little as a week ago, none would have dared do such a thing in John's presence, but circumstances were making them bold.

"I would trust Sir Guy's judgement on this matter, Sir Roger," said John, tersely. "And with regard to my stomach for a fight—if it is mine to which you refer—you will not be surprised to learn that I differ greatly from my brother. When Longchamp was cowering in the Tower, I knew I had only to wait. So my army did nothing. They sat and ate and drank in comfort. A good day's work, for them. None were injured, none died. Their bellies were full. My brother, the great warrior general, would have thrown them at the impregnable walls and wasted dozens of lives. Doubtless it would have rooted out Longchamp in the long run and been hailed as a great victory. But that is not my way. Much as I enjoy extravagance, I also abhor waste—as should you, in these straitened times."

De Percy's anger welled up. "Gisburne would do it if you told him to."

John smiled. "My, but you're a saucy fellow, de Percy... We'll have to keep an eye on you. Perhaps he would; but I have released him from my service. And I am a man of my word." A mix of laughter and disapproval erupted at his claim. "To those I respect, at any rate," added John above the commotion.

"Your word?" grunted de Montgard. "You've broken your word to half the men here!"

"Well, there you have it..." said John, and smiled. The laughter died; the grim mutterings did not. John pressed on. "The fact of the matter is that Gisburne is now his own man. Who else here can say that?"

De Percy had thought he could, until just moments ago. The evening had begun with him basking in the hard-won respect of his peers, brimming with confidence—in control. Now, all was in tatters. He brought his horse close to Gisburne again, his voice little more than a whisper. "I don't understand. You know you can do this. I see it in your eye. It could bring you wealth, success, respect—yes, even among those here. It could make you a man of influence. A man others would fight to know. All that is yours for the taking..."

Gisburne looked past him. "It is not whether a man *can*, Sir Richard, but whether he will."

And with that, he turned his horse and rode back into fog and darkness.

IV

The village to which no roads lead
February, 1194

MICEL STARED AT Hood's beaming smile and saw nothing behind it. The outlaw's big hand clapped him roughly on the shoulder, then those teeth—the whitest Micel had ever seen—flashed in the bright sunlight, and Hood turned and strode with fierce energy along the ranks of archers waiting their turn to shoot at the butts.

There were more fighting men here than Micel had ever seen. They were looking less like outlaws now, and more like soldiers. He was not party to Hood's grand plan, but one old man-at-arms who had seen service under King Henry spoke of it as preparation for war. He knew the signs, he said. Micel felt a strange thrill at it, and saw Hood's eyes blaze as he surveyed them. But it was a cold fire, and the thrill knotted his stomach.

Behind Hood's left shoulder walked the monk, Took. At the other, the cutthroat Will Gamewell—who they called "the Scarlet." Both were feared, if for quite different reasons. Behind them walked John Lyttel, and at his heels trailed Micel—now known to all by the name Hood had given him, Much. Lyttel had taken on the mantle of Micel's protector since the boy's arrival, and Hood had never ceased to find amusement in the odd pairing, with their ill-fitting names. "Lyttel understands Much, and Much understands Lyttel!" There were seemingly endless variations upon this theme. That John Lyttel was no longer greatly amused by these quips was plain to see; these days, he did not even pretend to smile. Now, the big man's head was bowed, and even from behind, Micel could tell his eyes were fixed on the ground. Micel worried about him—about his fate. He wanted to throw an arm about the big man, laugh and cajole a smile out of him. But somehow, in spite of everything, he lacked the will.

"Extra rations of the Prince's venison if you get all three arrows within the garland!" Hood slapped the nearest man on the shoulder as he passed—hard enough to almost knock him off his feet. But the man beamed. The rest gave a hearty cheer, and urged on those who were shooting with renewed vigour.

Micel felt his heart lurch at that cheer, and he understood, more keenly than ever, that he was alone. A failure. It seemed the harder he tried to serve his master, the harder it became. Sometimes he envied the others their unquestioning faith.

It had all been so simple when Robin Hood's band was a distant, seemingly unreachable goal. An ideal. It was easy to love him then. But then the dream had become reality; the ideal, a real man. As Micel had drawn closer to his idol—revelling, as everyone did, in the man's ability to inspire all around him—that vision had begun to blur. As the ideal faded, so other unwelcome details came into focus: the sweat on his shirt, the blood beneath his nails.

Then there was the occasional look in Hood's eye, beyond the heroic defiance. To Micel, it looked like cruelty, though it had not once been directed at him. After the escape from the Tower, Hood had even afforded him the greatest honour possible, admitting him to his inner circle; had given him the mark, shared only by the most trusted: Took, Lyttel, Scarlet, O'Doyle... and Marian. He looked at the crude tattoo upon his wrist—the snarling head of a wolf—and itched at it. Why he had been so honoured, he was not certain. A couple of those Hood kept close had fallen from favour of late, so perhaps he was looking to the future. Ensuring a supply of fresh blood. Whatever the reason, his master had shown him such favour that to disappoint him seemed, to Micel, the worst thing imaginable.

Lyttel had been some help at first, but not now. The big man had been withdrawn of late. Micel had no idea now what went on in that shaggy head, and, in truth, he feared finding out.

No. It was *his* problem—his failing—and he would fix it alone.

These were challenges to be overcome, like those God had sent to His most devoted, to test them, and he would serve Hood to the end. Apart from anything else, Micel yearned to recapture that heady thrill he had once felt when he looked upon his master. It was, perhaps, the one thing driving him on. He wondered if Christ's disciples underwent such struggles. Thinking so was a help to him.

Hood stopped before the rock that marked the far edge of the village, and turned and turned again, as if looking for somewhere else to go; but there was nowhere, except back again. Along the same ranks of archers. The gleaming smile faltered, and gave way to a flicker of explosive rage, as fingers flexed into claws. It was fleeting, but in that moment Micel felt he was looking upon a terrible beast pacing the limits of its captivity. Hood drew his leather gloves from his belt and slapped them against his palm in irritation.

Normally, Hood laughed through all eventualities, but his great plan, and their increasing activity, had involved restraint, a quality that did not come naturally. His mood had worsened in the past couple of days, when something had failed to come to pass. For some time beforehand he'd seemed expectant of something—something that filled him with almost child-like glee. Micel did not know what it was, although he had heard Hood repeatedly refer to a "guest." How a guest was to be welcomed in this secret place, or who it might be, Micel could not imagine, but for days, their master had refused all but the simplest food, saying he would feast when their guest joined them. Sometimes he seemed to speak of their unknown guest as an old friend, other times as an enemy. Often, both.

Then, two nights before, the joyous anticipation had suddenly been crushed. Micel had been in Hood's great hall, building the fire, when several of Hood's spies came to him with news of a clandestine gathering in the forest. Of Barons. Eyes flicked in Micel's direction, and the rest was whispers. Hood's eyes burned with fury. He bared his teeth and kicked a smouldering log across the rush-covered floor, sending a shower of sparks up to the rafters. Micel chased after the log, only barely managing to stamp out the burning rushes. Oblivious, Hood had snatched up his bow, stalked out into the night and, with a roar of wild rage, had loosed an arrow at the moon. The great, gnarled warbow was bent so far, and the arrow flew with such power, that Micel wondered if it would ever come to earth.

Hood had been like a caged animal ever since.

He turned and slapped his gloves against the towering rock, as if challenging the earth itself to combat. It was from this rock that Hood addressed the faithful, and he alone stood upon its pinnacle. Took and occasionally Will Gamewell had at times spoken from the rock—at one time, even John Lyttel had been afforded the privilege—but none presumed to stand upon the very top. That was Hood's place; a spot that Lyttel had once jokingly referred to as "the pulpit." None had laughed, and Lyttel had stayed quiet after that. The rest did not even dare to touch the rock, now. Not in plain sight. But every once in a while, late at night, Micel spied a ragged peasant place a surreptitious hand upon it, as if hoping to draw divine energy from a holy relic.

Something made Hood turn—notes of music piercing the excited chatter of voices. A jaunty tune, plucked upon an instrument; a man's voice, trilling some absurd lines of doggerel. A woman's laugh. Micel sought out the sound, and through the milling crowd, near the cooking fires, spied the Irishman Alan O'Doyle—and opposite, the Lady Marian. Micel had not seen either of them smile in days, and then only in each other's company. O'Doyle plucked the lute again and pulled a face. Marian laughed and placed a hand upon his arm. Looking back at Hood, Micel saw his master's eyes fixed upon them.

Hood grinned and nodded cordially as O'Doyle's gaze met his. The Irishman dutifully nodded back, and Hood's empty grin widened, his eyes glinting like black stones. Then Micel heard his cold voice mutter: "That minstrel's got to go..."

Something made Hood look up then—a sound Micel had not even heard. His master stepped forward and frowned as if to listen harder. There was, finally, a distant whistle, then another. A lone figure wove through the throng, which parted before him. The archers ceased their practice, and the chatter hushed. All eyes turned on the man as he fell to his knees at Hood's feet.

"Well?" said Hood, his eyes wide.

"The moment you have been waiting for has come, my lord..." panted the runner.

"I am not your lord. No man is." Hood knelt down and leaned his head forward to hear the messenger's urgent whispers.

Micel just had the opportunity to register a look of triumph upon Hood's face before his master stood suddenly and gripped him by the shoulder. "Rose!" Hood bellowed. Marian looked up in response. No one dared call her anything but Rose now. Micel saw her face fall, become drawn once more. "Come!" Hood gestured, and she hurried forward.

A moment later, Micel found himself standing by Hood's side upon the pinnacle of rock, with Marian upon the other.

"My friends!" called Hood. As he spoke, a silence fell, so total that even the wind in the trees seemed to abate. Micel had known there were many hundreds here—far more than this village could sustain—but seeing this multitude now stretched out before him, he felt his mouth go dry and his knees quiver.

"News has come to me that I must share with you," said Hood. "News for which we have been preparing these many months, and which cuts to the very heart of all we have become. In this place— upon nothing—we have built a family."

At that, Micel felt Hood's right arm around his shoulders, and saw that the outlaw's left was wrapped about Marian's slender waist. They were a tableau, an image of a perfect family.

"Who are we?" continued Hood. "We are the people that they did not want, the ones on the roadside, that they wished to imprison and kill. Is it because we are *evil* that they did this? No! It is because we are a reminder of their failures. Of their wilder natures.

"And who are *they?* They are the ones who flex their muscles to show their strength, their superiority. But those with real strength have no need to prove it. And we shall show them how weak they are. They eat meat with their teeth and they kill beasts that are nobler than they are—these things they have never truly had to fight for—and then have the gall to condemn those who possess *real* strength.

"They put you in a dark cell, and to them that's the end. To me it is the *beginning!* There is a world in there, and I'm free. It matters not what walls they build. Walls are nothing! We're all our own prisons, we are each our own jailer. A prison is in your mind... And can't you see I'm free?

"They expect to break me... Impossible! They do not know how Robin Hood thinks, because Robin Hood has not yet shown them his true self. I show people how I think by what I do, and do it I shall. There is pain along this path, to be sure. But pain is worthy. It teaches you things. And through it I have learned their game.

"They thought they could lock me in a dungeon and forget about me. But they can't forget. They will *never* forget. They think that if I am dead, their world will be better. But I'm what lives inside each and every one of them, had they but the courage to look. And it is because they lack that courage that I know we will win. They whimper and squirm and peep over the parapet at the shadow of their own death. They think of nothing else. But in my mind I live forever. I am not ruled. We are not ruled; *they* are ruled. By fear: of the dark, of the forest, of the wolf.

"My friends, the world is turned upside down. But we shall put it aright. This land is on the brink, on the very *edge* of chaos. And *we* may now tip the balance! I don't blame *them* for this precarious state. No, I blame King Richard! Yes, yes, it's true! This land is his, after all. His task was defending his people instead of deserting them to fight in foreign climes. What kind of king is it that swaps the rich garden of England for the desert, and leaves the tending of it to an outlaw like me? I'll tell you... It is one who understands that we must be *tested*. Like a new-forged blade, we must be plunged into the fire to emerge the stronger. He gave us this opportunity to show our mettle. He set an example to us—of iron will, of steel in battle. Of an unbending weapon with the strength to do what must be done.

"And so we must also be thankful to them—the rich, the high-born, the privileged, the weak, the pious, the pompous. For here we stand, because of them. We are all their children.

"They will say I made you do what we are about to do. But you will know that is *not true*. You know that we are a new and better kind of family—one they cannot understand. One founded on new rules. On *no* rules. A pack, bound by more than blood. And I will tell them: 'These children that now come at you with bows and spears and knives, *you* taught them. I did not teach them. I just helped them to stand.'

"And to you now I say this: if you are not strong enough to stand on your own, do not come and ask me what to do. I want no weakness around me. I don't tell people what to do, I simply... do. That is my one law. Be as you truly are. Become your true self. And do what you must do. And so, he who has no stomach for this fight, let him leave now. Freely.

"You have endured much to be here. This forest is wide. It can shelter, clothe and feed a band of good, determined men. Good swordsmen, good archers, good fighters! But we are not beasts born to cower—not boar or deer for them to hunt, for them to consume in pretence of supremacy. Nor were we made to grub a living amongst these dank roots, the stink and rot of dull nature. But this long night draws to an end, and from this forest we shall be reborn to a new life! A life in the full glare of the sun, where all is bathed in light and seen equally. I have heard it said that to see all at once with equal clarity is madness. Chaos. But those who say it are cowering in the dark dungeons of their own minds.

"We are sworn to despoil the rich. But you all know I do not covet gold. What means gold to me? Gold crowns are *trinkets!* There is a greater treasure: to *become* golden, to be bathed forever in sunlight, to live and be remembered in the mouths of men, and in their minds be forever bright. Let me tell you now: King Richard returns, and our day has come.

"Had I not seen the sunshine in the desert, perhaps I would be satisfied with the cell. It was the Lionheart first showed me the sun in all its glory, though he knew it not. And so I say, it is time to emerge into the light! To stand exalted by our King, to join with the lion, and show that the wolf, too, is strong, that like he we are not the ruled, but *born ourselves to rule!*"

As the speech had gone on, the chuckles, gasps and rumbles of assent had grown in volume and intensity, until finally, at Hood's last utterance, the crowd had cheered with such force that Micel felt his head spin, and the rock tremble beneath his feet. And yet, as the hundreds of voices battered him, he found his streaming eyes fixed not on the triumphant multitude, but on the distant, ragged, empty-eyed figures who lay dying or slumped against trees at the edges of the village—skeletal outcasts now too weak, or too old, to draw a bow.

V

Village of Gisburne
9 February, 1194

GISBURNE ARRIVED HOME exhausted. It had been a hard ride from Halifax, but despite the temptation to stop there, with night falling and the threat of imminent rain, he had pushed on. He yearned for his own walls about him, the satisfaction of his own front door closing at his back. And solitude; that too. Though that could be a mixed blessing.

Weary and damp as he was, his heart leapt when he finally caught sight of the squat, thatched manor house along the turn in the road. It was a feeling that had not changed since childhood—one he had often longed for on the battlefields of France, Byzantium and the Holy Land. These days, it came into view somewhat sooner, thanks to the newly built round tower at its western end. It loomed above the trees, its fresh-cut stones almost white in the moonlight; an addition his father had often dreamt of, but never had the funds to achieve. The old man's ambitions always had exceeded his means. He once nearly bankrupted himself to donate a pair of stone pillars to the local church. The privations it caused were felt by the family for months afterwards—but it was, he felt, appropriate to a knight of his station. Or, perhaps, of the station to which he aspired. Immediately after his encounter with the Red Hand, Gisburne had set work in motion; not for his own sake—he had no dream of being a castellan—but for his father's memory. The work was now almost complete, only the harsh winter weather had brought the masons' work to a stop.

The house itself was silent. No light burned in the window. No smoke issued from the chimney. Gisburne rode straight on to the stable. He knew full well that if he allowed himself to get settled inside the house, stirring himself to stable his horse would be all the harder.

Nyght, his mount, got short shrift all the same. He would sort him out properly tomorrow, though he had no doubt the stallion would show his displeasure for the whole of the next day. At times like this, he almost regretted having no groom.

There were no servants in Gisburne's house—no one to keep the hearth warm in his absence. This was something visitors would have found peculiar, but he never had any. Not that he was entirely bereft of help; the Horton woman cleaned and laundered, her husband cooked and maintained the property, and their elder boy tended the horses when needed—all tenants of the modest Gisburne estate. But they came and went, and of late he had given even them leave when he was in residence. Beyond that there were only the tenant farmers who worked the land, and by and large he left them to their own devices. Or rather, under the watchful eye of Old Oswald of Sawley, who had managed the day-to-day running of the estate since his father's day. And in turn, they left him to his. There were stories told of him and his ways, he knew—most of them pure fiction. Well, let them talk.

He did not mind doing things himself. It pleased him to keep busy, and besides, he liked things his own way. After years of self-reliance on the road and in battle, fighting for pay with not even a squire to support him, such ways had become ingrained.

Once, there had been a squire about the place, but he did not want to think about that. It served no useful purpose.

Rummaging in his purse in semi-darkness, he felt the distinctive, heart-shaped bow of the iron key. He turned it in the lock, feeling the dry grate of early rust, and pushed inside. The shutters were closed, the interior pitch black. Dumping his saddle bags, he stumbled in through the dark, thought about pushing the far shutter open, then changed his mind. His eyes would adjust soon enough.

He crouched by the hearth and made a token effort to light a fire, but the damp had well and truly set in and the tinder was having none of it. His will sapped, he pulled a sheepskin about him and sat in darkness, chewing on a chunk of stale bread and some dried meat until, finally, even being half-upright was too much, and he slumped down upon the musty straw pallet that he kept near the main fireplace.

DESPITE THE TIREDNESS deep in his bones, sleep eluded him. He lay for a long time, listening to the familiar sounds of the house. The creak and crack of timbers, the rattle of shutters. The whine of the wind in the thatch. Somewhere above him, a mouse or bird scratched. A fox barked in the distance. And, off towards the paddock, in harmony with the sighing of the trees, he could hear the squeak and clank of Sir Pell.

Sir Pell had been Gisburne's idea; but it had taken the genius of Prince John's enginer, Llewellyn of Newport, to realise it, and to christen it. Frustrated in his fight training by the bland simplicity of the traditional wood-and-straw pell—really, little more than a scarecrow—and seeking something more challenging than the quintain, Gisburne had determined to devise a new kind of device: one that would react, move and fight back. Llewellyn's initial suggestion, cutting as ever, was that what Gisburne needed was another human being. The challenge had fired his imagination and, after a month of discussions and experimentation by Llewellyn, Sir Pell was born.

It stood out there now, in the training yard, a curious wooden contraption with a multitude of swivelling arms upon complex pivots and gimbals, each of them made not only to swing in response to blows, but also to set others in unpredictable motion, and so constructed that Gisburne could place almost any weapon in each of its limbs. And challenge him it certainly did. Once, during a particularly energetic session, it had knocked him out cold. He had lain on the ground, undiscovered, for at least two hours before coming to. For a good few minutes more he had stayed where he was, taking stock of his injuries and imagining all of Llewellyn's possible comments. *Hm! Perhaps Prince John should have been sending Sir Pell on these missions rather than Sir Guy...*

The solitary life had its drawbacks, as he'd learned earlier that winter. It had begun with weary limbs and a throat like rusted iron, progressing to the inevitable cough and streaming nose. But when the cough had persisted for two and three weeks, bit by bit robbing his limbs of strength and his lungs of breath, he had finally taken to his bed. His chest began to throb. His head swam with fever, and for a time he had lost his certain grip on life.

For days—how many, he did not know—he lay, too weak to sit up, barely able to sip water from his flask; eventually, it ran out. He felt his mouth dry out, and then listened to his own rasping breath with detached fascination. For some time, he had strained to hear what he thought to be the distant voice of a child crying—only to realise the sound was coming from within his own chest.

During the fever, he thought he heard someone rap on the door, but only once. He supposed they presumed him to be away, or were respecting his fiercely-guarded privacy. He even wondered, in his distracted state, if they were a little afraid of him. Several times he heard the boy outside come to feed and clean out the horses, but was too feeble to call out. On one occasion, he had opened his eyes to see the twitching pink snout of a rat sniffing at his face. He hazily thought to swat it away, but he found that his arm, like the rest of his body, no longer belonged to him. He vaguely wondered if this would remain the case even when the rat started to gnaw at it. But, finding him of limited interest, it had turned and wandered off.

Strange visions came to him. He saw glossy black ravens, hundreds of them, perched all about the walls. A dead man paced the room restlessly, somewhere just out of sight—somehow he knew it to be the grey corpse of his dead mentor, Gilbert de Gaillon. At one time Gisburne looked down at his body and saw it covered not with a blanket, but by the shimmering, shifting bodies of a vast army of wasps.

Then, one day, he awoke suddenly stronger, and determined to venture outside, barely getting past the door before collapsing, breathless, in the blinding sunlight. He awoke again propped up in bed, with Richild the laundress coaxing spoonfuls of broth between his lips. Never had he felt so glad to see another human face, but it was the look upon it that told him that he had probably come closer to dying in these past few days than he had ever done in all his years of battle.

Gisburne had emerged leaner of body, and more circumspect of mind. In the weeks that followed, as he had returned to life, he had gradually resumed his training. He put Sir Pell through his paces. He set up targets throughout the wood west of the paddock, and practised his archery skills. The bow helped build strength in his arms and chest, and was good for his ailing left shoulder—weak since his ordeal at Hattin.

He saw no one, and often days passed when he spoke only with his horses. Sometimes at night he sat alone, the hurdy gurdy he had brought back from the Holy Land upon his lap, and cranked out a mournful tune. Gisburne was not normally one to be sentimental about objects—they were tools, solutions to problems—but the fact that this fragile thing had survived such an ordeal made it precious to him. Perhaps he saw in it his own ordeal, his own survival— especially after his trials that winter. The wood still had the ripe smell of Jerusalem's sewers when warm.

During his recovery there had been no demands on his time except those he made himself—not until de Percy's intriguing message had lured him to that absurd midnight gathering. But perhaps that had been just as well. Rehabilitation would not be rushed.

Even now, as he lay on the pallet that had once almost been his death bed, listening to the creaks and knocks of Sir Pell, he knew he was not back to full strength. Judging by the sounds, the mechanism was moving too freely, too wildly. One of the arms had worked loose in the wind. He knew he should probably go and tie it down, but the will eluded him. The wind wasn't strong; it would be fine until morning.

A horse whinnied. It sounded like something had upset Nyght. Maybe Gisburne would have to stop the clatter of Sir Pell after all. The sound came again, more insistent. Last time Nyght had made a fuss like that, it had meant rats in the stables. Gisburne groaned and lay for a moment, willing his horse to settle, listening to the pattering rain.

Then came a sound so familiar, yet so alarmingly out of place, that he found himself on his feet before his brain had even registered what it was.

The chink of a spur.

He pulled on his boots and his tattered black gambeson, fastened one buckle upon its front and threw his hauberk on over it. Then he drew his sword, let the scabbard and belt fall to the floor and felt the fine rain on his face as he cracked open the door.

VI

THERE WAS NO sign of movement in the yard, beyond the sway of the trees and the rhythmic clunk of Sir Pell. But he knew they were there.

Nyght whinnied again. Another horse answered his call—from somewhere in the depths of the woods. It would not be the only one. If what he had heard was indeed the chink of a spur, that meant a knight, and knights did not travel alone—nor did they come on social visits at night. Gisburne knew precious few who would even visit during daylight. Perhaps de Percy had dispatched men to try to persuade him further.

Or to kill him.

He moved across the yard, holding his sword low, the rain barely more than a mist, clinging to his face and hair, sending cold rivulets down his neck. He shivered, looked across at the weird shadow of Sir Pell, one arm appearing to wave in warning, and headed towards it. He had no doubt now they were in the trees at the northern edge of the yard; if they hadn't seen him before, they would now. Well, let them. He tucked his sword under his arm and turned to Sir Pell, pulling the rattling limb back into place and securing it to the frame with its wet leather thong.

"You might as well come out," he called to the trees. "We can't stand here all night."

For a moment, it seemed his voice had met with only empty gloom. But then came movement: heavy footfalls on the wet, gritty earth. Gisburne gripped his sword and turned to see a great cowled figure—over six feet tall and broad-shouldered—step out of the shadows. There was something immediately, disturbingly familiar about his bearing. Six yards from him, the figure stopped and threw back its hood.

So astonished was Gisburne at what he saw that his sword nearly fell from his hand. It was a face he had not seen in ten years—a face that no one within these shores had seen for at least five. The most well-known face in all the land.

Richard the Lionhearted, King of England.

"It cannot be..." said Gisburne.

"And yet here I am," said Richard.

The King took a step forward, and Gisburne felt the grip on his sword tighten. What kind of trick was this?

"How do you come to be here? How is this possible...?"

"I am a king. I do what others can't."

"That's no answer..."

"A year ago I was dead, or so my brother swore before God. But I stand before you all the same. How many do you know can do that?"

Good God. Did he really just compare himself to Christ? Without a hint of irony? "I suppose I should be used to people looming out of the shadows by now. But does no one meet by daylight any more? And out of the rain?"

Richard looked at the moon, now almost obscured by cloud, squinting against the icy rain. "You know, there's nothing I'd change about this dismal country more gladly than the weather. And yet I return to find it's one of the few things that is exactly the bloody same."

Gisburne heard a muffled snort of laughter from the trees to his left. Almost simultaneously, over to the right, deep in shadow, he sensed another movement. He had no doubt that Richard had him covered by at least a half-dozen crossbowmen.

"Is that what you're here for? To talk about the weather?"

Richard's countenance darkened. "Much has changed since I went away. But things are soon to be put aright."

Gisburne's mind raced. Much had indeed changed—much that could doubtless inflame the legendary Plantagenet temper. The question was, what in God's name was the newly returned King of England doing here, now, in the rain, talking to *him?* He wielded no power; he was not a bishop or a baron. Most did not even know of his existence, and many who did would sooner forget it. And yet, indisputably, Gisburne had been a key instrument of many of those changes. For three years he had served as right hand to the King's rebellious brother, during which John had all but waged open war against Richard's representatives in England, had hindered efforts to have the captive king freed and even sought the aid of Richard's most detested enemy, Philip of France, in his efforts to take the empty throne.

As far as Gisburne could see, just one possibility presented itself. "Are you here to kill me?"

Richard stared at him for a moment, the rain dripping off his neatly clipped red beard. Then the blank face broke into a smile, and the smile into a great, hearty laugh. From the shadows, his crossbowmen joined in. Ten of them, Gisburne judged.

"You think *you* are first amongst my enemies? No, Sir Guy, you do not have that dubious honour." The smile dropped, leaving no trace of its passing, and those in the shadows fell suddenly silent. "But there is one who concerns me..."

My God, he means me to turn against Prince John. Gisburne was no longer bound to the Prince by duty, but there was still a question of loyalty, of friendship. Of what was right.

"As it happens, you were right to doubt my presence," said Richard, pulling off his gauntlets. "In fact, I am not here. I have not yet arrived. But I shall." He wiped his bare hand about his beard and flicked the rainwater away. "On the twentieth day of next month, my ship will arrive on the Kent coast, to be met by my mother Queen Eleanor and a cheering crowd of loyal subjects. A hero's welcome. A day of rejoicing. It's all arranged."

"So what I see before me now is a just a ghost?" said Gisburne.
"Well, why not? Perhaps I'm dead too. It would explain a lot, such as why I only ever seem to converse with people at night."

"Consider this... reconnaissance. Life is a series of battles; my return is the next of them. And in battle, timing is everything. If I can also prepare the ground to my advantage, all the better."

"You forget, I've seen your methods, though I was just an ignorant squire and you a humble Duke." Gisburne wondered if he pushed the sarcasm too far, but Richard seemed not to have registered it at all.

"We have both come a long way since," he said. He smiled and narrowed his eyes. "You think this is about my brother, don't you? It is not. The Lionheart has nothing to fear from John Softsword." His men chuckled dutifully. "John's a weakling, always has been. His plays for support are increasingly desperate. And most of all, he is afraid of me. I don't need to do anything against an enemy like that. Left to his own devices, he will destroy himself."

"What, then?"

"I have a task for you."

Gisburne stared at him for a moment. "You? Have a task for *me*...?" It was his turn to laugh, now. He shook his head, cackling at the absurdity of it. "Outlaws at large in broad daylight, lords and kings creeping about under cover of night... And now the Lionheart seeks help from Sir Guy of Gisburne. I never thought I'd be so popular as I have been these past few days! The world truly is turned upside down."

Richard stared at him, steely and expressionless. "It is, Sir Guy. And that is precisely what I would have you remedy before my return to this Godforsaken land." The King drew closer, within range of Gisburne's sword—to remind him, he supposed, who was in control. "You know that I have no particular love for this country. I hate its damp and its constant rain, which turns everything to mud and mildew. I hate the damned English with their idiotically cheery ways. And most of all I hate their rebellious Saxon blood. So full of themselves, thinking they know better, arguing the toss. At least in Aquitaine and Limousin, they know their place."

"Because you remind them," said Gisburne, what remained of his mirth melting away, "by killing their families and burning their farms. Like I said, I was there. I saw for myself."

Richard leaned in closer still, poking Gisburne's chest as he spoke. "Yes, you know it yourself, because rebellion welled up in that heart of yours, didn't it? Don't deny it. There's Saxon blood in you, too."

Gisburne clenched his jaw. "My mother was of a noble Saxon family. My father of Norman stock."

"Then you are not totally devoid of good sense." Richard turned away and began to pace, his gauntlets clasped behind his back. "You also have a soldier's pragmatism. I respect that. You will know that rebellion cannot go unpunished. That it must be crushed without hesitation, without mercy. I may have little regard for this rain-sodden land of fools and weaklings, good for growing nothing but mould and discontent, but I fought hard to make myself King of it. Now I'm back, and those who fail to grasp this reality shall not do so for long."

Gisburne frowned, but he already sensed where this strange nocturnal conversation was going. "You say this does *not* concern John?"

"Not him."

"Who, then?"

"Your old friend," said Richard. "Your old enemy. The one they call Hood."

Gisburne felt the laughter well up again—bitter and humourless this time, dying in his throat. "My God. You too. You want me to catch him..."

"I don't want you to catch him," snapped Richard. "I want you to kill him."

VII

He stared at the King for a moment. "You know, it's funny... When I was determined to put an end to Hood, no one wanted to know me. I might as well have been a leper. Try to put the whole idea behind me, and suddenly it's all anyone wants."

"Circumstances change," said Richard. "I know he has built an army. I know, too, that he has become a hero of sorts among the common folk. They feel he stands for them. While he was seen as the enemy of my brother, he served my purpose, but when I am returned, well... There is no place for upstart outlaws in my lands."

"He has become much more than that," said Gisburne.

"You believe he poses a threat."

"Yes, I do. And so too must you, or you would not be here."

Richard grunted dismissively. "He relies too heavily on the bow. Good for skirmishing or hunting, but I see no future for it in open warfare."

"Hood does not *engage* in open warfare. He is a wolf. He hunts, draws out his prey, attacks, disappears back into the forest."

"I understand the tactics well enough," said Richard irritably. "And I know how to deal with them. You may not have approved of my methods, but you can at least attest to their effectiveness."

"It's more than tactics. A longbow costs not one hundredth of even the most commonplace sword. It is the weapon of the common man, beyond the means of no one. And yet, with it, a common man may kill a knight, though he be fifty sword-lengths distant."

The King appeared unmoved. "I prefer the crossbow. It requires no strength or training. For every man skilled in the use of a bow there are ten—a hundred—who can wield a crossbow. You can put it in the hands of anyone: a soldier, a cook, a boy. That is the future."

"You miss my point," said Gisburne, unable to hide his exasperation. "This is not merely a question of military superiority. It is about what people *believe*. The common longbow, fashioned by rough hands from wood cut in the forests of England—it is not merely a tool or a weapon. It is a symbol. It *is* rebellion. And Hood, who rules that forest, is its anointed king. You can kill a thousand men, break a thousand bows, but if you cannot break what drives them on, then you will only inspire more to come, and they will resist you with every last drop of that rebellious Saxon blood. That is why I gave up on this quest. I can fight a man, but I can't fight a legend. No one can." Gisburne stared into the cold, hard eyes of the King. "I have tried, God knows. But in the end... I tired of being part of his game, of fuelling that legend and being detested for it."

"If avoiding the hatred of others were paramount," said Richard, "we'd never get anywhere." Then, to Gisburne's great surprise, he gave a faint, fleeting smile. "I do not miss your point. I understand the situation exactly. And now I see that you do too—that you are indeed the right man for this task."

"But why?" He took a single step towards the King; in the dark, fingers tightened about crossbow grips. "Just two days ago, I said that no army in England could challenge Hood and his men in their own domain. I believed it then, but I was wrong. If it was under your command, it could. You are Richard the Lionheart, scourge of Saladin, the greatest warrior of our age. It's no secret I have little love for you, but your skills as a general are in no doubt, and, by God, you do know how to root out rebels. Those barons peck away at the problem, but you are the King. You could crush the man in a heartbeat—have all of Sherwood razed to the ground, if you wanted. And I know you would not hesitate to do so if it achieved your aim."

Gisburne saw Richard's fists clench. "Of course I could crush the man. But you yourself have identified the problem. I cannot..."—he corrected himself—"*will* not fight a legend." He drew in very close, then, whispering so only Gisburne could hear. "You know of Hood's reputation, how word of him has spread. Even my own men speak of him, sing songs of his exploits around their fires. Well, I, too have a legend to maintain. Posterity to consider. And for their sakes—and that of this fractured kingdom—King Richard cannot be seen to be Hood's destroyer."

Gisburne nodded slowly. "But I can."

"You are already known to be his enemy. It makes no difference to you."

"What makes you think I will do it, after all I've said?"

"You *will* do it. It's your destiny."

Gisburne laughed and turned his face up to the rain.

"All right," said Richard. "So neither of us believes that horseshit. But I can make life more comfortable for you. Better than this..." He gestured with contempt towards the manor house. "You have the skills, and you understand him better than anyone."

"So everyone tells me," said Gisburne. He thought for a moment. "There is one thing you should know about him... I do not believe he intends to fight you."

Richard frowned. "He has raised an army. What other use has it?"

"Not just an army. Disciples. And Hood is not a rebel. Not exactly."

"Not a *rebel?*"

"He does not hate you. He *idolises* you. Always has. I think he means... to *join* with you. To somehow gain your approval for all he has done."

"That is madness."

"It is. But mad or not, I believe he would fight for you. At least, at first."

"And later?"

But Gisburne had no answer. What if the wax in Icarus's wings had not melted, and he had continued to fly towards the sun? What if there had been nothing to stop him?

"If all you say is true," said Richard, "then you have just given up all your tactical advantages, and I have no need of you after all."

Gisburne knew it. They could kill him right now, in the rain, observed by no one, missed by no one. No one would even find his cadaver until the foxes and crows had had their way with it—if ever. But he no longer cared. He had been terrified of Richard as a youth; every word and action in his presence had been guarded. But he had grown tired of fear. Tired of it all. "It is true," he said.

Richard looked him in the eye. "You're right. I could make use of Hood. Use his legend to bolster my own. And I shall. But I am a practical man. That legend will be easier to control when he's dead."

"Legends prosper best when their hero is absent," muttered Gisburne. Richard could not have known that Gisburne was also talking about him.

"When he's dead and buried, then they can praise him to the heavens and back. But I will never join with him while he lives. I have always said: 'Choose your allies—do not let them choose you.'"

Gisburne stared at Richard, a strange numbness in his heart. "My master de Gaillon used to say that."

"Did he?"

"I heard it many times. I was there when he said it to you—less than one week before you sent him to his death."

Richard snorted. "Well, I took his advice to heart, clearly."

"You murdered him." Gisburne thought he heard another sound from the shadows. Something like a gasp. Well, let them send him to Hell if they wished. He had given them every excuse.

"There is no murder in war," said Richard, his manner disconcertingly matter-of-fact. "His loyalties were in question; he knew what to expect. If he'd kept his opinions to himself, he'd still be alive." He shook his wet shoulders and looked up at the night sky. "But we're wasting time, and I am being rained on. Here's the nub of it: all the resources I have are at your disposal, and while I will never acknowledge this arrangement openly, whatever reward you desire can be yours. Gold, land, a wife, all three. Name it."

"You know that I stood before an assembly of barons not two nights ago who brought me the very same offer?"

"I know it."

"Then you also know that I refused them. That their riches left me unmoved."

"But you will not refuse me."

"What makes you think so?"

Gisburne prepared himself for the predictable response. *Because I am your King.* But it did not come. Instead, Richard sighed and turned towards the shadows. "Sir Robert?"

Gisburne heard the clank of spurs. Into the feeble moonlight stepped Sir Robert Fitzwalter—and for the second time that night, Gisburne stared in disbelief.

Fitzwalter—and his daughter Marian—had been a constant feature of Gisburne's childhood. They had taken the trouble to visit him when he had been training in Normandy under Gilbert de Gaillon, and when he had returned home to see his parents, they had been there then, too. Though he did not know if it had ever been spoken of, at one time it seemed that Marian was the natural match for him—one both he and his father had dreamt of.

Then came the rift. When Richard turned against his father Henry II, intent on wresting the crown from the Old King, John had remained loyal. Fitzwalter had declared for Richard, but Gisburne's father—a loyal servant to Henry and participant in the young Prince's Irish campaign, and a man perpetually worried about his precarious fortunes—had aligned himself firmly with the King. It had proven to be his undoing. Not only had it brought to an end his long friendship with the more prosperous Fitzwalter—and the dream of a union between the two families—it had given Richard all the excuse he needed to seize Gisburne's lands when the crown became his. Gisburne's father, destroyed by events, had died soon after—and so it was that in that one moment, both Gisburne's past and his future had been utterly swept away. Until, at his lowest ebb, a chance encounter with an outlaw had led him into the company of John.

Though he had maintained contact with Marian in the years that followed—for all the fading dream had been worth—not once had he stood face to face with Sir Robert. Now that he did, he felt not anger—that had long ago burned out—but shame. Not because of a pointless feud, and not because of his service to the rebel Prince; but for his failure to save Fitzwalter's cherished daughter from her fate.

"If you will not do it for your King, then do it for me. For Lady Marian—or the memory of her. You will know that no word has been heard of my daughter since she was taken by Hood's men. No ransom has come; no threat, nothing. She may already be dead. But I will do my damnedest to prove otherwise and return her to safety, or at the very least see the perpetrators of this vile act brought to justice. Help me do this." Fitzwalter's voice cracked with emotion.

This, Gisburne found harder to refuse.

In spite of their differences, Gisburne had always regarded Sir Robert as a paragon of strength and constancy. When he was growing up, he had seemed somehow impenetrable. A giant. Seeing him now, in the depths of a despair that he fought to contain, he seemed suddenly small, and old. What made Fitzwalter's words pierce him to his core, however, was the knowledge that Marian was not only alive, but one of Hood's most fanatical followers. Only by the most strenuous of efforts had Gisburne kept secret the fact that she had also been instrumental in Hood's bloody escape from the Tower.

"There is one thing I would take in payment," said Gisburne.

"Name it," replied Richard.

"Restore the good name of Gilbert de Gaillon. Have his body taken from its pauper's grave and given a proper burial, with all due honours. Have a mass said in his name, an effigy carved. Make sure his story is told, that people know and think well of him."

After a long pause, Richard nodded in agreement.

"Then I will go to war for you, this one last time," said Gisburne. "But I cannot do it alone."

"You have your pick of my army," said Richard.

"I don't need an army, just a half-dozen fighters. But I choose them myself. They must be paid handsomely. And there's to be no argument about my choices. No interference or questioning of my methods."

"There will be none."

"And I need six weeks to prepare."

"In six weeks I will have arrived in England. It must be done before then. You have a month."

Gisburne sighed, and nodded reluctantly. "A month. But know this: when unleashed, this war will be total. No half-measures."

Richard's eyes glinted with satisfaction. "That is as it should be. When you're done, bring me his head. And his right hand. He has a distinctive scar upon it."

"I do not lop off body parts of my enemies," said Gisburne. "That is what the Red Hand did, and I am not him. Even Hood is deserving of greater respect."

"Then what assurance will I have that you have succeeded?"

"My word," said Gisburne. "And the songs that the poor folk will sing of his death." Richard's eyes narrowed. "I do this my way. You either trust me or you don't."

Fitzwalter drew out a heavy purse, and tossed it towards him. It landed with dull thump in the mud at Gisburne's feet. "That is my pledge," he said. "There is more. But that will get your fighters together."

Gisburne picked it up the purse. He stood for a moment, staring at the sheen on the wet, muddy leather and marvelling at the sheer weight of the thing. It had to contain a fortune in gold. Already a plan was starting to form.

He breathed deep. In spite of everything—of all he had said—anticipation of what was to come was changing him as he stood. It was a chance, after all, to put things right. Not the matter of Hood—Hood was just a detail. But all the others. All he had neglected, or let slip from his grasp. He knew precisely where this quest needed to start, and his heart pounded at the thought of it. He felt alive again.

"Well done, Gisburne," said Fitzwalter, for a moment sounding like his old self. "You are now in the service of King Richard of England."

II
WAR

II
WAR

VIII

Dover Castle
16 February, 1194

MÉLISANDE DE CHAMPAGNE placed her palms upon the cold stone battlement and looked out across the crimson ocean, the distant coast of France just visible in the early evening haze.

"Are you sure we are supposed to be here?" she said. She was rather pleased how utterly naive she made the question sound.

"Oh, fear not, my lady," said her companion, puffing himself up a little more. "The Constable of the castle—Sir Matthew—and I are very good friends."

It did not surprise her for a moment that Sir Jocelyn of Streynsham and their host, Sir Matthew de Clere, were friends. Such creatures, in her experience, flocked together.

"I thought you might appreciate a glimpse of your homeland, since you are so far from it," he continued. "A magnificent view, is it not?"

"Indeed." Mélisande flashed a bland, pleasant smile. A cold wind whipped across the parapet; she shivered and pulled the thick, emerald-green cloak closer about her. "How clever of you to arrange it."

Sir Jocelyn beamed at her words, thrust his chest out a little more, and looked about him as if the view itself were all his own creation. She did not fail to notice, however, how his eyes darted in her direction, and did not always come to rest on her face.

Well, let's give him something to look at, then. Throwing her head back a little, she turned her slender body slowly around, his furtive glances sliding about her as she moved. She was not looking at the view, however—no more than was her fatally distracted escort—although she made it appear so. She was looking at the castle itself. From the outer curtain wall below them, to the sheer walls of the great keep, she took in every detail—assessing, counting, measuring.

Dover, the jewel in Old King Henry's crown, was the most formidable fortress in England; the first line of defence against invasion—both royal palace and impenetrable stronghold. In truth, she had wanted for years to get up onto these ramparts and survey its defences. Once, it would have been in the service of King Philip of France. Now, that allegiance was at an end, but the urge remained. So, when dear Sir Jocelyn had suggested it in the hopes of impressing her out of her chemise, her initial eagerness had been impossible to hide—a fact that had clearly delighted him, and furthered her cause all the more.

She could not entirely blame the man for his interest. It had been with the express purpose of finding a suitable husband that she had come to England again—or so she told herself. That, after all, had been her father's final wish for her.

It was not hers, by any means. But she had been defiant all of her life, and had paid the price. Now, if she could just put one thing right...

The trouble was, with her father dead, the protection of the family name gone, her inheritance nonexistent and even her King turned from her, there were few among the nobility who looked upon her as marriageable. All they saw was a tarnished reputation, and an uncontrollable woman. She had many admirers—she had never wanted for those—but none, now, who would pledge their troth, none who were prepared to accept her as she was.

Well, one, perhaps; but a formal gathering of those most fiercely loyal to King Richard was the very last place she would find *him*.

As ever, she had determined to make her way despite her circumstances. Free of her duties to King and Country—carefree, but with precious few resources and little to lose—she found her restless mind occupied by new challenges, new opportunities. Opportunities of which her father certainly would not have approved—the most recent of which had occurred to her only in the last few excruciating hours. There was, after all, far more gold within Dover's walls than *these* idiots could put to proper use.

But first, there was the issue of good Sir Jocelyn.

"One question..." she said, almost sing-song this time. "Where are the guards?"

"I had them remove themselves. With our host's full accord, naturally. So we may enjoy greater privacy."

Privacy. She felt her stomach churn. *Oh, God...*

The wind gusted again, as if in response to the thought, tugging at her wimple. She firmed the gold circlet upon her head. "Do they not need to keep a watch for invasion?" she said, managing, this time, to sound like a lucky guess from an empty-headed idiot. "I have heard that Prince John is even now in France, seeking support from his friend, King Philip."

"Please, my lady," chuckled Sir Jocelyn. "Such talk makes enemies of us, and that is the very opposite of what I would wish."

Mélisande smiled sweetly, dropped her eyes, then looked back out across the sea, idly wondering what pattern would be made upon the stonework if she were to vomit over the parapet.

"To answer your very pertinent question, my lady," said Sir Jocelyn in his most reassuring, masculine tones, "the men atop yonder towers have their eyes upon the sea." He loomed in a little closer. "And they have strict instructions to keep them fixed there..."

Oh, Christ. Mélisande girded herself for what was to come. At that moment, she heard a curious, muffled *clank* of metal against stone. It seemed to come from a crook in the battlement, where the projection on which they now stood met with the main inner bailey wall. She slid sideways in the hope of getting a better look—just as Sir Jocelyn, who evidently had not heard it, chose to swoop. Instead of soft, feminine lips, he met empty air. It was all Mélisande could do not to laugh at the sight of him.

"I was sorry to hear about your father," he sighed, with all-too-obvious impatience.

Mélisande inclined her head in recognition of his sympathy, devoid though it was of any trace of feeling. Then he smiled to himself—a wicked kind of smile that unnerved her. "Is it true what they say about him—that he abducted your mother when she was a nun, and forced her into marriage?"

"Regrettably, yes."

"Oh, do not regret it, my lady. It is part of your heritage. Why, you would not even exist, had he not acted thus, so we can hardly wish it undone." He licked his lips and smiled. "Do you suppose such traits run in families? I believe they do. Look at your own escapades..."

"I'm sure I don't know what you mean, Sir Jocelyn," she said, her faux innocence somewhat slipping. She knew exactly what he meant, of course, and it did not please her. No more did the undisguised greed she saw in his eye, like a fox in sight of a chicken. She noted, without having to look, that his gloved left fist was twisting on his sword pommel. *So here it comes,* she thought, bracing herself.

"Where exactly is 'Streynsham,' anyway?" she said.

Suddenly, with all the speed of a predator, he was upon her—one hand about her waist, the other questing eagerly between her thighs.

"Sir Jocelyn!" she exclaimed, and thrust the offending hand aside.

"Come now, madam," he breathed, his face barely an inch from her own. "You know well enough why you are here..." The questing hand fought to regain its place.

"I come seeking a suitable match among..."

"Marriage!" scoffed Sir Jocelyn. "You dressed as a *man!* Cavorted with thieves and mercenaries! Brawled outside a dockside tavern in a London street with your hair flying free! Even your own *father* rejected you when he heard of it! What nobleman would wish to marry *that*... But I bet you could show them a thing or two..." He leered closer still, onion and sour wine on his breath. Mélisande felt the stone battlement cut into her back. "You're a woman of experience. I have heard that you spent time amongst the heathens in the East. That you learned a few nice tricks whilst there—the way the Saracens give favours..."

Mélisande's attention was no longer on Sir Jocelyn's monologue, but on the shape emerging from the shadows behind him. "Oh," she said, peering past her suitor's looming face. "Hello, Gisburne."

Sir Jocelyn recoiled as if struck across the chops, and, whirling about, reeled again at the sight of Sir Guy of Gisburne standing fewer than three yards from him.

"What the...? But how did you...?" Jocelyn's sword, drawn with impressive speed, waved in the air, its point inches from the interloper. Gisburne—hooded and black as a crow—did not move. Sir Jocelyn, his boldness returning, squinted at the shadowed face. "Gisburne, is it? Why, you're Prince John's hound... What business have you here? Are you even invited?"

"I need your help," said Gisburne. "I have been called to war and am gathering fighters, the best I know. A small band to carry out a challenging and dangerous task." He paused for a moment, then added: "It is by royal command."

Sir Jocelyn's eyes widened. His wavering sword drooped. His face flushed, and a smile that almost became a laugh spread across it. "Well... I am... honoured. Pray, sir, let me..."

"I wasn't talking to you," snapped Gisburne, and turned back to Mélisande. "Will you join me?" He stepped towards her, shoving the astonished Sir Jocelyn to one side as he did so.

She saw Sir Jocelyn's baffled eyes turn momentarily from Gisburne to rest on a shape in the shadows on the stonework: a grapple, sheathed in black, like a raven's claw, hooked over the parapet. By the time he turned back, she could see realisation dawning.

Then it happened.

Perhaps, she flattered herself, it was sight of her that distracted Gisburne—though, in truth, this thought was more annoyance than delight; she had no desire to be his weakness. Perhaps he simply underestimated Sir Jocelyn's martial skills; already she had noted the swiftness of the knight's reactions.

Whatever the reason, Gisburne did not hear Sir Jocelyn's sudden move towards him. He did not see the sword pommel raised, nor did he anticipate the blow that dashed upon his unprotected temple. Gisburne's legs crumpled beneath him, and in the next moment, Mélisande was again facing Sir Jocelyn alone.

Why he had not already called the guards, she could not fathom, but seeing him preparing to rectify that fault, she stepped over

Gisburne's groaning form, her face fashioned into an expression of eager gratitude. As predicted, he lowered his guard. She drew close—inches from his face, now registering triumph—and grabbed him by the balls. His eyes bulged.

"You want to know how they give favours to people like you in the East?" she hissed. Then she butted her gilded forehead into the knight's face. There was a crunch of bone, and blood spattered down his tunic; the gold circlet had cut his nose wide open. As he tottered backward, his face a picture of utter disbelief, she deftly twisted the sword out of his hand, brought the pommel up under his chin and kicked him in the groin. He went down like a sack of grain. She stood over him, holding his own sword point at his throat. But Sir Jocelyn was done.

It was almost dark now—a further blessing. There were no shouts of alarm. Behind her, she heard a shuffle, then an irritable grunt, and Gisburne rose unsteadily to his feet.

"Was that supposed to be a rescue?" she said.

"What were you doing up here with this idiot anyway?"

"Jealous, Sir Guy?"

Gisburne scowled, and she smiled sweetly in response.

"It's good to see you, too, Gisburne. I did have plans for the evening, but I suppose you'll do instead."

Gisburne shoved Sir Jocelyn with his toe. "*This* was your plan..?"

"No. Not him. He was just a means to an end." She reached out and touched Gisburne's face, then pulled away suddenly. "I was actually resigned to knocking him senseless long before you turned up." She glanced down at the sprawled body. "I had an idea to do something here. Something grand, memorable. But it will wait. For now, it looks as if I am to join you in your war. I take it it pays?"

"Handsomely."

"Good. I need it. My father left me nothing."

"But your brother..."

"Hates me. I shamed him into a fight in front of his friends when I was eighteen."

"I take it, then, that you won?"

She smiled a wry smile. "He was twenty-one and had been a

knight for precisely three days, and I wanted to prove a point. He never forgave me." With a great sigh, she hauled off her wimple and dented circlet and shook her hair free. "Well, I can at least be myself again, thank the heavens. Though you didn't have to pick a fight to get to see me. Where have you been?"

Gisburne side-stepped the question. "I didn't pick this fight. It picked me."

Looking Gisburne up and down, she frowned, then reached out and pinched his arm. "You're thinner."

"There's a famine. Hadn't you heard?"

"Ask them down there, in the great hall. The poor may starve, but the tables of the rich are still groaning. You've been neglecting yourself, Gisburne." She knelt by the insensible Sir Jocelyn. Out cold, not dead. He would come to in time. "Sir Jocelyn did you a great favour tonight. He had the guards removed from the battlement."

"That was indeed fortunate," said Gisburne, "since you turned out to be up here and not with the guests below. I wasn't expecting that." He looked about him anxiously. "Nor to have to remain exposed up here for quite so long. We must move."

"Tell me, where did you plan to make yourself known to me? In the great hall? In my bedchamber...?" In the deepening darkness, she wasn't sure if the expression on Gisburne's face was a smile or another scowl. "Do you ever consider simply knocking upon the front gate and being *invited* in?"

"I find it best not to rely on invitations," said Gisburne. "I get precious few."

Mélisande smiled. "The guards were gone *because* I was here. But you're right—we should move before someone in the tower neglects his duty and starts looking where he's supposed to." With that, she pulled open the deep neck of Sir Jocelyn's bloody tunic and shoved her gold circlet inside.

"What are you doing?"

"Leaving something for Sir Jocelyn of Streynsham to remember me by. Now, pull down his hose and braies..."

"What? Are you mad?"

"Well, *I'm* not doing it. Quickly now!"

With a shrug and a swift glance over his shoulder, Gisburne did as instructed. "'Streynsham'?" he said with a frown, whilst fighting with Sir Jocelyn's hose.

Mélisande shrugged. "I have no idea."

Gisburne yanked down Sir Jocelyn's braies and stood back, a look of slight distaste on his face.

Mélisande regarded the stricken figure for a moment. "Well, it's hard to see what Sir Jocelyn had to be so proud of."

"What will you tell them?" said Gisburne, nodding towards the great hall below.

"Them? Nothing."

"Nothing?"

She crouched, grabbed the hem of her bliaut—emerald green, to match her cloak—hauled it above her knees and tucked it through the belt at her waist.

"What's that for?" said a bemused Gisburne.

"I need my legs free so I can climb down the rope."

"What?" he looked suddenly panic-stricken. "No, no, no... You can't come with me."

"You don't think I'm going back in there?" She drew a pair of green leather gloves from her purse and pulled them on. "You said you needed me."

"I do. But not *now!*"

"Are you sure?" she said. "You needed me a few moments ago."

Gisburne glanced at the courtyard in nervous exasperation. "What about your entourage? Are you to leave them without a word?"

"You'll find my entourage has dwindled as dramatically as my income. All my loyal servants have been dismissed. Just three now—chosen by my brother, and paid to keep an eye on me—and they have access to more coin than I. Let's make them work for it..."

"You don't even know what I'm asking of you..."

"You can explain on the way."

Gisburne sighed and looked about him as if for some alternative, but she knew he had already admitted defeat.

"Now, quickly, before I scream." She hurried towards the grapple.

"Scream?"

"For help," she said, clambering without hesitation over the parapet. "Sir Jocelyn has assaulted me, remember? Robbed me. Perhaps even killed me. It's time for the guards to do their work. So..." She cocked her head to one side, and nodded towards the distant ground, above which she now hung like a spider. "This is an invitation, Gisburne, and you receive precious few."

Gisburne's booted feet swung over the battlement above her as she lowered herself down the great, blank expanse of stone into the dark of the advancing night. She thought she heard him mutter "God help me"—then she let rip with the loudest, most anguished scream that a wronged woman could muster.

IX

Ressons-sur-Matz, northern France
21 February, 1194

GISBURNE WINCED AS the big knight's lance smashed against de Rosseley's shield, sending shards of wood flying high in the air. The knights and retainers camped on the far side—now quite drunk— roared their approval, and fists were raised in triumph. Gruff oaths were bellowed out as de Rosseley turned his horse past their ranks and trotted back towards his attendants.

The sweet scent of freshly broken timber wafted on the air, mingling with the smell of horse dung, human sweat, mud and ale. These last two had formed an unlikely union, thanks to a split keg whose contents had formed a big, yeasty puddle opposite— prompting several of the big knight's entourage to begin a game whose sole object was to shove each other in.

"What does that make it?" said Gisburne.

"Even," said the squire, not once taking his eye from the lists. It was the most he had uttered in the past half-hour.

Each had now shattered one lance on the others' shield—in theory, the highest-scoring hit, short of unhorsing your opponent outright—but on both occasions Gisburne had failed to note what the opposing lance had been doing. He vaguely recalled something about the points varying according to how far along the shaft the lance had been broken, or was that only when both lances were shattered on the same pass? He couldn't remember. It seemed now that every tournament had its own arcane variation on the rules, usually made up that day by whoever was running the show, and not necessarily in the interests of either fairness or clarity.

To be honest, his grasp of this scene had always been sketchy. It infuriated him. Despite having stood at the lists in attendance of Gilbert de Gaillon as a young squire, this world—in which people fought for pleasure, and according to arbitrary rules—felt utterly alien. Perhaps what really made him angry was his own failure to grasp it.

De Rosseley was close now. Gisburne raised his head for a greeting, wondering if his old friend had spotted him standing there. But, as far as one could tell beneath the faceplate, de Rosseley remained aloof, his body language strangely still, as if concentration on the task at hand had shut out all else—as if hardly connected to his body at all. Gisburne knew that state, and envied him the ability to turn it on at will. Gaze fixed ahead, de Rosseley held out lance and shield to his attendant squires, even though to Gisburne they looked as good as new. Both were removed and replaced with such speed that their master's hands barely had time to open and close before being filled again.

His opponent—less patient than he—was already lined up for the final pass, and was roaring out some incomprehensible challenge. De Rosseley, however, would not be rushed. He walked his horse in a slow arc, affording the big knight no attention whatsoever. Gisburne could see how that infuriated him—even his horse seemed to stamp in frustration.

The knight was enormous: a monster of a man on a monster of a horse. His destrier was Friesian, each black hoof as big as Gisburne's face. The provenance of its rider, Gisburne could not guess. His armour was of decorated scales, in a Byzantine style. The blackened helm was Teutonic, with an ostentatious red plume upon the crown. The saddle had an Arab look to it. His shield—decorated with a red device that, to Gisburne, looked like a nun with a beak—was in a style he had never before seen: small and oddly shaped, and angled down the middle. The better to deflect a lance point, he guessed. And hanging from both the knight and his saddle were more weapons than Gisburne had ever seen on a single man: two fine swords, a variety of daggers, a short falchion, at least two maces, a flail and a long warhammer. These were just the ones he could see. Little wonder he needed a heavy horse for that lot.

The contrast between the two combatants could not have been greater. Everything about de Rosseley was light and sleek, not least his horse—a Cremello stallion of Iberian stock, unusually slender for its type but well-muscled and swift and silent as a ghost.

De Rosseley had barely signalled his readiness than the big knight was off—and at the first crash of its hooves, de Rosseley's mount leapt forward.

GISBURNE BIT HIS lip as they closed the distance. Worrying about de Rosseley's long-term safety was and had always been futile, but right now he *needed* him alive, and uninjured.

In the previous two passes, Gisburne had marvelled at how late, and how swiftly, de Rosseley lowered his lance. This time he was barely even aware of it happening. It struck dead centre of his opponent's shield and with a great *crack* flew into three parts, two of which went spinning upwards, leaving puffs of dust in their wake. Gisburne winced at the impact, but de Rosseley rode on as if through dry grass.

The big knight—whose own lance tip had barely clipped de Rosseley's shield—reeled and swayed dangerously in his saddle. His horse pulled hard to the right, snapping him upright. Gisburne wondered if he'd been trained to do that; it was a good trick if he had. But it mattered little now; the knight had lost. As he turned full about, Gisburne saw that his shield had split completely in two down the centre, its flapping halves now connected only by their straps and the linen covering.

Gisburne laughed, and clapped the squire on the shoulder. The young man gave a barely perceptible nod. Then, turning to look at the inscrutable young man, he thought he saw a fleeting frown.

Looking back across the lists, he saw that the big knight had thrown down both lance and shield, and—still shouting furiously—was now drawing his sword. Gisburne guessed that wherever he came from, he wasn't used to being bettered. It was only when the sword was raised in the air that he realised the knight meant to charge again.

"He can't do that..." muttered Gisburne, then turned to the squire. "Can he do that?"

The squire said nothing.

The big knight's supporters roared. There was venom in it this time. They wanted blood.

De Rosseley would simply leave the field. Of course he would. That would be the sensible thing to do. Or someone would intervene. He had won fair and square, and the unwarranted challenge obliged him not at all. He could leave now—honour, head, and limbs intact— and leave the blustering rutterkin listening to his own rant.

But as Gisburne watched, de Rosseley threw down his own shield and what remained of his lance, and drew out a mace.

"No, no, no..." said Gisburne. "What's he doing?"

The big knight lurched forward, sword drawn back. Gisburne could see he meant to pass along de Rosseley's right side. From such a position, his blade—with all the force the big man could muster and the added momentum of his horse—could strike de Rosseley square across the neck. At best, his mail might stop the blade, and his head would not be taken off, but the blow would still kill him.

As the crowd roared its approval, forwarded Rosseley advanced, mace held low by his right side, taking exactly the line that favoured his opponent's attack.

"This is madness," said Gisburne. "His mace has half the reach of the sword. He cannot possibly..."

Gisburne wanted to look away, but found he could not. The sound of the bloodthirsty crowd rose to a great animalistic snarl.

In the heartbeat before they closed Gisburne had seen something odd. Keeping it low, so as to be barely noticeable, De Rosseley had passed the mace from his right hand to his left. Gisburne barely had time to ponder the seemingly absurd gesture before its significance was made abundantly clear. With the pair barely three yards from their encounter, de Rosseley pulled his horse hard across his opponent's path. The big knight's destrier, fearing collision, lurched violently. The knight faltered, thrown off balance. His blow never fell. De Rosseley passed along his opponent's left—so close their stirrups clipped—and brought the mace up hard under the big knight's chin.

The black helm flew high in the air, plume trailing like the tail of a bird. The knight tipped back, swivelled, crashed down onto the mud and rolled over three times, limbs flailing, his many weapons strewn across the field.

The squire turned, gave Gisburne the thinnest of smiles, then headed off to attend to his victorious master.

"Gisburne!" cried de Rosseley cheerily, pulling the sweat-stained arming cap from his head and ruffling his matted hair. "What in God's name are you doing here?" As he dismounted, the inscrutable squire took his horse; another darted forward with a page in tow and received de Rosseley's helm, stuffed now with the arming cap.

"Guy of Gisburne at tournament? It truly is the End of Days..." He strode forward, grinning broadly. Keeping pace with his master, the squire passed the headgear to the page, then did the same with the mace that was shoved under his nose. The page ran off with both and disappeared into the striped tent from which de Rosseley's pennant flew. De Rosseley, meanwhile, unbuckled his belt and, without a glance, without breaking stride, held out his sword in its scabbard. This the squire kept for himself. Gisburne noted that once in possession of it, he strayed no more than three paces from his master, his arms folded about the sword as he cradled it against his left shoulder.

De Rosseley laughed and slapped his arms around his old friend, then stepped back and took a long look at him. "God's teeth, man, you look half-dead!"

"I thought you entirely dead not moments ago," said Gisburne.

De Rosseley shrugged. "Looks can be deceptive."

"A principle that you seem to have worked to your advantage." Gisburne nodded towards the lists where Sir Whatever-His-Name-Was—still out cold, or dead—was being attended by grey-faced squires.

As he spoke, the page returned at a scurry, pewter jug in hand, and offered up a silver cup to his master. De Rosseley did not speak, did not even look, but simply stretched out his hand, closed his fingers about the cup and raised it to his lips in one unbroken motion. As Gisburne watched, once again entranced by the seamless operation of a knight's entourage, he became suddenly aware of an identical cup hovering at his side, proffered by a second page. He took it with not half the elegance of his old friend.

"Welcome to France," De Rosseley said, "where they have the good sense to allow the *Conflictus Gallicus*." He clanked his cup against Gisburne's, and both drank. It was the finest wine Gisburne had tasted in months.

"Fear not," said Gisburne. "The tournament will return to England when Richard does."

"*If* he does," sighed de Rosseley, and drank again.

Gisburne was just about to follow this with some enigmatic comment when a raucous laugh from a party of knights nearby made de Rosseley turn, he regarded them with contempt.

"Look at these bastards," he said, thrusting his drink in their direction. "Every time, they do this..."

Gisburne looked, but all he could see was a group of well-to-do, unarmoured men enjoying some wine.

"They sit out the preliminaries as if they've no intention of taking part in the mêlée. They avoid injuries, size up the fighters, look for weaknesses. They watch them wear themselves out in the joust and single combat. Then on the day of the melée, these trundle-tails suddenly declare their intent and pick off all who they know to be weak or injured." He shook his head and snorted in disgust. "Vultures! It should be outlawed. In the joust they call lance-dodging 'failure to present.' You get thrown out for it. Ridiculed! But how is this any better?" He held out his cup. It was immediately refilled.

"Well, you know my thoughts on the tournament..." said Gisburne.

De Rosseley drank again—more irritably, this time—wiped his mouth and narrowed his eyes. "I'll be honest, it's making me uneasy seeing you here. Like bumping into a nun in a whorehouse."

"Do you speak from experience?"

"Just a figure of speech, old boy. Well, come on, out with it... I know you didn't set foot on a ship just to watch me joust. And you look like a man who's ready to leave before you've even properly arrived."

Gisburne's eyes flicked to the aloof squire and he lowered his voice. "I have come to ask if you would join me on a quest. A very important quest."

"What is it this time? The Ark of the Covenant?"

"There is a wolf in the forest that must be put down," said Gisburne. Then, realising he was talking in riddles, added, "An outlaw of my acquaintance."

"*An* outlaw?" said de Rosseley with a quizzical frown, "or *the* outlaw?"

"Yes. That one."

De Rosseley nodded slowly. "So, you've decided to finish business?"

"Let's just say it was decided for me." Gisburne drew closer. "Listen Ross, I must be honest with you. This is not ritual combat; not a glorious contest. It is war, and our enemy is to be hunted down and put to death by any means necessary. I dare say there will be little honour in it, and I know that is not to your taste. But I need good fighters. Those I can rely on. It will be a hard fight, too. If we all come through unscathed, I may be forced to believe in miracles again..."

"Why, you make it sound so enticing."

"Once done, it will rid England of its most vile pest—and earn more gold than a dozen tournaments, if you've a taste for it." Gisburne drew a gold coin from his poke and held it out to him. "See here."

At that, de Rosseley's face fell. He turned to the squire. "Go." The squire scampered swiftly away.

De Rosseley reached out to the coin—and closed Gisburne's fist back around it. "What the Hell are you thinking?"

Gisburne frowned. "I only meant..."

"A knight does not fight for pay. That's not how it goes."

"Think of it as a gift. Compensation, expenses. Whatever you like." Gisburne laughed, then gestured around him. "Come on, Ross, you spend your whole life fighting for money!"

"The tournament is different. You don't understand these things. You never took part. This is what a knight *does*. It's accepted. But fighting others' battles for gold, like a common mercenary..." He reddened slightly, then softened. "I'm sorry, Guy. I meant no offence. I cast no judgement on you, or..."

Gisburne raised a conciliatory hand. "I know, I know." He snorted and shook his head. "But we also both know that nearly every knight here has been bought by some lord or other. They call it loyalty, or service, or duty, but don't try telling me there's no pay in it. No silver, no horses, no fine swords. Food and shelter..."

De Rosseley looked about him nervously and drew in closer. "Yes, we do know this. And yes, there may well be a fine line between certain knights and mere pay-swords. But you cross that line at your peril; you step out of one class and into another. You know this better than most, my friend."

"It's all pretence," said Gisburne. "Deception. At least when I fought for pay, I did it honestly."

"I've lost count of the number of times I've tried to explain this, but you remain as bloody-minded as ever. Let me put it in purely pragmatic terms. Pretence it may be; hypocrisy, even. But if you ever wish to win them over, you have to let them *believe* in it. You can't fight everyone, Guy. Not all at once. De Gaillon taught you that much."

Gisburne nodded, reluctantly. "He did."

"He also, I hope, taught you that there are some for whom the knightly virtues are very real..."

Gisburne smiled. "Yes, that, too."

De Rosseley put a hand on Gisburne's shoulder. "We've got off on the wrong foot."

"I only meant to *show* you the coin, Ross. Did you not see what it was?"

"A dinar?"

"From the Holy Land, yes. Spoils of the Crusade, offered by the hero of the Crusade..."

De Rosseley looked at him in amazement. "*He* is your master now?" He shook his head. "No, I doubt anyone was ever that, but he really wants Hood dead?"

"Wouldn't you?"

"Well, what a turnabout..." De Rosseley drank, and pondered. "Hunted down, you said? I like a good hunt. How many are there to be in this company of yours?"

"A half-dozen. No more."

"This is a small war you wage, Guy..."

"Enough for a hunting party. We must keep it small. It may yet avert a far greater war."

"So, when is this hunt to take place?"

"We gather on the fifteenth of next month."

De Rosseley nodded slowly. "Tell me one thing. Am I the first?" Gisburne frowned. "That you have asked, I mean. Obviously, I'm hoping the answer is 'yes.'"

Gisburne thought carefully about his next words. "You are the first man I have asked."

De Rosseley narrowed his eyes, and looked hard at Gisburne. "*Man*?" He smiled. "What is it, Guy—was there a *woman* ahead of me?" He laughed then caught the look in Gisburne's eye. His face fell. "My God, there was... Wait... *A* woman, or *the* woman?"

"*The* woman."

De Rosseley looked him in the eye for a moment, then nodded. "All right. Fair enough. She brought down the Red Hand when I could not. Saved my life into the bargain. She was the better man that day. Did she agree?"

"She did."

He smiled, clearly glad at that news. "And where do you go next?"

"To find a Saracen."

"A Saracen?" De Rosseley raised his eyebrows. "Well, you'd better get going. It's a long way to the Holy Land." He waved his thumb towards the east. "And it's that way."

"This one is closer to home," said Gisburne, and nodded back towards England.

"So I am between a woman and a Saracen. I must confess I am mightily intrigued by this army of yours."

"So are you with us?"

De Rosseley sighed deeply. "I can hardly have it said a woman took up a challenge I would not, can I? *Or* a Saracen. But keep the gold. Grim as you may have painted it, this is a good deed. I'll do it for that. And for a friend." He smiled and knocked his cup against Gisburne's. "To our enemies' enemies."

Gisburne smiled. Ross always inspired confidence in him; he would do so in the others. There had been no guarantee they would agree to join him, but for the first time, he began to feel this thing was possible. "You know Clippestone?"

"Of course."

"Come there on the appointed day. Come alone. No squires, no pages; just you."

De Rosseley nodded, frowning, as if struggling to take in the strange instruction.

"And I know I shouldn't need to say this..." began Gisburne.

"Yes?"

"Don't make yourself fodder for the ravens."

De Rosseley laughed. "What in the seventy-two names of God is that supposed to mean?"

"Last time I saw you after a tournament, you looked like a pear that had spent a week in a royal messenger's saddlebag. Much as I know you abhor 'failure to present,' please—try not to die before our small war is even begun."

X

London
1 March, 1194

GISBURNE KNEW A cheat when he saw one. From his cramped corner, shaded by the rickety wooden stair of the heaving, sweaty inn, he had watched the same trick played out at least a dozen times, and he knew that all was not as it seemed.

It always went the same way. The victim was shown three cups and a ball, and the ball went under one cup. The cups were moved about rapidly on the barrel top, and the victim asked to tap the cup under which he thought the ball was hidden. The first time, he was always allowed to find the ball. Sometimes a second time, too. The trickster expressed amazement, hinted that the victim was too good at this, and then suggested they put money on it. Which the victim always did. From then on, the ball eluded him, no matter how carefully he watched, no matter how keenly he followed it. Finally, his money or his resolve would run out, then after a brief interlude another would take his place and it would start all over again.

It was a familiar enough trick, and it always involved cheating of some kind or another—a sleight of hand of some sort. But this was different. As Gisburne watched the trickster move the cups— sometimes only with his fingertips—it became clear something more was going on. Something that foxed even London's shrewdest street wretches. Something impossible.

At first, he hadn't been at all sure he would recognise that face again, not after all this time. It had only been a fleeting encounter, after all, and not exactly cordial. In the event, he spotted him immediately. Even if the face had not been familiar—the sharp nose, the piercing eyes, the crow-black hair—Gisburne's attention would have been drawn to that spot; the crowd gathered around the barrel, cheering and laughing and groaning as each victim's loss unfolded.

This was not at all what he had been expecting. In fact, that morning, he had set out seeking someone entirely different.

It had seemed a straightforward enough task: head for the docks, then ask for the big Saracen. Arabs were not exactly plentiful in London, and it had been Gisburne himself who had secured employment for his old friend among the merchants and wharf rats. He'd been looking forward to the meeting, too. Last time they had met had been far from England's cold and damp—in Jerusalem, in what now seemed like a distant dream. After that, there had been only a hurried message from London announcing his unexpected arrival there, and a favour that Gisburne had called in by way of help. That came courtesy of Ranulph Le Fort—one of those who had fought alongside him against the Red Hand, and whose life he saved—who also happened to have forged friendships among the merchants of London.

But today, Gisburne had arrived in London only to discover he was too late. The word on the docks was that the big Saracen had moved on—in a hurry. Eastward, they thought. But bit by bit, as Gisburne drew closer to the few the Saracen had trusted and who trusted him, the parts of the mosaic came together. A destination became clear.

As to why he had left, no one knew. He had disappeared overnight without a word, not even taking the wages he was owed. Most of those he had spoken to had shrugged it off as somehow inevitable. Daily life must be far from easy for an Arab in London, but for that very reason, any who did stay would command a certain respect, something this particular Arab generally achieved by his size and bearing alone. It must be something other than the usual trouble, and that worried Gisburne. Whoever had been responsible for his friend's flight to England may have followed him here.

But then, quite by chance, he had heard a quite different whisper;

another name familiar to him. And skills that had attracted some attention. The whispers had led him here. He could not have imagined, at first, that it was the same man that he had encountered in the Forêt de Boulogne. But now he'd seen him and was convinced. Well, if he could not find one recruit, perhaps fate could yet provide him with another—though quite what reception he would get, he couldn't say. How does one normally greet a man one has almost killed?

The game, it seemed, was drawing to a close. One by one, the roughs about the conjuror's barrel were melting away into the throng. Gisburne stood and began to weave his way across the crowded interior.

ALDRIC FITZ ROLF was gathering together his winnings—a tidy stash of silver pennies—when the mug of ale thudded down on the barrel top. "What if they were to find out the secret of your trick?" said Gisburne.

Aldric raised his head, and gawped in amazement at the face he saw before him. "You..."

"I have heard you're now an enginer, and it so happens I have need of one."

Aldric tried to stand, and Gisburne gripped his arm and dragged him back down into his seat. Aldric winced. Several pairs of eyes flicked warily in their direction, but at the sight of Gisburne, turned swiftly away again.

"Last time I saw you," hissed Aldric, "you shot me in this shoulder with a crossbow."

"And you were fighting for the madman Tancred de Mercheval, and shot me in the heart at his command. I'd say we're even, wouldn't you?"

Aldric shrugged irritably, then drank from the mug.

"When I left you," continued Gisburne, "I told you to find a better master. Did you?"

"Yes," said Aldric. "Me. But that was not so easy a route as you might assume."

"I never assume. Tell me."

"I hated Tancred. Who wouldn't? And when you arrived... Well, I knew he was done. Or if he wasn't, I was. So I ran, the bolt still in me. Or staggered, at least. It seemed an age that I plodded on like that, the flames of Castel Mercheval at my back. Then I ran into Lucatz."

"Lucatz?"

"Lucatz the Enginer," explained Aldric. "The one you tied to a tree. The one Tancred had brought from Paris to open your stupid box."

"Ah," said Gisburne. "Lucatz."

"He helped me—he was an able physician. And I him, as best I could. Together we made it back to Paris. I could not fight or find work with this injury, but Lucatz gave me a roof over my head and work I could manage. And so I healed."

"And showed an aptitude for the enginer's craft, it would seem."

"So it would seem. I became Lucatz's apprentice. Then he died. Robbed in the street." Aldric swigged his ale, his gaze fixed on the floor. "He was good to me. And I could not save him. Me—a man-at-arms..."

"There's fight in you yet, Aldric Fitz Rolf. I see it."

"No thanks to you," spat Aldric. "Anyway... Things didn't look good for me, so I took to the road. Just me, a bag of tools and my wits."

"And washed up here..."

"There are worse places to be."

"Last time I heard that was in a sewer."

Aldric eyed Gisburne, as if unsure whether to take him seriously. "How did you find me?"

"Truth be told, I came to London looking for someone else. Didn't find him. I may yet, if he isn't dead. But in the meantime, I heard a tale of an ambitious young enginer. One story led to another, each to a place a little humbler than the last. And here I am." Gisburne looked about him at the dark, sticky interior. "I have to admit, I'm a little disappointed."

Aldric narrowed his eyes. "What's it to you, anyway?"

"I have an interest. I set you on this path, for good or ill. I heard that the young man I encountered had grown, learned new skills. I was hopeful. And now I see *this* is how you put those skills to use—cheating pennies from strangers, when your wisdom could be winning battles."

Aldric scowled. "Cheating? How da—?" But before he could finish the sentence, Gisburne had gripped the barrel by its rim and turned it about, sending Aldric's mug flying. At its base, just where Aldric's feet had been, a small peg of wood projected from a slot. Aldric flushed red at the sight of it.

"Everyone checks the cups and the ball," said Gisburne. "No one suspects the barrel upon which they sit." He held up a coin between thumb and forefinger. "A silver penny. Old King Henry, bless him. Let's see where he ends up, shall we?" With that, he slapped the coin on a portion of the barrel top marked by a discrete scratch in the wood, then pressed his foot on peg. As if by magic, a tiny flap—so perfectly fitted it was all but invisible—yawned inward. The coin disappeared down the opening, flew out of a bung hole halfway down the barrel and bounced across the floorboards. Gisburne lifted his foot and the door snapped shut, invisible once more. "Everyone's so busy looking at the cups no one would think to look at your feet, nor at your hands retrieving the ball from the skirts of your tunic where your little device has deposited it. With the ball in your palm, you can lift any cup to your advantage, and it's a simple matter then to reintroduce the ball. They're all on the lookout for the ball being taken, after all; not for it coming back."

Aldric swallowed hard, and looked about him anxiously. Gisburne's antics had attracted unwanted attention. Several were men who had lost money to Aldric's game, and one or two now looked as if they were considering taking the matter up with him.

"Do you wonder how I knew? Because I was once acquainted with a man who was a master of conjuring tricks. The best. I watched him do his tricks a thousand times, in every tavern from Syracuse to Jerusalem. So I know what can and cannot be done." Gisburne peered over his shoulder and saw a muttering delegation of roughs forming, their eyes on Aldric and his barrel. He turned back, speaking swiftly. "I thought him a friend once. But it is he who is now my problem. I need to hunt him and trap him, Aldric, and I need someone who is equal to him in trickery. It's risky, I won't deny it. But the rewards will be great." He saw Aldric's eyes flit nervously to the door and back again; the roughs were approaching.

"Listen—I don't doubt you can earn good beer money with your disappearing ball trick, but what I'm offering will keep you in beer, wine and women for a lifetime. It's more than you have ever known. More than gold." He glanced over his shoulder. "But right now, unless you wish to lose your balls altogether, I suggest you make your exit..."

Aldric stood and ran for the door, and Gisburne turned to find himself face to face with a small mob of disgruntled, dangerously drunk ruffians—Aldric's victims, who now thought to make an issue of it. At the head of them was a big man with a face like a pig's thigh. The men behind him looked cautious, but not this one. He looked to the now empty doorway, and back again—and Gisburne could see he was unafraid. There was fight in his eye.

"Poor lad," said Gisburne, shaking his head. The big man's face creased in a frown. Gisburne nodded in Aldric's direction. "Leprosy."

The man's face fell, his eyes widened in horror, and as one they began to back slowly away.

OUTSIDE, IN THE mired, narrow street, Mélisande—hidden within a hood—was waiting with the horses.

"I want my barrel back!" cried Aldric as Gisburne emerged.

"Help yourself," said Gisburne. "They won't trouble you. In fact, I doubt they'll go near you ever again." He hauled himself up into his saddle. "Not that it's of any concern of yours now. You have business in the North, Aldric Fitz Rolf. Wealth. A future, should you wish it. I will see you there."

"I will not follow you..." protested Aldric.

"Clippestone. It's a royal palace near Nottingham. Be there in two weeks' time," said Gisburne, and he and Mélisande turned to ride away. "Come armed."

"I will not follow you!" Aldric shouted after him.

"The fifteenth day of March," Gisburne called without turning back. "No later!"

And they left Aldric Fitz Rolf staring after them in the muddy street.

"Will he come?" asked Mélisande as they turned east, towards Aldgate.

"He'll come," said Gisburne.

XI

"PUT YOUR BACK into it, you 'eathen shit-stain," said Udo, spitting a lump of mutton gristle into the mud.

"Now, now," said Jupp, turning his saggy face towards the younger man. "No need for that kind of talk. There's more than enough of that back there." He gestured over his shoulder, where the sprawling metropolis of the port of Dunewich spread south of the estuary. "You don't hear master Digory coming out with that kind of talk, do you?" He turned to Digory, seated on his other side, and patted him upon his meaty shoulder. Udo stared resentfully into Digory's vacant face for a moment, then turned his crossed eyes back to the sweating Saracen. "Our own little world here, it is, away from the hurly burly," said Jupp. "Our own little kingdom." He watched in satisfaction as the big man hefted the packed barrel of herring onto the back of the creaky wagon, then fetched a great basket from the quayside.

Jupp chuckled to himself and slapped his knees. "Oh, I could watch this all day, I really could! You see that, Udo, my friend? *That* is a talent. Most can only lift them baskets when they're half so full. And it takes two to heave them barrels on the cart. But *him...*"

Asif al-Din ibn Salah took a fish in his palm, slid the thin-bladed knife into its belly and slit it open. *Just keep going,* he told himself. *One fish at a time...* Pulling out the guts with his finger, he doused the fish in salt and tossed it into the next empty barrel.

"Oi, go easy on the salt..." called Udo.

Just keep on... He reached for the next fish and repeated the process, his eyes low. He had done this over a thousand times already, and would do five times that before the day was done. It had become his habit to keep count. Partly because it satisfied him to know what he had achieved—to set a goal and to try to better it. But, more importantly, it kept his mind off everything else. He needed to stay focused, to stay out of trouble. To be invisible. Although that, of course, was well-nigh impossible here. Back where he came from, he had been one of the crowd—judged for what he said or did, if he was judged at all. Here, he was and would always be different. Something to be stared at. Spat at.

He couldn't really blame them. Self-pity was not his way. They had been at war, after all. Not that any here had seen that for themselves, nor had they the slightest notion that there were Christians born and raised in the Holy Land who had regularly traded, laughed and broken bread with those they were called upon to fight. In his own small way, Asif had done what he could to make that possible. The fact that it was not *his* war was a possibility few seemed to entertain. None wished to. They preferred things simple. He understood that, too—his own people were no different, when it came to it. He laughed to himself. If they only knew. If only they understood that what he feared most was not the wrath of suspicious Christian hosts, but that of his own kind. These grumbling, petty-minded Christians may *wish* him dead, but there were others—here, now—who meant to kill him. And so, every hour, every day, he trod with caution.

"What's he got in this bag, anyway?" Udo's whining voice jolted Asif out of his meditation, and he nicked his finger on the knife. He looked up to see that the rangy, stooped figure had sidled over to his battered old scrip bag by the wheel of the wagon, and was now poking it with his foot.

"Leave it," he muttered.

"He never lets no one near it," said Udo, and continued to prod it until he got the metallic sound he was searching for. "I hears it clank and jangle when he carries it. I seen a glint from it, too. Silver, I reckon."

"Get away from it!" rumbled Asif, the gutting knife pointed towards Udo. It was a gesture only, but Udo blanched.

Jupp raised a hand. "That is his private business, Udo, and don't you go poking your nose, or you might find you lose it."

"Plenty of it to lose," said Digory, and snorted with laughter. It was the longest sentence Asif had heard the giant utter in three days.

Udo slunk sideways, and resumed his place next to Jupp. "Don't trust 'im," he muttered, then bit on the mutton bone he had been worrying, on and off, for most of that morning. Where he had managed to find that, Asif had no idea. He suspected a midden.

"Don't you listen 'a these two," said Jupp, cheerily. "It was a good day when you came amongst us, heathen."

Asif, his eyes still upon Udo, slit another fish open, dragged out its innards and threw them with a slap upon the heap of guts at his feet. "And there was I thinking you disliked me," he said.

"I? Dislike you? No, no, no!" He chortled, then shifted his large arse upon the plank of the makeshift bench they had constructed for themselves. "I didn't want you for this work, heathen, I'll admit. If it had been down to me, you would not be here. But there was a favour owed, and I honoured it. And glad I am that I did, for I learned a lesson, and a valuable one. And now... Well, I wouldn't change this for anything, would you, lads?"

They said nothing.

"Well, would you?" There was a hint of threat in his voice this time. Jupp tweaked Udo's ear with a laugh. Both shook their heads and muttered incomprehensibly. "Yes, you have changed my whole view of this world. I like you, heathen. Do you know why?"

"Because I do the work of three men, and yet am paid half as much as one?"

"Quite so, heathen, quite so! And what's more you can work on Sundays. On Holy Days. There's no stopping you! I see a bright future for you here, my boy." The bench creaked as he leaned forward. "You wonder how that is?" Asif had no intention of replying, but Jupp was not waiting on him anyway. "Well, I'll tell you. We are in a time of famine. Rain has drenched the land from summer to spring; made it wet as the sea, in some parts. Well, that's all right if you be a farmer of mould. But no Englishman ever lived off such fare, no. So, the harvest fails. Stores are sodden and mildewed. Cattle cry out for lack of feed and turn to skin and bones, their very feet rotting in the mud." He leaned forward again and raised a fat finger. "But what is not made bad by this wet? That's right, my heathen friend—the sea. *That* has not failed us. By the grace of the Almighty, it continues to give up its rich bounty, and those who farm its fields and reap its harvests are therefore kings."

He sat back, rubbing his palms upon his knees. "Now, can you tell me what day this is?" This time, it seemed a genuine question.

"It is Friday," said Asif. "When I should be at rest."

"At rest? We never stop work on a Friday, do we? Busiest day of the week, Friday is. Why? Because it is a fasting day. And here is my point. We are two days past Ash Wednesday. Now, I wouldn't expect a heathen to know what that means—but what follows it is Lent, a time of fasting. For six-and-forty days, no meat is to be eat. Nothing what lives off the land nor flies in the air. But fish... Ah, yes, fish may be consumed upon any fast day, and in any such quantities as you desire, provided the priest don't see it." Udo and Digory chuckled at that. "No, God has no qualms about the fishes. And that is our blessing. So, you gut those beggars as fast as you like, for there's old men and babes out there crying out for your handiwork—and though we'd never tell 'em, they would not even care not that those hands be godless, just as long as their bellies are full!"

His witless companions guffawed. Still laughing, Udo resumed his gnawing upon the mutton bone. He looked to Asif like a giant rat that someone had dressed in human clothes as a joke.

As he turned, a sudden, swift movement caught his eye—a half-familiar shape moving silently between the stacks of baskets and barrels. He froze, his mouth turning dry. They had found him.

"Asif..." Udo muttered contemptuously, tossing the bone into the mud.

"As if what?" said Digory.

"Eh?"

"As if what?"

"I dunno. It's his name."

Asif hardly heard them. He straightened up and took a step sideways, towards his bag.

"Hey!" said Jupp. "What you stopped for? There's twenty baskets to..."

"Get out of here," interrupted Asif, his eyes scanning the stacks. "Go back to the main dock, as fast as you can. Or better still, the streets of the town, among as many people as you can find."

Jupp glanced over his shoulder in the direction of Asif's gaze, then, seeing nothing, turned back with a sour expression. "Are you trying to mess with me, boy?"

"No, Jupp of Ledeston, I am trying to save your life."

Jupp had barely opened his mouth when a deafening *crack* stopped his reply, and one of the empty salt barrels stacked behind Asif leapt into the air, sending others tumbling. Asif hurled himself at the ground, landing heavily behind a jumbled heap of empty baskets. As he lay—half in the mud, half in fish guts—the barrel fell and spun to a halt by his head, shot clean through with an arrow.

It should have killed him, but some instinct had preserved his life. He took a deep breath and muttered a prayer. Asif was not one to depend on Allah's mercy, but he was glad of it this time.

He shuffled himself around, keeping low behind the rickety jumble of baskets. His mind raced, but drove out, one by one, all extraneous thoughts until a strange clarity descended. A single, simple truth: if he went after his attacker or tried to escape, he would be killed. If he stayed hidden and simply waited, his adversary would have to come to him.

But what then? It was by no means certain that Asif would see or hear him coming. And if he did? The man who was coming for him would be well-equipped for combat. What did Asif have? A knife to gut fish.

He peered out tentatively. No movement. The bench was empty, one barrel toppled and the plank askew on the ground. Jupp, Udo and Digory seemed to have vanished into the damp, salty air. The arrow had clearly come from one of the big stacks of barrels opposite, but if the archer had any tactical sense—and Asif was sure he did—he would already be trying to get around behind him. To his left was the more sheltered route. Asif crawled around the right side of his feeble wicker barricade, to keep it between him and his attacker. A movement to his other side made him turn: Jupp, Udo and Digory, cowering in the shadow beneath the wagon, against the wheel of which his bag still rested.

"Throw me the bag!" he hissed. Jupp started so violently at the sound that he hit his head on the underside of the cart. Asif could see his hands shaking as they curled over his balding scalp. "Throw it here! Quickly!" Udo looked at the bag, just beyond the shadow cast by the wagon, his eyes as wide as shield bosses, then back at Asif, and shook his head. "Throw me the damn bag!" he barked.

To Asif's great surprise, the lumpen frame of Digory then pushed forward between his quaking colleagues, and with apparent disregard for his own safety—or total lack of awareness—reached out, grabbed the bag, swung it and let go.

It landed with a clank less than a yard from Asif's hiding place. He darted out, dragged it back to him and clutched it to his chest—just as something struck him with the force of a horse's kick. As it did so, he glimpsed a dark, shabby figure disappearing behind the barrels to his left.

The second arrow had struck the bag and stopped hard against the metal inside; another near miracle. There would not be a third. Scrambling further round his meagre battlement, he pulled the arrow from the thick leather. He knew its type, and the mind behind it. Thinking him unarmed, his adversary would surely come for him now. They did not like to wait, and they did not waste opportunities. But he was no longer unarmed. With nervous fingers, wet with mud and fish blood, he pulled at the knot on the flap of the bag.

The attack came sooner than expected. It seemed impossible that his attacker could have covered such a distance without a sound—yet in the next moment the dark, cloaked figure flew at him from behind the barrels at his back like a great, silent bird, his sword arcing through the air, a dagger glinting in his other hand. Flat on his back, the bag still stubbornly tied, Asif had nothing.

As he braced himself for death, his outstretched hand met a familiar texture; the spilt load of a fallen barrel. His fingers closed about it, and he flung the contents wildly at the looming, shrouded face.

The black wrappings obscured all but the eyes, and it was at these that he hurled a fistful of the coarse salt.

The man cried out, and Asif rolled as his attacker's blade struck wet earth inches from his head. Before he was even fully to his feet, he slammed his fist into the man's side with every ounce of strength he could summon.

The blow should have broken ribs, but Asif's knuckle cracked against hidden armour. The man fell, nonetheless. Still blinded, he crashed into the heap of baskets, clinging to his weapons as if they were a part of him. Asif grabbed his bag and pulled again at the leather tie, but the attacker—as big as him, and far faster—was already on his feet, his streaming eyes red and burning with fury.

The sword sighed through the air, and Asif leapt back. It flashed back again, catching the bag that he held before him like a shield. The blow cut the tie—but the bag fell, spilling its contents into the mud. Asif felt the thump of the teetering stack of barrels at his back; there was nowhere left to go.

Everything slowed. As if in a dream he saw the blade draw back again—and stop dead. His attacker's eyes showed confusion. He seemed to be struggling, as if somehow unable to complete the gesture. And then, wrapped about the blade of the sword, Asif saw a gauntleted fist.

The dream broke. Everything accelerated—all action a blur. The sword was yanked down and raised to the attacker's own neck. He staggered backwards, the blade's edge close to his throat, his dagger falling from his hand. Then, over the killer's shoulder, Asif saw the face of an old friend.

Without a second thought, he made for the bag.

THE MAN'S STRENGTH caught Gisburne by surprise. He'd come into this fight with all the advantages, but now the bigger, stronger man—with a determination that marked him as more than a mere cutpurse—had locked Gisburne's grip in his own and was forcing him backwards.

The opportunity to close the blade on the man's throat was lost, and if he stumbled, and the big man fell on him, he'd be done for sure.

There was only one other way to break the impasse. Gisburne let him go.

The man whipped round, sword still in his grip as if nailed there, but Gisburne's own sword was already drawn. Up swung his blade. Gisburne saw the man's dark eyes follow it, ready to block—or stab him in the side before the blow could fall. But as it drew back, up came the seax in Gisburne's unregarded left hand. The man saw the feint—but too late. The short, heavy blade caught the attacker's hand on its upward swing, and his sword spun away, end over end, into the heap of baskets. With the agility of an acrobat, he leapt backwards out of the range of his enemy's blades, then drew a shortsword from beneath his cloak and turned on Gisburne again.

But he now faced two adversaries, to one side, Gisburne with sword and seax; to the other, Asif. He had availed himself of his attacker's lost dagger—but it was the weapons in his left hand that caught the attacker's attention: three flat rings of steel, their outer edges sharp as knife blades. He tucked the dagger in his belt, passed one of the rings to his right hand, and began to spin it about his finger. The metal rang as it gathered speed.

"Run," said Asif.

The attacker's eyes, framed in black, flicked from Asif to Gisburne and back. Then, fast as a fox, he turned and bolted for the heap of barrels.

Gisburne lurched forward, intent on pursuit. "No!" snapped Asif. He stepped ahead of him, drew back his arm and flung the ringing metal disc after the fleeing attacker.

It sang through the air, ending in a dull, sickening thud. The man jerked weirdly. The ring—embedded in the side of his skull—caught the weak sunlight for a moment and glinted like a skewed halo. Then his legs, limp as rope, gave way, his momentum sending him sprawling in the mud.

Both stood in silence for a moment. Behind them, the trio of wharf rats crept out from beneath the wagon.

"So, how are you liking England so far?" said Gisburne.

Asif gave a great laugh and flung his arms around his old friend. "It is... very green," he said.

"Green?" said Gisburne, stepping back and looking about him. "Asif, it's barely spring..."

"It's greener than I'm used to. Except for where it's brown."

"That would be the constant rain."

Asif stood back to look at him. "In Jerusalem we used to celebrate when it rained, remember?"

"If anywhere will make you tire of that habit, Asif, it's England." Gisburne turned and looked back to their fallen adversary. "I would have caught him, you know."

"You would not. And he had a bow hidden behind that pile." He strode towards the body, Gisburne trailing him. "But how did he find me here?"

The question knocked against another that had begun to niggle Gisburne: why this man had arrived on the same day as he—almost the same moment. The answer, all too obvious, struck him through like a blade. "Me. It was because of me. It's no coincidence, us both being here. I led him to you, or to those in London who gave me the information to find you. Damn it!" He crouched by the crumpled figure. "I was asking after you in London. And I was not discreet, not at first. I had no reason to be, until I began to understand what had happened..."

Asif held up a hand. "He would have found me anyway. Where else would a dock worker go after London but Dunewich? And had you not arrived at the same moment, it would be me lying face-down in the mud."

"So what brings you all this way?" said Gisburne. "Your message was vague on that front." He turned the body over and pulled apart the shabby, nondescript travelling cloak to reveal glinting scales of armour.

"You were always telling me what a beautiful country England was. I thought I should see it for myself."

"Aren't you supposed to be keeping the peace in Jerusalem?"

"I felt a change of career was in order. I have discovered my future is in fish. Also, Saladin's son wanted to kill me."

Gisburne stared at him in disbelief. "So, your life was in danger in Jerusalem, and so you—a Saracen—came to the Christian kingdom of Richard the Lionheart, scourge of Saladin and champion of the Holy Crusade. For safety?"

"Well, when you put it like that..."

Gisburne chuckled to himself, and began to unwind the bloody wrappings from the man's head, taking care to avoid the razor-sharp blade that still protruded from it.

"It has not been easy since the Sultan died," said Asif. "The sons are not like the father. They squabble. And the new Emir, al-Afdal..." He shook his head in disgust. "I had served under Christians as well as Muslims. He never trusted me."

The last of the wrappings revealed the face of an Arab, his neck covered in a distinctive pattern of tattoos. "So it would seem..." said Gisburne.

"*Hashashin*... I knew I had irritated the wrong people, but even I had not realised how much."

"Well, he's a dead *hashashin* now," said Gisburne.

Asif put his foot on the dead man's face and pulled on the disc. Metal squeaked against bone as it worked free.

"Still playing with those toys?" said Gisburne.

"They are good for more than tricks," said Asif wiping the blood from the smooth steel. "As you can see..." His expression turned sombre. "More will come."

"Then we'll stop them."

"Nothing will stop them. Except my death."

Gisburne gazed down at the lifeless figure. "Well, then... Perhaps it is the right time for you to die after all." He looked up at Asif, then back to the dead man. Yes. Similar enough. "Let's say I was never here. That our *hashashin* friend succeeded in his quest and rode away from this encounter alive. That you are indeed lying dead there in the mud. And they"—Gisburne nodded his head towards the three dumbstruck onlookers, still rooted to the spot in terror— "witnessed it all." He stepped closer, lowering his voice. "I can make you disappear, Asif, though where I would take you may yet prove more hazardous."

Asif grinned. "You always did like conjuring tricks. You and that friend of yours—that Locksley."

Mention of the name gave Gisburne a sudden chill. "Locksley is precisely why I am here, though he is now better known as Robin Hood."

Asif's eyebrows raised. "I have heard this name... The ordinary people idolise him. You say this is the same person?" Gisburne nodded, and Asif shook his head. "He is a dangerous man. I liked him well enough, but I learned things about him, even while the two of you were still in Jerusalem. I meant to tell you, but you were both gone before I had the chance."

"I found out in my own time," said Gisburne. "And you may yet have a chance to bring him to justice." He stood and strode off behind the barrel stack, returning a moment later with a black Saracen bow and a quiver full of arrows.

"Good bow," said Asif.

"It's yours, now. All these, too." Gisburne gestured to the weapons strewn upon the ground, then crouched and began to strip the dead *hashashin* of all that remained. "Put them on. The armour too."

Asif frowned. "Why the armour?"

"You're going to need it. I'm looking for good men, Asif, to help me hunt down Locksley. There's gold in it."

"Always happy to work for honest pay," said Asif. "And my opportunities elsewhere would seem to be diminishing." Asif held up the coat of scale armour. "This, though... This makes me feel like a thief."

"It's not robbery, Asif, but exchange. You must give him your clothes. Your belt, your purse—everything. There is no other way."

Asif questioned it no more.

When he was done, Gisburne threw the *hashashin*'s travelling cloak back over his friend's huge shoulders.

"Phew! He stinks!" protested Asif.

"Better the stink of the living than of the dead," said Gisburne. "But I'll be honest—the fish are hardly helping your case..." He turned to the wharf rats. "You! What is your name?"

"J-Jupp, sir. But I..."

"Go to whoever you answer to, Jupp. Go immediately and tell them Asif al-Din ibn Salah is dead. Set upon, in an attempt at robbery."

"But, sir..."

"No one here will question the death of an Arab, nor look too closely. Your skins will be safe. Tell his employer. Tell everyone. *Asif al-Din ibn Salah*—can you remember that?"

"Asif Adam... Eeeb..." Jupp's face contorted about the unfamiliar sounds.

"Just say the big Saracen, Asif," said Gisburne. "Now go!" They jumped at the command and scuttled away, evidently happy to escape with their lives.

Gisburne stared down at the prostrate body and clapped a hand on Asif's shoulder. "Well, you're dead, my friend. Now you must leave, with all possible haste. Avoid the town. Make your way north, to Nottingham. From there, travel west to Clippestone. It is a royal palace, everyone knows it, but be careful who you ask. If questioned, say you bring news from the East, and if doubted, show them this." He pressed a gold ring into Asif's hand. "It bears the symbol of Prince John. I'll not lie, there are more who hate him than love him, but even in these disordered times, few would dare incur his displeasure. We meet there in eleven days, on the fifteenth of this month."

With no more than a brief nod, Asif turned and was gone.

"Is THAT BLOOD?" said Mélisande as they rode past the Leper Gate and on towards the outskirts of the bustling town.

Gisburne looked at his sleeve. "Fish," he said, and wiped it away.

"I'm curious... Why an Arab?"

Gisburne noted that she did not use the familiar term 'Saracen' but the Arabs' own word for themselves.

He shrugged. "Because he's here. Because he's a friend. And because he is one of the most capable fighters I ever met. He even knew Hood a little, in the Holy Land."

"Our little band is beginning to take shape."

"It must," said Gisburne. "We will have only one chance. Hood's army is ramshackle—untrained, undisciplined, poorly fed—and I believe the ties that bind it will break under stress. But only if we can eliminate the source of its strength—the half-dozen closest to their master. There are many who will fight for Hood, but only a few who will stand with him to the last."

"So you mean for us to match them."

Gisburne nodded. "Man for man."

"And *woman*..."

Gisburne smiled and nodded.

"Do you know much about this core?" she continued.

"I have lived with them in my head for months. *Years*. Took, the rebel monk; John Lyttell; Will the Scarlet; O'Doyle, brother of the Red Hand; Much, who they call the Miller's son..."

He felt a pang of anger at the last; and also, perhaps, guilt. Once, he had attempted to part the lad from his infatuation with Hood. It had only been a fancy in the boy's head then. Weeks later, he was one of the Sherwood fanatics, instrumental in effecting Hood's escape from the Tower. Many had died that night—at least one of them by Much's own hand. Since then, Gisburne had heard that Hood was taking a special interest in the boy, doubtless fuelling his hero-worship. He was angry at the ruined life—the *stolen* life—and guilty at his own failure. Perhaps he had berated the lad too hard. Perhaps it was *he* who had finally driven him to seek a new master in the forest.

"And Lady Marian?" said Mélisande.

What of Marian? That, Gisburne did not know. Perhaps she could be rescued, returned to the fold. There was always the chance. Perhaps she was already lost. He honestly did not know which he feared more.

"I have sworn to restore Marian to her father, if it can be done," he said. He saw a pained expression upon Mélisande's face, and her gaze drop to the ground. It had been only a month since her own father had died—barely three, since he had banished her from his presence. By all accounts, he had recanted on his deathbed, but that came too late for Mélisande, and his death, too soon.

"What if it can't?" she said, irritably. Gisburne knew she hated any hint of weakness in herself; she was using anger to cover her grief. "What if she won't be restored—if she fights back? Whose task will it be to kill her? Mine? Is that why I'm here?"

"You know better than that."

She looked instantly regretful. "Perhaps I'll just take on Hood," she said with a conflicted smile. "Get it over with."

"Hood is mine."

At the crossroads, they passed St James' Chapel—the furthest religious house from the centre of the town, and a place of lepers— and there turned northward towards the humped stone bridge. A great graveyard opened up beyond the chapel, and Gisburne and Mélisande stared in silence across the crop of disordered grey grave markers—some wood, some stone, some already fallen—the only sounds the cawing of crows and the clop of their horses' hooves on the loose stones. Near the low wall marking out the hallowed ground were seven fresh graves, as yet unmarked.

"You know," said Mélisande, turning her attention ahead, "there was a legend among the pagans that told of the ultimate battle between divine heroes and their demonic counterparts—each matched in combat with their nemesis, to whom fate had always joined them."

"Who won?" said Gisburne.

"They all lost," said Mélisande. "Each side destroyed the other. It was the end of the world."

"We are not gods, and they are not demons. And if it takes our destruction to end them, well..." His voice trailed away, the latest in a string of gloomy thoughts overwhelming it. "You know you don't have to do this. I am not a general, and I do not give orders."

"Do you think I would take them if you did?" said Mélisande with a smile. She sighed. "Every army, no matter how small, needs its general. And there will come a time when someone looks to you. When we all do."

"But being there... That must be their own choice." Gisburne realised, even as he said it, how unconvincing he sounded. Mélisande knew it too. She always knew.

"Do you think this of all your soldiers," she said, "or just me?"

Gisburne found he could not meet her gaze.

"I don't need your protection, Gisburne. And you have no need to distance yourself from the responsibility this places on you. We all understand the dangers. We do it of our own free will—and out of respect and love for you." She blushed a little, then added: "All of us."

They rode in silence for moment.

"Anyway," she said, "why would a woman want to return to a life of privilege and luxury in the lush surroundings of her beloved Boulogne when she could be facing certain death on a fool's errand in a dank forest?"

They both laughed, despite themselves, the dark clouds broken.

"So, where next?" she asked.

"North. Fountains Abbey."

"To him?"

Gisburne stared straight ahead, his smile fading.

"You really mean to do it, then..." Still, Gisburne said nothing. Mélisande started to say something more, stopped herself, then began again. "You are sure about this?"

"I am sure."

XII

Fountains Abbey
10 March, 1194

"You say he still remembers nothing?" said Gisburne.

Ralph Haget, the Abbot of Fountains Abbey, watched as their subject deftly parried another blow, then turned his ice-blue eyes back to his guest.

"Nothing of his former life. He recalls his name, several childhood memories—some very vividly—and his early career as a knight, but beyond that..." Haget simply shook his head. "It is as if, for him, the years in between never existed."

"Perhaps that is the best thing that could have happened to him," said Gisburne.

He watched from the cool shade of the cloister as the slender fighter's wooden sword caught his opponent a sharp *thwack* about the side of his unprotected head. The big Norseman uttered a guttural curse. For a moment the pair locked weapons, then broke apart to take up their positions again, the slender man's closed helm glinting in the low sun.

They were an odd sight, these two. In part it was their surroundings. The small, cloistered courtyard—a place mostly used for growing medicinal herbs, but with an open, circular space at its heart—was undoubtedly a perfect space for close combat practice. It even afforded them privacy—which, given the nature of the combatants, was perhaps advisable. But it was the sheer incongruity of the scene that struck Gisburne. That this place of quiet contemplation in a house of God was ringing to the sound of clashing weapons—and under the stewardship of an Abbot who was an avowed pacifist— was strange enough, but then consider the men themselves. On the one hand, a broad Norseman whose plaited beard and hammer pendant marked him as a pagan—one of the very last of his kind; on the other, a graceful knight, in a domed, close-fitting steel helm whose locked faceplate—a lifeless, blank-eyed mask in parody of a human face—completely concealed the features beneath.

He announced his readiness, and battle was joined again. For a moment they danced around each other, then the Norseman tried a feint, and followed with a lunge—but his opponent, far swifter than he, and with movements more akin to a dancer or acrobat than a fighter, parried, dodged, spun full circle and brought his sword blade, two-handed, hard against the Norseman's ribs. The big man exclaimed again, stretched his aching sword arm and in a gruff, flat voice called the score. From within the mask, Gisburne heard what might have been a laugh.

"There is little more we can do here," said Haget. "Physically, he is as fit as one could hope, as you can see. Remarkable, when one considers what he has endured."

"The time has come for me to take him off your hands. I have a task for him."

"Are you sure this is a wise course, Gisburne? Those things he did... They are forgotten, but not gone."

"This is something by which he may yet redeem himself."

Weapons clattered again in the sunlit arena. The Norseman went in harder this time, with savage energy. He could not hope to match his opponent in swiftness, but Gisburne could see his ploy—to force an error. As he rained down blows, the helmed warrior danced and spun—until his foot caught a patch of green upon the still-wet stones and half slid from under him. His arms flailed momentarily as he righted himself—but the Norsemen, seeing the gap, caught him square on the helm with a clang of wood on metal.

He went down with the sheer force of it, and sat for a moment on the ground, his breath rasping beneath the mask. The Norseman extended an arm and hauled his opponent to his feet, a look of grim satisfaction upon his face. He was now only trailing by seven strikes to one. Still panting, the masked man reached up to the catches on the faceplate of his helmet.

There was one sharp click, then another, and with a grating squeal the expressionless face swung open. For a moment the weirdly disconnected non-face hung in the air, a hollow-eyed silhouette obscuring what lay beneath, until he grasped the helm upon either side and slowly eased it off his head.

Even Gisburne, who knew well enough what to expect, felt his flesh creep at what was revealed.

There was the living skull, its dark flesh burned and withered until it barely covered the bone. There were the lips drawn back across the blackened teeth, and the lidless eyes that stared without cease. And there, beneath it all, were the two misaligned sides of what flesh remained, divided from right brow to the left of his chin by a near-vertical scar.

That life could exist behind such a shattered visage seemed impossible. It was a face that belonged in the grave—in Hell. But even they had spat it out.

As if sensing something, the vision turned and looked directly at Gisburne. Gisburne, chilled to the bone in spite of the balmy weather, looked back into the face of Tancred de Mercheval.

IT HAD BEEN over three months since he had seen him last, when he delivered him into Haget's care. Then, he had been a broken man. Not physically—he had injuries, yes, but God knows he'd already had a lifetime of those. It was what was *within* that had changed. Something new was emerging. Or perhaps something already there was falling away—Gisburne could not be certain. He only knew that some metamorphosis seemed to have occurred—that the vile grub that was Tancred was somehow transformed; into what, he could not exactly say. But now, his decision to keep the one they had called the White Devil alive when all thought him dead suggested new possibilities—possibilities he could never have grasped when he had first brought him here.

Haget had accepted Tancred without argument that day—the only living being Gisburne knew who would. Gisburne trusted Haget completely, but there were other reasons why Fountains seemed appropriate. Many among Haget's brotherhood were former soldiers—they gravitated towards him, and he gladly accepted them—and if it came to it, were far better equipped to handle Tancred and his pagan manservant than the average pasty cleric.

In the event, no such precautions were needed.

"Model residents," Haget had told Gisburne when he had arrived that morning. "Tancred observes every office, day and night, and prays in between. He shames some of the brothers with his devotion. And his man sees to his every need without a word."

Haget had nevertheless made a point of taking Gisburne via a circuitous route through the infirmary—a reminder, he supposed, that the Abbey was not here just to grant favours to the well-connected.

It seemed much changed since his last visit. The place was now packed with ragged, grey figures—old men, young women, barefoot children—some pale, many thin and hollow-cheeked, some merely looking lost.

"All these people are ill?" he had asked as they passed through.

"Hunger is a sickness," Haget had said. "Rest assured, the tables of their lords are replete with food. It's not they who suffer, just the poor souls who helped put the food there." His eyes blazed with a pale blue fire. "There is a familiar cycle to these things. When the harvest is good, those above merely take the best part of it. When it is poor, they take it all—and demand more work to make up the shortfall. The people who work the land tire and hunger. They entreat their lord, who tells them to tighten their belts—that it is *necessary*. The priest tells them that it is good for the soul, that it will make them stronger. So they tighten their belts. What choice have they? But they do not grow stronger, only the hunger does. They begin to eat the fodder meant for their animals. Now their animals hunger. Their lord tells them to work harder still, for his table must not be wanting. They forage the hedgerows—but their lord takes that, too. Bereft of nourishment, they seek out the plentiful deer in the forest, whose meat furnishes the royal tables. When caught, they're flogged if they're lucky, hanged if they're not. Those not bold enough to poach begin to look to the ailing ox, and think how many mouths its flesh might feed, until, finally, they give in to temptation. Well, why not? It was going to die anyway. Its meat is tough and meagre, and soon gone. And now they have no food to eat, no seed to grow, no ox to plough. And what does their lord do? He punishes them over the death of the ox. And here we are..." He spread his hands wide, then shook his head in anger. "It almost makes me want to take up my sword again."

"Now you see why outlaws flourish," said Gisburne. "The monk Took thought as you did—and he *did* take up his sword."

"That is where we differ, he and I," said Haget with some asperity. "Took is not one with whom I am happy to be compared, though neither can I wholly blame those who follow him, or his master. Man does not live by bread alone, but he dies without it. And anyone who promises it—he is a king in the eyes of the starving."

"Famine is fertile ground for some," said Gisburne as they moved on past the gardens.

"We provide what alternative we can. The wheat and barley may have failed across the land, but at least here we have a fair crop of root vegetables. We forage, we fish. We should be getting some spring crops soon, God willing. The land almost turned to marsh in the rain, but we have built up the beds so they drain. People here will not starve, but I fear more will come—and we cannot provide for everyone."

Then they had turned into the small, cloistered courtyard, and there had been Tancred, fit and capable and practising swordplay.

TANCRED STARED AT Gisburne for several long seconds before finally turning away and seating himself upon a simple wooden bench. Gisburne had held his gaze, looking for signs of recognition, uncertain whether he really wished to see them or not. But his look conveyed nothing. The Norseman brought water, and Gisburne watched as the two of them drank.

"I admit I am surprised at you allowing this," he said.

"You mean the sparring?" Haget gave a gruff half laugh. "It's true I have made no secret of my feelings about war and bloodshed. About so-called 'holy crusades.'" He almost spat the words. "That puts me out of step with most of Christendom. But how many of them, I wonder, dare to ask themselves what Christ would do? Would he take up the sword, and slaughter his brothers? Kill those who did not believe the same as he?" Haget shook his head in disgust, his fists clenched in anger. Gisburne guessed he did not get to air these views often.

Haget sighed deeply. "I also do not forget that I was once a soldier. I detest killing, most of all in the name of God." He held up a hand as he said it, as if to fend off objections. "I know you will say that it is sometimes necessary, even good, and we can argue that point from now until doomsday, but my point is that while I abhor killing, I nonetheless understand and respect the disciplines of knighthood. The ideals, the physical challenges, the patience they teach... The restraint... These things are good, for mind and body. And so, yes, we allow this. *I* allow this. It is good for him. It has restored his health; and he finds himself through it, learns again who he is. One must know that before one can embrace anything else. A man is not a hollow vessel to be emptied of one set of ideals and filled with another. This, the mason understands better than the bishop. The ground upon which we build must first be firm."

"And what of him?" Gisburne nodded towards the big Norseman.

"You will not be surprised to learn that many of the brothers are uncomfortable having a pagan in their midst. But where else should he be? Where better than here?" He shook his head. "You know my views. The truth of Jesus Christ cannot be forced on anyone. God gave us free will; one must choose, or it is meaningless. I would even venture that there are lessons some of my Christian brothers might learn from him. Rarely have I seen such devotion." Haget's brow creased into a frown, as if contemplating an impossible conundrum. "Though given what you have told me about Tancred—and what I have heard—it seems hard to credit."

"Tancred always had something about him," said Gisburne. "As a youth, he was charismatic. Everyone wanted to know him, to be in his company. I'm not sure even we entirely knew why."

Haget looked at Gisburne in surprise. "You knew him?"

"I was just a boy, starting my training in Normandy, under Gilbert de Gaillon. Tancred was older. A squire, still, but a model of all we aspired to. And a great fighter. But now I see that there was more to it than that. He is, in a sense, two men. He changed, you see, after his injury."

"You mean the burning..." said Haget. As he gazed upon Tancred's wrecked, skull-like visage, Gisburne saw him—this veteran of a dozen battles—give an involuntary shudder.

"No," said Gisburne. "Not that. As a young knight he took a sword blow across the face." He ran his finger from forehead to chin.

"A sword blow to the face?" Haget looked at Gisburne in astonishment. "You will understand that I have seen many such injuries, but none from which the sufferer fully recovered. That he survived at all is a miracle."

The word "miracle" rankled with Gisburne. It hardly seemed appropriate to one such as Tancred. "In a sense he did not. It disfigured him, of course. But far greater was the damage done to his mind. By all accounts, the Tancred we now know—the mad, cruel, heretical Templar—was born that day. The old Tancred, it seemed—the good-natured boy I had known—was dead."

"And the burning? The destroyed flesh?"

"That came later," said Gisburne. Haget turned his searching blue eyes upon him, and Gisburne did not wait for the question. "He took those close to me prisoner, and the burning was my response. Quicklime, then fire. He should have died. But he refused."

"Refused? How does one *refuse* to die?"

"I don't know. But something similar happened during our last encounter. He should have died, but did not. They used to say he had the Devil's luck. Even when he lay at my feet, defeated, defenceless... I could not finish it. At last, I gave up trying to kill him and instead brought him here."

"Once is luck. Three times is something else."

"Perhaps," said Gisburne. "What is certain—and what I never understood—is that, no matter what evil he did, people saw something in him that they wished to follow. The Norsemen do not give their loyalty to just anyone."

"Only one being has true power over life and death, Gisburne. Perhaps that is what they saw in him."

"You mean God?" Gisburne laughed. What a cruel twist that would be. "Tancred always believed God worked through him. I'm not sure his victims felt the same."

Haget nodded sombrely. "Such men do pose a problem for the theologian. God favours the good; that is a fundamental principle of our faith. Why then do evil men flourish?"

Gisburne looked him in the eye. "You have an answer to this question?"

"I do. It is a challenge, one by which we all may be tested."

Gisburne looked back at the weird figure of Tancred, sitting bolt upright upon the low bench. Certainly this man had tested him. "You know he made the journey from England to the Holy Land in just thirty-two days?"

Haget shook his head. "That's not possible..."

"Yet he did it. The voyage from Brindisi to Acre alone took me fourteen, and that was considered swift. Tancred did it in seven. Flat seas, clear skies. The most favourable winds one could imagine. And overland, the weather smiled every step of the way, though it was winter." He gave a bitter laugh and looked up at the sky. "Even today the sun shines on him."

"Well, then, I stand by my claim of a miracle, for clearly someone was looking out for him..."

"How do you know it wasn't the Devil at his back?"

Haget, for once, said nothing. There *was* no knowing, only faith.

Gisburne did not know what he believed about Tancred. He had seen enough of life to have abandoned the belief that God granted favours to the living. One thing he could not deny, however—that he had seen with his own eyes, time and again—was that when it came to luck, good or bad, some seemed to possess far more than their share.

Hood was such a man. In the desperate battles on the way to Thessalonika and at Hattin, there were many who had felt their chances improved simply by standing with him. That was Hood's great secret—the reason for his growing following. Good God, hadn't Gisburne felt it himself? And hadn't it proved itself to be the truth at Hattin, where they both had escaped impossible odds? For the first time Gisburne wondered if he had survived that ordeal only because of Hood—if he owed his life to him. He shuddered at the thought.

"Put aside the petty acts, the small deeds that brought us all here, and see it for what it is," said Haget at length. "What was it that stayed your hand as you stood over him? I believe his redemption—your mercy towards him on the battlefield—was part of a greater plan."

"I don't know about th—"

But Haget waved an impatient, dismissive hand. "We don't need to know. We are not *meant* to know. Believe or don't believe; we must get on with life regardless, and make our choices, each according his conscience. More than that, we cannot do."

Gisburne gestured back towards the infirmary. "So, those starving in there—are they part of a great plan too?"

He'd sounded more spiky that he intended. The Abbot sighed heavily, as if answering for the twentieth time that day. "If God chooses to challenge me in this way, it's because He wishes me to fight. And fight I will. Metaphorically, I mean. It's those who say 'It is God's will' and do *not* rise to it who have failed Him the most. We are not all ascetics here, Gisburne. We do not simply pray and contemplate. We *do*. I thank God for my food, but I don't expect Him to bring me breakfast. I suspect that underneath it all, you and I are not so different."

Gisburne could not disagree with that. Pragmatism was the quality he most admired in men. Not just in men.

"Well, then," he said. "I suppose it is time to see if this gift of Tancred's can be put to good use."

* * *

"DO YOU KNOW who I am?" asked Gisburne.

The skull-face, with its perpetually staring eyes, gazed back at him, a perfect blank.

"The Abbot tells me you are Sir Guy of Gisburne. I have heard of you. A noble knight." The rasping whisper of a voice was chillingly familiar, yet its character was altogether changed—entirely devoid of the spite and bitterness Gisburne associated with the White Devil. "They also say you saved me from destruction."

Gisburne nodded slowly. Tancred did not need to know that the destruction he had saved him from was Gisburne himself. He glanced at the big Norseman, who looked on in stony silence—expressionless and implacable. He had been there, had seen Tancred's downfall. Would he tell him? Had he already? And how much, he wondered, was really destroyed that day? How much of the man remained? How much of the knight? How much of the mad Templar?

"Tell me," said Gisburne. "What is the role of a knight?"

"To serve one's lord and Almighty God, and to protect the weak and innocent."

"And do you know who you are?"

At this, Tancred faltered. "My name is... Tancred. My father was Hugh de Mercheval. They tell me he is long dead. My mother too. My memory of this is... unclear." He stopped, thought for a moment, then—his eyes boring into Gisburne's own—said: "Do I know you?" Something like a frown distorted the features of his wrecked face.

"Do you?" asked Gisburne.

The glassy, unblinking eyes studied him intently, his head, for a moment, cocked to one side.

"In Jerusalem, perhaps?" Gisburne prompted.

"Have I been in Jerusalem?"

"You have."

"You would think I would remember that," he said, a curious note of sadness in his voice.

"It was... memorable," said Gisburne. It had been Tancred's plan to set the entire city ablaze—an ambition he had come within a hair's breadth of achieving. But the face before Gisburne remained resolutely blank.

Then, without warning, Tancred's eyes seemed to widen further still, and there came a sudden horrible, hissing breath. *Oh, God*, thought Gisburne. *He does remember.* Tancred's bony finger raised, and pointed at Gisburne three times, his face once again distorting weirdly—this time, in a manner Gisburne had never before seen. As the dry chuckle clicked in Tancred's throat, Gisburne understood that this haunted, agonised grimace must be a smile.

"Fontaine-La-Verte!" hissed Tancred in triumph. "When we were boys. You trained there under Gilbert de Gaillon. A great man. Is he well?"

Gisburne dropped his gaze. "He, too, is gone. Taken before his time."

"That is indeed... sad."

"I fight now to restore his good name. And to rid this land of its greatest villain—an outlaw, thief and rebel. So, tell me, Tancred de Mercheval—will you fight with me, to protect the weak and serve your God?"

At that, Tancred suddenly dropped to his knee, his domed scalp bowed.

"All I have to give is yours," he said.

"ARE YOU SURE about this?" said Mélisande, frowning at the mounted figures of Tancred and the Norseman ahead. They were flanked by two monks, provided by Haget as an escort. He had made light of it, saying the brothers had business in Nottingham anyway, but their size rather suggested they had been hand-picked for the task.

"That is now the fifth time you have asked me that," said Gisburne.

"Do you wonder at it?"

Gisburne sighed. "Tancred remembers nothing of the man he was. As a young knight, he was a good man—an inspiration to others. I saw it myself. Perhaps this new injury has undone what the other did—returned him to the man he once was."

Mélisande, who for several minutes had been mesmerised by the bobbing bare skull ahead, tore her eyes away and grimaced. "Your mercy is... admirable. Especially in the heat of battle. But to take him in with us? Into a new conflict? And one of such importance..."

"Tancred is the best swordsman I have ever seen," said Gisburne.

"And...?"

"And... He is the only outsider ever to have returned from Hood's lair."

"Ah."

"I know everything about Hood and his gang—everything except where to find them. There are scraps of information, even a map of sorts. But it needs knowledge to unlock it. It is my hope that when we are upon the path, Tancred will recall something of it, and guide us—that our old enemy may become the key to Hood's defeat."

"Are you sure you want him to remember?" She sighed, and looked about, her gaze finally coming to rest on the Norseman. "And what about him? You trust him?"

"He is loyal to Tancred unto death. As long as you don't attack his lord, you'll have no trouble from him."

"And if his lord attacks us...?"

Gisburne said nothing.

She sighed once more, her eyes drawn back to the ghastly, yellow-grey pate of bone ahead of her. "So, is this to be the view all the way to Clippestone?"

"For you," said Gisburne. "I am headed north. To Durham." He smiled at her inevitable, outraged scowl. "I yet have one last piece of business." His smile faded at the thought. "One more to gather to our band."

Mélisande nodded. "And how do you suppose *he* will take to fighting alongside Tancred de Mercheval?"

Gisburne had no answer. He would find out soon enough.

"Even convincing him to talk with you will be difficult," she said. "Unless..."

"Unless?"

Mélisande sat up in her saddle. "Brother Dominic! Brother Samuel!" The monks turned. She smiled sweetly. "You seem most capable men. A word, if you please..."

XIII

Durham
11 March, 1194

GALFRID COULD TELL they were going to be trouble. He could *always* tell. They'd been rowdy most of the night, and although the banter had been good-natured, he had sensed something brewing.

He knew a couple of them slightly. They shared the same employer; they were men-at-arms in the pay of the bishop, and although garrisoned elsewhere, he'd seen them around. Their chief task, he'd deduced, was to guard the lead transported from the mines in Weardale, over which the bishop held the rights. It was not a great leap, considering they had twice delivered a load to the cathedral where he himself had taken receipt of it—and it told Galfrid that they also earned considerably more than he did.

This fact had grown in significance when, just a few nights before, their nodding acquaintance had led to him joining their game of dice in this very hostelry. On that occasion, he had redressed the balance by relieving one of them of a substantial amount of his pay.

They'd been a jovial bunch then—good, uncomplicated company for the most part, which had exactly suited his mood. He'd had a skinful, but felt good on it, and his luck was clearly in. In fact, it had been a pretty fair night all round. Even the one he'd roundly fleeced had taken his losses in good part and slapped him on the back at the end of the evening, cursing his own bad luck with a smile. Tonight, however, the same man had been raising his mug at him, trying to catch his eye and flashing a drunken, over-friendly grin that teetered on the edge of something more threatening. Several times he'd nudged his fellows, and nodded in Galfrid's direction, and muttered something that had caused his companions to burst into raucous laughter.

Doubtless, when Galfrid had stopped acknowledging these signals, he'd made it worse. But tonight all he really wanted was to sit in this corner and enjoy a quiet drink. Well, 'quiet' was impossible—the clamour in the place was enough to stir the dead in the neighbouring graveyard—but Galfrid could shut that out easily enough. Just as long as he was left alone, to drink himself stupid and forget about fucking masons for five minutes.

The only reason he came here at all was because it was one of the few inns near the cathedral where masons and their apprentices never drank. He didn't know why. Probably there was some dark reason for it—some omission or slight on the part of the landlord that had caused the place to be forever shunned by the masons' guild. They were a bloody odd bunch at the best of times; and these were not the best of times.

Galfrid's current quest for alcoholic oblivion was inspired by an ongoing dispute between a pair of masons working on the cathedral. Relations had never been cordial between Master Godric and Master Hubert, but when Master Hubert had reported that three stone blocks bearing his mark had been stolen from the cathedral precincts, things were brought to a head. Galfrid, as captain of the watch, had expressed doubt as to whether anyone could have carried such weighty things out of the precincts without a single guard being alerted. He wasn't even sure why anyone would try. When he had further suggested—quite logically—that the blocks had never left the cathedral, and that therefore—also quite logically—they had been moved by someone on the inside, Hubert had pounced on the idea, and pointed the finger at Godric. The old man was trying to discredit him, he said. At Hubert's insistence, Galfrid then had the joy of examining every side of every one of Master Godric's stone blocks for signs that Godric had ground out Hubert's carved mason's mark (a pentagram) and replaced them with his own (a fish) whilst the opposing apprentices glared at each other across the masons' yard.

All of which had left Galfrid not a little depressed. Not because it was proving difficult to untangle. It had been blindingly obvious to Galfrid almost from the first moment that the culprit was Hubert himself, and that he had stolen his own blocks and secreted them somewhere—if indeed they had ever existed—with a view to disgracing Godric. Nor because it was proving impossible to produce hard evidence of this—although that was indeed a problem. Mainly, it was because he was struggling to give a rat's arse about any of it.

It had not begun that way.

The reasons were complicated. Galfrid was not what you'd call a religious sort—never had been, and probably never would be— except when he found himself in a cathedral. Then, he felt his soul come alive. It was not exactly an orthodox faith; he had no idea if it had anything to do with the presence of God, and to be honest, he didn't much care. All he did know was that when he stood among the silent columns and gazed up beyond those soaring arches, he felt at one with the world. At these times, like no other, it all seemed to make sense—for if men could achieve this, he thought, they could achieve anything.

Then he had spent three months in the company of the men who were achieving it, and their petty-minded squabbles had wrung all the wonder out of him. In fact, it was fair to say that he had come to regard masons with the same contempt that he had previously reserved for the clergy. All things considered, perhaps his choice of employment hadn't been the wisest. He'd been lucky to get it, but he had no doubt that his luck would eventually run out—if he didn't go stark raving mad first. Maybe it was time to move on. But where? And to what?

The serving girl—she was thirty-five if she was a day, but in here, perpetually, a 'girl'—protested as one of the party opposite slapped her on the arse. They guffawed. She swatted at Galfrid's drunk friend, who made a big show of ducking as if terrified. They hooted and whistled.

Galfrid called her over. Partly because his stomach was gnawing at him and he thought food would give him—and it—something else to focus on. Partly to get her out of the paws of those who were driving him to distraction. But it seemed somehow to break an invisible barrier between him and the soldiers.

Galfrid saw his drunk, dice-losing friend crane his neck as the serving girl approached. "Oi Gal!" he called, trying to make eye-contact with Galfrid. "Gal! Oi! Oi Gal! Gal!" Clearly he thought the nickname, repeated relentlessly, utterly hilarious, to the extent that he collapsed into periodic fits of laughter. "Oi Gal! Gal!"

The serving girl rolled her eyes. "What can I get you?"

"Bread and ham."

"There's ham, but no bread," she said.

Galfrid shrugged and then nodded. He just wasn't in the mood to converse further.

"Go on, luv," called his drunk neighbour. "Give 'im one from us! 'E could do with some cheering up! Eh, Gal! Go on—he's got a nice big staff!" This time, one of them laughed so hard that a stream of snot flew from his nose.

"Do pilgrims do girls?" chimed another.

It was a reference, Galfrid understood, to the pilgrim staff he carried, and which was now leaning against the wall behind his right shoulder. The girl rolled her eyes again, shook her head and left.

"Ooh, not impressed," commented his neighbour, and shrank in faux fear as she swept past.

Galfrid drew his eating knife and stabbed it into the table top with a thump. This drew an "Oooh!" from the party opposite. It hadn't been meant as an aggressive gesture, but if they were determined to take it that way, then let them. Still he studiously avoided eye contact; if he engaged, the evening was over.

Then, as he stared down into his mug of ale, he became aware of a figure drawing closer. The girl, bringing his ham, or so he assumed—until she sat herself opposite him at the table.

There was a buzz of excitement from those nearby. "Hullo! Who's your friend?"

Galfrid stared in disbelief across the rough tabletop at Mélisande de Champagne. "Do you just put up with that, these days?" she said, cocking her thumb towards the rowdy crew.

"What in God's name...?" He could not resist a laugh.

"Who's yer friend, Gal?" called his nosy neighbour. Another one called out "Galfriend!" More fits of laughter. "I'm not really sure we can say who's the 'gal' here..." said the ringleader, and gave Mélisande a good look up and down.

Galfrid leaned to one side and did the same: rough boots, riding hose, a man's cloak, leather brigandine. A variety of knives. It was a far cry from the delicate, demure vision he had first encountered in Paris.

"I see you're not hiding your light under a bushel these days."

"No point," she said, her voice hard but her eyes suddenly sad. "Those days are gone." Her eyes slid sideways to the eating knife stuck in the table top. "You really shouldn't do that, you know. If you break the tip..."

"Yes, yes..." he raised both hands in protest. "Christ's boots, you've hardly been here long enough to warm the seat..."

Meanwhile, Galfrid's gambling friend was leaning dangerously towards them. He pointed at Mélisande. "So, what is it?" he slurred. "A man with the manner of a woman, or a woman who dresses like a man?"

"Which are you?" she shot back. Another "Oooh!" from the assembled men. He slumped back down in his seat, red-faced and momentarily chastened.

"So, what the Hell brings you here?" said Galfrid.

"I'm happy to see you too," she said with a pleasant smile. "I understand you're working for the Bishop of Durham, these days."

Galfrid shrugged and took a drink.

"God's hooks, Galfrid. The Bishop?"

"I like cathedrals."

"But Hugh de Puiset is a vicious opponent of John's—and one of the most dangerous men in the land."

"Also one of the richest," said Galfrid, deadpan. He slurped his ale.

"Until just a few months ago, you had been one of Prince John's most trusted agents—and now, somehow, you're in the employ of the Bishop of Durham, who also happens to be one of King Richard's Chief Justiciars. How does that happen?"

Galfrid bobbed his head from side to side. "I may have glossed over some aspects of my previous experience."

She leaned forward, lowering her voice. "That experience is needed."

"Needed?" said Galfrid, mulling the choice of words. "Do *you* need it? Or does someone else?"

"There is a task left undone. In Sherwood."

"Sherwood..." Galfrid's eyes narrowed. "Did *he* send you?" He scanned the dim interior, until finally his eyes came to rest on a familiar figure deep in the shadows. "Christ..."

"Just listen..."

"Not interested," said Galfrid.

"Galfrid..."

"It was low of him to send you to do his dirty work."

"It was my idea." She drew in closer. "And it is by royal command."

"Really?"

She raised an eyebrow.

"Then why does the Prince not command me himself? He knows I would answer the call."

"Not Prince John."

"Not...?" Galfrid frowned. If it was not Gisburne's former master, then...

"No, not the King of France either, before you ask," she said. "But a king, all the same... Closer to home. Or soon to be."

Galfrid could only stare at her. "No. No that's not possible."

Mélisande simply nodded.

"Gisburne, working for... him?" whispered Galfrid.

"He's full of surprises."

A scrape of furniture against the boards alerted them that their neighbour was out of his seat. Galfrid saw him edging towards them as his fellows giggled in the background, his cheeks flushed, a stupid grin on his face. But it was no longer Galfrid he seemed interested in.

"So, what is this strange creature?" he said, his voice low and husky, and he poked a finger at Mélisande's sleeve. "Definitely real," he said, shooting a glance back at his gang, who tittered. Mélisande did not turn, but Galfrid saw her fists clench upon the tabletop. The interloper prodded at her again. "Excuse me, Mrs Man..." His fellows chuckled uncontrollably. "Mrs Man..."

"If that finger, or any other part of you, touches me again," snapped Mélisande, "I'll break it off." The grinning idiot recoiled and yet another "Oooh" issued from his cronies. But then, to Galfrid's dismay, he began to creep towards her again.

"Don't..." muttered Galfrid, as the finger extended once more, and jabbed at her sleeve.

In the blink of an eye Mélisande grabbed his hand, bent the finger back until it snapped, then slammed his face into the table. He slithered to the floor, blood streaming from his nose and mouth.

The whole place fell silent. Galfrid, his trusty pilgrim staff gripped in his hands, was already on his feet, but so too were the six—no, seven—men-at-arms. They stood, staring at each other across three feet of ale-soaked boards. No one was laughing now. Galfrid's eyes darted to the shadow in the far corner, but the familiar figure was gone.

"I see you're still using that old staff," muttered Mélisande.

"Only a knight is permitted to carry a sword within the city walls," said Galfrid.

"I fear I may have broken that convention," said Mélisande, and drew back her cloak to reveal a Byzantine blade with a gilded hilt.

"My lady, when you walk in the door, convention goes out of the window."

If the gesture was meant to warn off their opponents, however, it failed. One—the biggest—drew a long dagger. The rest filled their hands with weapons—knives, two maces, a halberd that had been resting against the wall.

The big man grinned a gap-toothed grin. "Seven against one-and-a-half. Looks like the odds are in our favour tonight."

"Not any more," said a voice.

The big man turned, and the nervous crowd hastily parted. There stood Gisburne, sword in one hand, seax in the other.

Not wishing to waste the opportunity, Galfrid swung his staff and clouted the big man while he wasn't looking. The man-at-arms went flying, his great bulk hitting the floor with such force the whole place shook.

The interior of the inn exploded. Mélisande rushed forward before any could respond, driving her shoulder into a guard's chest and swinging his mace about so it broke the nose of another. As customers scrambled for the doors and windows, the man with the halberd charged at Gisburne. He forced the blade upwards with his crossed weapons, letting its own momentum drive it hard into the beam, then stepped forward and cracked its owner about the temple with the blunt back of the seax before turning his attention to the second man with the mace.

Another two of them, knives drawn, had Galfrid backed into a corner, where he couldn't swing his pilgrim staff effectively. He raised one hand to the top of the staff and twisted until it clicked, revealing a concealed sword blade, and their resolve faltered. As one of them stepped back, Mélisande's foot thrust hard against the back of his knee and brought him crashing down. She wrested the knife from his hand as he sprawled, and drove it through his palm, pinning it to the boards.

The other looked at Galfrid on one side and Mélisande on the other, the howls of his companion ringing in his ears, and knew he was outmanoeuvred. "Come on, then!" he cried, spit flying from his lips, his blade shaking in his hand. "Come on!" The knife whipped around, glinting in the dim lamplight as the pair circled him. "You'll not take me, not without me taking one of you. Which one's it gonna be, eh? You? Or you? Even then, you'll not be safe! Not from the bishop! Oh, no! 'Cause after me, there'll come others. Yes, after me..."

A thrown mace bounced off his forehead, bringing the tirade to an abrupt halt. He folded into a heap at Galfrid and Mélisande's feet as Gisburne stepped into the arena.

"Let's get out of here," he said. All looked up as a distant horn sounded; someone had alerted the city guard. "Fast..."

As they headed for the door, Galfrid hesitated. "Wait!" He ran back inside, pulled his eating knife from the tabletop, then—after a moment of thought—crouched over the groaning drunkard still lying among the ruins, nursing his broken finger and crushed nose. "Don't do it again," he said. Then, after rifling in the stunned man's poke, he dashed for the door, flipping a silver penny into the serving girl's hands as he passed. "Sorry for the mess."

They ran until they could hear the cries and the sound of the horn no longer, then leaned against a dank wall in a dim side street, panting and laughing. Galfrid felt the pounding in his head and chest—the grazes, the cuts, the bruises. For the first time in weeks, he felt truly alive. He caught Gisburne's eye—then remembered himself. His laughter died away.

Gisburne turned to face him. "Help me get Hood," he said. "Fight with me one last time."

Galfrid stared hard at his former master. There was passion in the entreaty, but he would not do it for him—not just like that. Then he looked at Mélisande, saw the pleading in her eyes and felt himself nod in agreement. Mélisande threw her arms about him, hugging him in delight. Over her shoulder, he caught sight of Gisburne's face, half in shadow.

"Many miles have been travelled to reach here..." sighed Gisburne with a smile of satisfaction. "Now, we're complete."

Galfrid held his gaze. He did not return the smile. "I will fight to the last, just as I ever did. But do not think this undoes what has been done."

XIV

Clippestone Royal Palace, Sherwood Forest
15 March, 1194

ALDRIC WAS THE first to arrive at Clippestone.

It was the afternoon of the fourteenth—one day before the company was due to gather—when the guard called Gisburne to the gatehouse battlement. Through the haze of driving rain, heavy drops drumming against the horse-leather of his hood, he saw the lone figure of Aldric trudging up the gritty path, wrapped like a pilgrim and with a huge, heavy-looking bag over his back. Gisburne ordered the gates to be opened and his guest, pale and soaked to the skin, mud-caked to his knees, plodded in. He looked like he had been sleeping rough—and, thought Gisburne, was not very good at it.

"You win, damn you," whispered Mélisande in Gisburne's ear. It had been she who'd suggested placing bets on who would be first to arrive. Gisburne had gone along with it; it helped to distract from the foreboding that had clouded his mind for the past few days. Those days here with Mélisande—away from the eyes of those who might judge them and temporarily free of responsibility—had been idyllic. But the very preciousness of the time had only served to trouble him further. He had fought the feeling, and pushed it as far down as it would go. But some things, he knew, would not stay buried.

De Rosseley had been Mélisande's choice—the clear favourite, she felt—and she had scoffed when Gisburne had nominated Aldric.

But Gisburne understood Aldric's situation. He had nowhere to go and few funds to buy a bed, and these days food was scarce even for those of moderate means. By Gisburne's reckoning, if Aldric made it at all, it would be early, and he would not wait before knocking.

Gisburne sat him by the fire, where he ate and drank eagerly and rapidly returned to life. Even when engrossed in his meal, however, he never let the bag leave his side, nor allowed anyone but he to touch it.

Asif appeared later that night, also on foot. The rain had held off for an hour at most, but Asif somehow had managed to stay almost completely dry—and had also reached the main gate without the guard seeing or hearing him. Gisburne smiled to himself. It was little wonder the city fathers of Jerusalem—Christian *and* Muslim— had so valued his services.

Gisburne suspected Asif had been travelling under cover of darkness for at least part of his journey; a wise precaution, in these troubled times. Although bereft of sleep and left leaner by the past ten days, he carried it better than Aldric. In extremis, thought Gisburne, the training always showed.

The very first thing he did—almost before he was through the gate—was to press Prince John's gold ring into Gisburne's palm. "You'd better have this back," he said. Whether it had served him well, or he could not wait to be rid of it, Gisburne could not be sure. But it didn't matter now. He was here.

The exhausted Aldric had already retired to his bed when Asif took up his place by the fire, but the Arab soon fell into animated conversation with Mélisande, who surprised him—and Gisburne— by conversing with him in his own tongue.

All three stayed up far later than intended.

De Rosseley arrived bright and early next morning as Aldric and Asif were eyeing each other cautiously over breakfast. He looked rested and fed, and was immaculately dressed and freshly shaved, with all his gear packed neatly on his horse. Gisburne guessed he had stayed at the nearest inn with the object of arriving as early as possible. It was typical of Ross; he had turned up on the appointed date, exactly as instructed, with the full potential of the day ahead.

"Did we say first to arrive," muttered Mélisande, "or first to arrive *on the day?*" But Gisburne would have none of it.

He introduced the knight to the others, and they ate together, although De Rosseley partook only a little and, Gisburne guessed, purely out of politeness. While perfectly courteous to his fellow guests, he talked almost exclusively to his host, then afterwards sought permission to take a tour of the grounds on Talos, his chestnut stallion. Almost the only time de Rosseley was content to sit still was when he was on the back of a horse.

"There are some areas you may not go," explained Gisburne, "but the guards will stop you before you get there. Other than that, the place is yours."

De Rosseley bowed his head, a model of good manners, though the gesture clearly amused him. "My lord... My lady..." he said with a smile, then took his leave.

The pair watched from the battlement as he put Talos through his paces out by the still, swollen lake—walking him backwards, then making him stop and kick, spurring him sideways in a full circle with the lance point maintained perfectly at its dead centre. Occasional shafts of sunlight crept through the clouds as he did so, making the stallion's flanks shine with a coppery fire.

"Whatever does de Rosseley do when the training stops?" asked Mélisande.

"For him, there isn't anything else," said Gisburne.

"Perhaps it should be you out there. We haven't even sparred in a week." She shot him a mischievous look. "A sword achieves nothing in its scabbard..."

It was a mark of his preoccupation that this made him look to the east wing of the palace, where the roofs of the enclosed courtyard were just visible. One of those forbidden areas he had spoken of. For now, at least. Mélisande followed his gaze.

"When will you tell them?" she said.

"When everyone is together."

"Most know him of old. And all have reason to hate him."

"It will be a test of their resolve."

"Undoubtedly. But do you think this the right way to test it?"

"It's... necessary." Mélisande had accepted it, after all, and she had more reason to hate him than most. But the nature of her dedication was altogether different. He stood silent for a moment, wondering what she made of his hesitation. "If it proves too much... Well, it will show we cannot stand together. Better here than out there."

"And what then?"

Gisburne did not reply, but turned and glanced nervously past the north gate and along the length of the road, tree-lined and empty.

XV

GALFRID WAS THE last to arrive. On this, both would have laid money, but neither mentioned it. There had been no question in Gisburne's mind that his old squire would come. Galfrid was a man who set great store by his word—something Gisburne recalled, with a pang of guilt, eleven or twelve times a day. In the event, Galfrid left it just late enough for Gisburne to start doubting—just late enough to make the point.

It was late afternoon. The light—what little there was of it, beneath the now-thick cloud—had started to fade. In the great hall, Aldric was entertaining de Rosseley with magic tricks while Asif looked on. Most depended on an array of tiny bottles, which sat neatly sorted within a lidded box that Aldric had produced from his precious bag and unlocked with a tiny key. First, he threw a powder in vinegar and made it fizz. Then he tossed other materials into the fire and turned the flames to a rainbow of colours—much to his audience's delight. Next he took the knight's drink, dropped a pellet of some substance in, and set it alight with a taper so a blue flame danced above its rim. De Rosseley was laughing and clapping enthusiastically when the horn blew from the gatehouse.

Galfrid's palfrey plodded with weary resignation through the dun-coloured puddle permanently established beneath the arch of the north gate.

Gisburne hurried across the muddy courtyard as the squire dismounted, the gates closing behind him with the heavy thud of damp wood. Galfrid acknowledged him with a curt nod. There was no smile. Not today.

A groom hurried forward to take Galfrid's horse. Another servant went to unload the bags, but Galfrid stopped him. "I'll do that," he said. The servant hesitated and looked to Gisburne, who dismissed him with a nod.

"Good," said Gisburne with a weak smile, his manner made all the more awkward by his attempts at nonchalance. God, he hated this. "Well, you know your way around well enough. We're the only ones in residence, but for the servants, guard and steward, so you have your pick of lodgings. There will be food in the great hall presently. And a good fire, too. We will all gather there."

Galfrid nodded once more, and walked away without a word.

XVI

GISBURNE SPENT THE next half hour avoiding what must come. He had been glad to see them all again—even Galfrid. The fact that all had, indeed, come now seemed remarkable to him. His response to their show of dedication, however, was as unexpected as it was unwelcome.

He arrived in the great hall to the sound of laughter. He had made sure that there was good wine, ale and sweetmeats laid out on a table for them, and already Aldric, Asif and Mélisande were being entertained by some outlandish tale of de Rosseley's. The clear tones of Mélisande's laugh—a sharp contrast to Asif's deep boom—rose above the cheery clamour, ringing about the great hall. For a moment, as he approached, Gisburne found himself overwhelmed by a feeling that, he now realised, had become almost alien to him. These were the people he loved most in the world, together. Happy.

As he looked upon them gathered there, another, tangled emotion writhed in him—something that he now understood had been there from the very start, but which he had smothered with preparations and practicalities. What was before him now, however, was not hypothetical, but flesh and blood.

Mélisande turned and shot him a bright smile, the light of the fire making her eyes glint like glass beads. Others turned in welcome—good cheer on every face. Or almost every face; Gisburne, unable to meet their eyes, sought out Galfrid. The squire, standing apart from the others, was hunched over the fire with one foot on the hearth, stabbing at the crackling logs with a poker as if he meant them harm. He, too, glanced up at Gisburne's approach, but there was no love in that look.

And the feeling that rose up in him now was so overwhelming it seemed to engulf him in shadow.

All had fallen silent. They sensed something wrong, as if a shadow had cast its chill over the entire room. He could have hidden it from others, but they knew him too well. That his weakness was so plainly visible gripped him with panic.

He stood for a moment, his eyes flitting anxiously. So many preparations, yet still he was not prepared for this.

"I..." he began. Mélisande regarded him with a puzzled frown. Even Galfrid looked concerned. Gisburne found he could not look either of them in the eye. "I..."

"Well, come on man, spit it out!" said de Rosseley with forced cheer.

Gisburne sighed heavily. His head drooped. "I meant this to be a welcome," he said. "But I fear..." He shook his head. "This has been a mistake."

"Mistake?" De Rosseley laughed, thinking it a joke. Then the laugh died. Gisburne saw Mélisande shake her head in disbelief, and mouth the word *No*...

"I should not have brought you here," he said. "If any of you wish to leave..."

"Why on earth would we wish to leave?" said Asif.

"You said there was a job to be done," said Aldric, his irritation barely contained. "That my services were needed."

"You will be paid in full."

"That's not the issue!" snapped de Rosseley.

"If honour is the issue, it is satisfied by your being here. I release you from your obligation."

"Was it an obligation?" said de Rosseley, looking about him. "I came of my own free will."

"The issue is," said Galfrid, "there is still a job to be done."

Gisburne looked him in the eye. "I can find other means."

"Don't..." said Mélisande, still shaking her head. "Don't do this..."

"There are plenty who will fight for pay."

"Hirelings?" said de Rosseley. "They won't risk their lives to protect you."

"Perhaps that's better."

"So you squander your gold on us, then go cap in hand back to the Lionheart, asking for more?" said Mélisande. The bitterness in her voice pierced him like a blade. "If ever there were a man who collected on his debts, it is he."

"The gold was not from him."

"Who then?"

"Sir Robert Fitzwalter," said Gisburne. He immediately regretted saying it. Had he revealed it under other circumstances, when Mélisande felt she had his confidence, its effect may have been quite different. But the discovery that Gisburne was in the pay of none other than Lady Marian's father stunned her into silence.

De Rosseley took a step towards him. "We've travelled the length of England for this. For *you*. Do you think we did so lightly?"

"No. No, I do not."

"Gisburne..." began Asif, but Gisburne raised a hand to silence him.

"Hear me out... Then you can do as you wish. You came because you feel duty bound to do so. Because you... trust me." He stumbled, as if struggling to find the right words. "And I asked you because I knew you would say yes. But that certainty is precisely why I should not have."

"You're talking in riddles, man..." said de Rosseley.

"It is highly likely this venture will get you killed, Ross," said Gisburne.

"Do you think we don't know that?"

"Actually, *I* didn't know that," muttered Aldric.

"It seemed great wisdom to gather you all together in this great enterprise—until I entered this room. Then I was struck by its immense folly. The folly of leading *you*, of all people, to the most deadly place I know. To a man who would see you all dead, killed for his pleasure, and for my torment." His eyes were on Mélisande's when he spoke these last words. Her expression changed as he did so. He believed—he hoped—she understood.

"Certainly, this is a sword with two edges," said Asif. "But the better for it, I would say."

"Well, now we know," said de Rosseley. "You say all will be recompensed. Fine. That means if we stay, we do so only because we want to." He turned to the others. "So, are we doing this or not?"

"Without question," said Asif.

Galfrid nodded slowly. "It's my fight as much as anyone's."

"Nothing would drag me away," said Mélisande.

Aldric looked about him and shrugged. "Why not? I've nothing better to do."

"Well, there it is," said de Rosseley. He thrust a cup into Gisburne's hand and raised his own. "To death!" All drank—although Gisburne's reluctance was clear. Their response moved him, but his fears remained.

"I hope you do not think I said these things in order—"

"You have no further say in the matter," interrupted de Rosseley. Gisburne cast a glance at Mélisande, and saw her expression had mellowed. At the sight of it, even he managed a weak smile.

"Well, can we at least find out what it is we're supposed to be doing?" said Aldric.

XVII

De Rosseley frowned. "You mean you really didn't know?"

Aldric shrugged. "We're to catch someone. That's all I heard."

"God's teeth," muttered Galfrid. "So what promise did he make, to get you here?"

Aldric looked defensive. "Gold," he said. "And more than that..."

Galfrid sniggered. "More than gold. That's a good one. Well, perhaps you should have found out what that meant and what you were being asked to do before you came."

Aldric's face reddened. "What did he promise you?"

"I'm not here on any promise," said Galfrid. "It's personal. Unfinished business." His eye lingered on Gisburne for a moment, then turned back to the glow of the fire.

Aldric surveyed the faces surrounding him, and for the first time seemed to realise the disadvantage he was at. "Am I the only one who...?"

"For God's sake, tell him, Guy," said de Rosseley.

Gisburne sighed heavily. There was no point pussy-footing around the issue. Not now. "I brought you here to kill Robin Hood," he said.

Aldric first stared, then looked incredulous, then burst out laughing. "Robin Hood?"

"You have heard of him, then?" said Gisburne.

"Of course, but... But he's not *real*..."

"Tell that to those he's killed and robbed," muttered Galfrid.

Aldric's laugh withered under the squire's cool gaze. "Good God..."

"Trust your soul to God's safekeeping, if it pleases you," said Galfrid. "For the rest, wear armour."

Aldric turned to Gisburne. "You're serious?"

"Gisburne is always serious," said Mélisande. "Even when he jokes."

Gisburne looked intently at the young enginer. "Before this month is out, no matter who stands beside me, I will either see Hood dead or be dead myself. Those are the facts of the matter, Aldric Fitz Rolf. If they do not please you, you remain free to leave—to take the gold promised you and be thankful for an uneventful life. You'll not be judged. I have no wish to lure anyone on a false promise."

"Hm!" snorted Galfrid, and spat in the fire.

Aldric looked nervously at the silent faces about him, then swigged his drink. "I served under Tancred de Mercheval," he said. "After that, everything is easy."

"We have a strategy, I suppose?" said de Rosseley.

Gisburne stared at the ground. "I go into the forest, find Hood, kill him, take with him as many of his closest lieutenants as I can. Then burn his village to the ground."

"That's it?"

"That's it."

Each looked at each other, as if wondering who would be first to respond. "No more need be done," continued Gisburne. "Without him, his army will fragment."

"Army?" said Aldric. "Wait... You said we were after one man..."

Gisburne shrugged. "It's not really an army. A robber gang. A rabble, really."

"And how many make up this 'rabble'?" asked Aldric.

"Over three hundred, at the last count," said Galfrid without turning to face them. "Most of them armed with bows."

"Five hundred, now," said Gisburne. "Or so it is rumoured."

For a moment, the only sound was the crackling of the fire.

"And you propose we just walk into this camp of five hundred archers?" said Aldric. "In broad daylight? That's not a plan, it's suicide!"

De Rosseley gave a reluctant nod. "He's right, Guy. They'd pick us off before we got within a hundred yards."

"That's why I mean to go in at night."

Aldric's eyes widened. "That's madness!"

Asif shook his head. "No, it is wisdom."

"You don't know these forests, friend," said de Rosseley. "Christ, Guy... Moving through that—the enemy's own domain, to boot—in total darkness? No attacker would choose that course."

"And that's precisely why I chose it. If one does what an enemy expects, then one is finished before one starts."

"Seven of us against five hundred?" said Aldric. "We are finished anyway!"

"Do you wish to reconsider your position yet, lad?" said Galfrid.

"We need to keep in mind this is not a pitched battle," insisted Mélisande. "It is a raid."

"This is how the *hashashin* would do it," said Asif.

"We are not *hashashin*..." said de Rosseley.

"To do this, it is necessary to become like them," said Gisburne. "Asif knows their ways. First-hand."

De Rosseley looked askance at Asif.

"I know them, too," said Mélisande. She blushed—one of the few times Gisburne had ever seen her do so. "A little."

Both Asif and Aldric looked stunned—Aldric suppressing a nervous snigger.

"She may not be the strongest of us, nor the biggest," said de Rosseley. "But you will learn, if you did not already know, that Lady Mélisande is no mere bystander." He turned to face Aldric. "I saw her bring down a man bigger than our Saracen friend here—one covered in iron plates and armed to the teeth. A murderer of knights. He had got the better of my guards—of me, too. I was down, and would be dead and buried but for this good lady's actions. In her native France, she is a legend."

"For all the good it has done me," muttered Mélisande. But she could not resist a sly smile at the knight's testimonial, nor at the way Asif and Aldric now regarded her with amazement.

No less amazed was Gisburne, who was still mulling over the words she had uttered. Did she really mean that she had learned from the *hashashin* first-hand? How? When? He had discovered much about her in the past few days, yet so many things remained unknown between them.

"Lady Mélisande is proof that the smaller force can defeat the greater," he said, "but only by attacking in ways the opponent does not anticipate." He looked across to Galfrid. "Like Inis na Gloichenn..."

"Inis na... what?" said de Rosseley.

Galfrid sighed heavily. "The defeat of Tancred de Mercheval," he said in a monotone. "Upon a lonely Scottish isle of that name. Don't worry that you haven't heard of the battle; hardly anyone has, outside of this hall, and I doubt anyone else ever shall. We walked right in, were on him and his men before you could say 'knife.' We chose the harder course that day. I suppose you could say the aim was achieved." With that, Galfrid poked at the logs again, sending a burst of sparks up the chimney.

Gisburne silently thanked the squire for his grudging intervention. "The plan is this," he said. "We go into Hood's village under cover of darkness, when their every instinct tells them no one will come. When they are unprepared.

"We find Hood. It will not be hard: he will be at the very heart of the nest, and has never considered himself in need of protection. Leave him to me. You will take down his generals, and then we set the place ablaze. Fear and panic will do the rest. Those five hundred will have no idea how many are attacking them, whether we are seven or seventy times seven. And they are not soldiers. Most will flee as soon as the confusion hits. The rest will not stand their ground for long when so many of their fellows are put to flight. A handful will fight to the last—the core of men who Hood calls the Wolf's Head—but with Hood dead, even they will falter.

"All of us here have different skills; all will be needed to get us there, and to get us out alive. But I believe we can do it. We can get him. We *will* get him. I have no desire to send anyone to their deaths, least of all the people in this room, but I need those about me I can trust. The Wolf's Head—those Hood can call upon when his life is threatened—is no more than a half-dozen strong. The rest will scatter. Thus, we are a match for them. More than a match. And we will have surprise in our favour."

De Rosseley nodded at his words, and smiled. "You've changed your tune," he said.

Gisburne frowned, and saw de Rosseley and Asif exchange grins.

"You said 'we,'" explained Asif.

"And 'us','" added de Rosseley.

Mélisande raised her cup. "To us," she said, her eyes on Gisburne's. "Together." Asif, Aldric and de Rosseley joined the tribute.

"This is all well and good," said Galfrid, "but there is one thing you have failed to mention..."

XVIII

THIS TIME, GALFRID turned from the fire to face Gisburne. "How do we attack when we don't even know where he is? When there is not one person outside of the robber gang who can say *where*, in these thousands of acres of forest, Hood's village lies?" There was a challenge in his tone—or perhaps he suspected there was more to Gisburne's plan than he was letting on.

"Is this true?" said de Rosseley.

"We do not know precisely," said Gisburne. "Finding his lair will be our first task."

"And how, tell me, is that to be done?" said Galfrid, not addressing Gisburne, but the whole of the rest of the party—a rhetorical question at his expense. "Many of you may feel you know forests; some may even think you know this one. But you do not. Much of Sherwood is open woodland, heath and pasture. Plenty of space for a horseman to pass. Good for hunting. That is the purpose of it, after all. Doubtless you know other places much like it. But that is not Hood's forest."

He stepped closer, his eyes still on Gisburne.

"There are parts of this woodland where the trees close in and block out the sunlight, the shrubs and vines twist together till passage is choked, the rocks rise up on either side or fall away at your feet into fissures and caves. Into these places, no horseman may go. We must make our final approach on foot—into this realm where wild boar and wolves roam free. March is Mud-Month, and this year has seen rain like no other. Even if we knew *where* we were going, the going would be hard."

"What *do* we know of its location?" said de Rosseley.

"They call it 'the village to which no roads lead,'" said Galfrid. "It is the stuff of legend, for it has never been found. No one who has ever been there has returned, or if they have, they will not speak of it."

"But the very fact it has not been found tells us much," said Gisburne. Galfrid laughed dismissively, but he pressed on. "We know it is far from roads and paths, well away from the hunting courses— out of sight of all who might pass. Not even the Foresters venture here. It needs water, so we know a stream must flow nearby. That narrows the possibilities all the more. And like wolves, Hood's men have a range. They will go so far, and no further. If we consider all their attacks over time, they will define an area at whose heart their nest will surely be found."

"But that area must still encompass dozens of acres," said Aldric.

"Hundreds..." corrected Galfrid.

"If it is as you say," said Asif, "we could pass within fifty yards of his camp and not even know it."

"Why do this now?" said Aldric. "Why not gather more knowledge first?"

"It must be now," said Gisburne. "Or never."

"Do we really not know any more than this?" asked de Rosseley.

Gisburne drew a small scrap of dirty cloth from inside the battered black gambeson and flung it on the table. On it were marked crude lines and smudged shapes. "This was drawn by someone who was there. A guide to its location."

There were no names upon the map, no numerals. Nothing to indicate scale or orientation. "This could be anywhere..." said de Rosseley.

"Or nowhere," added Aldric. He frowned at it, then pointed at a curious row of uneven dots. "What are those?"

"I believe them to be traps," said Gisburne. "That's why my meeting with you was so fortunate, Aldric. We will need the skills of an enginer to pass them safely."

Aldric, Asif and de Rosseley exchanged uneasy glances.

"When we encounter them," continued Gisburne, "we will know for sure we are close."

Galfrid—the only one of them to have seen the map before—eyed it suspiciously. "Traps..." he said. "Have you divined the map's meaning, then?"

"Not yet," said Gisburne. "Not entirely. But there are other sources that I believe may yet make sense of it."

"Other sources?"

"There was another agent of Prince John. Richard Fitz Osbert—a veteran of John's Irish campaign, whose name was also on the Red Hand's list of intended victims."

"Good God," said de Rosseley. "I knew him, back then."

"He was a member of Hood's band. He lived among them for weeks. They knew him as 'Hereward.'"

"'Was'?" said Aldric. "You said 'was'..."

"He was betrayed. Killed. But he managed to get some fragments scraps of information out. It was he who said that the village was protected by traps."

"Scraps..." said Galfrid.

"On their own they mean little, but combined with what else we know..."

"They mean *nothing!*" snapped Galfrid. "We know nothing." He stepped towards Gisburne. "Hearsay. And dots! Face it—if his intelligence was worth anything, we'd have been about this task months ago when he was still alive, when he was still some use. What good is he to us now? The only outsider to ever see Hood's camp, and he's dead and gone."

"No," said Gisburne. "There is another."

Galfrid stared at him, mute, his expression slowly turning to one of dread. For the first time since his arrival, the cynical mask had fallen entirely away. He looked shaken, uncertain. Perhaps some part of him knew.

Well, it was as good a time as any. Gisburne craned his neck, looking past the gathered company to the door at the hall's far end, and gestured to the servant lingering there. He disappeared from view before the others could turn, but as they did so another, taller figure filled the doorway.

And as they looked upon it, every one of their faces fell in horror.

It walked forward slowly, the firelight glinting off the cold metal that encased its head, then some half-dozen yards from them stopped and gave a bow, and in a muffled voice that was barely more than a low hiss, said: "God save you all..."

XIX

ALDRIC DROPPED HIS cup and took three steps back. Wine splashed red across the flagstones. Asif—suddenly finding himself in the company of the monster who had almost beheaded him in the sewers of Jerusalem—uttered a prayer, or perhaps a curse. Even de Rosseley, to whom Tancred was little more than rumour, recoiled in horror at the extraordinary vision. "Gods..."

But it was Galfrid to whom Gisburne looked. The old squire turned fully to face him.

"Why would you do this?"

"Galfrid..." began Gisburne.

"*Why would you do this?*" Galfrid's eyes were wide. He looked ready to commit murder.

"This is not the Tancred you know. If you will only listen to him..."

"Listen...?" Galfrid let out a loud, disconcerting laugh, utterly devoid of mirth.

"I understood this meeting might be difficult..." breathed Tancred.

Galfrid, incredulous, stared at Tancred, then beyond to the door by which their unexpected guest had entered, and a tall, muscular, bearded man who looked on with grave inscrutability. The last surviving Norseman of Inis na Gloichenn.

The squire laughed again—a grating, joyless sound—and threw up his hands in exasperation. "This is insane. Does no one else think this is insane?" But all were too stunned to speak. Galfrid threw what remained of his drink into the fire, ale hissing on the hot stones of the hearth, then slammed down his cup and turned on Gisburne, his whole body vibrating with fury. "Keep your gold; keep your mission. I'm done with it." He turned for the door, but before he had taken two steps, turned back. "Second thoughts. I'll take the gold. Have my share brought. Coming here cost me dear. I'll have that back, at least."

"Galfrid, please..." Mélisande tried to take hold of his arm, but he shook it off and headed out without looking back.

Mélisande caught Gisburne's eye, and he shook his head solemnly—but she pursed her lips in defiance and went in pursuit.

HE WAS ALREADY turning into the small chamber when she caught up with him.

"Galfrid. *Galfrid!*"

"I don't want to hear it."

She followed him in. "It's not what you think. And we *need* him. He is the only man alive who knows where we will find Hood."

Galfrid was already stuffing his belongings into his bag. He did not look up.

"You knew, didn't you?"

"There was never going to be an easy way to tell you..."

Galfrid was struggling to cram everything back into his bag in his haste, and slapped a pair of hose back down on the bed in frustration. "I'd only just unpacked this bloody stuff..."

"Leave it unpacked," she urged, and placed a hand on his arm. "Stay. Please."

"I should not have come. Should not have trusted him..."

"Then trust me."

"After this?"

That sparked a flash of anger in her. "I was Tancred's prisoner too—or have you forgotten? I was there, in that same dark place, with the same horrors..." She calmed herself. "I was doubtful, just as you are. But I tell you, he *is* changed. I have seen it."

"It's an act," scoffed Galfrid.

"No. This is something different. That's what Gisburne saw in him. The blow he took to the head—it wiped away years of his life. The bad years. Please. Let him prove himself. He deserves this chance."

"Deserves? He *deserves* to be dead!" spat Galfrid.

"Tancred *is* dead. The Tancred we knew. What stands in that hall is what was hidden beneath. The good man he once was."

"Then what use he had died with him!"

"We have to try. Hope that he may remember..."

"Remember? You *want* him to remember?" Galfrid screwed up his face and shook his head, as if his thoughts buzzed at him. "Gisburne knew I would have nothing to return to—that I would have burned my boats with de Puiset in Durham—but if he thinks that will stop me riding back out of that gate, he's mistaken."

"Please, Galfrid. Stay. If not for his sake, then for mine. For the one who suffered alongside you."

Something in her speech pierced his defences. He sighed heavily, and rubbed a hand over his face. Then he turned to face her, his expression altered.

"This mission is madness," he said.

"Isn't everything we do?" She smiled. "It will be a little less mad with you than without you."

GISBURNE AND THE others were seated about the table when Galfrid returned. Little had been said during his absence, and the atmosphere had remained awkwardly charged—with Aldric glancing every few minutes at the looming Norseman, who simply stood in the doorway unmoving, like a sentinel. None, so far, had seemed keen to acknowledge him.

In some respects, it had gone far better than Gisburne could have expected. It had been Tancred himself who had led the stilted conversation, first apologising—in the most humble and courteous of terms—for his horrific appearance. It was not, he said, what anyone wished to look at over a meal.

De Rosseley, with equal grace, thanked him, then added—perhaps a little too pointedly—that he tried not to judge people by appearances. Tancred's simple honesty and unaffected manner carried an unexpected, near-unbearable poignancy—all the more so because Tancred himself seemed entirely unaware of it. Gisburne could see it struck all about that table. Their resistance softened, they even began to talk. Hatred was easy to maintain at a distance—far harder face-to-face, no matter how monstrous that face may seem.

The awkward silence returned with a vengeance when Galfrid walked back into the hall. Gisburne's heart leapt at the sight of him—then sank again at the thought of the work that was still ahead. He could not imagine how Mélisande had achieved it. Such tricks of persuasion had always eluded him.

Galfrid stopped short of the table. For a moment, Gisburne thought the squire had returned with the express purpose of delivering another damning speech—but his demeanour said otherwise. His head was held low. The fire had gone from him.

Then Gisburne realised.

The only places remaining at the table were the seats either side of Tancred, which the others had carefully avoided. Gisburne stood and offered his own place. "Here," he said. "I need to go anyway." He looked to the door, in the hope of seeing Mélisande, but there was no sign.

Galfrid said nothing. He simply took his seat and set about the food.

It was Tancred who spoke first. "Squire Galfrid," he said, pleasantly. Galfrid froze, but did not look up. "I have wronged you. I was told this. More than that, I see it in your face. I remember none of these things. That is my curse. I can only pray that the Good Lord forgives them, and gives me the power to put right what I have done."

"Pass the mustard," grunted Galfrid, and stabbed his eating knife into the table.

Another small obstacle had been negotiated. When Mélisande entered and saw Gisburne on his feet and making to leave, she stopped.

"You're going?" she said. "Do you not eat with us?"

"Things to do," said Gisburne.

"Please, join us, my lady," called de Rosseley.

She smiled sweetly, but for the moment remained by the doorway.

Gisburne turned to address the table. "Eat. There is more being brought: poached fish and potage; pickles and fruit, too. Simple Lenten food, but good. In the morning you will find more food upon this table. Make the most of it. When you are all gathered tomorrow morning and have breakfasted, meet me by the Great Pond—and then we shall begin in earnest."

"Begin what?" said Aldric.

"Training," said Gisburne.

"God's teeth... All I ever do is train," said de Rosseley. "I'd hoped for a holiday. At least tell us what type of training. We do need to know how to dress, Gisburne; not all of us wear the same clothes for everything we do."

"Dress for war," he said. Then he turned to leave. "From now on, I want you ready for battle day and night."

As he passed Mélisande, he paused. "I don't know how you did it," he muttered, "but thank you. Now, please join them. Enjoy this moment."

Mélisande caught his sleeve before he could hurry off again. "'Ready for battle day and night'?" she whispered. "What exactly do you have in mind?"

Gisburne did not return her smile. "From now on, you will have the Queen's Chamber to yourself. I will sleep here, in the great hall."

She raised an eyebrow. "It's a time of fasting, Gisburne, not total abstinence."

"It's just—"

"Don't worry," she said. "I understand. There must be discipline. And I shall be good. But you need to *eat*, Gisburne." She pinched his arm. "Without your strength you have nothing."

Gisburne avoided her gaze. "Make sure they are all there tomorrow," he said, and walked away.

XX

THE NEXT MORNING was cold, and a low mist hung over the lake. But the rain held off—and no-one had chosen to leave in the night. Another obstacle overcome. Gisburne was grateful for the smallest achievement.

They had dressed as instructed. De Rosseley, predictably, looked magnificent in his armour. Hardly less formidable, though, was Asif, clad in the *hashashin*'s scale armour beneath his black cloak, or Tancred—startlingly transformed into the man they had once fought so viciously. Galfrid stood a respectable distance from him; the last time he had seen Tancred with a sword, it had been at his throat. The squire's gear was as simple and practical as ever—but next to Aldric's ramshackle garb, it appeared luxurious. Mélisande, meanwhile, maintained an air of mystery. Her hair—uncovered—was back in a single tight plait; the rest of her was covered, literally head to foot, by a fine, green wool cloak.

Many carried bows. On their belts were edged and blunt weapons of all kinds, each according to taste. And there were helms of all descriptions—some worn, some carried.

Gisburne cut straight to the meat of the matter. "Some of you know each other, some do not. But over the next few days, we will all get to know each other much better. Our lives may depend on it." He happened to catch Galfrid's eye as he said this, then looked swiftly away.

"You have all brought arms and armour. Good. Aldric, Ross: I note you have no bows. You will need them. What you do not have, the armoury here can provide."

"I prefer the crossbow," said Aldric.

Gisburne smiled. "The last person to tell me that was Richard the Lionheart."

Aldric frowned at that. "I have my own," he added, as if anticipating protest on Gisburne's part. "I made it myself. And it's a match for any bow." He looked around, suddenly aware that all eyes were on him.

Gisburne nodded. "If it's what you know, then use it. Just as long as it's up to the task." He stepped forward, and looked Aldric up and down. The short-sleeved haubergeon—which showed signs of repair where Gisburne's own crossbow bolt had struck it over a year before—was of excellent quality, and the sword at his side was keen and well-fashioned. But as for the rest... Gisburne put his hand on the top of Aldric's helm and wobbled it from side to side.

"Hey!"

"The lining is shot," said Gisburne, then poked Aldric in the chest with a finger. "And that gambeson is barely thicker than my grandfather's shirt. You're not a guard on a battlement now."

"It's all I had," said Aldric defensively.

"To the armoury. Galfrid will help you find what you need. Galfrid?"

The squire grunted his assent.

Gisburne turned then to Mélisande. "Is this what you call 'dressed for battle'?"

"Not exactly," she said—then she pulled off the cloak and flung it upon the wet grass. "But this is."

Asif gasped, but even Gisburne was taken aback. In the past, Mélisande's fighting gear had been minimal and discreet—designed to blend in, to keep her hidden at night. Those considerations were now cast aside. She was clad in a hauberk and chausses of blackened mail with bronze detailing around its edge, over which was belted a surcoat of green, a gilded Byzantine sword at her waist.

Many times Gisburne had seen her wear armour and ride and fight like a man. But none here had ever seen a woman dressed so entirely in the manner of a knight.

"Is that strictly legal?" said de Rosseley, clearly conflicted on this point.

"I think we are beyond such considerations, Sir John," said Mélisande.

Galfrid gave a gruff chuckle and pointed south. "The law ends five miles that way," he said. "And if you're heading into it, you'd best go prepared."

"Here is how it will be," continued Gisburne. "Half the day, we train. The other half, we hunt."

"Hunt!" exclaimed de Rosseley, rubbing his hands in delight.

"After today, we eat only what we hunt or forage for ourselves."

"There's deer and boar aplenty in the forest," said Aldric. "Wild rabbits, too. On my way here a stag came within ten yards of me, bold as you like."

"What of the Lenten fast?" said Tancred.

"Do as your principles dictate," said Gisburne. He gestured to the lake. "In the waters of the Great Pond, roach and pike abound— perfectly acceptable Lenten fare. There are bows, there are arrows, there is twine. And, at the end of the jetty, a boat. But know this: if God has chosen you for this task, then he also wants you strong for it." He thought for a moment, then added: "More importantly, so do I."

De Rosseley slapped a hand on Asif's huge shoulder. "Well, you have one advantage, my Saracen friend. Your conscience is not troubled by Lent. Tell me, does your religion permit you to eat boar, or does that count as pig?" Several among the company chuckled.

Asif shrugged. "If it looks like a pig, and sounds like a pig, it probably is a pig." And with that he lurched forward with a great grunt, causing de Rosseley to recoil. Asif led the laughter this time; de Rosseley reddened, unused to having the tables so roundly turned upon him.

"Fasting be damned, I say," said Galfrid. "The people of England have done fuck-all but fast since last Michaelmas—and it's been an age since I tasted venison."

"But they are the King's deer," said de Rosseley. "It's hanging or a flogging to take them."

"We have royal dispensation," said Gisburne.

Each looked at the other—some with bemusement, others with delight. "Consider it archery practice," he said. "But keep in mind what our ultimate prey will be." He turned and paced before them. "Why do we carry bows, Aldric Fitz Rolf?"

Aldric shrugged. "Because Hood's men do so."

"Exactly so. And if they see us, they will shoot us—so learn how to hide. They certainly will. They are animals of the woods, now. Not game, but wolves—for so they style themselves. And that means they bite. So accustom your eye, and if you see them, shoot first and deny them the pleasure of making you their prey. And if we should encounter them on horseback, I hardly need to remind you that your horse needs to be as ready for the fight as you are."

He turned to de Rosseley. "Ross, you are to be tutor for all matters of the horse and related combat." De Rosseley bowed, happy to accept that mantle. "All except the longbow. On that, Asif shall be your schoolmaster."

Asif looked at de Rosseley, both equally bemused, then the Arab turned to Gisburne with a frown. "Are you su—?"

"Completely. Ross, we both know you're terrible with a bow. And Asif is the best there is. We can all learn from him."

"The Saracen way?" said de Rosseley, with a hint of mockery in his tone.

"I can lower myself to shoot the European way, if need be," said Asif, then gave a broad grin.

De Rosseley looked the hulking Arab up and down. "But can you raise yourself to the level of one of our horses?"

The laughter was at Asif's expense this time, and Gisburne smiled. It felt good at last to be *doing*, rather than endlessly thinking, planning speculating. Gisburne knew he could lose his doubts in simple, day-to-day tasks—even if those tasks meant deadly danger. And part of him, he began to realise, craved that too.

Even as he thought it, he looked at Mélisande, and something gripped him inside. He pressed on.

"For hiding in plain sight or moving undetected, let Lady Mélisande be your guide. And when it comes to turning a fight to your advantage, without the advantage of size and strength, no one knows better." Mélisande bowed in imitation of de Rosseley, who chuckled—partly out of disbelief, partly out of sheer delight.

Gisburne began his pacing again. "We will all spar with each other. Starting today."

"Even him?" said Mélisande, and nodded towards the distant figure of the Norseman who looked on, cool and impassive. Such a constant presence had he become that Gisburne had forgotten him.

"Never mind him," said Gisburne. "As far as the rest of you go, I want everyone to spar with everyone. Everyone..." He eyed Galfrid. "We must *all* learn from each other. Get to know each other."

Galfrid's gaze slid to Tancred, his expression resolutely grim. Gisburne had not singled out Tancred, although his skill with a sword surpassed anyone he had seen. There was only so far he could push. They would see it; they would learn. Even Galfrid.

"Everyone is different. Embrace those differences. They are why you are here. Work to your strengths. Look for the weaknesses. Sometimes our differences can get us killed." His gaze lingered for a moment on Asif. "But here, they may be what keep you alive."

XXI

On the first day, the lesson was archery.

"No, Sir John," said Asif, yanking de Rosseley's arm about. "Grip it. *Grip it!* It is a bow, not a bottle of wine."

"Dammit!" said de Rosseley, fighting to get the bow into the position Asif indicated.

"Think of it as a poisonous snake," said Asif. "Hold it firm. Yes, better!" Then he slapped the knight's forearm. "But angle it. Like this. Or the snake will bite."

De Rosseley began to draw.

"Do not aim!" said Asif. "Just *look...* And do not..."

But it was too late. The moment the string touched de Rosseley's cheek, he had released it. The arrow whipped past the bowstave. De Rosseley gave an exclamation of pain—and the arrow sailed past the target's top left corner and glanced off the top of the earthen butt to land who-knows-where.

"No, no, no..." Asif stepped forward, shaking his head. "You're rushing."

"Last time, you said I was too slow," said an exasperated de Rosseley.

"Too fast, and you do not focus on your target. Too slow, and you think too much. And you do not *pluck* the string, Sir John. You release it. You are trying to kill a man, not play a tune."

Mélisande and Aldric stifled their sniggers.

"All right, all right," sighed de Rosseley, glaring at both. "I told you I was no archer."

"And the string—it hit your wrist, yes?" said Asif. He was making the most of it.

"Yes..." said de Rosseley, irritably.

"A bow is like a lady, Sir John. Fail to show it the proper respect, and you are likely to get slapped."

Aldric laughed aloud at that one.

De Rosseley fumed. "It's all right for you, with your damned crossbow!"

"But his damned crossbow is hitting its target, whilst you—you are now being killed."

"Aldric," said de Rosseley. "Pass that here, would you? At least I might have a chance with it..."

"No," said Aldric, and clutched the crossbow to him. "No one must touch this..."

"All right, all right..." De Rosseley, for whom failure was his most hated enemy, found this excruciating. "Tell me honestly," he said. "How bad am I?"

"Honestly, Sir John?" said Asif, "I could do better throwing a stone."

De Rosseley held his gaze for a moment, then stooped, picked up a stone the size of a small apple, opened the Arab's palm, and slapped it in. He waved towards the target.

There was a moment of expectant silence among the gathered company as Asif regarded the missile, and turned it about in his hand. Then he suddenly whipped his arm around, and the stone flew and *thwacked* against the dead centre of the target. There was an "Oooh!" from the audience. De Rosseley gave a reluctant smile and clapped his hands slowly.

Asif turned back to the whole company. "There is nothing magical about a bow, nothing mysterious. It is a stick of wood and a string. What makes an arrow find its target is in here"—he tapped his forehead—"and in here." He tapped his chest. As he spoke, he drew out a short knife from his belt and flung it towards the target. It struck the edge of the gold in its centre.

"Many things may be turned to the same purpose," he said. "Even things you would not expect." And he drew from his bag the large, sharpened ring of flattened steel.

"What the devil *is* that?" said de Rosseley.

"I acquired it in Aqaba from an old man with a turban the size of a goose. He called it a *chakkar*. He had brought it from the East."

"I thought *you* were from the East?" said Aldric.

Asif smiled. "You will find that even the East has an East." And he snapped his hand like a whip, sending the disc ringing through the air. It embedded itself next to the knife.

He turned back again. "How do I know a stone will land where it does? Or a blade? Or a lance point?" Here looked at de Rosseley. "I don't know how. I just know. I look at where I want it to go, and there it goes. We all of us know this."

Asif walked towards the weapons rack, talking as he went. "So re-acquaint yourselves with the bow. Get to know it—its limits, its tolerances. How it may be used, and how, perhaps, it may be cheated." He chose a lance from the rack and turned to them again. "But always remember what you already know." He held out the lance to de Rosseley. "Try this."

With a smile, the knight hefted it, found the balance point, drew back, and hurled it. Its point drove straight through the straw target's centre, tearing it clean off the butt as its weight pulled it to earth.

Asif nodded approvingly. "Now, he is *not* killing you." And with that, he spread his arms wide. "You see? We all know, from childhood. From throwing a ball, or a stick. We just have to allow ourselves to *remember*."

ON THE SECOND day, de Rosseley got his revenge on Asif. It came with the startling discovery that the Arab hated horses.

"I never really rode in Jerusalem," he protested, struggling to heave himself into the saddle, a lance gripped awkwardly in one hand. "There was rarely the need. And anyway, the saddles were different."

"But I have heard you speak of Aqaba, Tyre and Acre," said de Rosseley. "How did you travel? Did you walk? Were you *carried*? Or did you travel in a wagon like a woman?"

"I can ride perfectly well!" protested Asif. He made another attempt at hauling himself up, got half way, and gave up again. "It's just getting on and off... And I am certain our horses were lower."

"Try this," said de Rosseley, and signalled to a stable boy, who ran forward and put a stool by the horse's flank. "It's normally for young boys and old men, but, you know..."

Asif teetered on the stool and put his foot back in the stirrup, pulling on the cantle and pommel so hard that the whole saddle began to skew—at which point the grey stallion decided that enough was enough, and walked off.

Asif hopped three times on the stool as he watched his other foot, stuck in the stirrup, drift away from him, then overbalanced and fell backwards, arse first, into the mud.

"A horse is like a lady," said de Rosseley. "Fail to show it the proper respect and... Well, you get the idea."

The grey stallion walked around behind the prostrate Asif, and gave the Arab's head a sharp nudge with his nose.

"Ow!"

"He's checking to see if you're still alive," said de Rosseley. "He assumes the reason you're on the ground is because you're wounded. I've seen horses drag their masters from danger at times. Not sure this one is quite prepared to render that service yet..."

Asif sat up. The stallion snorted in his face, then wandered off.

De Rosseley rode around Asif a couple of times. "You're lucky you didn't impale yourself on that lance, too," he said. "Normally you'd get in the saddle first, then have someone pass it to you. But I admire your ambition. Anyway... You seem to have dropped it..."

Then he urged Talos forward, and spoke a barely audible command. Talos dropped his head, clamped his teeth about the centre of the lance shaft, and lifted it up. As de Rosseley leaned forward, he turned his head and the knight took it from him.

"Work with a horse, and it you'll find it can be far more to you than just transport."

And with a broad smile, he turned and left Asif sitting in the mud.

XXII

OVER SUBSEQUENT DAYS the company tested themselves, one against the other, each taking their turn as schoolmaster.

Galfrid showed them how to use a bowstave as a weapon. Tancred demonstrated sword moves that even those experienced in the art had never before seen—while Galfrid looked on with detached cynicism. Aldric showed them how to improvise deadly weapons from the most unlikely of resources.

De Rosseley became a reasonable archer, and Asif a fair horseman.

And Aldric Fitz Rolf even began to overcome the obstacle that had dogged him these past two years, thanks to his sparring with Mélisande.

"You think you cannot fight well because of your injured shoulder," she said. "I can see it. But you just have to fight a little differently. And fighting differently is good; it is an advantage. Training develops reflexes, but it also breeds habits, patterns. Introduce surprises, and your adversary's own patterns may be his undoing. That is how Tancred wins. How Hood outwits his enemies."

He lunged at her with a knife. She sidestepped and grabbed his left arm, twisting it, and he froze, helpless.

"Fear is your first enemy," she said, her face close to his. "You fear this shoulder will fail you. You try to keep it from harm, hold it back, and I see that. So I target it." She released him. He stood back, flexed his left arm and straightened his tunic. "Don't give your enemy such a gift. You may spare your shoulder only to lose your life."

She stood ready for a fresh attack. Aldric crouched, dagger at the ready. "You know Gisburne also has an injured left shoulder?" she said.

"Gisburne?" said Aldric. He swiped at her. She saw it coming and dodged back. "I see no sign of it."

"Precisely my point."

"How bad?"

"He almost lost his arm at Hattin."

"Gods... He was there? I had no idea." Aldric tried a feint, then brought the dagger swiftly up, but Mélisande did not fall for it.

"He keeps it to himself. The injury, too."

"Does it trouble him much?"

"Every day," said Mélisande.

Aldric brought his hands together, shook his shoulders, then lunged at her with his right arm. She caught it, pulled him forward and locked it in a tight hold. Only then did she realise his right hand was empty. The knife was inches from her throat, in his left hand.

She grinned. "You're learning, Aldric Fitz Rolf!" Then she ducked and twisted, throwing him clean over her shoulder so he slammed down on his back.

He lay for moment on the damp grass, regaining his breath. "Where *did* you learn to fight like that?"

"Here and there," she said. "Mostly there."

GISBURNE HIMSELF KEPT a quiet distance from proceedings. He sometimes ate with them, and from time to time joined their activities—the sparring or riding—but for the most part he left the company to their own devices. To "get to know each other," he said. Mélisande understood his reasoning. She also understood why, for now at least, it was better—for the sake of the whole company—that the two of them maintain a respectful distance. She found it strange, nonetheless: him being there, yet not there.

Occasionally she spied him off at the archery butts, taking practice shots on his own, or taking Nyght, his black stallion, out across the grounds. It troubled her; there had always been a solitariness about him, but of late he had retreated further, and she wondered if it were something he could ever truly overcome.

In some ways, she missed him more now than when he'd been a thousand miles away.

One day, when they were resting between sessions, taking a drink about a fire they had built, she spotted him standing in the circle of dead earth beneath the great yew tree. He was leaning against its trunk, studying something—Tancred's map, she thought. She wandered over and stood beside him. As she approached, he screwed the cloth into a ball and shoved it inside the half-open front of his battered, black gambeson.

"Do you care to join us?" she said.

"Better not," he said. "I must get back to the palace. I am expecting a delivery from Llewellyn today."

She smiled. "What is it this time, an apparatus for flying? A cloak to make you invisible? A sword that can cut through steel and stone, perhaps?"

He smiled back. "Nothing so elaborate."

She looked at him intently for a moment. "Why are we here, Gisburne?" she said. "Doing this?"

He shrugged. "Always hone the blade before a battle."

She narrowed her eyes. "Is that one of de Gaillon's?"

"Is it that obvious?" He smiled. "It's not just about that. It's about the strengths and weaknesses. The alliances, the rivalries, the resentments... It's not enough to throw ingredients in a pot—you have to boil them together."

"Honing the blade. Boiling the pot. Is this really how de Gaillon spoke? I'd have screamed."

"If there is a weakness, I don't want to discover it out there." He nodded his head towards the dark edge of the forest. Then, after a moment, he added: "How is Galfrid?"

She glanced back at the sombre squire. "He refuses to spar with Tancred," she said. "He will not even speak with him. Every time he has a bow in his hand and the Templar in his sights, I see him fighting temptation like St Anthony in the desert. But he hasn't killed him yet, so..."

"He'll come round," said Gisburne.

"You'd know all this for yourself if you were more involved."

Gisburne, staring off into the trees, did not respond. Mélisande frowned and drew closer. "Why so distant, Gisburne? You're as good a rider or swordsman as anyone. You understand stealth and tactics at least as well as I, and we both know you are the best bowman here. You will lead us into battle, so why are you not with us now? Leading us?"

Gisburne shrugged. "I don't want to be the focus of attention. I want each to see the others' skills, not just mine. To see their true worth, beyond status, sex, the colour of skin."

Mélisande nodded. "I see that, and understand it; but an army also needs its general. It's he that pulls it together." She looked more intently at him. "Are you sure there are no other reasons you seek to separate yourself from us? Those things you said, when the company was first gathered, when you were for sending us away..."

Gisburne shook his head, and shifted awkwardly. "I was foolish. Not thinking."

"Perhaps you were thinking too much. Perhaps you still do... When I asked why we were here, I meant also why are we *still* here? Time is wasting, and Hood also prepares. The pot has been boiling for days, now. You can't put it off forever, Gisburne."

"I am not putting anything off..."

"You fear you will fail us. All those months languishing in an empty house have made you doubt yourself."

"Don't worry about me," said Gisburne, irritably.

"I know you were ill over the winter."

"How did you...?"

"Because I find things out. Though it pains me to have to find them out that way. Christ, Gisburne—you could have died. Alone."

"I've got through worse."

She reached out and moved a strand of hair from his brow. "The capacity to survive is not infinite. There comes the day when it abandons every one of us. But others can help, if you let them."

He looked her in the eye, and for a moment seemed to realise the impossibility of hiding from her. "It will all be over soon," he said.

At that moment, a shout went up; Gisburne looked towards the palace and saw a page running headlong towards him. The rest of the company turned at his approach and De Rosseley and Asif stood, all watching in anticipation as the lad knelt and offered up a tiny, tightly-folded parchment. Gisburne looked upon it with a grave expression, then, crushing it in his fist, strode across to the others and threw it into the fire.

"It's time," he said. "Richard has landed on the south coast and even now marches his army north. At dawn tomorrow, we ride into the forest, ready or not."

XXIII

IT WAS LATE when Gisburne found himself climbing the stairs to the Queen's Chamber, the single candle throwing a huge shadow behind him. He had waited until certain the others were abed; whether Mélisande would also be asleep, he did not know, but he would wake her if he had to. He knew he must see her now, or miss his chance. He stopped for a moment and listened: no sound, no movement, just the wind gusting outside, driving a light rain before it. Tucking the wrapped steel plate tighter under his arm, he resumed his steady ascent.

The thing under his arm made his mind drift back to the last meeting with Llewellyn. The old enginer had been sat in a chair in his perpetually smoky workshop hidden away in the bowels of Nottingham castle, trying to decipher a parchment with the aid of a glass, and failing. "Damn these eyes!" he had said, flinging it upon the bench.

He had looked old. He had *always* been old to Gisburne; it was something he took for granted, much as one might of a grandparent. But today it was different. Age was no longer just a quality of his— the same today as it was yesterday and would be tomorrow. Now it seemed to truly weigh upon him. Reducing him. Perhaps for the first time, Gisburne understood that Llewellyn would not live forever.

Gisburne could not remember once seeing Llewellyn outside of this chamber, or its equivalent in the White Tower. So oddly severed from the world was his experience of the man—made more profound by the bizarre, improbable devices that perpetually surrounded him in this chamber—that it almost had the quality of a dream. But today, he was flesh and blood, both of which were failing him.

"Oh, it's you," he had grunted as Gisburne entered. He then tried to rise, but Gisburne had waved him back to his seat, and he had slumped back with a wheezy cough. The grumpiness was reassuring, but as the old man's hands were less steady, his eyes less quick to focus—if they could focus at all. In every one of their meetings up to now, there had come a point when Gisburne's requests—always challenging, and sometimes impossible—had awoken a spark in him. But not today. He noted the requirements, scratching them upon a slate, then, as their meeting came to a close said, "I am not long for this world."

The sudden candour shocked Gisburne. All traces of irascibility were, for that moment, quite gone. He seemed suddenly without guile—child-like, almost. And a little afraid.

Gisburne had dismissed the words, of course, and said that Llewellyn would outlive him—a standing joke between them, given Gisburne's exploits. But today was the first time he felt certain it was not true. "You need to get out of this dark dungeon," he told the old man. "Get the sun on your face and some fresh air in your lungs."

"You mean for good," said Llewellyn.

"Yes," said Gisburne. "For good."

HE STOPPED AT the top of the stairs and hesitated outside Mélisande's door, his fist poised, ready to knock.

It opened before he could make another move.

"You know your right boot has a distinctive squeak?" said Mélisande. She stood before him like a ghost in the candlelight, her long red-gold hair contrasting sharply with the pure white of her shift. He gazed at her for a moment, caught up in her beauty—unadorned and bereft of the hard shell of recent days.

She put a hand on her hip. "Well, are you coming in, or not?"

Gisburne did not answer the question—but neither did he step over the threshold. "I just wanted you to have this," he said. "Before tomorrow. Before we leave here." He held out the wide, flat thing, crudely wrapped in plain linen.

"A gift?" said Mélisande, taking it from him with a smile and a frown. She took it, registered its weight, unwrapped the cloth. The polished steel breastplate sent dancing reflections about the dark corridor. She turned it over. It was shaped to fit her, its leather straps—dyed green—ending in bronze buckles. "Well..." she said, almost lost for words. "Most men just give a girl a ring."

"The buckles are shaped like dragon heads," said Gisburne. Quite why, he wasn't sure; it was self-evident. He felt rather foolish, but he wasn't at all sure what she was thinking.

She ran the tip of her finger over another tiny dragon stamped into the metal. "Llewellyn?" she said.

Gisburne smiled. "Who else?" Then, in case the gift were being misunderstood, added: "It's not a mere trinket. It is made to be worn. Put to use."

She sighed, and shook her head a little. He thought he sensed scepticism in her—even, he thought, irritation.

"Do you not like it?"

"It's wonderful."

"But?"

"You do know I already have armour? Among the finest in Europe, in fact?"

"This will provide extra protection against arrows," said Gisburne. "Much more than mail alone. Where we are going..."

She put a finger to his lips, silencing him. "And if I came to you, suggesting—insisting—you change your tried and tested armour the day before a battle, how would you take that?" He did not know how to respond. She held his gaze for a moment, then relented. "I'm sorry. I appreciate it, I really do."

Gisburne felt the moment slipping from him. This had seemed so simple in his mind. "I need to explain..." he said. "Do you know what happened at Inis na Gloichenn?"

Mélisande shrugged. "You captured Tancred."

"But do you know how? How we knew him to be there? It wasn't deduction. We were told."

She frowned. "Told? Someone betrayed him?"

"Hood," said Gisburne, and her eyebrows raised in wonder. "Tancred had collaborated with Hood's gang—helped them effect his escape from the Tower. Then Hood helped us. Made us a present of Tancred's whereabouts, so we might bring his reign of terror to an end."

"It is hard to believe that altruism was behind that act..."

"You are right to think so."

"Was it meant to eliminate a rival?"

"Perhaps. But I think there was more to it."

"What then?"

"I think..." He pondered for a moment before continuing. "I think he wants me all to himself. To have... my undivided attention."

She nodded slowly. "And that is why you starved him of it these past months. Why you were reluctant to pursue him..."

"It was all I could think to do—the one course from which he could make nothing. But I knew that one day the confrontation would come. And when it did, I also understood what his strategy would be. That he would target not me, but those around me. That he would hurt them, kill them. To keep me dangling on the hook. That is why I had this made."

Finally she seemed to understand. He sighed heavily. "I have been told that putting others before yourself is a weakness. Perhaps it is. But I cannot simply let it go. I know no other way."

Mélisande touched his face, then remembered herself and withdrew her hand. She pressed the elegantly curved armour against her, shuddering as she did so. "It's cold!" Looking down at herself, she twisted and moved from side to side, her long hair swaying. "Impressive. The proportions are true. It will fit well over a gambeson. Doesn't cut into the waist. Should even work well for riding."

"I had to guess the dimensions..." said Gisburne. "Working mostly from memory."

"It seems they were exceptionally clear in your mind." She smiled coyly. "And I am glad of that. It is perfect. Thank you." And she kissed him—a chaste kiss, for now, upon his cheek. "So, how good was your guesswork when it came Asif, de Rosseley and the others?" She gave him a mischievous look.

Gisburne reddened, and looked away.

"Gisburne?"

"There is no armour for the others. Just this."

"No..?" Her face fell.

"There was time for Llewellyn to make only one. So I had him make it for you."

"For me? Me alone?" Her eyes flashed with anger. "I did not ask for special treatment." She took the breastplate off. "You could have had one made for yourself. Why did you not?"

"He doesn't want to kill me. That is not his game."

"Then what of the others? Do you consider them of less value than me? Or simply more capable? I'm not some damsel in distress, Gisburne. I have faced a dozen enemies without your protection. A hundred."

Her anger baffled and exasperated him. "Hood is no ordinary enemy. I have seen him snatch an arrow from the air and shoot it back. This is not magic; it is real. And it is what we face, come tomorrow."

"Everyone in my life from my father onwards has tried to protect me." She fumed. "Or, more often, some *idea* they have of me. And each and every one has ended up doing the utter opposite."

Gisburne grew more insistent. "Don't you see? I do this only because I have no wish to see you die..."

The anger that had welled up in her seemed, momentarily, to turn to something else. "And don't you see that I feel exactly the same? That if we were facing a hail of arrows, I would place that armour on you before myself?"

They stared at each other in cold silence.

"Please," he said. "I only ask..."

"No one tells me what to wear," she snapped, and slammed the door.

He stood for a moment in the corridor, listening to the swish of the rain. She would come round, somehow. Galfrid too. And Tancred would prove his worth. These things he had to believe, for tomorrow he would lead them to victory—or to death.

III
CONQUEST

XXIV

Inis na Gloichenn, off the West Coast of Scotland
November, 1193

GISBURNE'S STOMACH HEAVED as the boat rose on the swell. His eyes were fixed on the dim light that burned in the tower window—the one sign of life on the dark island. That light was their guide now. Not that the island's inhabitants had any idea of it; nor would the realisation last long when they did.

He glanced back at Galfrid—who winked at him from beneath his armoured brow—then beyond to the dozen other glinting helms within the boat.

Against his better judgement, he let his gaze stray further, beyond the confines of their craft to the other boats strung out along the tether. The lead boat dipped and the remaining five, one after another, rode up on the swell in a graceful arc, the faces of their crews—stark and clear but weirdly expressionless—like ghosts in the moonlight.

His stomach felt like it was dropping out of him. Every muscle clenched, and the reality of his situation—which he had mostly banished from his mind—crashed in afresh. His insides lurched, his head spun. He turned hastily, fixing his eye back on the single light ahead, gloved hands gripping the prow. He tried to focus on the steady rhythm of the oars—the one note of order in this immense, black chaos. Breathing deep, he felt the ache of icy air, laden with salt spray, hitting his lungs; the pain was a relief. It would be over soon, one way or another. Almost there. Almost there...

Ahead, the rocks loomed black as shadows, like a jagged row of teeth: the island's maw, waiting to consume them. Along the gumline, the water—churned white by the crashing waves—seemed to glow in the cold light of the moon. The landing would be treacherous; it was likely at least one of the boats would be smashed. But the boats did not matter. If all went to plan, they would soon have their enemy's ship. If it did not... Well, nothing would matter then.

As Gisburne watched, cloud passed over the moon, plunging the rocks ahead into shadow. But they would know where they were soon enough.

They had given themselves all the advantages. They had approached from the island's far side, beyond which was nothing but the great northern sea. There was no watch upon this jagged shore. Only a madman would approach from that direction.

They had come under cover of darkness and had no lights upon their boats. If anyone had happened to look out in their direction, the chances of them being spotted were remote.

They had been informed of their enemy's hiding place by one Tancred had not once suspected would betray him.

The risks were high. Merely being on the sea was the very last thing Gisburne wanted. But if successful, they would catch their enemy completely unawares.

An old adage came to mind: *To defeat your enemy, you must think like your enemy.*

Tancred was mad, of course, but so was the man who had betrayed him—a fact Tancred had not properly assessed. If any among the assembled army of Templars and Hospitallers had thought Gisburne's strategy mad, none had expressed it, but, at the moment, that, too, seemed a fair assessment. But to win, one had to do what others were not prepared to—even if it meant facing one's worst nightmare. And Gisburne meant to win.

The time spent on the Scottish mainland, waiting for the right moment to strike, had been close to unbearable. For three days Gisburne had looked out upon the churning grey ocean and tried to picture enacting his plan upon it.

He could not.

Back in Nottingham, it had seemed a work of bold genius. Now, with the salt wind lashing his face and the waves pounding the rocky shore, it looked utterly impossible. Not that he could let his doubts show. His Hospitaller and Templar comrades had faith in him. Quite why, he wasn't sure.

The Templars weren't here because of him; that much he knew. They were here because of Tancred, whose heresies and outrages had brought shame upon their order. And the Hospitallers were here because of the Templars. Pragmatic as ever, neither order seemed unduly troubled that Gisburne's Scottish campaign had only been possible thanks to the support of Prince John. What John had promised the King of the Scots in return for safe passage, Gisburne did not know, but he suspected William the Lion was as happy as anyone to have Tancred swept from his threshold.

He had sensed a grudging respect amongst the knights nonetheless. The Templars knew of his early campaigns against Tancred, and—in spite of one or two past altercations between them and Gisburne—were prepared to support his efforts to the hilt if it meant ridding them of the hated madman. He supposed they must have forgiven him for stealing the skull of St John the Baptist.

The Hospitallers—or, at least, *these* Hospitallers—had stood alongside him once before, following the murder of one of their brothers by the Red Hand. That fight had also brought the death of one of their worthiest members, Theobald of Acre, and to honour his memory the Hospitallers of Stibenhede had pledged to stand by Gisburne if needed—especially if there was a chance to show up the Templars.

Still, all this did not sit well with him. He was no commander. It had been years since he had led a company into battle. The last occasion had been at Hattin, and Robert of Locksley had been among them. The wounds inflicted in that disastrous clash still lingered—on his body, in his mind, on the world.

Most gathered upon that shore seemed remarkably unconcerned about the battle ahead. They spoke of it in purely practical terms: the terrain, numbers of men, their opponents' training, the visibility upon their approach.

These aspects of the plan worried Gisburne not at all. For him, all was overshadowed by the prospect of a short sea voyage in a small boat—and each day as he looked out upon the lead-grey sea, it was all he could think of.

Several times, while they had been waiting on the mainland for the weather to abate, Gisburne had taken out the tiny scrap of parchment that had brought them here—the clue that Hood had delivered to him on the shaft of a green-fletched arrow. It said simply:

TANCRED

And, below that, the name of the island upon which the rogue Templar had established his fortress:

INIS NA GLOICHENN

The simple words had nothing more to yield. Studying them was pointless, a nervous habit. Yet every time he looked upon them, the same thought occurred: Hood knew the whereabouts of Tancred, yes, but Tancred also knew the whereabouts of Hood.

One day, as he and Galfrid had stood watching the setting sun turn the sea to red beyond the distant island, the squire had touched upon this same thought. "Do you think this is what Hood wanted?" he said. "For us to kill Tancred?"

"Partly."

He shook his head. "A stupid risk on his part. How could he know that Tancred would not give us information on him?"

"He doesn't," said Gisburne. "In fact... I think he's depending on it." Galfrid frowned at him. Gisburne sighed and looked to the bloody horizon. "A reckoning is coming between Hood and me. It's what he wants, what he expects." He did not relish doing what his enemy wanted—it went against his every instinct, all his training— but he knew, somehow, that it was inevitable.

Galfrid had simply shrugged. "Let him expect what he likes. Tancred would never give up that information. Although, in a way, that's a good thing."

"Why?"

"Because it means there's no possible good that can come of him." He had nodded as he stared into the distance. "No reason not to kill him."

Three days they had stood, battle-ready. Three days doing no more than watching the atrocious weather. They were waiting on the word of the gruff old Scottish fisherman who had agreed to act as their guide. On the first day, as the wind and sea raged, Galfrid had asked when the storm was likely to pass. The old man—who spent words as sparingly as silver pennies—looked at him with a frown and said: "Tha's nae a storm."

"God's teeth..." Galfrid had muttered to Gisburne. "What if this really *is* as good as it gets?"

Gisburne did not even want to think about that.

The old man's eyes—the only part of him to move—scanned the horizon. "Calmer water is comin'," he said. "Two days, maybe three."

And he was exactly right.

The boat struck something. It heaved forward on the swell, rock grinding against wood, and lurched sideways, and suddenly a jagged black shape was looming ahead of them. Gisburne—whose first instinct was to grip the prow tighter—gritted his teeth and let go. As he did so, the boat scraped over the reef and butted its bows against the low black rock. The port side of the prow splintered where his hand had been. Had he hesitated, his mission would already be over.

The two men behind him sprang up and hurled grapples into the dark, the leather-clad metal clanking dully against stone. One was pulled tight on its rope; the other dragged free and crashed against the starboard bow, narrowly missing Galfrid's shoulder. Without pause, the knight hauled it up and swung again, riding the boat's pitch and roll with all the ease of a master horseman on an unbroken stallion. This time, it caught, and they heaved the boat hard against the rock.

Gisburne gripped the rope and pulled himself onto the sea-smoothed outcrop, the crunch of mussel shells beneath his feet.

In a moment he was upright, relishing the feeling of solid ground beneath his feet and slinging the small, teardrop-shaped shield off his back. The moon emerged from behind the clouds and he ducked to his knees—no movement up on the cliff; no light, no cry of alarm. Glancing to his right he saw the other boats strung out along the shore, all pitched at crazy angles on the surf, their crews hurling ropes in the cold light or already scrambling ashore, the shields on their backs making them look like a swarm of beetles.

He waited until all seventy-seven men had made landfall, then thrust his arm through his shield's straps and began to move forward.

Not a word was spoken. There was no sound but the waves, the quiet clink of arms and armour and the soft footfalls upon rock. As the ground flattened out and rocks gave way to earth, Gisburne shouldered his shield for a moment, unbuckled his helm from his belt, put it on and pulled the strap tight beneath his chin. He had painted it black for the occasion; if he was to be first above the parapet, he had no intention of signalling their presence to the enemy.

The faceplate made it harder to see where he was putting his feet, but already he could make out the path winding up the low cliff. It was far narrower than expected; they would have to go up in single file. If for any reason they were discovered before they had made the clifftop, they would be done for. But if they could all make the climb unobserved—and if the old fisherman's description was correct—there would be nothing but a low, dry-stone wall between them and their goal. That, and an unknown number of pagan Norse warriors.

Once the scourge of the English coast, they were now a rare breed. The last of them had fled to ever more remote regions to escape the rule of kings and the taint of the White Christ. Somehow, that had led them into the service of the fanatical Tancred. So uncommon were they that not a single man here had fought their like before. None knew what to expect of their combat. And as yet, it was unclear whether they would find ten, or a hundred.

Gisburne went first, shield ready, sword drawn, and Galfrid followed close behind. The climb went quickly, and his impressions as he picked his way up the rocky path were weird, unreal. The helm separated him from the world in a way he did not like. But it was better than getting your head staved in.

The path ended with a narrow squeeze between the rocks. Gisburne and Galfrid eased themselves through. Gisburne stepped over a rise—and threw himself flat on the soft, mossy ground.

Directly ahead, he could see the roofs of a clutch of strange stone dwellings, along with more recent huts built from boat timbers. From the heart of them rose a thick, grey stone tower shaped like a bee skep—a *broch*, built by the ancient peoples of these islands, taken by Tancred as his castle. Before them stood the dry-stone wall—little more than waist height—that the old fisherman had promised. And standing before that, with his back to them, was a Norseman in a belted sheepskin, pissing against the grey stones and humming quietly to himself.

Gisburne lay for a moment, weighing up the situation. Clearly, this was the watchman of this shore—he was dressed for the weather and his spear was propped against the wall. No other figures were visible. The lone guard was utterly oblivious to the nearly eighty elite knights and serjeants poised behind his back. Yet ahead of him—and just a shout away—was the island's entire garrison.

The time for thought was over. Gisburne launched himself forward, sword held wide and low. He could hear Galfrid—adept at anticipating his master's moves—close behind. Their gear rattled with every step—but before the guard could turn, Gisburne was on him. He brought the sword up and drew its blade across the Norseman's throat, cutting to the bone. The guard's cry was lost in a gurgle of blood as Gisburne spun him around and let him fall. Galfrid jumped back, but not fast enough to avoid the still-flowing stream of urine splattering across his feet. He gave Gisburne a dirty look, then signalled to the others to move forward. Swords were drawn, shields gripped, as they slipped over the wall and spread out among the huts.

The plan was simple. Each group would target a dwelling, blocking all but one entrance, and, when the alarm was raised, capture or kill the men as they emerged. Neither of the knightly orders relished such brutal tactics, but the fact that these were pagans salved any troubled consciences.

Gisburne and his crew, meanwhile, would head to the *broch*, and to Tancred.

They were almost at the door of the tower when a big Norseman appeared from its far side, a great log on his shoulder.

At the sight of them, he bellowed at the top of his lungs, hurled the log at them and ran headlong for the door.

The fight had begun.

Gisburne side-stepped the log as it crashed to earth and took off after him, with Galfrid and the others close behind; they had to get to the heavy wooden door before it was closed and barred.

Gisburne crashed into it just as it was closing, stopping it with barely a finger's width to spare. Beyond it, mere inches from him, harsh voices were shouting. He shoved with his shoulder; the door gave, then shoved back at him, his booted feet sliding on the gritty ground. Galfrid's shoulder joined his and the door gave again, allowing the squire to jam the point of his shield in the gap. Two Hospitallers joined the struggle, but so confined was the space that they could only get their hands, not their shoulders, against the door.

As it quivered back and forth, iron hinges squealing in protest, sword blades struck out from within, stabbing blindly. One sliced a Hospitaller's upper arm, forcing him to retreat. Gisburne responded in kind, jabbing into the gap. On the third thrust, his sword point met with something; there was a cry and the door fell back, opening a full eight inches. Wide eyes glinted in the dark, and then one of the Norsemen gave a deafening roar of defiance, and the gap closed once again.

They were at an impasse—and all the while, those inside were entrenching themselves for the fight to come.

Gisburne looked at Galfrid. "Llewellyn," he said.

Galfrid understood. From a leather bag on his back he pulled out a globe of terracotta, barely bigger than an apple, the wooden bung sealed with wax. A gift from the workshop of Llewellyn of Newport, enginer to Prince John.

Gisburne gripped Galfrid's shield, twisted it hard, and with a great cry of his own put every ounce of strength into his shoulder. The injured Hospitaller, blood coursing down his arm, forgot his wound and put both palms against the planks, his roar joining with Gisburne's.

The door slid open five inches, eight, then suddenly gave another four. Galfrid hurled the globe low through the gap, and it smashed on the grey stone floor. The squire ducked aside as the space beyond the door lit up, and a wave of intense heat burst through the opening, making the Hospitallers recoil—but the door did not close, and the cries from beyond it were now those of agony.

Gisburne waited until the glow had abated, then pushed hard. The door flew open, stopping half way against a soft form slumped in the entrance; they hauled out the smoking body, tongues of flame still licking about his legs. Another—alive, but barely conscious— lay slumped in the dark, and Gisburne stepped over him, the bitter stench of burnt wool and seared flesh in his nostrils, and advanced up the narrow stone stair.

At the top was the orange glow of an open doorway. They would be waiting for him—but he was fully armoured. He held his shield close, lowered his head and charged into the chamber.

He felt something crash against his shield. Another blow battered his head. A third struck his right shin.

He did not stop.

The rain of blows ceased. Glancing back, head still low, he saw four Norsemen being overwhelmed by the invading Hospitallers. They fought back viciously; though lacking armour—one even had no shoes—they seemed entirely without fear. Gisburne keenly felt the tragedy of their inevitable defeat, but his pity was short-lived.

He turned and lifted his head. Galfrid was at his right shoulder. And he was staring.

In the centre of the floor was a broad circular hearth, in which a great fire was in its dying stages. But beyond, on the far side of the dimly-lit interior and partly obscured by woodsmoke, stood a large, peculiar apparatus, the like of which Gisburne had never seen. It had a chamber made of copper, and wheels and weights of iron, articulated arms and a framework of wood. On some of the parts were gleaming copper plates bearing arcane symbols and letters: some Hebrew, some Greek, some utterly beyond his comprehension.

Up higher, closer to the vaulted wooden roof through which the rising smoke filtered, something else caught Gisburne's eye: a movement, and a glint of silvery metal. He nudged Galfrid and advanced toward the stone steps that wound up to the upper floor.

Gisburne had never known Tancred run. He did not shrink from danger, nor fear death or pain. Such things seemed to have no meaning for him. And as they stepped onto the timbers of the gallery, there he stood, unmoving and unmoved. Armoured—because he always was. Sword drawn—because he would never surrender. Within the dark holes of the expressionless steel mask, unblinking eyes gleamed.

"Let's get this over with," said Gisburne, and strode forward.

Gisburne raised his shield and drew back his sword—then from nowhere a stocky Norseman with a forked blond beard blocked his path, long axe swinging in great, sweeping arcs before him. He had no mail, no plates, not even a gambeson to protect him, but the axe made an impenetrable barrier. Gisburne braced himself against the attack.

Galfrid, beyond the axe head's reach, did not wait, but rushed at Tancred. The mad Templar whirled, his blade glinting in the air. Galfrid—unused to Tancred's unorthodox attacks—was forced to parry with his sword blade. Iron bit iron, Tancred's blade scraping across Galfrid's with a squeal that made Gisburne shudder.

Galfrid was a fair swordsman but, Gisburne knew, no match for Tancred. He knew, too, that the squire, fuelled by rage and revenge, no longer cared. He might get lucky, but Tancred had the Devil's luck.

Gisburne stepped to one side, and the Norseman, his reflexes sharp, did the same, still blocking his path. Gisburne dodged again, looking for an opening, knowing it would be fleeting, if it ever came. The Norseman matched his move. Yet only slowly did Gisburne realise that the Norseman was not advancing; that he seemed to have no intention of doing so.

Then he understood. It was a show. The Norseman's purpose was not to kill him—not even to attack him—but to keep Gisburne there, powerless, forcing him to look on as Tancred gutted his squire.

For a fleeting moment, a wild idea entered Gisburne's mind: that Tancred had somehow predicted their coming. That he had allowed them to get this far precisely so he could so this.

Galfrid parried again, then attacked—and missed. Tancred whirled about and struck the squire across the helm. Stunned, Galfrid fell to his knees.

The axe head whooshed past Gisburne's face. He heard its passage, felt the breath of air against his eyes.

A memory flashed before him: a bright summer's day, and he no more than sixteen. The place was Fontaine-la-Verte. Gilbert de Gaillon was before him, swinging an axe—as he had told them the Danes and the English used to—and was challenging him to attack. But the young Gisburne simply stood, rooted to the spot. "You think you will parry an axe with a sword?" said de Gaillon. "Think again. I would not even trust a shield. I have seen a man stop an axe with his shield and still lose his forearm. You cannot stand; I will cut you down. You cannot run; your fight is over, and your worth with it. And I will be after you. So, there is only one way to go..."

Gisburne snapped back to the dank, smoke-filled *broch*—and as the axe swung up, he lowered his head and charged forward.

The crown of his helm smashed into the Norseman's teeth. He staggered backwards, the axe—now useless—still tight in his grasp. A warrior's instinct: never let go your weapon. But Gisburne did not stop. He drove his opponent backwards with the flat of his shield, sending him stumbling in great awkward strides that could not hope to save him, till he overbalanced and fell, full force, against the rough wooden rail at the edge of the gallery platform. The rail gave way.

The Norseman sailed out into the void, eyes wide, still doggedly gripping the axe. Gisburne fell forward onto his shield, stopping just short of the brink, his head—heavy with the helm—hanging over the cavernous space below. He had a clear view of the pagan as his legs turned over his head and with a horrid thud he stopped hard, face down on the stone slabs. By some fluke, the axe flipped back up in the air and came down, blade first, in the back of the Norseman's skull. It stood perfectly upright for a moment, then began to topple, turning the dead man's head as it did so, until he stared with empty eyes at Tancred's infernal device.

As Gisburne struggled to his feet, his helm twisted, obscuring his vision. The buckle had broken. He threw down his shield, pulled off the helm and turned on Tancred.

Then he saw it. Galfrid, panting, his nose bloody, flat on his back, Tancred's foot pinning his right wrist, sword point at his throat. The bag of Greek Fire grenades lay on the floor, far out of reach.

"You cannot win," hissed Tancred.

"Can't you hear?" said Gisburne. "Your castle is overrun. It's only a matter of time before..."

"I don't talk of the battle," said Tancred. "I will die here. But *you* cannot win. I see the future, Gisburne. You can *never* win. Can you not sense it?"

"What makes you think..."

"Because you care," snapped Tancred. "Look at you, frozen to the spot. Only because you have things to lose. I... I have nothing. I am free."

"Don't listen," said Galfrid. "Just take him."

"If I move, he'll kill you."

"He'll kill me if you don't! It doesn't matter any more... Take him and damn the future!"

Gisburne stood, unable to move, wishing to God he had a bow in his hand. Tancred's sword point pressed harder against Galfrid's gorge, and the Templar chuckled to himself, his horrid, clicking laugh muffled behind his mask. "The future is damned already. And so are you."

Gisburne let his shoulders droop, and his sword arm fall. He saw the despair in Galfrid's eyes—the disbelief at his master giving up, at him being in Tancred's power, if only fleetingly. Yet all the while, Gisburne was thinking: *There's only one way to go...*

Without warning he swung violently, hurling his helm at the Templar. If Tancred *could* indeed predict the future, he didn't see this coming. Before he could react, the helm smashed into his faceplate, knocking him off his feet. Galfrid scrambled away, but Gisburne was already on the Templar. As he rose, his mask yawned open, revealing the ghastly, skeletal face beneath. Gisburne swung at the ghoul's neck, both hands upon the sword grip.

An inch lower and it would have taken Tancred's head clean off—instead, it struck metal. Tancred went down again, but this time rolled away and back up onto his feet. He raised his weapon, but Gisburne intercepted, his blade striking Tancred's hand and sending the sword spinning off the gallery and clattering on the floor below.

He advanced on his foe, raining blows upon him, heedless of where they landed. There was little aim, and no finesse; it was pure rage. Tancred's mail saved him from the blade's edge—but beneath, every part of him was battered, his helm beaten out of shape. He reeled under the barrage, staggering backwards until he, too, was teetering on the brink, yards from where the Norseman had pitched to his death. Gisburne stopped, panting hard as the dazed Templar swayed there—then Galfrid's foot sank into Tancred's midriff, sending him plunging off the platform.

Gisburne stepped to the edge in time to see Tancred, arms and legs spread out like a starfish, crash flat into the hearth. The impact sent a plume of sparks up towards them, and he shielded his eyes, felt the burning flecks on his face. When he looked back, he saw a great circle of smoke and ash rolling up and away on the hot, billowing air.

The fire was extinguished. Tancred did not move.

Gisburne and Galfrid exchanged fleeting glances, then turned and scrambled back down the grey stone steps, as fast as their feet would allow.

Below, the Norsemen lay dead. The door hung off one hinge. The Hospitallers had turned to other tasks outside, on Gisburne's orders, but everywhere the shouts and noise of clashing weapons had abated. A single harsh cry pierced the air, then was silenced.

Gisburne's heart beat faster. Victory was theirs. Leaping the last four steps, he ran into the smouldering circle of smashed embers and gazed down at the smoking, cadaverous form, scarcely able to believe it was really over.

As they stood, the captain of the Hospitallers approached, his face cut and bleeding, closely followed by a fellow Hospitaller and a Templar dragging a Norseman between them. The blond giant was on his knees and tied up like a hog.

"They're beaten," said the captain. "We tried to take them alive, but none would yield. I fear he is the only one left."

The Templar pointed to a wound on his face. "Gave me this whilst the three of us bound him—with his teeth, if you can believe that." He gave the Norseman a kick in the ribs. "Filthy pagan!" The big warrior growled and hauled at his captors, the ropes biting his flesh, but to no avail.

"I can believe it," said Gisburne. "But I'll thank you not to kick him again."

The Templar stared at him, utterly wrong-footed.

"The Lionheart beheaded nearly 3,000 Saracen prisoners who were under his protection at Acre," said Gisburne. "And Saladin killed all the Templars and Hospitallers he captured after Hattin. I think we can do better, don't you?"

The Templar dropped his head and said no more.

A gust of icy wind through the broken door sent the smoke curling up the gloomy interior, and it was then that the Norseman saw the ashen figure collapsed at Gisburne's feet. The fight seemed to drain from him, then, the defiance extinguished.

Gisburne turned back to the captain. "Search everywhere," he said. "Bring everything to me—look especially for anything written or drawn, be it on parchment, wood or stones, however insignificant it may seem." He turned and looked at the weird device looming in the haze. "Have that loaded onto the ship, too."

The Hospitallers looked at the incomprehensible thing, then at each other. The captain puffed out his cheeks at the prospect.

Gisburne pointed at the Norseman. "And keep this one alive."

They hauled the Norseman to his feet, and the captain nodded towards Tancred. "And him?"

"He's ours," said Gisburne.

Gisburne and Galfrid stood in silence for some time after they'd gone, looking down at their vanquished foe. Gisburne felt the exhaustion wash over him, his wounds making themselves known. In a way, he was grateful for it; it was the one way he could tell this was real. Finally Galfrid knelt and started to search the Templar's crushed body. From the pouch on his belt, now stained with Tancred's blood, he dragged a small, grubby scrap of material. There were marks upon it.

"Is this it?" said Galfrid.

"That's it," said Gisburne.

"Then it does exist," said Galfrid, struggling to make sense of its symbols. He passed it up to Gisburne. "It's not quite what we'd hoped."

Then Tancred groaned, and Galfrid recoiled, muttering a curse. The Templar's limbs stirred. Both stepped back, involuntarily. For a moment, Gisburne—his sword still gripped in his hand—was paralysed with horror. This man should have been dead a dozen times over. His body had been hacked, burned and beaten, in places stripped to the bone. Yet still it would not die.

"Finish him!" said Galfrid.

Gisburne, startled out of his grim reverie, looked at Galfrid, then back at the mad Templar, the glassy eyes—moving now—staring back up at him. He raised his sword—and hesitated.

"Do it!" bellowed Galfrid. But Gisburne could not move. Galfrid stepped forward, his own blade raised. Gisburne gripped his wrist and shoved him back.

"We'll take him alive," he said.

Galfrid stared at him, wide eyed, his face sweat-streaked and flushed from the heat of the fire. "You swore! You *swore!*"

"He *knows*," said Gisburne.

"I don't care what he knows," cried Galfrid, tearing his arm free. This time, as Galfrid raised his sword, Gisburne raised his own. Galfrid gripped Gisburne's fist, and the pair struggled. Hands and blades flailed—and the pommel of Gisburne's sword struck Galfrid across the brow. Galfrid's legs buckled under him. He fell back and for a moment sat, stunned, rubbing the bloody spot with an ashy palm.

The look Galfrid gave him then was one Gisburne would never forget. It felt like a stab in the gut. All his instincts told him what he'd done was right, but he was anguished by it.

"He's been there. To Hood's hideout," he said, as gently as he could. Then he held out a hand. "Help me carry him to the boats."

"Carry him yourself," spat Galfrid, staggering unaided to his feet. "Do it all yourself. I'll help you no more." Then he turned his back and walked into the darkness.

XXV

Sherwood Forest
23 March, 1194

"I DON'T WISH to alarm you gentlemen," said Mélisande, "but we have for some time been followed by a very big man on a very stocky pony."

Gisburne's eyes stayed fixed ahead. "Our friend the Norseman."

"He's been there for the past two hours," said de Rosseley.

"Since dawn," corrected Asif.

Aldric sat up in his saddle, turned and squinted into the far distance. The boy with the pack horse, his face pale and anxious, did the same. There, far behind them on the track, framed on either side by trees, was the distant but distinct shape of the Norseman.

"Don't look back," said de Rosseley, "you'll just encourage him." Both heads snapped forward again.

Aldric looked about him, throwing his hands up. "So, were you going to share this information at any point?"

"We had bets on when you'd notice," said Mélisande. De Rosseley and Asif sniggered.

"I thought you told him he couldn't come..." said Aldric.

"What I actually said was that he could not *accompany* us," said Gisburne. "He's taking us at our word."

"I wonder at what I must have done to inspire such dedication," said Tancred. His tone was one of genuine bemusement—but Gisburne caught Galfrid's eye as the Templar spoke, and his look was as cold and hard as stone. "I do not believe he will act unless I call upon him."

"Is that meant to make us feel better?" muttered Galfrid.

"This isn't his fight," said Aldric. "Why is he here?"

"To protect his master," said Asif.

"Well, I hope he isn't after a share of the fee."

"Honour is his reward," said Mélisande. "And a place at the table of his gods."

"Should I command him to return?" asked Tancred. "I think if I were to give him a direct order..."

"Would he fight for us, if needed?" said de Rosseley. The question was directed at Tancred, but it was Gisburne who answered.

"With every fibre of his being, if so instructed," he said. "I've seen it for myself."

"Because you fought others like him yourself," said Galfrid. "As did I. And we were lucky to come out of that one alive. As was he." His eyes landed on Tancred.

Gisburne glared at his old squire. Until now, he had avoided speaking to Tancred of the events on Inis na Gloichenn. It was not a discussion he wished to have here, on the road.

"He is merely being loyal to his master," said Mélisande.

Galfrid gave a humourless laugh. "Well, I wish him all the best with that one..." This time, Gisburne felt the squire's eyes on him, but did not meet them. Galfrid gave a grunt, and looked away.

"This loyalty naturally extends to my friends and allies," said Tancred. He turned and looked directly at Galfrid, his perpetually staring eyes holding the squire's horrified gaze. "He will not harm you. You have my word. And he will fight for you." It was bizarre to hear Tancred's eerily metallic voice attempting reassurance. He turned away again. "We are united in our goal."

"Then let him come," said Gisburne.

Galfrid spoke no more, but simply fumed in dark silence. Gisburne knew what he was thinking, all the same. The Norseman's loyalty was not in question. But with it came two circumstances in which he presented a threat. The first, if Tancred turned on them. Gisburne had wondered a thousand times what might happen if those lost memories started to return—but with all he had seen, he refused to believe it possible. Tancred, he was sure, was a changed man. A good man.

The second was if one of them turned on Tancred. On this front, he was less certain.

He yanked his gauntlet off with his teeth, then pulled out the map.

He read it again discreetly, the deceptively heavy gauntlet—its fingers sewn with metal plates—still hanging from his teeth.

It remained as enigmatic and impenetrable as ever. The stream; they needed to find the stream. He knew the general direction lay to the west of them. He had plotted the positions of Hood's attacks, and, on the assumption that they rarely ventured beyond a day's march, had charted an area within which he was certain Hood's lair lay. But Galfrid was right. It was still hundreds of acres, some of it dense, choking forest.

He heard one of the riders pick up the pace behind him, shoved the map back into hiding and pulled his gauntlet back on.

Mélisande came up alongside.

"Is all well?" she said.

"All is well," he replied, perhaps rather too cheerily.

"Sir Robert Fitzwalter..." she said at length.

Gisburne had been expecting her to raise the matter, some time or another. Could he really blame her for doing so?

"Why did you not tell me before?"

Gisburne shifted in his saddle. "I did not think it relevant," he said. "The mission is the same."

"Is it?"

Gisburne had no answer to give.

"He clearly believes Marian can be saved," continued Mélisande. "No parent wishes to give up on their child."

"Is she alive?"

"As far as anyone knows."

"But do you believe it? That she can be saved, I mean?"

Gisburne spoke in a monotone. "I believe her journey is the very opposite of Tancred's. That she is now too far into darkness to find her way back to the light."

"And if you are wrong? If she *is* saved? What then? Sir Robert's gratitude will know no bounds. And her admiration..."

"I do not believe it will happen," said Gisburne. "That it *can* happen." But still her question troubled him in ways he had not anticipated.

Mélisande nodded slowly, and fell back behind.

The going had been good that day. The rain had held off; the sky was overcast but bright. The day had warmed up, without losing its refreshing crispness—perfect conditions for travel. Even the muddy track, dried by high winds in the early hours, was firm enough not to hinder them unduly. For the first two hours, progress had been swift. The air smelled like spring and the band was invigorated. Had they been certain of their destination, perhaps they would even have reached it by now. But road had shrunk to track, and track would soon become path. Then, there would be no path.

Already they were feeling their way—perhaps more so than Gisburne was willing to let on. Of the route up to this point, Gisburne was certain; of what lay ahead, far less so—and each new turn added further uncertainty. In his mind he had an image of a great oak tree: the road upon which they had travelled that morning was the trunk. After a way, the tree had diverged into three or four boughs, each spreading into a dozen meandering branches, which in turn radiated into a hundred gnarled twigs—and from every one, a thousand buds and leaves sprouted.

One of these was their goal—Hood's lair. But the closer they got to it, the less clear the path ahead.

They had awoken in the early hours to prepare and pack their horses. An icy wind whipped across the courtyard as Gisburne arrived to join the others. All were fully armoured, travelling cloaks pulled tight, straps and cords cracking in the wind.

Mélisande had immediately greeted him with a broad smile, and as easily as that, their skirmish of the night before—and the worry that had accompanied him to his bed—was instantly dismissed. He'd smiled back, glad of any crumb of good feeling. But of the gift from Llewellyn, there was no sign.

Each packed their own gear upon their horses, at Gisburne's insistence. In this straightforward task, only de Rosseley seemed to struggle, swearing as he tried to fit everything back where it had been on his arrival; evidently he had not packed his own horse on that occasion. Gisburne wondered if he ever had. At the sight of Robert, the head groom's boy, prepared for travel and loading up a pack horse, de Rosseley's eyes lit up. Gisburne was quick to disabuse him of the notion that he could palm any of his gear off on the beast. De Rosseley watched glumly as feed and waterskins for the horses were loaded upon it.

"Are we taking the horses far?" he said with a frown.

"Not far," said Gisburne. De Rosseley caught Asif's eye, and the pair exchanged looks of bemusement.

"So, what's in the box?" he asked. All had noted the cylindrical wooden case—at least a yard long and a hand's-width across—that Gisburne was now securing behind Nyght's saddle.

"Nothing you need to worry about," said Gisburne.

"I wasn't *worried*..." said de Rosseley. This time, he caught Mélisande's gaze and rolled his eyes.

"Just as long as it isn't that fucking hurdy gurdy," said Galfrid. Mélisande sniggered. Even Gisburne smiled—but when he looked, Galfrid's expression was as grim as ever.

"Do you need help with that?" said Aldric, scurrying over.

"No!" snapped Gisburne, positioning himself firmly between Aldric and the box. He pulled the strap tight, then added, after a pause which was a little too long: "Thank you."

Aldric nodded slowly and backed away. Then, as he turned and looked back at his own horse, it was his turn to shout. "Hey!"

Asif, who was turning Aldric's crossbow over in his hands, looked up. "Sorry, my friend," he said. "I couldn't resist. It is a good weapon."

Gisburne could not resist a snigger at how Aldric's nosiness had left him open to someone else's. But Aldric did not look amused.

"Please," he said, his hand extended, a look akin to panic on his face. "Put it down. Gently."

Asif frowned and looked over the bow again. "What is so special about this weapon of yours?"

"It bites," said Aldric. Asif laughed, but Aldric did not. "Hidden in the stock, just where you grip it, there is a spike," explained Aldric. "It is attached to a spring, and charged with a powerful poison. I alone know how to disarm it. If anyone other than me picks it up and attempts to use it, they are dead..."

Asif, needing no more convincing, placed the weapon gingerly on the cobbles.

Aldric snatched it up. "It's my own design," he said. "Someone took my crossbow once and turned it on me." His eyes met Gisburne's briefly, then he looked away. "I swore I would never allow that to happen again. But it's meant for enemies. So, please, all here, be warned."

"Consider it done," said de Rosseley.

"Consider yourselves told not to poke your nose in another's business!" said Galfrid. "We all have our odd ways, our secret weapons." He shoved his pilgrim staff through the straps on his saddle. "Like those damned rings of yours." He gestured to the *chakkars*, now hanging from a loop on Asif's cantle.

"This is why we pack our own gear," said Gisburne, slinging his shield across his black. It was freshly painted for the occasion— black, with a diagonal yellow band. Smiling, Mélisande had asked him why he wanted to look like a wasp, and he had replied—in complete seriousness—that it was because he had once been terrified of them. "Check everything yourself," he added. "Know where it is. We all need to be as self-reliant as possible."

"Just as long as there aren't *too* many secrets," muttered Mélisande. Whether anyone heard it but him, Gisburne could not tell.

And with that, they had mounted up and ridden on out of the palace.

XXVI

MÉLISANDE SURVEYED THE row of men, backs turned, each pissing against his chosen tree. "Remind me not to drink downstream of here," she said with a sigh.

"It's good for the nettles!" called Galfrid.

They had found the stream an hour before—or rather, Nyght had. Their progress had slowed to a creep, with Gisburne peering anxiously this way and that, checking the map obsessively. The forest had grown dark, the trees close—in places, enclosing them like a leafy tunnel. It was quieter here: the birds and beasts were more timid, and the sounds strangely muffled. It was then that Gisburne had seen Nyght's ears prick up, and swivel to his right. He stopped and listened. Mélisande stopped too, then the others.

"I hear it," she said. A trickle of water—so sweet of sound it was almost musical.

There, some twenty yards from the track, had been the stream, snaking between moss-covered rocks and disappearing beneath a blanket of brambles. The relief on Gisburne's face had been plain to see. And there, having achieved at least one goal, they had stopped for refreshment, and calls of nature. With the light already fading, it seemed that here they would stay, for tonight, at least.

"Why exactly does it have to be against a tree?" said Mélisande. "That's something I have never understood."

"It's one of those things we men prefer to keep a mystery," said Galfrid. "Just as you women keep yours. By the way, if you have need..." He gestured towards the tangled, thorny bushes.

"I'll wait, thank you," said Mélisande. "Anyway, someone has to watch your arses whilst you are all... exposed."

Galfrid, hauling up his braies, guffawed. "It's been a long while since I was complimented on it, my lady."

"Didn't say I liked it, Galfrid. Just that I was keeping watch on it..."

Galfrid chuckled to himself. Against expectation, and in spite of their slower progress, the squire's mood had brightened with every mile they had put behind them. He was like Gisburne in that regard, thought Mélisande. Give him something to do—something practical—and his worries melted away. And he rarely remained unhappy for long when on horseback.

"We make camp here," said Gisburne, and signalled to the boy Robert to see to the horses' needs. "Tomorrow we leave the horses, and strike into the forest."

He patted Nyght on the muzzle, then, while the others busied themselves with unpacking their mounts, pulled out the map. His finger traced the line of what he hoped was this very river, and he looked about him. He could not see far ahead, but could tell the stream curved around to the northwest. Did *this* bend in the line correspond to it? How could he know if its span was meant to be ten yards, or a hundred? Sometimes he looked at the grubby, smudged marks and saw rivers, trees and tracks, but now he saw nothing but impenetrable scrawl. That curve could be mere embellishment, or an unsteady hand.

Or a lie.

"It is making sense at last?" said a voice by his side: Asif. Gisburne looked at him and gave a sort of shrug that said neither "yes" nor "no". The Arab squinted at the scrap and frowned.

"What is that?" he pointed to a black mark near the map's edge.

"A scorch mark," said Gisburne. It had been a relic of Inis na Gloichenn. "Ignore that."

"And this?" Asif indicated a reddish brown area close to the stream.

"Blood."

"Yours?"

"No." Gisburne glanced over at Tancred. The Templar—yet to relieve his horse of its burdens—was on his knees, apparently engaged in silent prayer. He cut a bizarre figure, kneeling in that glade. With his clasped hands and glinting mail he looked the very image of the pious Crusader knight, until one looked into his blank, staring skull of a face. Gisburne had seen all manner of grotesques carved into the stones of the Abbey at Vézelay: shrieking visions of Hell, contrived to shock all who looked upon them into penitence. Yet the most fevered hallucinations from the darkest imaginations of men paled utterly next to the flesh and blood reality that was Tancred.

A hand clapped on his back jolted him out of his reverie. "But we have found the stream, yes?" said Asif, with a deep laugh. "You said it would be here, and you have found it!"

Asif, still laughing, drifted away, and Gisburne crept over to Tancred.

A twig cracked, and the Templar turned and looked at him.

"I was giving thanks," he explained. "For our safe arrival here."

"Do you recognise this place? This stream?"

Tancred cocked his head on one side. "Recognise?"

"Remember," said Gisburne. "You have been here before."

"Have I?" Tancred looked about him, his head turning very slowly, as if taking in every detail.

"Here," said Gisburne, and held out the crude map. "Is it here?"

Tancred took the scrap between bony fingers, and stared. So long did he look that Gisburne began to feel unnerved. Was he remembering? Without a word, he handed the map back, then shook his head slowly, the lips drawn back from his teeth in a parody of an expression—neither smile nor grimace.

As Gisburne looked at Tancred, a curious shudder passed through him. He felt, for the first time, the stirring of doubt. *Are you remembering? If this really were the place—if you began to*

*recognise after all—would you tell me? Or would you lead me
ever further off the path?*

He peered closer at the Templar, holding his relentless gaze, as
if daring him to reveal himself. But no matter how hard he stared
into those eyes, he could not read the slightest thing in them.

XXVII

THEY WAITED UNTIL darkness before lighting the fire, to avoid their smoke being seen. By that time, all were feeling the chill of the night in their bones, but the fire, and food and drink—simple though they were—put the blood back in their veins.

"Come closer to the flames, boy," said Gisburne in a low voice. He cracked a dry stick in two with his seax and threw both parts upon the fire. "No need to sit apart. You're one of us now."

Robert crept nearer and settled himself between Mélisande and Aldric. De Rosseley—who'd had the foresight to bring a flask of good wine—filled a small, horn cup and passed it to the lad, who sipped at it eagerly, then shivered.

"To tomorrow," said de Rosseley, tipping his own cup at Gisburne.

They drank, then Aldric wiped his mouth and sat staring into the flames. "I suppose it may be the last time we do this."

No one responded. It was not done, to speak of an imminent battle in these terms, but Gisburne could not blame Aldric for doing so. He drew his eating knife, cut a slice off the dry, smoked ham, and slid it in his mouth.

"Still with that old eating knife?" said de Rosseley.

"It never leaves him," said Mélisande.

"And it never shall," said Gisburne, with a smile. He turned the knife around in his fingers as he chewed the firm, salty meat. The black, riveted bog oak of the grip had seen some knocks, and the slender, tapering blade—thick as a sword at the back, keen as a razor at the front, and with a point as sharp as a needle—carried a now-irredeemable patina from nearly twenty years of daily meals, but he could imagine no replacement. It was not just that the knife, simple as it was, seemed so perfect to him in form, so right in his hand. It was that this knife had taught him something.

He had loved this knife before it was his. Coveted it, in fact; so much that as a callow squire of barely a year's service to Gilbert de Gaillon, he had contrived to steal it. The night that he had done so, only to be discovered by his master, was seared into his memory. It could have been the end of him, destroying both career and reputation before either had even taken shape. Yet de Gaillon—the paragon of fairness and pragmatism, to which Gisburne always aspired—had given the boy a chance. Gisburne, sickened and shamed, had grasped it. All was put right again. None knew of it, or would ever know, other than himself and de Gaillon—and neither would speak of it again. The next morning, it was as if nothing had changed.

And then, that same day, the knife's owner—an older lad named Nicolas, whose respect all the younger squires strove to earn—gave it to Gisburne as a gift, just like that. Nicolas knew nothing of the attempted theft, and had nothing to gain by his generosity. It was an act of pure kindness. His father had given him a fine, new eating knife, and he felt Gisburne—who had always shown admiration for the older one—deserved the blade.

There had been many critical moments in Gisburne's eventful life—turning points, forks in the road, revelations and brushes with death. But somehow, this moment, so small by comparison, eclipsed them all.

From then on, the value of that knife changed and grew—and Gisburne and his values with it. He had come to be a man who hated thieves, liars and cheats above all else. Of all the evils in the world—many of which he had seen first hand, and up close—it was dishonesty he detested most. And all because of one night, when he had been made to glimpse it within himself.

"There have been times I wished he cared about it less," grumbled Galfrid. "Nearly got us killed, last time we were in London."

De Rosseley frowned and looked from Galfrid to Gisburne and back again.

The squire shoved a bit of cheese in his mouth. "Had a spot of bother in a tavern full of Germans. Not one of 'em under six foot. Things turned a bit... fighty. Made it out by the skin of our teeth, then"—he pointed his eating knife at Gisburne—"realises he's left that damned knife in there. So back in he goes. A minute later he comes flying out the door and the fight fills the entire street."

Gisburne chuckled, glad of the memory. This was the most convivial Galfrid had been for months.

"I can attest to it," said Mélisande with a slight blush. "I was involved myself, against my better judgement."

"It was because of this that something of Lady Mélisande's real character was revealed at court," explained Gisburne.

She sighed. "You might say that knife has a lot to answer for."

"Well, if any of you see him without it," said Galfrid, "you'd best start saying your prayers—for that day you'll know the world is ended."

Gisburne, still smiling, caught Galfrid's eye. For a fleeting moment they connected as of old, then the squire's smile withered, and he looked away.

"That sword of yours," said de Rosseley, gesturing at the blade that lay beside Gisburne. "I've had my eye on it. It looks a fine specimen."

"My father's," said Gisburne, glad of the diversion. "Given to him by Old King Henry, for services in Ireland. Almost as old as me."

"It deserves a better sword belt, then," said de Rosseley in slight disgust. "How many times has that been repaired now?"

"Enough to make it the way I want it," said Gisburne. He chuckled to himself. "My father was so proud of that sword. Never saw much use. I don't think he ever used it in anger, and then it lay idle for a long time after his death. I never thought myself worthy. But when I came to face the Red Hand... I felt it was time."

"That, and you'd left your previous sword in a sewer," said Galfrid.

Gisburne smiled. "Yes, that too."

"May I?" said de Rosseley.

Gisburne gestured for him to help himself. De Rosseley hesitated. "Before I pick this up, is there anything I should know? Will it poison me? Or burst into flame? Or turn into a serpent?"

"Not that I am aware."

De Rosseley drew it from its scabbard and turned it over in his hand. It had been a sight to behold when Gisburne's father had first brought it home, and had thrilled him as a child; the simple crossguard and pommel were covered in silver, the three ridges upon the black grip perfectly fitted to the hand. The crossguard had now lost most of its silver coat, the pommel was pitted, and the grip worn and hardened by sweat, but its quality shone through nonetheless.

"A good blade," said de Rosseley. "And with a history. Does it have a name?"

"A name?" Gisburne looked at his friend as if were suddenly speaking a foreign language.

"It deserves a name."

"What purpose does a name serve?"

"Purpose? Come on!" cajoled de Rosseley. "Every great sword should have a name. And this *is* a great sword—a king's sword." He raised it, moved it, felt its balance, the blade reflecting the orange light of the fire, then levelled the point at Gisburne. "How will the ballads sing of it if it hasn't even a name?"

"If my story troubles any balladeers, then let them make up a name to fit their metre. They'll make most of it up anyway."

"You surely don't want to leave that responsibility to *them*," said Mélisande. "Who *knows* what monstrous epithet they'll come up with?"

"They've already done that," said Gisburne, and poked the fire irritably. "Such things are out of our hands, anyway."

"Already done it?" said de Rosseley.

"'The Dark Horseman,'" said Mélisande with a smile. "Sir Guy's nickname on the Continent."

"Of course..." said de Rosseley. "Just as you were known as 'The Shadow', my lady."

"That legend persists, even though I am now revealed." She snorted dismissively. "There are those who refuse to believe it was me—some who have claimed my exploits for their own."

De Rosseley tutted in disgust. "Such things truly are out of our hands... What of you, Arab? You already have more names than the rest of us put together. Did your time in Jerusalem earn you a nickname, too?"

"Not I," said Asif.

"Oh, yes it did," said Gisburne. "*Al Akrab*." He looked around the others. "The Scorpion."

Asif scowled. "What did I do to deserve that? I was only ever fair towards the Christian—"

"It was your own men called you it," interrupted Gisburne. "And I *believe* it was a compliment—your skill with a knife was legendary."

The Arab grunted.

De Rosseley lay the sword across his lap and rubbed his hands. "The Dark Horseman, the Shadow, the Scorpion... We are shaping up to be quite a colourful crew. Squire Galfrid? Any colourful names to add to our list?"

Galfrid sniffed. "Many. None repeatable."

"Master Aldric?"

"Not that I know of," said Aldric.

"You'll earn them," said Gisburne. "Of that I am sure."

"But what of you, Sir John?" said Mélisande. "I can't believe, with all you do, that you have avoided this dubious honour."

De Rosseley reddened slightly.

"His French rivals at tournament call him *le Martel*," said Gisburne.

"'The Hammer'...?" said Mélisande, eyebrows raised.

De Rosseley shrugged. "What can I say? I hit things."

Only Tancred now remained to be asked—but there the conversation died, and with each passing silent, glaring second, the omission became the more uncomfortable.

"Am I to take it," breathed Tancred, "that I also had such an epithet—one that you would sooner avoid?"

The excruciating silence returned.

"They called you the White Devil," said Galfrid at last. He looked Tancred full in the face. "It was not meant as a compliment."

"Devil..." Tancred looked into the fire and gave the word long consideration. There hung about him an air that, in spite of himself, Gisburne found almost tragic. "Did I deserve it?"

Galfrid bit a sliver of dried meat and shrugged. "You had me tortured. And her." He pointed at Mélisande with his eating knife. "You stole a holy relic. Aided the escape of England's most notorious murderer. Then you tried to destroy Jerusalem. I'd say you deserved it."

Gisburne found himself once more studying Tancred's features for signs of recognition. Of memory. Of anything.

"Well, this is not solving our sword-naming problem," said de Rosseley, with determined cheer.

It immediately broke the spell. Ridiculous as Gisburne found the notion, even he embraced it. "Come on, then," he sighed. "Do your worst..."

"Are there rules?" said Aldric.

"It should embody some particular quality," said de Rosseley. "Of itself, or its owner."

"*Joyeuse...*?" said Mélisande, with only the mildest hint of irony.

"Taken, I'm afraid," said de Rosseley.

"Foe Taker?" said Aldric.

De Rosseley nodded approvingly, but Gisburne just winced.

"Foe Dodger, more like," muttered Galfrid under his breath.

"Vengeance," suggested Asif.

Gisburne shook his head. "Too lofty..."

Aldric smiled. "Spike!"

"Too plain!" protested de Rosseley. "It should have something about it... It should bring something... Something..."

Aldric snapped his fingers. "Lightbringer!"

"Oh, please..." said Gisburne. "I'm a man with a sword, not the Archangel Michael."

"*Ladghat*," said Asif.

"What?"

"It means 'Sting'," said Mélisande.

"Like a scorpion's sting," explained Asif.

Gisburne sighed in despair. "This is almost as bad as naming a horse."

"Naming a horse is easy," scoffed Galfrid.

"You only think so because you called yours 'Mare'..."

"Quicksilver?" ventured Aldric.

"That *does* sound like a horse," said Mélisande.

"I like Quicksilver," said de Rosseley.

Gisburne shook his head again. "No."

"It should be something poetic, at least," the knight insisted.

"What use is poetry on the battlefield?" said Gisburne, tiring of the game. "I don't need words. My sword speaks for me."

"Irontongue," said Mélisande. Gisburne stared at her. The others, suddenly silent, did not quite dare. She gave him a little smile, then shrugged. "Because it speaks for you."

Since Gisburne failed to raise any further objection, de Rosseley— with all-too-obvious delight—declared Mélisande the namer of the sword. Irontongue it was.

They settled down to sleep then, each in their own manner—each sheltering from the elements in their preferred way.

De Rosseley watched in fascination as Asif—an apparent stranger to this environment—heaped up leaves and twigs into something like a grave mound, drew his sword, and lay down upon the pile.

"You mean to sleep with your sword in your hand?" said de Rosseley. He looked impressed.

"The scorpion sleeps with its sting," said Mélisande, hooking her thick woollen cape over a branch.

With no further word of explanation Asif pulled his cloak around him so it completely covered his head, then drew the sword underneath and hoisted the fabric upon its point like a tent. "An old Bedouin trick," he said, grinning through the slim gap at the bottom. "Meant to shelter from sun, but I have found it works for rain just as well."

De Rosseley shook his head in wonder. "Never would I have believed that a Saracen had something to teach me about rain."

And with that, they settled down to sleep, wrapped in cloaks and under improvised canopies, Gisburne with Irontongue nestled by his side.

XXVIII

MÉLISANDE DID NOT know how long she had dozed; the fire still glowed, its warmth reaching her face. The hunched figure by the stream jolted her, reaching for her dagger and casting about for Gisburne, until she realised it *was* him. He was sitting, gazing into the water.

She crept over and sat by him. He held Irontongue, scabbarded, in the crook of his arm.

"You should sleep," he said, without looking up.

"Shouldn't you?"

The stream was fast and strong here, its racket amplified by the night. His gaze was fixed intently upon it, but look though she might, she could see nothing.

"What do you hope to see?" she said. "The future?"

He smiled, still not taking his eyes off the tumbling water, and she looked upstream, where it faded into total darkness. If it did lead to Hood's lair, then all their fates lay somewhere along its course.

"Actually, I was hoping to see the past," said Gisburne.

She frowned. "Memories? That's not like you."

"More often of late. But this is something more pragmatic. If this stream passes through Hood's village, and they make use of it, then it stands to reason some of their waste will find its way past us."

Mélisande nodded. "So, if you see it, you know for certain where it leads..." She looked at him, frowning. "You're *not* certain, then?"

Gisburne said nothing.

"Well, never let it be said the life of Guy of Gisburne is not glamorous. Picking through middens, wading through sewers, and now watching for turds in a stream."

He smiled. "My mother would have called this a 'burn.' That's what my name means, you know—*gisel burna*: 'rushing stream.'"

"Really? So, a rushing stream, watching a rushing stream."

Gisburne pondered this for a moment, as if some profound truth were contained within it.

"Well, it was really your idea," he said at length. "That comment you made about not drinking the water downstream..."

"But you could sit here all night and see nothing. And seeing nothing proves nothing, one way or the other."

He nodded slowly, gazing somewhere far beyond the water. "Our course is set," he said. "We must follow this stream tomorrow, no matter what."

"Then leave this. Come to bed."

But Gisburne did not respond.

She looked at him for a long time, then said: "Let me ask you honestly; who are you doing this for? You? Richard? Marian?"

He sighed heavily, shaking his head. "Honestly? I don't know."

"These doubts you're having, Gisburne... they will cripple you."

"Doubts are necessary," said Gisburne. But he sounded defensive.

"Of course," she said, "but not all the time. Look at what you've done, what you would never have done, had you doubted. You forced your way back into Castel Mercheval—one man, against an entire garrison."

"I came back for you."

"And Galfrid..."

"And Galfrid."

"But you're missing my point. You had a plan to get in, but no plan to get out. None at all. There could *be* no plan. It looked like suicide, but some part of you believed, against all reason, that it could be done. That it would happen if you simply willed it enough."

"You're saying I'm like him. Like Hood?"

"I am saying that you have become so afraid of being like *him*, that you no longer allow yourself to be *you*. All these things that have happened... They have shaken you. Your estrangement from Galfrid, Prince John's fall from power, being drawn back into Hood's game. Fighting for his hero, Richard—yes, especially that.

"But you are *not* Hood. You could never be him. And to occasionally be *like* him, well... At times, we all are. And perhaps we *need* to be; to screw our doubts and fears into a ball and hurl them back in the face of fate. What I'm saying is, we need that old Gisburne. The one who was not afraid to be a little mad. The one who destroyed Tancred's men in the Forêt de Boulogne and took Castel Mercheval. *You* need him."

"It was easier, then. I was alone."

Mélisande laughed. "Alone? What reason would there have been to go back to the castle if you'd been alone? You were never alone."

Gisburne looked at her, as if struggling with these thoughts, then turned slowly back to the stream.

"Come to bed," she urged. But Gisburne did not move.

She placed a hand gently on his back, then, and left him, absorbed once more in the flow of the water.

XXIX

Sherwood Forest
24 March, 1194

NEXT DAY, THEY rose early and ate a simple breakfast. Dried fruits, salted and dried meat, scraps of bread. They spoke little.

Gisburne sat, silent but for the scrape of the whetstone along the edge of his old seax. He heard de Gaillon's voice: *always hone the blade before a battle...* It was testament to his old mentor's pragmatism that his advice worked as well literally as figuratively.

Gisburne gazed at the grey, pitted blade, losing himself in the whetstone's steady rhythm. The seax had belonged to his mother's grandfather, forged back when Saxons had still ruled this land. If ever there were a blade with a history, it was this. He twisted the wrapping cord back under itself where it was coming loose from the grip, and wondered, idly, if it had ever been given a name. Impressive though Irontongue undoubtedly was, he loved this solid, functional blade more. He thought then about the eating knife that hung from his belt. It seemed that the smaller and more prosaic the blade, the more he cared about it.

Mélisande emerged from the forest's edge, adjusting her hose, and returned him to reality. Shoving the seax in the scabbard that hung across the back of his belt, he stood, his mail hanging heavy upon him, and looked up at the grey sky, barely holding back the rain. "Time to move," he said. "Leave the shields here. They'll only get in the way."

"I thought that was the whole idea," muttered Aldric.

Mélisande re-buckled her belt and pulled her surcoat straight. "Is all quite well with you, Master Fitz Rolf?" she said. Aldric had been staring, and now reddened and looked rapidly away. "I am aware that my presence here, and my garb, take a little getting used to," said Mélisande. "Just try to think of me as one of the boys."

"That *is* rather a challenge," said de Rosseley, looking her up and down.

Mélisande looked him straight in the eye. "I may not relieve myself standing up, Sir John, but I can take a kick to the goods better than any man here." Aldric nearly choked on his drink, while Galfrid chuckled quietly to himself and tied his sword belt.

De Rosseley looked mortified. "I meant no offence..."

"I'm teasing, Sir John," said Mélisande with a sweet smile, throwing her arrow bag across her back and taking up her bow. "I grew up in a household of men and boys, all obsessed with knighthood, all determined to outdo each other. In that environment, a girl either becomes a shrinking violet or a fiercer fighter than all of them."

De Rosseley raised his horn cup and smiled. "Here's to shrinking violets, then," he said. He drained the cup, shook out the dregs and kicked dirt over the embers of the fire.

Gisburne, whose eyes were back on the map, sensed Mélisande beside him. "You must know that thing back-to-front by now," she said.

He hastily screwed it into a ball and thrust it back into his gauntlet. "Map or no map, we follow the stream." Then he lifted Llewellyn's cylindrical box by its strap, heaved it over his shoulder and turned to the boy Robert. "At any sign of danger, sound the horn," said Gisburne. "We will hear it, and if we can come, we shall. Have you been practising?"

The boy nodded.

"And with what are you charged?"

"Stay here for two nights, and if none are returned by then, lead the horses back to Clippestone."

Gisburne smiled, and ruffled the lad's hair. "You're a brave boy. Just remember: drink from the flasks, not the stream."

The boy nodded.

Galfrid, meanwhile, stood in an apparent quandary, looking from his bowstave, which occupied one hand, to his pilgrim staff, which occupied the other. Only now, it seemed, had he realised that he could not manage both. He turned to Robert, and held the staff out to him. "Look after this for me, boy," he said. The boy took it, looking bemused, and Galfrid came in closer. "Should you have need, twist the top and pull. You'll find a sword concealed in the shaft. It's got me out of many a tight spot." Galfrid winked and tapped his nose and then withdrew, leaving Robert looking thrilled with his new acquisition.

"Will we really turn back, if we hear that horn sounding?" said Galfrid as they left the glade behind them.

"Let's hope we don't have to," said Gisburne.

XXX

THE STREAM TURNED northward, and they followed it. As they picked their way through the trees, keeping the plash and purl of the water at their right hand, the forest began to change. The ground became uneven and rocky, the air strangely still and heavy, with the musty scent of fungus. The oaks were huge and ancient here— like something out of an old legend, de Rosseley said—great roots bulging and entwining beneath their feet, and everything about them furred with green moss, as though all were part of one giant, slumbering creature.

They walked using bowstaves for staffs—all except Aldric, whose crossbow was slung across his back. Here, under the canopy, the six-foot lengths of yew caught on every branch and bramble.

Still, they served the purpose well enough. The spike on the foot of Gisburne's bow, which bit satisfyingly into tree roots, sank disconcertingly into mud, which was a small irritation. Mélisande's bow, by contrast, had been without a spike or ferrule of any kind, so Aldric had improvised by tying a stuffed leather pouch about the nock. "A boot for the bow," he called it. It didn't sink into any but the softest mud, leaving Mélisande, who had begun with a disadvantage, ending up better off than any of them. Gisburne admired the ingenuity; they would have need of that.

For a long time, nobody spoke, their footfalls cracking and rustling in steady rhythm. After perhaps an hour, the ground began to broaden and flatten, and they were again able to walk side by side. Their spirits lifted. There was even an little dappled sunshine sneaking between the branches. One could almost imagine they were out for a spring stroll, or on a morning hunt.

"So," said de Rosseley. "Tell us more of Hood. I know all about what he is *now*, but not how he got there. What of his history?"

"Now that is a tangled tale..." said Galfrid.

"One hardly worth telling," said Gisburne.

Mélisande snorted. "Gisburne once claimed he had lost all interest in Hood." She gave him a sideways look. "And yet, here we all are..."

Gisburne smiled a little uncomfortably. "That never was *entirely* true," he said. "For all I might have wished it were. After Hood's escape from the Tower—after the Red Hand—I was obsessed with him. We were, by then, making plans for Inis na Gloichenn, but in truth my mind was only half on that task."

"I remember it," said Galfrid, casting a glance at Tancred, who walked in silence on the far side of the group.

"Even then, I was reminded daily how we came by the information, that it was by Hood's pleasure we were able to act at all. But, strange though it may now seem, it was not the idea of *finding* him that possessed me, or not exactly. Rather it was finding out who he was. *What* he was. Where he had come from. I had known him for years—fought by him, shared food and drink and lodgings with him—and yet, I came to realise, he remained an enigma."

De Rosseley sighed. "A pity your enigma will not be solved before we finish him."

"But it was," said Gisburne.

Galfrid missed a step; Aldric almost walked into him.

"It was?" Galfrid moved up closer. "You said that knowledge was lost."

"Hood had gone to great lengths to obscure it, but everything leaves a mark somewhere. I just had to learn to stop looking for the *tracks*, and start looking for the hiding of them."

"Well? Come on, man—who is he?" said de Rosseley

Gisburne shrugged. "No one."

"That's it? *That's* your answer?" de Rosseley looked far from satisfied.

"He's not a god, not a devil—though both have been claimed, from time to time. Just a man. Born to a woman, like everyone else. Like I said, hardly worth telling."

"Born to a woman?" repeated Mélisande. "My God. You found his mother..."

Gisburne nodded. "I did."

"Well, come on, man, tell us," said de Rosseley. "We've little else to entertain us."

And so, as they trudged on through the forest, Gisburne related the story.

"It was ten years ago when I arrived in Sicily to fight for William the Good, in his war against the Byzantines. That was where I met Robert of Locksley, as he was then known, in an inn marked out by a blue boar. I took him as I found him; a charismatic if reckless character, a fearless fighter, and a matchless bowman. Only years later did I learn that, before Sicily, he had gone by the name Dickon.

"Dickon Bend-the-Bow was a master archer—some say the greatest who ever lived. He had emerged from the Forest of Dean one day and joined with a troupe of entertainers bound for London. Within a month, people from near and far were clamouring to witness his tricks—before he disappeared without trace.

"I went to the Forest of Dean. I spoke to some who claimed to have known him. They described a quiet, reclusive man, who lived alone in the forest. He'd had no great archery skills back then, they said. When asked how he had suddenly acquired them, they claimed he had made a deal with the Devil by a crossroads."

"A reasonable assertion..." said de Rosseley.

"He had also, rather *less* reasonably, grown by six inches. What became of the *real* Dickon—the quiet, reclusive Dickon—is anyone's guess. I dare say his bones lie somewhere in that forest. He was a man who had a use, and who would not be missed, much like the poor soul from whom Hood stole the name Robert of Locksley. But then, quite by chance, I happened upon stories of another great archer, further north, who had been accused of poaching deer and made a daring escape. He exactly fitted the description of Dickon Bend-the-Bow, and Locksley, and Hood. I followed the stories north, forgetting names—he used so many—and trying to look beyond them, to something else. There are many things Hood is good at hiding, but his talent is not one of them.

"By degrees, they led me to an account of a young adopted boy, of prodigious talent and unpredictable temperament, who had left his father dead in Skipton and fled into Bowland forest. I talked with the mother—the widow Godberd. I could see that the one she spoke of was Hood, as clearly as if he were before me. She, too, could tell that I knew him without it being said. But in her eyes was no desire to see him: no yearning, no sadness. Only fear."

"Skipton?" said Galfrid. "But that's..."

"...less than a dozen miles from my home, yes." He laughed at his own words, as if hearing them aloud made them absurd all over again. "We could have met, played together as children. All this searching, all these travels—from here to the Holy Land—and it leads me right back to my own doorstep." He sighed and shook his head. "From there, it was but one more step. The child that Godberd took in had come from the priory at Kyrklees, the bastard child of a young nun. A nun who is there still."

"And the father?" said de Rosseley.

Gisburne shrugged. "Only she knows the answer to that. De Gaillon always said that to know your enemy was to have power over them. That's what the Red Hand taught me—to turn the skills of the hunt to the discovery of the truth. Following the signs to their source. But as I was asking those questions, working my way back, putting the mosaic together piece by piece, I discovered that Hood was doing the same. Our paths almost crossed a number of times. I met with several people who said they had spoken to another on the same matter. Sometimes he went in disguise, but I knew it was him. Doubtless there were times when he heard stories about me. And finally he, too, found the truth about Kyrklees. About himself."

"You went there?" asked Mélisande. "Met her?

"I lingered outside the gate. For near half an hour, I pondered what I would say, what I would ask."

"And then...?"

"I turned and rode away." He shrugged. "What was the use? What purpose would it serve? All this time, I had thought if I could only find out who he *really* was, where he really came from, then I would know something of true value. But it meant nothing. I understood him no better than I ever had."

Another great sigh left him. "From that moment, I decided I was done with him."

"Until the Lionheart turned up..." said de Rosseley.

"But what of Hood?" said Mélisande.

Gisburne shook his head. "It would seem that, having discovered the truth, he too went no further. I think perhaps he was protecting them. The priory can cover up a bastard child, hide the odd indiscretion, but not that."

"Protecting?" said Galfrid. "That doesn't sound like the Hood I know."

"There are other things," said Gisburne. "The priory has received regular, generous gifts from an anonymous donor."

"Not unusual for a religious house," said de Rosseley.

"But the manner of their delivery is. Silver and gold deposited upon the ground outside the gate. Left in a heap, like household rubbish. The nuns of the priory take the gifts and utter prayers of thanks, and doubtless know better than to question them too closely, but here's the thing... Empty though their bellies are, the local people know better than to touch the gifts. To do so means death.

"None would even speak of it that I found—none except one, who I eventually persuaded with a promise of bread and meat. He told of another poor soul—starved half out of his mind, by all accounts—who filched a single silver cup from the pile. It was stolen anyway, why not have it? He disappeared that same night. Not a trace; not until two days later, when his flayed corpse was found nailed to a tree, his eyes pierced by Hood's green-fletched arrows.

"Anyway... What all this told me was that Hood had taken an interest, sought the answer to the great mystery—which had been a mystery even to him. He had begun to do something he had never done before: to question who he was, his place in the world. And I have come to understand, in recent weeks, that this makes him a hundred times more dangerous."

All walked in silence for a while, until they became aware of a sound ahead: the roaring of water. Gisburne's heart sank at it, and what it might mean.

The trees thinned, confirming his worst fears. Ahead was a wall of sheer rock, from the top of which tumbled the source of their stream.

"Is that on your map?" said Galfrid.

Gisburne strode from one side to the other in agitation, his eyes scanning the rock face. "There must be a way. Aldric? Can we scale this?"

Aldric pulled a pair of lenses from his bag and squinted up at the cliff edge. It was not high, but it was high enough—as impenetrable as a castle rampart. "Well, we have a grapple and rope, but nothing that could get it up there." He sighed. "Even if we did, the rock is crumbling. We couldn't trust it."

De Rosseley threw down his bow in frustration. "Dammit!"

"Look for steps cut into the rock," said Gisburne. "Caves, fissures, anything. This *is* the path. It has to be."

"It doesn't have to be," said Galfrid, irritably. "We know the village is on a stream, but it doesn't mean that the path follows it."

"Then there's a way around," insisted Gisburne. "We have to find it."

"You do that," said Galfrid, gloomily. "I'm going for a piss."

XXXI

GALFRID PLODDED OFF until the voices behind him, hotly debating God knows what, had faded almost to nothing. Rather further than he needed, not as far as he would have liked. It occurred to him that he could simply keep walking; double back, collect his horse and pilgrim staff from the boy, and then ride off to a quiet life somewhere far from here. An apple orchard, perhaps, with space for a few pigs. Maybe some bees. He'd always fancied keeping bees.

But he wouldn't do any of these things. Couldn't.

He selected a suitable tree and hoisted up his mail and tunic. As he stood, his urine splashing and steaming against the green trunk, half whistling a tune he'd heard the Durham masons singing, his eye settled on a sprig of broom. It was long dead, desiccated. Not much to look at. An unremarkable bit of grey-brown foliage in a hundred thousand acres of the stuff.

What was not the same, however, was that this tiny fragment—this insignificant atom of Sherwood. It was fastened to a low, broken branch with woven grass, twisted into a secure knot.

Frowning, he reached out to pluck it up, but stopped himself. Tied. It had been *tied*.

He withdrew his hand, and stood a moment. "Over here," he called. No response. "*Over here!*"

Gisburne looked around this time.

"I have something..." said Galfrid.

He made himself decent as the group hurried up to him, Gisburne a good three strides ahead of the others.

"Common broom," said Mélisande as they gathered around it. "What is broom doing so deep in the forest?"

"We passed a patch of it early this morning," said Aldric. "But there's none around here. Not for miles, I'd say."

Gisburne peered closer. "So, it has not only been put there deliberately," said Gisburne. "It has been chosen, *brought* here."

"To what end?" said Asif.

"Perhaps it's nothing," said Aldric. "A charm. A traveller's idling."

"Who but Hood's men travel through here?" said de Rosseley.

"You're missing the point," said Galfrid. "This is *planta genista*. The emblem of the house of Anjou. Old King Henry. King Richard. Prince John."

Gisburne's eyes lit up. "Fitz Osbert..." he whispered. "Hereward! It cannot be a coincidence..."

"A message?" said Mélisande.

"A marker," said Gisburne. "One few would notice and none think strange."

"Unless they were looking for it..." added Galfrid, nodding.

Gisburne laughed and clapped his hands together in delight. "You said he was no use to us, Galfrid, but you were wrong. Dead he may be, but he speaks from beyond the grave. I am certain of it!" He pushed past it and turned about. "Look around. Look everywhere. If it is a marker, there must be more."

They spread out, eyes hunting every tree, every branch.

"Here!" called Aldric. Gisburne ran to him. The young enginer was crouched by a holly tree some twenty yards further into the forest. "No broom, I'm afraid, but this has been tied." The now empty loops of grass about the slim branch were twisted in identical manner to Galfrid's discovery.

"Follow the line these make," said Gisburne. "Look for a third."

They crashed through the dead leaves and broken twigs for another forty or fifty yards—so far that Gisburne convinced himself they had missed it and was ready to turn back.

"Here!" called Asif up ahead. And there it was—another sprig of broom, carefully tied like the first.

"That's three," said Gisburne. "And they form a straight line." He pointed. "That way."

"Westward," said Mélisande carefully. "Away from the stream."

The stream had been their only lead, but this felt right—the first real glimpse of their quarry.

"We follow this track now," said Gisburne.

XXXII

TWO MORE SPRIGS of broom marked the way, extending the straight line through the oak trees; each a little further than the last. Then, for what seemed an age, there was nothing.

Gisburne stopped in a small clearing lined with oak and beech, amidst thick, tangled undergrowth.

"No more markers," said de Rosseley.

"Or we've missed them," said Aldric.

"There *must* be something," said Gisburne, eyes alighting on a rough break in the foliage at the edge of the clearing. He turned to Galfrid, and saw his gaze already fixed upon it.

Eyes narrowed, the squire walked towards the dark opening. "Here... The branches have been pushed back. Some have been broken—and over time, too." He peered through. "And... Yes, I see a beaten path beyond."

"An animal?" said Asif. "A deer, or a boar?"

Galfrid shook his head. "People have passed this way."

"They've been careful up to now," said Gisburne. "This means we're drawing close." He turned to the others. "Nock your bows. Keep arrows to hand."

They bent and strung their bows, then Gisburne led the way towards the opening.

But then a voice—harsh and insistent—froze every one of them in their tracks: Tancred's. "No!"

It was the first time he had spoken in hours, and it seemed to Gisburne that he was sounding a little more like his old self. He stood, motionless, staring with unblinking eyes at an unpromising patch of bramble and ivy that filled the space between two entwined oak trees. He raised a bony finger. "This way."

"You remember..." said Gisburne. Galfrid looked at Gisburne, then back at the Templar.

"These two trees," said Tancred. "Like lovers embracing—reaching out for one another. Their shape is distinctive."

"But the beaten path is this way," said Mélisande.

"It is meant to appear so," said Tancred. "But that way are deadly traps."

De Rosseley stepped up to Tancred and pushed aside the curtain of ivy-covered brambles with his bow. Beyond it, the forest opened up, and Gisburne made out a faint line where earth and litterfall had been compacted.

"There is a trail," he said. He turned to Tancred. "This will take us there?"

Tancred nodded.

"Do you really trust this?" said Galfrid.

"He's been there. He remembers."

"And if he remembers *wrong?*"

"The image in my mind is clear," said Tancred. "I would stake my life on it."

"And ours too?" said Galfrid. "What if *this* way is the trap?"

Gisburne held Galfrid's gaze for an age. "We go this way," he said at length. "Because it was hidden. But we go with caution."

"I'll scout ahead," said Mélisande.

Gisburne took her arm. "No..."

"Trust me," she said. "I know what to look for. And they will not see me before I see them." She shook him off and pushed past the tangled stems.

"Well, at least we seem to have lost our Norse friend," muttered de Rosseley, close to Gisburne's ear, and they plunged in after her.

The forest was open, but eerily still. Gisburne fought the urge to break into a run, his heart pounding beneath his armour now they were so close to the end. They would find it now; they could afford to wait their moment.

But no sooner had Mélisande disappeared from sight, barely a hundred yards from the clearing, than Aldric stopped and looked about him, listening intently. "Is that thunder?" he said.

"That's the waterfall you're hearing, lad," said Galfrid.

"No, there *is* something," said De Rosseley with a frown, and peered above, through the towering trees. "Is it rain?"

Gisburne heard it too—and something about it made the hairs on his arms stand up. Mélisande's pale face emerged between the low boughs. She was running headlong back towards them, dodging between the trees with a terrible urgency, eyes wide and hair flying. She had made no sound of warning, and, as she neared, still running, pressed a finger to her lips.

Gisburne needed no more to understand what was coming. He looked around. "Up into the trees," he said.

Aldric stood, momentarily bemused, as Mélisande swung up into the boughs of a squat oak like a squirrel.

"Up!" hissed Gisburne. "Now!"

From the forest ahead and to either side of them, the sound intensified—a rumbling, a pattering. Not rain, *feet*. Hundreds of feet.

There was no more hesitation. Weighed down by gear and mail hauberks though they were, they hauled themselves up into the trees. Twigs whipped their faces, and straps and bowstaves caught on every branch, but there was no time to debate or complain.

Gisburne had pulled himself up into the same tree as Galfrid, who, with astonishing agility, was already yards above him. He pulled himself up onto a thick, green-dusted limb almost parallel with the squire, the cylindrical box hugged beneath him, and shuffled into a more secure position, flat on his stomach.

Suddenly struck by the absurdity of their situation, he looked though the branches at Galfrid with a broad grin, only to be met with an expression of horror. Gisburne followed the squire's gaze to his own belt, just in time to see his eating knife, its scabbard upended—caught up in the strap of his bag—slide free of its sheath.

It fell slowly, as if through water. Gisburne watched as it bounced on the ivy-covered bough, spun around several times, and stuck, point down, in an exposed root directly below him.

His mind raced. The knife would be seen; they might as well have raised a flag.

He peered into the distance as far as the trees would allow, then back down at the knife. The host was not yet upon them. If he could just reach it...

As he began to make his move, he again caught Galfrid's eye. The squire shook his head sharply, as the noise of many trampling feet rose up around them like the rush of an incoming wave. Gisburne, unmoving, stared back down at the knife, its blade glinting in the feeble light—and saw as the forest floor was blotted out by a dark swarm of men.

XXXIII

HE SAW NO faces—most were hooded for travel—but could see there were young and old and everything in between. Some carried spears, and a few had swords, but there wasn't a one who did not have a bow across his back and a quiver stuffed with arrows; some clearly carried more in plain canvas bags, which rattled as they ran. Many of the bows were thick about the middle, and the shoulders of the archers were thick, too. From the look of them, they had spent the past two seasons doing little more than preparing for war.

He hardly dared to take his eyes off the knife standing proud of the tree root, every moment expecting a cry of discovery. But they were everywhere, filling every space, every gap—a great trampling horde stretching as far as the eye could see, the rhythmless rumble of their footfalls so relentless that he felt it was crushing him.

Gisburne's fingernails dug into the green bark as he watched a dozen, a score, a hundred oblivious feet brush past the slender blade. He and his company were horribly exposed—perched only yards above the horde, with the trees barely in leaf. One of the outlaws had only to look up... Not until he began to feel dizzy did Gisburne realise he was holding his breath.

The buzzing swarm passed as suddenly as it had come, the racket gradually merging with the sighing of the wind in the trees. Not until the birdsong had returned did anyone move.

Gisburne swung down first, and plucked the cherished blade from the tree root. One by one, the others dropped to the forest floor.

"We're too late," said Gisburne. "They've heard the King is back. They're on the march." He cursed and kicked the tree that had harboured him.

"That was more than five hundred..." said Aldric.

"It's hard to be sure," said de Rosseley, "but I'd say no fewer than seven."

"And they are equipped for war," said Asif.

"*Damn!*" cursed Gisburne, his boot slamming the tree again. "If we had only set out a day earlier. One day!"

"Well, it proves one thing," said Mélisande. She looked at Galfrid. "Tancred was right."

The squire looked away, not wishing to acknowledge it.

"But what now?" she continued.

Gisburne looked first in the direction the army had taken, then where they had come from. "This way lies a clearly trod path to their village," said Gisburne. Then he turned in the opposite direction. "And this way, the road to Nottingham..."

"Their camp is undefended," said de Rosseley. "We can follow the trail and destroy it. Their homes, their stores..."

Asif nodded. "That is the tactic the Lionheart would use."

"It doesn't help Nottingham much," said Galfrid.

"The camp means nothing now," said Gisburne. "To us *or* to them. Our mission is to kill Hood. We must follow him."

Mélisande took a step towards him. "You are certain he is with his army?"

"He is with them. Right at their head. You can count on it."

"And you believe Nottingham is his goal?" said de Rosseley.

"Hood knows the King will come there. I believe he means to wrest it from the grasp of those loyal to John before Richard arrives."

"And make a prize of it to him?"

"More than that. To show he can do it."

"And then?" said Mélisande.

Gisburne looked grave. "If he can take the most powerful castle in the north and bloody the nose of the hated Prince, how many more of the free folk of England will flock to his banner? A thousand common archers can wreak havoc—rain fire arrows down upon a city until it is reduced to ash. Imagine what he might do with ten times that number. Much as he idolises Richard, Hood has neither friends nor enemies; only worshippers or competitors. And he will not stop the game—not now, not even for a king."

He clenched his teeth, burning with frustration that their adversary had passed so close. "No time to waste," he said. "We at least have a clear trail to follow. Stay together. But keep a safe distance from our quarry."

"And when we find them?" said Galfrid.

Gisburne's every plan was in ruins. But there was only one way this could end. "If I can get a clear shot, one arrow will finish it. Then we can all go home."

Aldric stared in the direction the army had taken. "Our horses are somewhere back there," he said. "And the groom's boy. What if they are discovered?"

"Let us pray they are not," said Gisburne.

XXXIV

THEY FOLLOWED THE trail southeast. For an hour or more, they saw and heard nothing—just the trampled forest floor, sticks crushed to splinters, earth and leaves churned to mud. Amongst the thousand overlapping, layered tracks—somewhere—was the mark of Hood himself—and of the monk Took, Will the Scarlet and all the others. It struck Gisburne then, more than ever, that Hood's time of hiding had come to an end. They were marching out of the shadows and into the light.

Finds tantalised them: a leather gauntlet trodden into the mud, the detached goose-feather fletching of an arrow caught in a briar. Once, a green hat with a feather in it, lying unblemished on the ground. Whether their owners missed them was impossible to judge, but there was no stopping now. No going back.

The army must have been moving fast, but Gisburne was wary of running into the back of them. In the event, he needn't have worried; after a while they began to hear, waxing and waning upon the gusting wind, the sound of many hundreds of voices raised in song. It was a cheery, earthy ballad that throbbed and swayed with the rhythm of their feet. A song of praise, not to God, nor their sovereign King, but to the King of the Greenwood. Their beloved Robin.

They trudged on, listening to the raucous sound as it came and went on the breeze, resisting as best they could, the urge to fall into its rhythm. Round and round it went, seemingly without end. Gisburne was growing to detest it when, just as the forest was thinning, he felt Galfrid tug at his sleeve. The squire pointed to their left—and Gisburne, hearing the clear sound of running water, understood.

The stream. The horses. He even thought he saw the moss-covered rocks through the trees. They were near. He signalled to the others, and they cut away from the trail.

The clearing where they had left the horses was only minutes away. Gisburne's heart pounded hard as they approached. They had heard no blast upon the horn, but a cut throat or an arrow in the back could come without warning.

As they drew closer to the clearing, swords at the ready, they saw their horses, standing calmly, still tied up just as they had left them.

And, in a bloody crumpled heap, collapsed over the smouldering fire and wreathed in smoke, a body.

"No," said Gisburne. "Please no..." and he ran forward. But as he did so, beyond the smoke, another figure emerged from the trees, a long blade clutched in both hands.

The boy Robert.

He was breathing hard, his face pale and his eyes wide. He stopped at the sight of them, and lowered his sword.

Gisburne grabbed Robert by the shoulders. "You're alive! Thank God..."

The others gathered around. The boy glanced across at the dead man, then stifled what might have been a sob.

Gisburne turned the body in the fire. His clothing was rough and patched. Upon his belt, a quiver full of arrows smouldered and smoked, and by his side lay a bowstave of yew—thick as a woman's wrist, at the grip. He turned him over with the point of his boot. The beard and hair were quite gone, the flesh of his face sizzling. Not even his own wife would recognise him now.

"They passed close by," said Robert. "So close I could hear them—singing, their feet trampling. I drew Squire Galfrid's sword—the one hidden in the pilgrim staff—then hid and stayed quiet, prayed the horses would do the same, and that they would not see the smoke of the fire. I thought they had not..."

"Their minds are on other things now," said Gisburne.

"Then I came out of my hiding place and saw a man. Strayed from the pack, he must have. He was sort of turning about, looking at the horses, looking for whoever owned them. He had his back to me. I don't know why he didn't call out right away. I think he was afraid. But I had Squire Galfrid's sword. And I knew he *would* shout, in time. So... I charged." He shuddered. "It went straight through. I felt the blade grate against bone. Then he staggered forward. Slid off the sword. Fell on the fire." His face creased into an expression of horror and disgust. "That smell..." He looked away, and steeled himself. "I thought to sound the horn, but did not dare for fear they'd hear."

He took a deep breath, and swallowed. "The horses are all well, Sire, and I saddled them up ready soon as I heard them coming. Just in case."

"I am more than happy to see my horse safe and sound, Robert of Clippestone," said Gisburne with a smile. "But no less am I glad to see you. Take your horse now and ride back to the palace. Have them double the guard, on my orders." Robert nodded, and bowed and began to back away. "And do no work for two days. I insist upon it. When this is over I'll talk to your father about your future. It'll be grooming horses if you want it. Perhaps something more, if you don't."

Robert smiled and turned—then, remembering himself, turned back and held out the sword to Galfrid upon both palms.

The squire let his face crack into the slightest of smiles. "You keep it, lad," he said. "You've earned it."

Gisburne turned to the others. "Someone must ride ahead to Nottingham, to warn them of what is coming."

"I'll go," said Mélisande.

Gisburne hesitated.

"My horse is the fastest here," she added.

He nodded. "Circle around until you reach the road, then go for your life. Ride hard and you'll be there within the hour. Ask for Sir Radulph Murdac, Constable and now High Sheriff. He's an officious bastard, but he'll listen. Galfrid—you go with her."

Galfrid, past the point of putting up arguments, merely nodded.

"Do you not trust me?" said Mélisande. "Or do you think they'll not trust the word of a woman?"

"Galfrid knows the roads. And these are troubled times—merely getting past the gate will be hard enough. Galfrid is at least known there."

"Is that a good thing?" muttered the squire.

Gisburne pulled open the purse on his belt and rummaged inside. "And here—take this..." He handed her a heavy gold ring.

Mélisande gazed at it and smiled broadly. "Why, Gisburne," she said, with faux delight. "What does this mean?"

Gisburne heard de Rosseley snigger behind him. "It means you have the seal of Prince John in your possession—just in case they need any persuading."

She slipped it over a gloved index finger.

"Go!" said Gisburne. Galfrid and Mélisande mounted their horses, and with a last fleeting glance, she reared her horse and the pair of them leapt into a gallop.

"And us?" said de Rosseley.

"I'm tired of being at Hood's tail," said Gisburne, slinging his shield across his back. "Being one step behind, breathing his wind. Now, we have horses and they are on foot. We follow no more. Soon they will reach the Nottingham road. Once we're certain they're on it, we'll ride around and get in front of them. Get a look at them head on. Hood himself is at the head of that army; take the wolf's head, and the rest will die."

"Just like that?" said de Rosseley.

"Can you think of a better way?"

"And him?" said Asif, pointing at the dead man.

"Let him burn," said Gisburne. He grabbed Nyght's reins and tossed them up over the horse's ears. "No time to waste. Mount up. We ride immediately." Gripping the reins and a handful of mane in one hand and the pommel of his saddle in the other, he swung himself up onto the horse's back. "But, Sir Tancred..." he called, bringing Nyght about.

Tancred's skull face swivelled to him.

"Helmet on, I think. We will soon meet the road. No point in frightening the locals."

And with their shields and bows on their backs they thundered off after their prey.

XXXV

HE WATCHED THEM mount up and ride off, cursing under his breath. Removing the bolt from his crossbow, he slid it back into the quiver, slung the bow and began to clamber down.

The past few minutes had been entertaining to watch, at least. He had missed the boy skewering his intruder, which was a shame, but Gisburne's reaction more than made up for it. There was the joy of discovery—the boy was alive!—and the touching moment when he hailed the boy as hero. Then the debate about their next move. They were too far distant to hear, of course, but he could imagine every word. He even caught himself muttering their dialogue under his breath in silly voices: gruff, masculine Gisburne; the common, yokel squire; the breathy, squeaky woman. He got so engrossed in the game that, like an idiot, he missed his one chance.

The woman had left the scene far sooner than expected. It was good she was there, of course—for some time, he hadn't been at all sure that she was. Then the obvious truth about the oddly slim, shapely knight in the green surcoat had struck him.

His position was good. He had judged well. He had a clear line of sight, and had correctly anticipated where they would stand. The body on the fire had helped him there, of course.

What he had not anticipated was how quickly they would move on. There he had been, nocked and loaded, with the woman clearly in his sights. Then the Saracen had blocked her. He judged that from this distance—assuming both stood still at that moment, and that he aimed high enough to clear the Saracen's scale armour—that he could shoot straight through the Arab's neck and still hit her head. But it was a risk. He'd decided instead to wait—but in the next moment, she was on the move, on her horse and away. Then Gisburne and the others had ridden away too, and at such a pace that it would take him some time to catch up again. And so, yet again, he would have to un-nock the crossbow, pack up and move off. He was used to it. For every successful shot actually taken, there would be at least two dozen lost opportunities.

It meant, he supposed, that he still had the element of surprise. And he was in no hurry. That was what he kept telling himself. He had waited this long, after all—he was not about to let impatience ruin everything. Still, he was only human. It frustrated him.

He thought about alternative targets. There was the boy, who had gone north with the pack horse. Back to Clippestone, no doubt. He would be easy enough to pick off—but to what end? Likely as not, Gisburne would never hear about it—once this was over, he would be dead as earth.

He gave it due consideration, nonetheless. The plan was not set in stone, after all. It couldn't be. But it would take him out of his way. He would have to leave off stalking his main prey, and that he was not prepared to do. He had to be focused, cool-headed. Keep the overall objective in mind and not be distracted by more petty matters. He had seen that mistake made a hundred times over. No, he would just have to bide his time, and let the opportunities come—as he knew they would.

He swung down from the bough, gently released the string of the crossbow, and packed bow and bolts neatly upon his waiting horse. Then he heaved himself up into the saddle and rode towards the south.

XXXVI

Nottingham
24 March, 1194

"LOWER THE GATE, in the name of Guy of Gisburne!" called Galfrid across the moat.

The pasty face of the guard atop the rough stone tower—barely more than twenty feet above their heads—peered down at him, then at the cloaked and hooded rider by his side, then back again.

"You are not Sir Guy of Gisburne, sire," said the guard, his voice thin and nasal—a match for his face.

"He's too short, for starters," said another, somewhere out of sight. Galfrid pictured a porker of a man. He then pictured his own boot making repeated and forceful contact with his oversized rump.

"I didn't say I *was* Guy of Gisburne," said Galfrid. "I said to open the gate in the *name* of Guy of Gisburne. I am his squire, and bring important news to your Constable, Sir Radulph Murdac."

"He looks a bit old for a squire," said the disembodied voice. Galfrid clenched his fists tight about his reins.

"I thought you were known here," whispered Mélisande. "Do you get this often?"

"All the bloody time," sighed Galfrid gloomily. It had been nearly three months since he'd had occasion to come to Nottingham, but even when a regular visitor he had rarely entered unchallenged. Perhaps it was something about his face. There were a few he knew among the castle guard, it was true—but they were mostly within the keep, and out here, on the cold, draughty outer defences, was where they sent the 'barbican fodder': the new, the young, the idiots.

The simple round tower served as gatehouse for the castle's outer bailey, a deep ditch and simple wooden stockade that circled all but the south and west of the great rock upon which the castle stood, where the sheer cliffs formed their own defence.

It was before the sharply sloping bank of this ditch that Galfrid and Mélisande now stood, a green, stinking channel of dead water— growing more pungent by the minute, in the sun's warmth—between them and the raised drawbridge.

"You do know that Sir Guy is a loyal servant of Prince John, and answers directly to him?" called Galfrid. This was not quite true— not any more—but Galfrid thought it best to keep things simple.

"I know it well, sire," said the guard in his bored monotone, "and would open this gate to him in a heartbeat, were he here. But this castle is under siege."

"Siege?" said Galfrid. He drew himself up in his saddle and looked about. The road stretched away behind them, empty. From somewhere above in the bright sky came the twittering of a skylark. At the far corner of the moat, a lone crow flapped. "By whom? There's no one here."

"With respect, sire, you are here."

Galfrid stared up at him. The day's sun had made for a sweaty ride, his arse ached from the saddle, his stomach growled for food and drink, and now this was making his brain hurt. "You think *we* are the siege?"

"There are forces who even now plot against the authority within this castle," said the guard, as if reciting from memory. "I am sorry, sire, but all comers must be challenged."

"Ask him why the other one's face is hidden," said the second voice.

"May we please see your companion's face?" called the guard.

"Better yet, let me show you this..." Galfrid leaned across, took hold of Mélisande's wrist and raised aloft the hand bearing Prince John's ring. "Upon this hand is the seal of Prince John, Count of Mortain, Lord of Ireland, master of this shire—and this castle."

The guard leaned forward, squinting down at them. "I can't see that from up here."

"Then lower the bloody gate, you numbskull!"

"I am sorry, sire, but I can't do that. This castle is und—"

"Perhaps you'd like me to send it up there to you?" snapped Galfrid.

"Can he do that?" said the voice.

"Can you do that?" asked the guard.

"Easy as pie," said Galfrid with a smile. Then he slung his bow off his back, uncovered his quiver and drew an arrow from it. "Lean out a bit more, will you?"

"Lean out, sire?" said the guard, suddenly wary. "What for?"

"So that when I send this ring up, the arrow it's tied to will have something to stick into."

The guard's head snapped back.

"He's gonna shoot!" he said to the other. "Quick! Sound the horn!"

"Good work, Squire Galfrid," said Mélisande, her patience exhausted. "Perhaps a different approach is called for..." And before either could wet their chops and sound the alarm, she threw off her cloak, her voice ringing out with such severity that it put the wind up Galfrid better than a hundred arrows.

"I am Isabella, Countess of Gloucester, wife to Prince John..." The guard reappeared, then gasped, boggle-eyed, so terror-struck by this revelation he actually clapped a hand over his mouth. "I come accompanying a valuable relic to the safe-keeping of the castle." Her eyes flicked sideways to Galfrid, who was trying hard not to look too stunned.

"My lady, I—" began the contrite guard.

"Never mind!" she snapped. "You are tasked with challenging all who come to this gate, and that you have done. Excellent! What is your name?"

"Cuthbert, my lady,"

"Cuthbert..." repeated Mélisande. "I shall mention you to the Prince. But there are more pressing matters. As you see, the dangers upon the road have required me to travel in disguise, but now that you have forced me to reveal myself outside of the castle's protection, I stand vulnerable to enemy arrows. So, before this encounter ends with your lord made a widower, I suggest you lower the drawbridge!"

Galfrid, who had traversed this gate more times than he cared to remember, had never seen it opened so fast.

"Who are you calling a relic?" whispered Galfrid as they clattered across the wooden bridge.

"Well, at least I said you were valuable," muttered Mélisande.

Almost before they had passed through the gateway, the counterweights either side were lowered and the bridge drawn back up—then the guard, every bit as skinny as Galfrid had anticipated, his mail ragged-edged and ill-fitting, came bowling out of the door at the base of the tower.

"I shall announce you, my lady," he said. And with that the guard—already out of breath, but keen either to curry favour or avoid further disaster—ran ahead of them up the winding, gritty path to the gatehouse of the inner bailey.

"So," muttered Galfrid as they went, "what happens when they find out you are not Prince John's wife? Isabella is known here, and believe me, you are very little alike—in either looks or temperament."

"But if and when they do, we shall already be inside," she said. "And if we haven't got Murdac's attention by then... Well, I'm sure we'll think of something."

"Assuming we don't get killed first," said Galfrid.

She gave him one of those sweet smiles with which she was so adept. "Well, I could just tell them that my father was the Count of Boulogne and my grandfather King Stephen of England," she said, then she geed her horse and trotted on past the panting guard. "Come on, Master Cuthbert!" she called, cheerily. "Keep up!"

Galfrid watched Cuthbert toiling behind her, then glanced back at the barbican and idly wondered how these outer defences would fare when Hood's men came knocking.

XXXVII

Sherwood Forest
24 March, 1194

"CAN YOU SEE?" called Gisburne. "Is it them?"

Aldric shifted from one swaying branch to another in the treetop, and squinted through his eye-glasses. "There's a dust cloud. A big one, past the river. Heading north—towards the town."

"How did they get there so fast?" said Asif. "Are you sure those glass-eyes of yours aren't deceiving you?"

"I've never seen them put to such a use," said de Rosseley. "I thought such things were to help half-blind monks illuminate what was right under their noses."

"Well, these are to help illuminate what is far away from mine," said Aldric. "And yes, I am sure."

So keen had he been to use his lenses, in fact, that when the opportunity arose, he had been up the tree like a squirrel. Gisburne had commented upon the apparent improvement in Aldric's shoulder, and allowed himself a smile. Mélisande had been right; pain meant nothing if you had the right motivation.

"Then we've found them..." said Gisburne, smacking a fist into his palm, as much in relief as in triumph.

He hadn't thought it possible to lose close on a thousand men, yet somehow they had managed it. His plan had seemed simple enough. Once Hood's army were set upon the Nottingham road, they would follow them as far as Basforde, then strike out east, turn south again, and lie in wait just past the crossing with the western road—where Gisburne knew there was a copse of trees that could provide good cover.

All had gone well. Not far beyond Hemps Hill, with the town almost in sight, they had made their move. The going was swift— there had been no rain now for three days—and they reached their goal in good time. Here, the approach broadened out into meadow, with an isolated copse of very ancient trees—their chosen hiding place—at the meadow's southern end. The meadow itself was far more open than Gisburne remembered it, with the low-lying shrubs and grasses barely into their spring growth. That was good. Hood would have no cover.

Gisburne placed himself behind a massive bough, which over the decades had dipped so low from the main trunk that the end had sunk into the ground. From here, he could turn his bow a full third of a circle, commanding a broad sweep of the road ahead. The sun was almost directly behind their backs—and directly in Hood's eyes.

The plan was unchanged since Clippestone. Gisburne would target Hood; Aldric would back him up with the crossbow. Both would then move on to secondary targets. The others each had targets of their own. Gisburne had carefully described Hood's inner circle to them—the hard-liners of the Wolf's Head who had kept things going even when Hood was languishing in the Tower. Asif, Tancred and de Rosseley would go for Took, Lyttel and Will the Scarlet; and—in Galfrid's and Mélisande's absence—Aldric would target O'Doyle, and Gisburne himself would deal with Much. From there, with all Hell breaking loose, they would take out as many of the lesser lieutenants as they could—David of Doncaster, Gilbert White Hand, Arthur a Bland and others—taking off to a safe distance on horseback if things became too hot.

It almost seemed too easy. As they stood, bows ready, arrows nocked, a feeling rose up in him, as unwelcome as it was unexpected; nagging at his innards, and pulling his mind from the task. Something he had not experienced with such force since the day he had stolen the eating knife.

He felt ashamed.

Gisburne was a practical man, a pragmatist. It was what he prided himself on, what he had most admired about Gilbert de Gaillon. But no matter how he thought about what he was about to do, how he justified it in terms of the greater good—and, by God, there was plenty of justification to be had—it felt dishonest. It felt wrong.

It was, after all, what Hood would do. What the old Tancred would do. What Richard would do.

Two faces loomed in his mind, accusing him. One was the boy Much, as he had once looked: a driven and passionate youth for whom Hood was as yet only a dream. He could not, no matter how he posed it to himself, feel good about the boy's imminent death. But Hood had forced his hand. Word was that he had accepted him into the Wolf's Head—and a chance survivor of a raid upon the Great North Road had seen the tattoo, fresh on the boy's wrist.

The other was Marian. Whether she would be with the band was a possibility he had entirely avoided. Yet a possibility it remained.

He had done worse things, more desperate things, but always out of necessity—in extremis. *This* was calculated, a strategic choice to render the enemy powerless. And it was this, perhaps, to which his soul objected: it felt less like battle than slaughter.

But he had to do it. Inasmuch as anything could be considered right, in this grey, grey world, this was right.

The feeling, he now understood, had been with him from the very start of the mission. He'd thought it would ease as things progressed, but it had only grown more acute. This was, he supposed, how it felt to be a general.

And, so, these thoughts churning in his breast, they'd waited.

And waited.

The realisation that Hood was never coming dawned only slowly.

Gisburne had paced back and forth in fiery agitation, for the first time entertaining the idea—surely impossible—that Hood knew he was being pursued. If so, the rules had undergone a radical change, and surprise—their most valued weapon—was lost. But he could not believe it was the case. He would not.

He had dispatched Aldric and de Rosseley—one north along the road as far as Hemps Hill, the other northeast, back across White Moor—to track them down.

De Rosseley had returned first, horse steaming from the ride. No sign. Then Aldric; also nothing. It was, said Aldric, as if the road—the very earth—had simply swallowed them up.

They had, evidently, done what no one could have anticipated and turned west—*away* from Nottingham.

It made no sense. Every step Gisburne had taken in the past few hours, every decision he had made, had been built on the absolute certainty that the great castle was Hood's goal.

"He *has* to come there," said a baffled Gisburne. "It is the last great symbol of Prince John's authority, and where the Lionheart will certainly head. There is no other place it makes sense for him to go."

"I am forced to agree," said de Rosseley. "Though it appears there is something he wishes to do first..."

De Rosseley's insights—he had the keenest soldering instinct Gisburne had ever known—were at times profound, but this time, Gisburne could make neither head nor tail of it. There was something else, that much was clear. But what it could be was beyond him.

"What is to the west?" said Asif.

Gisburne shook his head. "Villages. Just a string of villages..." There were no castles, no rich barons, no challenges. Just people. People of no consequence—without power, without wealth, without even food to put in their...

And that was when he began to understand.

They had headed south, skirting around Nottingham, feeling their way. Of Hood's army, there was no sign—yet Gisburne could almost sense them out there to the west. Like wolves, circling at a distance. Mocking them. Was it really possible that Hood knew? Had the game swung back in the outlaw's favour?

Gisburne remained convinced Hood's ultimate goal was Nottingham—but his opponent, mercurial as ever, seemed in no great hurry to get there. And Gisburne now believed he understood why. Hood would be going from village to village, taking in as many as he possibly could along the way, striking out west and following the villages in a great arc around the town, before turning back northwards to make the final move. It would take time—days—but put Nottingham under far greater threat than Gisburne had ever realised.

Hood had never led an army into battle. What he would do with it, when he finally had the chance—inspired by the example of the merciless, butchering Lionheart, whose legend he sought not to match, but to exceed—made Gisburne shudder.

He thought then of Galfrid and Mélisande—who by now must be there—and how things might unfold if he were to fail.

But then, courtesy of the most trivial of things—dust on the breeze, spied by chance from the top of a tree—fortune had swung back in their favour: the opponent's move revealed.

Gisburne mused on his fragile luck. Had the past few days not been the driest for weeks, there would have been no dust, and they might never have found Hood's army again—or not before they struck.

As Aldric swung down from one bough to the next, Gisburne leapt back on Nyght. "They're on foot and have had a long march. But even if their fervour has them break into a run, they cannot reach Bridgeforde before we can. We'll cut ahead of them there. I know a way through the woods—a forester's path—it'll take us straight to the road north of the bridge. And then... we'll have him."

De Rosseley mounted up, shaking his head in bafflement. "They must have circled right around the town and crossed the Trent near Cliftone. For what? What possible purpose does it serve?"

"It makes little difference now," Gisburne said, turning Nyght about.

This was not quite true. But if it made the kind of difference Gisburne suspected, it was not the kind of news he wished to give. Get the job done first. Kill the one they had been sent to kill—take the head off the wolf, then worry about whatever came after. The plan remained the same.

"Hey!" called Aldric, dropping down from the tree. "Don't leave without me!"

They rode at a gallop, following Gisburne's lead. After a few moments, he turned east off the road and plunged down a narrow path through dense trees and scrub.

It was tortuous for the horses, and no less so for the riders. So dark was it that the bumps and hollows in the damp, sheltered earth were impossible to see, and the lower branches battered and threatened to unhorse them.

Yet they neither stopped nor slowed—if anything, their hooves pounded faster, Gisburne putting on a burst of speed as they drew close—until they were almost on the road upon which Aldric had seen Hood's men advancing.

Only then, as Gisburne spied the ragged hole of daylight ahead, did a rogue thought intrude on his singleminded pursuit. It was something Asif—who knew these lands the least of all of them—had said: *How did they get there so fast?*

At the time, so eager had he been, he'd dismissed Asif's objection out of hand. But now, as they hurtled towards the light, he was suddenly gripped by a terrible doubt.

They burst onto the wide road; Nyght reared wildly, and the others almost piled into the back of him. Talos whinnied in complaint as Asif's horse butted into his flank and the Arab lost a stirrup.

For there, surging past them towards Nottingham, filling the road in both directions as far as the eye could see, was a multitude of armed men, some mounted, many on foot, banners flying, helms and blades glinting in the sun, near-blinding them.

The nearest soldiers recoiled at the sudden appearance of the horsemen, barging into others as they drew back and gripping their weapons tighter. A shout went up. In an instant, Gisburne understood his dreadful error.

It was an army, but it was not Hood's army.

XXXVIII

Nottingham Castle
24 March, 1194

FOR ALL HIS ineffectiveness at the barbican gate, Cuthbert proved an invaluable asset once inside. He saw them safely past the porter and watchmen to the inner bailey, where he made sure their horses were led away to be fed and watered. Then—much to their surprise—he accompanied them further still, securing their entry to the courtyard of the great keep itself. Mélisande had requested he did not reveal her true identity, a secret with which, for now, only he could be trusted. Cuthbert, seeing the logic of it, and clearly happy to be co-conspirator to the Prince's wife, had readily agreed.

Galfrid sensed the poor lad was rarely, if ever, the centre of anyone's attention, and was making the most of the situation—perhaps dreaming of advancement. Whether his superiors would think him worthy of it if they knew what he had done, Galfrid frankly doubted. But right now, as so often in the past, he had occasion to thank God for stupidity.

Once they were in the keep, no one seemed interested in them. They faced no challenges, and no one rushed to welcome them either. The only thing that attracted any attention was Mélisande's outlandish garb—and few seemed to know quite how to respond to it.

The castle courtyard was buzzing with people; more than Galfrid had ever seen here, and few of whom he recognised. Those he did tended to be grooms, cooks and buttery staff—good if you needed food, drink or your horse looked after, which Galfrid very often did, but not for much else. A good number of these fine fellows, upon seeing the squire, gave him a smile and a cheery greeting as they went about their business. Some, on catching sight of Mélisande, paled and scurried away in a kind of uncomprehending, existential terror.

"Do you not know any people of real consequence around here?" grumbled Mélisande.

"I know the daughter of the Count of Boulogne," said Galfrid, deadpan, "granddaughter of King Stephen of England..."

Ignoring him, Mélisande scanned the milling crowd, hurrying about on various tasks, none overly keen to make eye contact with the odd-looking strangers. When a grey-haired man whose size of hat marked him as someone of importance—a steward, perhaps—saw Mélisande looking his way, clearly about to address him, he hastily dropped his eyes.

She took a step towards him. "Pardon me, but..."

He looked at her, terrified, and without a word fled from the pair of them, almost careering into a scullery maid struggling with a pair of full buckets.

"Well!" said Mélisande, in genuine disgust. "I've never seen such rudeness. Is this what passes for a welcome in Nottingham?"

Galfrid chuckled. "Had you been you in a fine gown, he would now be fawning at your feet..."

"Do you have a gown?" said Mélisande, irritably.

"Not on me," admitted Galfrid. "Perhaps if we—"

But she had already made another move—straight ahead, this time, and directly into the path of a grandly armoured man in a mail coif, greying beard jutting from his chin. Galfrid recognised the captain of the castle garrison, the very man who, less than a year ago, he had given a black eye in a local tavern. The captain stopped, startled, Mélisande blocking his progress, and Galfrid lowered his head and pulled his hood a little more over his face.

"Pardon me," said Mélisande, sweetly. "I am in need of assistance..."

The captain looked Mélisande up and down with a baffled expression, and—finding it impossible to tell what class of woman she was—decided to hedge his bets. "Madam," he said, bowing his head an inch or two as a afterthought.

"I am a French noblewoman and close ally of Prince John," she said. This much, so far, was true. "It is essential that I see Sir Radulph Murdac as soon as possible."

The captain, unable to judge the truth of the claim, was clearly not eager to get into negotiations. "Sir Radulph is taking counsel and cannot be disturbed," he said

"But I must get a message to him," she said, with a degree of breathy pleading in her voice.

The captain visibly softened. "I cannot grant that privilege, my lady. Sir Radulph has asked for there to be no interruptions. They are also taking lunch and likely to be some time yet. But if I may find someone to see to your needs in the meantime..."

"May I know where this consultation is taking place?" she asked, as if the question were no more than an idle fancy.

It was evidently a great deal more to the captain, who stiffened again. "I am not at liberty to say." But as he spoke the words, his eyes flicked upward to the main tower, and swiftly back again. "Please wait here..."

"Thank you," said Mélisande. "You have been most helpful." She smiled her most courteous smile, and curtsied—a gesture that, under the circumstances, looked decidedly strange. Certainly it was the first time Galfrid had seen a curtsey performed in full armour.

The captain bowed again—several inches lower, this time—and his eyes settled on Galfrid. The squire tensed, and tried to look as unlike himself as possible. The grey eyes stayed on him for a moment, narrowed slightly as their owner struggled to place a memory, then evidently dismissed the attempt—and he turned and strode away.

Mélisande turned to face Galfrid.

"The main tower," she whispered.

"I saw it too," said Galfrid. "There is a chamber at the top of it, spacious and well-lit, with clear views in all directions. Well away from prying ears and eyes. If I were discussing matters relating to the defence of this castle, that is where I would do it." He hardly needed to add that the chamber was probably the most secure location in the entire castle. The narrow stone steps up to its entrance were now guarded by three armed men—clearly cut from stouter cloth than Master Cuthbert—and in between the bolted door they were guarding and the upper chamber was the entire castle garrison. Galfrid looked across the courtyard and saw the captain now conversing sternly with two more armed guards, and occasionally gesturing back towards the two of them.

"Whatever we do, we'd best do it soon," he said. "The captain is discomfited at having strangers rattling around in his castle." Galfrid knew him as the sort to put you in irons first and ask questions later. It was as well, from this point of view, that they had left their swords with the horses, but he'd still feel a lot better with one by his side.

"So, the person we need to see is at the top of a guarded tower," mused Mélisande, tapping her fingers against her chin. "And the only person who can grant us access... is at the top of that guarded tower. Tell me, what would Gisburne do if he were here?"

"Just walk in, probably," said Galfrid with a sigh. "And they would most likely let him. He has that air about him, like it or not."

"And if they didn't let him?"

Galfrid puffed out his cheeks and widened his eyes. In his experience, that situation usually ended in a fight. But even as was thinking about a suitable response, he noticed her eyes darting about, studying every window, parapet and stair as if committing each to memory—or matching them to one already in mind. It was as if she were already formulating a plan, and one that would end in a fight.

"This is stupid," he said, glancing nervously across at the captain, who was now deep in conversation with the man in the important hat. "Skulking about like criminals... If Murdac himself clapped eyes on us, he'd want to hear what we had to say."

"Then we must make sure that he does," said Mélisande. Her eyes had now settled on a low, insignificant-looking doorway in a far corner of the courtyard, tucked in shadow where the round south tower met the wall. "And there is one other person here who can get us up there... Wait here."

"One oth—?" began Galfrid.

But Mélisande was already heading towards the door.

XXXIX

THE WAIT SEEMED to last forever. Not comfortable being so exposed, Galfrid dodged out of sight behind a stack of barrels. There, a cellarer of his acquaintance had been toiling with a pair of exhausted-looking scullions, and Galfrid now struck up a conversation with him—whilst keeping half an eye on the courtyard.

The cellarer—whose name was Bartholomew, and whose cheerfulness knew no bounds even when he was complaining—related, several times and in a variety of different ways, exactly how many barrels he had shifted that morning, and what each contained. He was especially keen to point out how some of these were, technically speaking, not his responsibility, since their contents were actually not food or drink at all and therefore, by rights, outside of the province of the cellarer, but that those in charge just thought a barrel was a barrel, when in fact, as should be obvious to all, a barrel wasn't just a barrel—oh, no, not at all—for they could be very different from one another, each according to the purpose for which they were intended, and that if one knew barrels as intimately as he did, one could tell with some precision exactly what contents...

Galfrid's attention—half-engaged at best—slipped its anchor and drifted away, never to return. One thing was of interest to him, nonetheless: there was some truth to Cuthbert's claim about a siege. Murdac was provisioning the castle. He sensed trouble.

It was then that Galfrid saw Mélisande reappear from the doorway, bearing something very large, long and clearly heavy under one arm. She looked about, then, not seeing him, was off again like a hound on the scent, heading straight towards the foot of the great tower.

"Good to see you, anyway!" said Galfrid, cutting Bartholomew off in mid-sentence, then clapped him on the shoulder and was off.

To the casual observer, Mélisande was just another figure amongst many, carrying another burden as nondescript as Bartholomew's barrels. As he caught her up, however, the thing beneath her arm—wrapped in sacking—began to take on a half-familiar shape. It clunked ominously as she shifted its weight under her arm. It looked like... But surely not?

"I thought you'd gone to find a gown," said Galfrid.

"And I thought you'd abandoned me," she replied. "Actually, the one gown available to me would not have enhanced my reputation."

He peered nervously at the ungainly package. "So, what's in the..." He would have finished the sentence, had it not then dawned on him that she meant to walk right up to the tower's three guards, and that a smile of greeting was already on her face.

Of the three guards, the two standing either side of the stair bore polearms, while the third—clearly the more senior—wandered from side to side, fist on the pommel of his sword, making occasional glances up at the closed door. Waiting for his master to reappear, Galfrid guessed.

It was he who Mélisande now addressed. "Why, captain!" she said.

The guard—red-haired beneath his helm, with neatly trimmed beard in the style of the Lionheart—turned, and gave a bow.

"Not captain, sir—I mean ma'am..." He negotiated the correction with admirable ease, and seemed remarkably unfazed by the figure now before him. Amazing what a pretty face could achieve, thought Galfrid. "I am merely guard to the Constable. How may I—?"

"Please excuse my ignorance!" said Mélisande with a beaming smile, and dumped her burden at her feet. The guard frowned at the heavy *clank*, but Mélisande did not let the thought linger.

"Tell me, have we met previously? Only your face... It seems..."
She frowned, and twiddled her fingers.

The guard actually blushed a little, struggling to recall an occasion that had never existed. "I don't believe..."

"Your name. What is it?"

"It is Henry Rousel, my lady," he said with a bow. "'Rousel' on account of this red hair of mine."

"Really?" she said, eyes wide, almost absurdly engrossed.

Galfrid had no idea where this was going. Nor, he suspected, did the guard—but the man seemed not to care.

"It must be a very great responsibility, guarding the Constable himself," said Mélisande, her eyes full of wonder. "In a way, you are the most important man in the whole castle."

Henry Rousel smiled and blushed again. "Oh, I wouldn't quite say that... But I did have the honour of forming a guard for King Richard, when he once visited here."

Mélisande was a picture of admiration. She took a step towards him. "Sir Radulph is such a dear friend," she said. "I would dearly like to get a message to him, if you were able to convey it."

"I'm afraid I cannot just now, my lady."

"Not for *anything?*" she said, crestfallen.

Rousel's face and voice were all apology. "Only the castle being under attack is sufficient cause, my lady."

The words, coupled with the mysterious object at Mélisande's feet, made Galfrid suddenly uneasy.

"But if you can wait an hour or so," Rousel continued, gesturing towards the top of the tower, "he shall be down, and then perhaps—"

"So, he *is* up there, then?" interrupted Mélisande, the warmth and wonder suddenly diminished.

Rousel frowned as she pulled on a pair of heavy gauntlets, aware that things were not quite as he had thought.

Galfrid had seen many extraordinary sights in his life, but what unfolded in the next few moments would rank with the best of them.

Rousel spoke—Galfrid did not catch what it was, nor could be certain it was even comprehensible—but Mélisande was already crouched over her sacking bundle.

She stood, holding one of the largest crossbows Galfrid had ever seen, cocked and ready to shoot, a bolt with a grapple already loaded upon it. And, in an instant, all was suddenly clear to him—where she had been, who the mysterious other person was. Llewellyn, of course. Who else? Somehow, she had sought him out in his workshop deep in the bowels of the castle—not an easy task, even for those who had been told the way. Then she had somehow convinced him to hand over one of his precious creations. If anything, this was an even more incredible achievement. There had been times when the crusty old tinkerer had been reluctant to hand them over even to Gisburne. Galfrid found himself chuckling like a child.

Rousel, meanwhile, had recoiled at the sight of the great bow—but Mélisande, her eyes now fixed on the tower battlement, had by that time already taken three steps away from him. So bold and unhurried were her movements that neither he nor his comrades seemed quite able to take them in. Before any could make a positive move, she heaved the great bow up, took aim, and shot.

There was a dull *thunk*. The bow jumped almost out of her hands, the bolt zipping from it. A thin rope whipped through the air behind it. The grapple fell with a *chink* of metal on stone and Mélisande pulled the rope tight. Then, just as the three guards were finally coming to their senses, she hauled herself up, booted feet against the tower's stones, and started climbing towards the tower battlement.

Galfrid—his own part in this done, if indeed it had ever existed—burst into loud, uncontrollable laughter. *Yes,* he thought, *that's about what Gisburne would have done...*

Rousel, his sword now drawn—though to what purpose, Galfrid could not guess—could only stare as the slender, silhouetted figure disappeared up the tower wall and clambered over it like a spider. Somewhere, people were shouting in alarm.

Galfrid saw crossbowmen on adjacent battlements fumbling with their weapons and quarrels, but they were already too late.

Rousel, apparently lost for words, turned back to Galfrid as if for some explanation. "Don't look at me," Galfrid said, almost incapable with laughter. "I've told her time and again to stop doing that."

XL

Sir Radulph Murdac leaned upon the table and regarded the three men before him, expression grim. "William de Ferrers will be first to come hammering at the gate," he said, stabbing his finger at the table top, "of that we can be certain. He scents blood."

"It is personal for him, brother," said Philip of Worcester, Murdac's brother. "I hear he is still calling himself Sheriff."

Murdac gave a dismissive laugh. "I don't doubt it... Perhaps he *would* be Sheriff still, had he not turned against the man who granted him that position." De Ferrers was no fool, but he was playing a dangerous game. It was John, not some spurious, scheming Council, that ruled this county. It was John who appointed its officers. "Well, he can call himself Sheriff all he likes," said Murdac. "I have possession of this castle. De Ferrers can do his worst."

Roger de Montbegon nodded his head slowly. "Others will come," he said. "The Earl of Chester, for one. He already counts himself half-royal, through his connections with Richard."

"De Blondeville is a scheming, swivelling bastard," spat Philip, "and nothing would give me greater pleasure than to see him dash his pitiful brains out on these castle walls." He laughed and punched the table in satisfaction, then glanced at Sir Fulcher de Grendon, who merely appeared uncomfortable.

De Grendon was a petty knight who Philip had befriended and was obviously seeking to impress—probably, if Murdac knew his brother at all, having promised to aid his social advancement. Murdac resented de Grendon being here at all, especially when there were others of far greater moment who were not. But, on this occasion, he had chosen to indulge his brother rather than embarrass him. At least the nervous Sir Fulcher kept his mouth shut.

Roger de Montbegon folded his arms. "There are many more looking to win favour with the King, now his return is imminent. To show their true colours."

"Or swiftly change them..." muttered Philip.

Murdac raised his palm towards his brother. "The King is not here yet..." he said.

"And when he is?" said de Montbegon.

Murdac narrowed his eyes. He liked de Montbegon; trusted him, even. But he wondered, when push came to shove, where the baron's loyalties would ultimately lie.

As if reading Murdac's thoughts, de Montbegon added, perhaps a little too earnestly: "You know you have my full support, no matter what."

As he said it, a metallic clatter rang out from somewhere close by. De Grendon flinched, and Murdac turned with a frown. It was unfamiliar; or *half*-familiar. Like a poker dropped in a hearth. Whether it had come from above or below, he could not tell. Some clumsy oaf in the garrison, Murdac supposed.

De Montbegon, meanwhile—who had either not heard or chose to ignore it—was not yet done. He glanced at de Grendon and leaned in closer. "We do have a sensitive issue here, my lord. You are Constable of this castle and sworn to defend it—as I know full well you will—but in whose name?"

Just then, shouts rose from the bustling courtyard below. Murdac momentarily wondered at them—but still de Montbegon pressed on. "The Council claims that when the King granted Nottinghamshire to John, he excepted Nottingham castle."

"What a nonsense!" blustered Philip. "How is one to administer the county without it?" As if in answer, a distant laugh rang out.

De Montbegon sighed—his first outward sign of impatience—and cast a withering look at Philip. "Nevertheless," he said slowly, as if addressing a child. "That is the issue we face, like it or not."

Murdac clenched his fists and leaned on his knuckles, glaring at de Montbegon. His brother was a hothead, but he was still his brother. The trouble was, De Montbegon was right. The issue regarding ownership of the castle was... hazy. But possession was nine tenths of the law. *All* of the law, if none could take it from him. He took a deep breath. "To fight the King is treason," he said in measured tones. "And when—*if*—the King himself comes to our door and I hear the command from his own lips, then and only then will I bend."

There was further clamour from outside, and a thud. Irritated at the distraction, but wishing to give de Grendon a proper show, Murdac stood up straight and thrust out his chin in defiance. "As for the others... well, I say, let them come."

The moment the words left his mouth, there was a violent crash—this time mere yards from him. Murdac saw astonishment on his companions' faces. De Grendon froze, but the other two had their swords drawn before Murdac could turn. As he did, he saw the door to the chamber flung open, and, framed within it, advancing slowly, fully armoured, one hand held aloft, a woman—her red-gold hair flying half-loose, her face flushed with exertion.

"Sir Radulph," she said, speaking rapidly. "My apologies for this rude interruption. Please be reassured that I am unarmed."

Murdac blinked. He felt his mouth work, but no sound came out. A disordered swarm of thoughts battered his brain, but just one—seemingly trivial—rose above the others. That was how much this—whatever it was—resembled the Count of Boulogne's daughter.

Worcester, de Montbegon and de Grendon, equally at a loss as to how to act, stood motionless and staring at the woman's raised fist, upon which glinted a heavy gold ring.

For a moment, no one spoke.

"Well, I have your attention, at least," she said at length.

There was a clatter from the stair below and the intruder moved around so her back was away from the door. They turned with her.

"But how did...?" said Murdac.

"Never mind about that now," she said. "I am come here with Squire Galfrid and have urgent news from Sir Guy of Gisburne."

Even as she said it, two guards from the garrison below—both armoured and helmeted, and with drawn blades—burst into the chamber.

"Hold!" barked Murdac, and held up his hand. The guards skidded to a halt.

"Thank you," said the woman, as if she had just been handed a cup of wine at a feast. "I may not be armed, but I am armoured." Her eyes flicked to the guards, still frozen mid-charge. "I probably wouldn't survive your blows, but I dare say I'd wear you out."

"Gisburne, you say?" said Murdac. "Last I heard, he had withdrawn from political affairs."

"Perhaps this can persuade you otherwise?" she said, slowly turning her raised hand. Murdac's eyes went to the gold ring, as she let it slide off and caught it between thumb and forefinger, then took a step forward. The guards tensed, but Murdac kept them in check. Her eyes flitting between each one of them, she edged forward until finally she was able to place the ring upon the table and raise her hand, fingers spread to show it was empty.

Murdac snatched up the ring and made a show of examining it, but he had already recognised John's seal.

"Lower your weapons." Every man hesitated, and Murdac sighed heavily. "I see Gisburne's methods remain as unorthodox as ever. What is this news that is so urgent?"

"Hood is coming," she said. "With an army. We believe he means to take the town in the name of King Richard."

Murdac stared at her, then at de Montbegon and Worcester, and burst into laughter. "The outlaw? Coming to take this town? This castle?"

"Yes," she said. His laugh died away under her severe gaze.

"How many men?"

"We estimate seven hundred."

"How equipped?"

"Bows."

"Just bows?"

"Mostly bows."

"Siege weapons?"

"None.

"Mining gear, perhaps?"

"None that we know of. They are travelling light. On foot."

"On foot? Not even horses?"

"No."

Worcester sniggered.

"Then what possible threat is this outlaw rabble?" said Murdac. "Seven hundred common folk, armed with sticks? They'll break against these walls?" There were chuckles from around the room, but not the woman. Her stern, defiant demeanour unnerved him. He had seen that only a few times in women—in Queen Eleanor, for one. He had also, now he thought of it, heard some wild story about the Count of Boulogne's daughter and sometime associate of Sir Guy of Gisburne, Mélisande—a story which, at the time, he had dismissed as fantasy, but which he now suspected to be only a pale shadow of the truth. "Lady Mélisande... It is Lady Mélisande de Champagne, is it not?"

"In the flesh," she said, giving an elegant curtsey.

"Much as I appreciate Sir Guy's warning. I hardly think that—"

"Have you studied mathematics, Sir Radulph?"

Murdac, irritated by interruption and the irrelevance of her question, gave an exasperated laugh. "Mathematics? I *know* it, but I don't see..."

"I studied it in the East, amongst other things. I can tell you this: once they have sunk their fire arrows into your outer defences and burned them to the ground, they will be in a position to rain down arrows upon the inner bailey, the keep and all the timber and thatch contained therein at a rate of four thousand, two hundred arrows every minute. Accustomed as we are to rain, Sir Radulph, that is a storm I doubt even this mighty edifice could simply shrug off."

Murdac stared at her for several moments, contemplating these words. No one was laughing now. He turned from her. "I am grateful to you, my lady. I don't doubt you have risked much to bring me this information, and I shall respond in kind. Both you and Squire Galfrid—who is well known to me—will have the protection and freedom of this castle..."

Worcester made to protest, but Murdac shut him down. "The *protection* and *freedom*," he said, looking his brother hard in the eye. "And we shall consider your words. But know this: the castle has withstood far greater threats than the one you describe. It shall do so again—and perhaps soon. Now, go freely." He waved his guards away. Then, looking her up and down, he added: "Perhaps now you are here you could also find some clothing that is... more suitable."

Mélisande gave him a pleasant smile, and curtseyed once more. "I wish to stay alive, Sir Radulph," she said. "And find this most suitable for that purpose."

Then she plucked the ring from the table top and descended the tower steps, the two guards following close behind.

XLI

Sherwood Forest
24 March, 1194

THERE WERE THOUSANDS of men of every possible class—boys to fetch water and arrows, cooks, quartermasters and camp followers, miners in wagons, archers and men-at-arms, companies of mounted serjeants and noble knights. There were earls and bishops—Gisburne recognised some of the colours that whipped and fluttered in the wind—and far, far up ahead, many hundreds of men distant, one pennant in particular stood out, for so it was designed to do. Larger and taller than all the rest, it was red as fresh blood, and on it, in gold—not mere yellow, but actual glittering gold—were three lions. The banner of Richard the Lionheart, Duke of Normandy, Aquitaine and Gascony, Count of Poitiers, Maine, Nantes and Anjou, Overlord of Brittany, Lord of Cyprus and King of England—and the most feared warrior in all the western world.

Gisburne had marched under Richard's banners once before. But that was far from here, and many years ago, in the days when Old King Henry was still very much alive. Never once did he dream he would do so again—least of all, that he would be marching upon Nottingham.

It was Gisburne's quick thinking that had saved them. In the confusion of that sudden, unexpected encounter, two courses of action would have spelled disaster for them. If they showed—or appeared to show—resistance, or if they attempted to flee, they would be killed, as enemies or deserters.

So he had done neither. Without hesitation, he had turned and barked "Fall into line!" His comrades had immediately done so and—barring the odd muttered curse from the footsoldiers closest to them, whose heads had been under threat from Nyght's flailing hooves—had been immediately accepted. They now walked two abreast, part of the King's army.

Doubtless it was the sight of Tancred and de Rosseley—both clearly of the knightly class—that had sealed the illusion. But now, as they rode, Gisburne found himself thinking about Asif. He prayed to God, Allah and anyone else who might listen that the Arab had had the good sense to cover his face, but did not dare look back, for fear of attracting further attention. Gisburne could see several nationalities from where he sat—English, Welsh, some Flemish; Normans, of course—and did not doubt there were many more. Perhaps even the odd turcopole was a possibility. But an out-and-out Saracen knight? Such a thing was hardly commonplace in Richard the Lionheart's army. Yet not one man here now seemed of a mind to pay them the slightest regard.

Gisburne glanced at de Rosseley, riding beside him, and the pair exchanged looks, conducting an entirely unspoken conversation.

What now? said de Rosseley's slanted eyebrow and tilted head.

Your guess is as good as mine... said Gisburne's imperceptible shrug.

There was nothing to be done. De Rosseley craned his neck and looked ahead. He was, Gisburne guessed, wondering whether they might simply leave the column as casually as they'd joined it; Gisburne had been thinking the same. Perhaps it could work, but he had seen how Richard dealt with deserters.

He could, of course, seek out Richard and make himself known. But, given the nature of their arrangement, he did not know whether Richard would acknowledge him openly—or at all. Even then, getting close enough to converse with the King himself seemed utterly impossible.

There was nothing to be done. And so they marched on.

The light was already beginning to fade. Tomorrow, they would reach Nottingham; then they would see. Then, the siege would begin. Perhaps Murdac would do the sensible thing and capitulate at the sight of the royal standard. But, much as he hoped for it, Gisburne knew Murdac better.

As he rode, heart strangely numb, he took stock of the situation. He had lost Hood's army, and become stuck with Richard's. He had split the company, stranding two of them on the wrong side of a siege. He stood to be publicly rejected by Richard for his past associations with John, and by John's supporters for his current association with Richard.

In his mind, he saw Hood, somewhere out there, as he laughed and laughed and laughed.

XLII

He cursed Gisburne's name. His stupidity, his stubbornness, his infuriating ability to survive whatever was thrown at him.

It was far from the first time he'd cursed the man, and nor, as he watched Gisburne and company merge with the great swell of humanity heading north, would it be the last. There would be a last time, though. Soon, perhaps.

Gisburne's movements after leaving Sherwood had been erratic—stopping, starting, splitting, joining, backtracking. Part of him was amused to see Gisburne so desperate, so clueless, so utterly at sea. Nothing amused him more than Gisburne's suffering. It was, after all, what had brought him all this way. But the practical side of him was driven to curses. All that to-ing and fro-ing had complicated matters, and tracking him without discovery had been difficult. Not that he did not relish the challenge. He enjoyed being tested; it allowed him to hone his skills, and would make the completion of his task that much more satisfying. But still, he was not thankful for it. He refused to be grateful to Gisburne for anything.

For some time he had watched them at the copse north of the town. This also amused him—watching these would-be *hashashin* taking up careful positions and waiting to murder their prey, while *he* had *them* in his sights. Like a hunter stalking a deer, he had squinted down his crossbow at them, observing their movements—which were minimal—and their patterns of behaviour. Nothing fascinated him more than watching people when they were thought they were alone. In it was a kind of truth.

Each was very different in their inactivity. The knight seemed the least comfortable; in fact, he was never completely still, perpetually stretching or flexing his shoulders as if stillness were abhorrent to him—or as if movement were all that kept him alive.

The Arab was quite the opposite, sitting motionless for so long in his black cloak that he melted into the shadows. Only twice did he move: once to carefully smooth the fletchings on his arrows, once to kneel and pray. He chuckled to himself at that; this ancient copse had seen its fair share of pagan practices in its time, he was certain, but surely never that one.

The enginer, partway up a tree and peering this way and that through some glinting sliver of glass, interested him greatly. At one point, it looked like the glass might even be turned in his direction, and he dropped his head in panic. The possibility that his concealment was not total and inviolable did not please him. But the moment soon passed and fascination took over once more. Did the glass really help him see further, or better? What a boon such a thing would be! Perhaps, later, he could take it off his body.

Only the one with the skull face *truly* never moved, to such an extent that finding any sign of life in him at all—anything that marked him as human, with real blood in his veins—became a challenge. As the hours passed, he grew ever more determined to catch the one twitch, one sniff or itch. But he never did. He might as well have been staring at a discarded puppet, waiting for it to sing and dance.

Then there was Gisburne. For a long time he was still, but gradually his agitation grew until, once it was clear he had been denied his target, he began to pace. It was this sight that pleased him most of all.

Each one he had had in his sights for minutes at a time—he could have shot them ten, twenty, a hundred times over. This was his favourite time. As his aim roved around different parts of them— sometimes settling on the head, sometimes the back, occasionally, for variety, an extremity—he imagined pulling the trigger. He pictured the bolt striking, saw them jerk or spin as they were hit, saw them fall, saw the blood flow. He imagined how they would react after the first death—who would run and who would stand still, how many he could bring down while still making a clean escape. He felt his heart pound at the thought.

Not with pleasure, exactly. That first moment, with the shot taken, the bolt committed and his presence announced—he liked the least. Then, all that mattered was that he get away—to disappear again. He was at his most content when disappeared. Perhaps one day he would not pull the trigger at all. Perhaps one day those odd fears that befell him—which thrust him back into the world with such force and which were nothing to do with killing and everything to do with being exposed—would conquer him. But not yet.

Still, he did not shoot. Frustrating as it was, this was not the time or place. It was not enough to kill one of them; the others had to know who had done it, and why.

Then they had been on the move again. He almost lost them when they had disappeared suddenly into the forest, but then had watched with a kind of fascinated horror as they had run headlong into the King's army. For a moment, he really thought that was the end of it. The end of them, the end of his task. The thought both amused and infuriated him. He wanted this done with, certainly, but on his terms. He would not be robbed of that. It was what had motivated him from the start: revenge.

But as he watched them drift away, in the stream of men and horses and coloured banners, alive but untouchable, he knew he would have to wait all over again. He would withdraw, bide his time, keep an eye on his prey, and hope they would once more be drawn to the forest. And, of course, they would.

If the worst came to the worst, well, there was always the secondary plan. Even if his main goal was achieved, this other would remain to be completed. Just thinking of it made the hairs on the back of his neck prickle. It was little different from any one of his other missions; a shot from a crossbow, no more. Yet it had the potential to make him the most famous man in England. Perhaps the world.

XLIII

**Nottingham Castle
25 March, 1194**

"AT LONG BLOODY last!" said Edmund de Levertone, rubbing his gloved hands. "I thought you'd got lost on the stairs."

Will Cobbe stepped out onto the tower battlement and yawned. "You do know you say that every time?"

"And one day it'll be funny. Mark my words, it'll get to you in the end."

"I'm not that starved of conversation," said Will. "Not yet, anyway."

"You want to try a night up here," said Edmund, puffing out his cheeks and rubbing his hands together again with a shudder. "Starved of everything, I am, and chilled to the marrow. That wind cuts through you."

"Nothing to report, then?"

Edmund nudged his helm further up on his head and knitted his eyebrows in mock concentration. "A goshawk was mobbed by a bunch of crows over Fishpond Woods nary an hour ago." He nodded towards the interior of the keep. "Then Bartholomew was mobbed by Mrs Bartholomew. Not a pretty sight. Other than that, a quiet night."

"No pretty young ladies climbing the tower today, then?"

"More's the pity!" They both chuckled, Edmund shaking his head in wonder. "What I wouldn't give to have seen that!"

"You and me both, brother..."

"Hey," said Edmund, nudging the other, and pointed to the corner of the battlement. "See that?" Will Cobbe could just make out a freshly chipped patch of stonework between the two end merlons. "That's where her grapple bit."

"She can grapple me any time. Most exciting thing to happen in years, and we bloody missed it. Who was it up here, anyway?"

"Lambert."

"No!" Will chuckled. "Had to be him, didn't it? Poor bastard!"

"Just stood there, apparently, eyes wide as platters, no idea what to do or even what he was looking at. Then she says to him: 'Don't mind me, my good man...' and before he can blink, she's headed straight down to the Constable's chamber."

"God's teeth!" laughed Will. "Has anyone seen him since? It'll be a wonder if he's still marriageable after one of Murdac's bollockings."

"Just be glad it *wasn't* you..." said Edmund with a laugh. He slapped Will on the shoulder and headed towards the stone stair. "Anyway, the day is young—who knows what it might bring? So, you dream on about your pretty intruders, my friend—I've got a pressing engagement with a bowl of hot potage. And not before time, neither. Looks like a storm's brewing."

Will held his hand above his eyes and squinted up at the sky. "Storm? You sure?"

"Sky's clouding up to the south," said Edmund, cocking his thumb.

Will turned, stepped up to the battlement and looked out over the River Leen towards the Trent. There, hanging in the air over the trees between the two rivers, was a dark haze. He looked first to one side of it, then the other.

"That's not cloud," he said with a frown. "Looks more like... smoke."

Edmund stepped up by his side, and for a moment they stared in silence.

Not cloud. Not smoke. Dust; and beneath it now, advancing along the forest road—filling it, and shimmering with the glint of metal—something far worse than rain.

"Holy Christ..." said Edmund.

They should have recognised the signs earlier, but they had not. A rider from the bridge outpost should have come and forewarned them, but they had not. But before either Will Cobbe or Edmund de Levertone could move, someone on the lower battlement blew three blasts upon a horn.

And then all Hell broke loose.

THE ALARM BROUGHT Murdac running, Galfrid and Mélisande close behind. "If this is your supposed 'rebel army'..." muttered Murdac as he emerged from the stairway. But when he reached the battlement, his jaw dropped.

The great army was already crossing the Leen bridge. Soon, Murdac knew, they would wheel around and advance up the hill towards the castle's eastern wall, overrunning the houses beyond the outer bailey. Accompanying them now, drifting in and out on the wind but growing stronger with every minute, was a clamour such as Murdac had never before heard: voices bellowed and chanted, drums battered and throbbed, and the sounds of trumpets rent the air. Even at a distance, Murdac could hardly believe themselves less assaulted by noise than the doomed inhabitants of Jericho.

Flying above the advancing forces were the colours of the Earl of Huntingdon, the Earl of Chester, and—just as Murdac had predicted—William de Ferrers, Earl of Derbyshire and rival for the title of Sheriff. But there were many more besides: the crosses of the archbishops of Canterbury and York; the banners of the bishops of Lincoln, Ely, Hereford, Exeter and Whithorn; the standards of Earls Warenne and Salisbury, of Roger Bigod and William Marshall; and there, flying more prominently than all others, were the flags of King Richard.

Murdac blanched.

"They're not the rebels," said Galfrid, turning to him. "We are."

Worcester, de Montbegon and Fulcher de Grendon burst onto the platform behind them—and they, too, stopped dead at the sight stretching before them.

"Gods," muttered de Montbegon. "The King himself is come."

"We don't know that," said Murdac.

"But the banners..."

"It's a ruse," said Murdac. "The King is not with them." There was a distinct quiver in his voice.

"The King is returned," insisted Galfrid. "Five days ago. I know this for a fact."

"This is just the army come from taking Tickhill," said Worcester, dismissively.

"Tickhill is north," said Galfrid, as if addressing an idiot. "This army approached from the south."

Murdac gathered himself. "The King is returned," he said. "That much is true. But he remains in the south. I have good reports to that effect. These barons, come to do his dirty work or to win favour, want us to think otherwise. And why? Because they know full well they cannot take this castle by force. Their only hope is if we give in."

"Perhaps we should consider..." began de Montbegon.

"We will not!" snapped Murdac. "That is exactly what they are hoping for. What they rely upon. We have stores enough for months, perhaps years. They have a great army to feed, in a land that provides scant fare even for its own people. Let them dig in. We'll see who starves first."

"The King will see to their provisioning, by whatever means necessary," said Galfrid. "And you know he will not be content to simply wait it out. There is nothing he likes better than to break a castle. None have yet resisted him." Galfrid drew in closer. "And you know what he did to the rebels in Aquitaine, Angoulême and the Limousin?"

Of course Murdac knew; *everyone* knew. Many had nothing but awe and admiration for the Lionheart's uncompromising, brutal methods. They made him a great general, and a great king. But it was a rather different matter, mused Murdac, when those methods were turned on you. To those outside, Richard was a robust, decisive leader; to those in the regions themselves, he had been the very reason they were perpetually in revolt.

"Well, where is he then?" said Murdac, suddenly defiant, and gestured wide across the battlement. "Do you see him out there, riding before his army? Of course not."

"The fact we have not see—" began de Montbegon.

"Others may be frightened by stories, Sir Roger," said Murdac, turning on him, "but I left those fears in my crib. I was charged with holding this castle for Prince John, and hold it I shall."

He stepped to the edge of the southern battlement and looked down into the courtyard of the keep, where vast numbers of his men had now turned out, nervous eyes on him. Leaning out over them, hands on the cold stone parapet, he bellowed out in a hard, clear voice: "Prepare for siege!"

XLIV

Nottingham
25 March, 1194

"WELL, THIS IS a pretty pickle," said de Rosseley. It was an English expression—one Ross could only have picked up from one of the grooms—but certainly it captured their situation.

They were sitting about a flickering fire in a muddy yard on the town's shabby outskirts, chewing on their meagre rations, cloaks pulled about them against the spotting rain. In the near distance, the jagged edifice of Nottingham Castle loomed. The stones of the great keep and inner bailey glowed orange in the night, illuminated by the flames from the blazing barbican.

Gisburne looked up at the besieged fortress, and the drifting column of thick, black smoke before it, twisting a bent, discarded arrow shaft in his hands. "A pretty pickle," he repeated. He poked at the blazing logs and spared a thought for the citadel's defenders.

Why they had not immediately capitulated when they saw Richard's banners, Gisburne could not fathom. Surely even Murdac could not be that stubborn. Formidable as the castle was, they could not hope to win; this was no mere upstart baron at their gates, but the King himself, the great conqueror of castles, and in his own domain. By resisting, all they guaranteed was death—and a traitor's death did not come swiftly.

Immediately upon arrival—even before the last of his army had left the road—Richard had set about breaching the wooden stockade of the outer bailey. The reports Gisburne had heard were sketchy and at times fantastical—so it ever was, with the Lionheart's exploits—but from what Gisburne could gather, a large force had pushed forward behind thick shields, the King himself among them. The first objective had been achieved swiftly, but not without considerable bloodshed on both sides. There was little the crossbowmen on the stockade could do to halt the advance, but once the outer bailey gate was breached, resistance—doomed though it clearly was—had been fierce. A group of defenders had even made a bold sortie from the castle itself in support of their beleaguered comrades, but were soon beaten back. It was said that the Lionheart himself had killed a knight with a crossbow. Later, men from the castle had again crept out, this time to set fire to the captured barbican—a gesture of defiance, but really no more than a gesture.

Gisburne and his company had heard it play out—the bellowed commands, the blasts upon horns, the clash of weapons and the cries of agony and alarm—but had seen nothing. Then, finally, the evidence of it began to reach their eyes. One by one at first, and then many at a time, carried between pairs of men like sacks of wet grain, the wounded and dying were brought for the attentions of the barbers, the priests or the gravediggers. It was a sickening parade, even for one used to such spectacles: faces hacked, extremities gone or hanging, bone exposed, bellies, limbs and heads stuck with shafts of ash and oak, and so much blood and gore that a red trail was left in the mud and dung of what passed for a street.

The women of the whorehouse opposite—among the select few to have stayed when the army pitched up, risking ruin for the sake of opportunity—stood and watched in glum silence, their hair askew, the ragged hems of their skirts caked in mud. The sounds of their sisters plying their trade drifted from the tiny, uneven windows above, and for a time had merged with the groans and babblings of the battle's casualties.

Battle had ceased until the next morning, but around them still were the sounds of a busy camp: the hammering of timber and metal, the cutting of wood, the rasp of blades against stone, and above all, voices—hundreds, thousands of voices, laughing, cursing, singing, praying, but most often raised in command or protest—sometimes English, sometimes French, occasionally that curious mixture of the two that made sense only to an Englishman. They were the preparations for siege, and in the sounds alone, one could divine a strategy. This was to be no mere waiting game; Richard did not starve castles into submission, he broke them. And this—the rebel castle, held in defiance by his upstart brother—was in for particular punishment.

Gisburne looked again towards the castle walls. Somewhere in there—if they had made it that far—were Galfrid and Mélisande. In there also—still living, he hoped—was the old enginer, Llewellyn of Newport. It was entirely possible, tucked away as he was, that the whole siege could come and go and the castle change hands and Llewellyn wouldn't even realise it. But he thought of the last time he had seen him, the old man's fragile health, his own advice that he get out of his workshop, and worried for his wellbeing.

Nottingham, a town Gisburne knew better than any other, had never been so full—nor, perversely, so wholly abandoned. Upon hearing the blasts of the horn from the castle guard, the inhabitants had all either taken refuge in the castle—if useful enough to warrant feeding—or fled. Now, the great sprawling army, with its dozens of factions, was camped in and about the town's buildings—fine houses for the lords; humbler dwellings for the knights, serjeants and other men-at-arms; barns and stables for the common soldiery, where they could get them. The meadows beyond the town limits were dotted with tents, many reserved for those of status. The rest had to make do where they could.

Gisburne and his company, at least some of whom looked like knights, had been offered accommodation that was at least warm and dry, but Gisburne had eschewed it in favour of a quiet corner away from the main army—and prying eyes.

A quiet corner... Gisburne laughed to himself, assailed as he was by the raucous carousing from the packed hovel behind him, where a company of Flemish crossbowmen had taken root. It had, in part, dictated Gisburne's decision to camp here—mercenary companies tended to keep themselves to themselves, and he doubted they understood enough English to make sense of anything they might overhear. *If* they heard anything; in celebration of the day's successes they were making enough noise to raise the dead.

Judging by the state and stink of it, the yard had until recently been occupied by a pig, something that evidently did not delight Nyght and the other horses, who were now tethered to the fence rail and drinking—reluctantly—from its trough. The fate of the creature itself could was hinted at by the smell of roasting pork now wafting from the hovel. The row of tumbledown cottages the Flemings had commandeered included an alehouse, and clearly the new residents had also discovered its abandoned wares and duly liberated them.

All in all, they had far better things to occupy themselves than Gisburne's gloomy band—and that was just the way he wanted it.

"So, what now?" said Aldric.

"There is no other course left to us," said Gisburne. "I must get to King Richard by any means possible, and before battle is joined tomorrow."

Earlier in the day, they had again considered slipping away. Aldric thought it eminently possible—one might whitewash the archbishop's wagon unchallenged, if one did it with confidence, he had said.

Perhaps he was right, but Gisburne refused to countenance it. He had no qualms about putting himself at risk, but the others? De Rosseley might bluff his way out, but what of Asif? As long as he lay low, attracting no attention, no one in this chattering chaos was likely to notice him or care much if they did. But who here would look at a dark-skinned man acting suspicious and believe he *didn't* have malice in mind?

The lives of the rest of his company—now separated from them— also concerned him. They now found themselves among people who Richard, if true to form, would skewer, burn or publicly eviscerate for their treachery. Once before, Gisburne had put Mélisande and Galfrid in danger within the walls of a castle. He had not abandoned them then, and could not abandon them now.

But the main reason Gisburne had to seek out the King was brutally practical.

Some time during that afternoon a wild thought had occurred to Gisburne: that Hood might already be among them—that his men might have merged with Richard's. It was a mad idea, but once thought, there was no ridding himself of it. Though they had searched for signs of Hood's men, they found nothing.

But as they plodded about the camp, he had begun to accept a harder truth. The element of surprise was now lost. The swift, lighting strike they had planned would fail—worse, it would lead them into the jaws of a trap.

The plan had been bent further and further from its original shape to accommodate every change in circumstances. But like a bowstave, there was a point where it would break, doing harm only to the one wielding it.

It had been painful to admit, for the course it led him to was one he dreaded. But it was clear, with Hood drawing steadily closer, there was only one option remaining.

He needed to get to Richard, because only Richard could give him an army. And he needed an army to go to war with Hood.

It was the very last thing Gisburne wished to do, and therefore the very last thing Hood would expect. And that was why he had to do it.

He hated that he had been driven to this—that he had to go cap in hand to that most detested man, that lover of war. But understanding that it had to be done—committing to it, not reluctantly, but completely—inspired another, entirely unexpected feeling in him. One he had all but forgotten. Here, in the midst of disaster, surrounded by mud and death, he felt suddenly alive. It was as if some part of him, long ago fallen into slumber, had begun to wake up.

The new plan was simple.

All he had to do was get to Christendom's most ruthless crusader in the midst of his own army, accompanied by a Saracen and a skull-faced heretic, admit his total failure to carry out what had been asked of him, and ask to draw a huge military resource from a siege inspired by decades of familial hatred.

He had faced worse odds. It had been Mélisande, by a stream in Sherwood, who had reminded him of that. Something else was occurring to him now—a mad idea inspired by a mad idea—that actually made him smile.

"This is all very well," said Aldric. "But one does not simply walk up to a king."

"Especially when he is engaged in a war," added de Rosseley.

"And he must be alone," said Gisburne. "If he has company, I can't guarantee that he'll even acknowledge me." He spoke as if, in some grim fashion, he actually relished the challenges ahead.

"That's impossible," protested Aldric. "We should just make for the forest. Nothing's stopping us."

But Gisburne was smiling, an idea forming in his head.

"There is one time it might be done," he said.

XLV

Nottingham Castle
26 March, 1194

RICHARD SETTLED HIS arse over the hole in the board, then turned and glared at the groom. "I don't need help," he snapped.

The groom bowed, gave a final anxious glance around the unfamiliar surroundings of the walled garden, then scuttled away to leave the King to the King's business.

Richard sat back on the worn commode, his mail gathered in his lap, his sword leaning against his thigh, and smiled to himself. Ah, yes. Perfect.

He was back in armour. He was back at the head of an army. He had a rebel castle under siege—a good one, too—and prisoners ready to hang. His eyes flicked up to the castle walls, where he could make out guards shifting nervously on the battlements—little more than a bowshot away. Richard had taken the house closest to the castle walls for his lodging, much to his barons' alarm. They had urged him to move further back, but even when he had stepped out and two of his men had been shot dead by crossbow bolts, he had refused. He had simply put on a coat of mail and an iron helmet, and continued to stride before the besieged walls. He meant to show these upstarts—and his own men—that he was not afraid.

Now here he was, in the open air on a fine spring morning, the smell of burnt, blackened earth in his nostrils, the birds singing and the carpenters hammering at the gallows. Only one thing could possibly improve matters—and that was a good, satisfying shit.

In an uncertain world, it was something Richard knew he could absolutely rely on. When it came to regularity, there was nothing to match the King's bowels. It didn't matter where he was, what stresses or strains he was under or what he had eaten—it was always the same, every morning, like the rising of the sun and the crowing of the cockerel. Even on campaign, when others were dropping like flies, their innards turned to quivering jelly by dysentery, he alone remained firm and true. It was a sign, he felt—to him and to others—of the great strength within him. He had no doubt it struck fear into his enemies, whose own weak bellies liquefied in terror at the prospect of facing him.

He took a deep breath, taking pleasure in his brief seclusion—a pleasure that had only grown since his incarceration. Privacy was not something Richard often experienced, or indeed particularly valued, but there were times, he had to admit, when solitude was best, and this was assuredly one of them. Occasionally, his one-time clerk and now physician Mauger had tried to get in on it—examining what was produced for the purpose, he said, of "ascertaining the King's good health." Richard had said, with all the firmness he could muster, that Mauger could poke and prod all he liked afterwards—he could make them into a damned hat if he wanted—but if he ever wished to be a bishop, something the King knew he coveted, he would have to go against tradition and keep his face out of the King's arse.

So it had become sacrosanct—and for this moment, everything stopped. One might say his day revolved around it, as surely as the sun revolved about the earth. Nothing was planned to clash with the daily occurrence, and all else took second place. Had the Pope himself come knocking, threatening excommunication, even he would have to damn well wait until nature had taken its course. In the Holy Land, Richard had kept King Philip of France waiting thus on more than one occasion—often rather longer than necessary, it had to be said. He chuckled to himself at the memory. So finely wrought were his guts, so predictable the movements, that it rarely took more than a few minutes to complete the process satisfactorily; but having the King of the French waiting on his turds amused him too much for the opportunity to be wasted.

There were other, more profound reasons why he so relished this moment, however. It was still. It was without interruption, without strife, without any kind of demand upon him: perhaps the only moment this was really true. Apart from when he was asleep, of course, but that Richard largely regarded as an irritating waste of time. To be at stool, however—to have his old travelling commode brought out by his grooms, the one that he laughingly referred to as his "throne"—and to be in this state of sublime isolation, that was glorious. A perfect, still moment—a moment of prayer, almost—in which all was right. It was, he had come to realise, the only time he truly enjoyed peace.

The sound of boot leather scraping on the wall shattered his reverie. It came from behind him, and he knew immediately what it was. It was followed by the heavy thud of feet landing on earth.

His hand crept to the grip of his sword. Every day of his life, he had been prepared for someone to come and kill him, or to try. He was not afraid—he was never afraid—but he knew *they* would be. They were afraid because they were about to face the Lionheart. And he was not—because he *was* the Lionheart! Let them come.

But the man did not move. Then Richard heard more sounds from further along the wall—another man clambering over and dropping into the garden. Then another. Then two more. At the edge of his vision he saw the last slide over the top of the wall and drop like a shadow. Great God! Could it be?—it looked for all the world like a Saracen...

Still he did not turn. He would not give them the satisfaction. The helm was still upon his head and the mail coat upon his back—they would have a job felling him. And he could take five if he had to. "Well, come on, then," he called in a strong, unwavering voice. "Let's see what you've got."

"My lord," said a half familiar voice. "We need to talk."

Richard turned upon his wooden throne and frowned. "Gisburne?"

XLVI

"WHAT IN THE name of Christ's holy bollocks d'you think you're doing?" thundered the Lionheart, hauling up his drawers. "How dare you disturb my repose!"

"I am sorry, my lord." Gisburne's voice was firm, but as spoke he looked nervously to the tiny windows and back door of the house, wondering if Richard's shouting would bring a flood of armed men, and whether the King was in any kind of mood to stop them killing them. "It was the only time I knew you would be alone. The only time we could get to you."

"The worst possible time!" bellowed Richard, tying his waistband, his face red with rage.

"But now we are here," said Gisburne. He saw Aldric wince at the words. Everyone's instinct before the raging Lionheart was to grovel, but Gisburne knew Richard of old. To do so was to dig one's own grave.

"We have news," Gisburne said.

To the astonishment of all, Richard's fury actually seemed to abate.

"There are other methods of delivering news, Gisburne," he rumbled, and buckled his sword back on. "This one was likely to get you killed—perhaps rightly!"

"But we weren't. And other methods could not be trusted."

"And it takes five of you to deliver it?"

"We stay together," said Gisburne—thinking anxiously of his comrades behind the doomed castle walls.

Richard nodded and took a step closer to Gisburne, casting his eyes about conspiratorially. His gaze came to rest on Asif.

"God's nails, man! A Saracen? You brought a fucking Saracen to *me?*"

"He came of his own free will. I merely invited him."

"A Saracen," said Richard, as if unable to believe the evidence of his eyes. "Here. In England. In the Lionheart's own camp..." He laughed, and shook his head. "I can see why my brother likes you, Gisburne. Though quite what you saw in the chitty-faced windsucker is another matter." He turned to Asif and, thumbs tucked in his belt, looked him up and down as a trader does a horse.

"Who is he, anyway?"

"A friend," said Gisburne. "Lately of Jerusalem. He has enemies in that city now."

"As do we all," muttered Richard.

"I am honoured, my lord," said Asif, bowing very low.

Richard appeared taken aback by this direct address—as if the horse had just spoken. "Honoured?" Richard said. "You're lucky to be alive. You must be a special kind of Saracen to thrive this far from home. And to be so trusted. Tell me, since you fight for me now: what is your opinion of Saladin?"

"He was a very great man," Asif said. "Fearsome in battle, but also wise. Magnanimous to his people, harsh when necessary. Brutal, sometimes. But fair when it was possible to be so."

The Lionheart held his gaze for a long time, his eyes expressionless. "A lesser man might have said he hated him, thinking it was what I wanted to hear. But it is not. People think I must have hated Saladin because he was my enemy. Not true. I loved him like a brother. Rather better than some brothers, perhaps... We understood each other, as only kings and warriors can understand each other. You know he sent me two horses when my own was killed? And iced water, from the mountains? Just because you have to kill someone doesn't mean you can't love them."

Gisburne saw Asif almost laugh at this, thinking it was a joke. But it was no joke.

"When you go back," said Richard, "tell your people that I, too, was fair to you. That I showed respect." Asif bowed his head low—but his eyes slid to meet with Gisburne's just for an instant.

"And you," said Richard, turning. "De Rosseley, isn't it?"

De Rosseley bowed.

"Hm. Good choice. A great competitor in the tourney. Marshal speaks highly of you. He is here, you know. You two should get together."

William Marshal, fast becoming the King's right hand, was regarded by many as the greatest knight who ever lived, and in his tournament days was unsurpassed. De Rosseley bowed again, blushing a little.

"My dead brother was the one obsessed with all that play-fighting," continued Richard. "I prefer the real thing. But when there's no boar to be had, I'll settle for pork!" He laughed and clapped de Rosseley upon the shoulder.

Richard turned, for a moment allowing his gaze to rest on Tancred. At Gisburne's insistence, Tancred had donned his helm, the faceplate of which obscured his features. Thank Christ—God knows what Richard would have made of him.

Aldric, meanwhile, was afforded not even a moment of the King's attention.

"Well, Gisburne," said Richard, "you have so far today invaded my privy and upset my natural rhythms. Let's see if you can win back your King's favour." His voice turned grave. "I hope your news is good—that you have succeeded in your endeavour...?"

"The situation... has changed," said Gisburne.

Richard's expression turned cold as stone. "That's the kind of thing people say when they have *not* succeeded."

"His army was already on the march. And his spies work hard for him. They got the news of your arrival even before Nottingham."

"How many?" said Richard.

Gisburne hesitated.

"Seven hundred, we believe," said de Rosseley.

"More," said Gisburne. De Rosseley stared at him. "I believe there may be more. The route he has followed, round the villages—there can be only one reason for it. To win more followers to his cause. That, and to bask in their adulation."

"Well, what are you going to do about it?" snapped Richard.

"You said it yourself: you cannot be their destroyer. But I can. And you have the means here. Ten times over."

Richard stared hard at Gisburne. "I offered you an army once," he said. "You turned it down. Just now, that army is a little busy."

De Rosseley stepped forward. "These men we face—they are common folk, on foot, lightly armed and barely armoured at all. If we hit them hard, just fifty knights might see it done."

Richard looked from one to the other, studying each, but his expression had thawed at de Rosseley's entreaty.

"Walk with me," he said, and headed off towards the house.

All fell into line behind their King.

"For a moment I thought he was going to kill us," whispered Aldric close to Gisburne's ear.

"For a moment I thought *I* was going to kill *him*," muttered Gisburne.

"Will he give us the men for the task?"

"I have no idea."

The King threw the door open with a crash and, ducking under the lintel, strode in.

The gloomy, uneven passage led past a low doorway on one side and a winding wooden stair on the other, then opened directly into the room at the front of the house. This, it was obvious, was the chamber Richard had taken for his own. Its windows gave an unimpeded view up to the castle, and immediately impressed on Gisburne how perilously close the King had chosen to be to his enemy.

In half of the room, several men—now caught off-guard by his unscheduled appearance—stood about a table, upon which were a drift of documents and a jug of wine. It was here that Richard drew up his plans for the siege. They snapped to attention and bowed as he entered, and he dismissed them with an irritable wave.

The other half of the room served as his bedchamber. There were none of the soft touches of luxury that would have accompanied his brother John. The bed was simple, as were the two pallets in the corner—one for a groom and one for his physician, Gisburne guessed—but upon two walls had been hung rich tapestries depicting, on one, the King spearing a boar in the guts, and on the other, the King decapitating his enemies.

Among those in the now-crowded room were a groom, a herald, Mauger the physician and a handful of fully-armoured serjeants and knights. Gisburne could not help wondering why none of them had come to their King's aid when he and his comrades had dropped over the wall. He had fully expected it—surely it was their duty to watch and protect their lord? Perhaps Richard—the most arrogantly self-reliant and untrusting man Gisburne had ever met—had ordered them not to. Perhaps they were afraid to. Or perhaps even they—especially they, the ones who really knew the man—wished him dead? Maybe all three.

Richard ignored them all and barged straight through to the front door which, despite the desperate scrambling of a groom to get there first, he opened himself.

"Well?" he said, when Gisburne did not follow him outside.

"You wish me to accompany you?" said Gisburne. "In plain sight?"

"If one man has seen you in my company, then all have," said Richard. He did not sound pleased at this prospect. "So let them see you. They will think you are coming round to the side of right."

De Rosseley raised his eyebrows at Gisburne, who felt his innards squirm.

They marched out, several of the armed knights scuttling after them, strapping their helms upon their heads as they came. As they emerged—the reek of burning hitting Gisburne's nostrils, the sounds of clattering and hammering assailing his ears—he was reminded again of their proximity to the castle walls.

Directly opposite them was a tall house in a rather fancy, continental style, but this and the one they had just left were the last of the street, which stretched away to the right of them. A short distance to their left, past the street's end, was a great ditch, and just beyond it the smoking stumps and tarry black earth where the burned stockade had stood. Beyond that, at the top of the sloping hill, rose the walls of the castle itself.

Richard strode straight towards it, then veered off to the right, to pass around the end of the fancy house.

"You know what they call me in the Limousin?" he said. "*Oc e No*. 'Yes and no.' Because for me the world is black and white. There is no grey, no in between, no compromise or indecision. I say no when I mean no and yes when I mean yes."

Gisburne had not the slightest clue why he was being told this, but as they drew around the end of the house, evidence of his words came into view. There, in a neat row before the smouldering embers of the stockade, were erected six tall gallows, clearly and immediately visible from the castle walls. Limp bodies swung from them, swaying in the wind, their heads crooked at impossible angles, the first flies of the season already buzzing about them. One turned slowly upon its rope as if in response to the King's approach—flesh livid, eyes bulging, tongue lolling. Like his fellows, he was armoured, and wore the colours of the Nottingham garrison.

"Captured them yesterday," said Richard, pausing to admire his handiwork. "Now they're working for us again!" He laughed at his own joke. "You should have seen their faces when they finally realised the person standing before them was their *King!* Well, now those up there know what's in store for them." And then he turned and walked on, parallel to the ditch, past the ends of the houses and yards at their right hand. A crossbow bolt whirred and smacked into the grass at the ditch's edge, not five yards from him. Richard paid it not the slightest heed.

It was a moment before Gisburne—faced with the horror that was to befall his besieged comrades—fully realised the significance of the King's words.

"They don't know..." he muttered to himself.

"You'll have your knights," Richard said, still striding ahead, then added, with greater force: "But when I am done with them. We have business to see to first."

Gisburne drew closer, and said: "They don't know. They don't know it's you. Or they don't believe it—that you are really here."

"They'll know soon enough," said Richard flatly.

"But if you could show yourself—clearly, so they could see your face—they would yield. Knowing for certain the Lionheart himself was at their gates would be enough, I am sure of it. All this could be avoided. It could be over within the hour."

"You want me to move closer?" said Richard, cocking his thumb at the castle. "They'd like that, their crossbowmen. Perhaps you would too. But I'm not a complete fool. Do you think I don't know how to handle a damned siege?"

As they rounded the last of the houses and stepped into the wide, open space before the collapsed gatehouse, a great cheer went up, and Gisburne and his company saw exactly how the Lionheart handled a siege.

For a forty-foot stretch at least, the great ditch had been filled and flattened, ready for the feet and hooves of the besieging army, and about the approach road, that army was now gathered in vast number, saluting and shouting for their King, weapons glinting in the daylight. But it was not these that took Gisburne's attention, but the three huge siege engines that towered behind them—two mangonels, flanking a great trebuchet.

"Master Elias! Master Roger!" called the King. "Bring them forward!"

And as the crews hauled the engines into place, the footsoldiers chanting them on, Gisburne realised his hope for a peaceful surrender was an utterly lost cause. Richard doubtless understood Gisburne's reasoning, but he didn't *want* them to give up. He wanted a fight.

The King stepped up onto the back of a broken cart, and turned to address his men.

"See those men in there?" he roared, pointing his sword back towards the castle towers. "They think this castle is theirs!" A great cry of protest and derision went up.

"Well, we'll take their castle!"

A cheer.

"Then we'll take their traitorous hands and their traitorous balls!"

Another, louder this time.

"Then we'll take their women—while they look on!"

The loudest cheer of all.

Swept up by the wave, bathing in its glory, Richard bellowed on, spittle flying from his lips. "They have been excommunicated – infidels now – so you may do as you please to them! But before we taste, I say we tenderise the meat. What say you?" And he thrust his sword at God.

With a frenzied roar, all raised their weapons; hundreds— thousands—of swords, spears, polearms and lances were shaken at the sky.

Richard smiled, bearing his white teeth like a predatory animal. "Begin the bombardment!"

And then Gisburne remembered why he hated the Lionheart.

XLVII

THE TALLOW CANDLES flickered and spat as Galfrid and Mélisande descended the spiralling stone steps into thick darkness, the world rumbling around them.

Neither spoke. Galfrid had long ago tired of the impacts of the missiles from the siege engines. Over the hours, the sound had become insidious, oppressive, the hammering of fate at the door. The engines were not just for breaking walls; they were for breaking spirits.

For a time, as they had vainly courted sleep beneath a bench in a corner of the packed crypt, the walls about them booming and quaking, he had tried to read a pattern in those impacts. It was not a question of where the great stones were being aimed—that much was obvious—but it seemed to him that if he could work out what adjustments the engine operators were making, then he might predict where the next missiles would fall—or, more importantly, where they would not.

At length, the futility of the task overwhelmed him. There was nothing that could be done; nothing at all. He had only convinced himself otherwise because the alternative—cowering helplessly in a corner—was too much to bear. The rain of stones and rubble continued to pound the castle, each impact driving him deeper into despair.

He had actually dozed for a while then, until Mélisande had tugged on his sleeve and suggested an alternative place of refuge for the night—one so obvious, he cursed himself for not thinking of it before.

They were close to the dark, open doorway below when something struck the tower above them with a thunderclap. The stone stair shook so violently beneath them that Galfrid fell against the curved wall. Mélisande held her candle aloft and raised her eyes upward. Galfrid grasped her hand—and as she turned back to him, frowning, a great shower of dust and grit and crumbling mortar rained down. The rumbling subsided. Mélisande unhunched her shoulders, brushed the dust from her hair and gave Galfrid a nod of thanks.

The steps ended suddenly, opening into a dank, airless, vaulted chamber into which the weak light barely penetrated, the interior so crammed with barrels that to enter it seemed at first an impossibility.

Galfrid knew this place of old—knew its air of damp earth, spiked with the sour tang of vinegar. Today, however, the smell, heavier than ever, was accompanied by an undercurrent of sewage—a stink that immediately transported him back to Jerusalem, in whose sewers he had so nearly perished. He heard, rather than saw, pools of water on the floor, and upon the walls—in the few places they were visible—he could see some sort of moss growing. It glowed faintly when cast into shadow. The constant heavy rain had evidently taken its toll, seeping into the deep cellarage and bringing the stink of waste with it.

He crept forward, Mélisande close behind, weaving his way through the maze of barrels and crates. Long, deep shadows slid about them as the moved. At a cranny between two teetering rows of puncheons, Galfrid stopped, and peered within, candle held before him. Assured this was the place, he edged in. It was so narrow he had to turn his shoulders, but there, in a small archway concealed by the heaped stores, was a familiar narrow door. Galfrid pushed on it, and it creaked open. From within, carried upon a heat like a desert wind, came the smell of sulphur and woodsmoke. Galfrid and Mélisande stepped inside.

In one corner, an all-but-extinguished furnace. Set before it, an incongruously elaborate wooden chair, one side of it burned completely black, and by its side a small rustic table on whose surface were a number of human finger bones, a gauntlet constructed entirely of metal, a quantity of iron nails and a jar filled with something the colour of blood. In the other corner, hanging from a cord stretched beneath the vaulting, was a huge flap of brown leather screening off a tiny section of the room, whose surface was marked by silvery flecks of molten lead. Against one wall was a cluttered bench, strewn with tools and pieces of sculpted wood and cast metal; on the other, shelves packed from floor to ceiling with every kind of curiosity, from bottles of liquids and jars of coloured powders to animal skulls, antlers and lengths of bone. In between, every inch of the cramped space was filled with sacks, barrels, boxes and chests—and over all of it lay a veil of gritty dust.

"The crossbow worked, then," said a gruff voice. Llewellyn of Newport shuffled out from behind the ragged flap partition and coughed. "I suppose it's too much to ask for it back?"

"Murdac has it," said Mélisande, apologetically. "I tried, but..."

Llewellyn grunted. "That bloody fool hasn't the first idea what to do with it."

"I think he mainly objected to the idea that I did," said Mélisande.

Llewellyn chuckled, coughed again, then spat into a rag and looked away. "What can I do for you?" he said, suddenly officious.

"Nothing, really," said Galfrid.

Llewellyn frowned at him. "Nothing?"

"We really just wanted a safe haven from all that." He looked up. As if on cue, another great impact shook the castle.

The jars rattled on the shelves, and dust drifted down from the ceiling. Galfrid had thought they might feel less vulnerable down here, but in some strange way, he felt more exposed. This place had always seemed so separate from the everything outside, as if it existed in a dream. The trembling ground seemed to drag even this, their last refuge, and Llewellyn's entire universe—a realm that had always seemed as constant as the stars—into the mire of reality.

"Sounds like the end of the world," muttered Llewellyn.

"Perhaps it is," said Mélisande.

"Murdac refuses to yield," added Galfrid. "Soon that option will be closed to him, whether he wants it or not."

"Stubborn bastard," said Llewellyn. "So, who is it? The French?"

"You mean you don't know?" said Galfrid.

"Of *course* I don't know! It's a trifling detail that my thousands of visitors must have neglected to pass on."

Galfrid and Mélisande exchanged glances. "It is the Lionheart," she said. "The King is returned."

Llewellyn stared at her, so still he might have turned to stone. An unbearable sorrow seemed to pass behind the old man's eyes. All knew how Richard dealt with enemies. With prisoners. "And you say Murdac refuses to yield?"

"He doesn't believe it's true," said Galfrid. "Thinks Richard's barons are trying to trick him."

"And Gisburne?" said Llewellyn, looking around, as if he might see him lurking in a corner. "Is he alive?"

"Perhaps," said Mélisande. "We don't know. He's out there somewhere."

Llewellyn shook his head in dismay. "Then we'd better have a drink. I've a bottle here somewhere."

Crossing the room, colliding with nearly every obstacle as he did so, he stooped over a willow basket near the table and drew out an oddly-shaped glass bottle. He winced as he straightened, and groaned. A frown creased his brow as he cradled the bottle in his hands and slapped the dust off it. Bobbing about within it was a greenish object, as big as his fist—and bigger by far than the neck of the bottle.

"What in God's name...?" said Galfrid.

"French," said Llewellyn, and sniffed, as if that answered everything. "A novelty produced over there, given to me as a curiosity. They tether the bottle to a tree branch and grow a pear inside it, then cut it free and fill the bottle with distilled liquor. The spirit preserves the pear, and the pear imparts its flavours to the spirit."

"Is it any good?" said Galfrid.

"Revolting. I swore I would drink this wretched ornament only in a dire emergency. All things considered..." He went at the bung with the point of a knife.

Then they sat, deep below the earth, and drank in grim silence as the dust of ruin rained down upon them.

XLVIII

Nottingham Castle
27 March, 1194

GISBURNE HAD NOT expected to sleep, despite the fine lodgings the King had given them, but somehow the clunking, relentless rhythms of the siege engines had lulled him into dreamless oblivion.

A blare of trumpets awoke him, and he raised his head from Llewellyn's wooden cylinder—it made a poor pillow, but he wanted it where he could see it. There was a second fanfare, closer this time. In a moment he was off his pallet and at the window where Aldric was already positioned, both shutters open.

"Reinforcements," said Aldric. "As if we need them..."

Gisburne strained to see what was happening; de Rosseley and Asif stirring in the room behind him. Far down the muddy street men and riders were moving, but he did not recognise the banners. A small party broke from them and advanced up towards the King's lodgings, and he spied the man at its centre. His bearing was arrogant—swaggering, one might even say—and the pouting lip and sour, jowly face were familiar.

"Oh, Christ," Gisburne said. "Hugh de Puiset, the Bishop of Durham."

"That is bad, I take it?" said Asif at his shoulder.

"It's bad."

Gisburne threw on his armour and hurried down below.

It was a strange state of affairs. So distracted was he by the siege, and how to aid Mélisande and Galfrid, that Hood, at times, slipped his mind entirely. Then he would remember that Hood's army was somewhere out there, moving from village to village, being fed, being watered, and steadily swelling its ranks, and he was gripped by panic.

The previous day had been excruciating. Richard, excited by his new toys but frustrated at the lack of direct contact with the enemy, had amused himself by finding unusual things to hurl within the castle walls. He had experimented with one of the bloated, hanged corpses of the castle guards. Flushed with the success of this, but not wishing to further diminish the gallows, he had his men haul more bodies from the burial pit and flung those—until Mauger had advised against such actions, for the sake of Richard's own men. Richard sulked, and had a wounded prisoner hurled against the battlements instead.

By great good fortune, it seemed, a horse died that same morning. Being unfit for food, Richard had ordered its fly-blown corpse to be flung into the castle, too, curious to see whether Master Elias's trebuchet could cope with it. When it had proved too bulky, he'd had it cut in half, and shot it at the enemy a bit at a time.

He had called on his most loyal to name the engines. On crusade, he said, the King of France had a trebuchet named "Bad Neighbour," something that amused Richard no end, though he insisted the name had been his idea. Amongst the idiotic suggestions from the sycophants and hangers-on that day were: *Richard's Revenge; The King's Spoon; Pride of Nottingham; God's Right Arm; Tree-Bucket; Zounds!* and *Wall Banger.*

Richard had ultimately chosen *The Lion's Roar,* and dubbed it such in a quasi-religious ceremony. He had insisted on doing so without interrupting its operation, and stood so close to the swinging counterweight that the engine crew had paled.

By the time Gisburne and de Rosseley emerged from the house, de Puiset was nowhere to be seen. But Gisburne heard the trebuchet's great counterweight being ratcheted back into position, having made an early start on the day's shooting, and was sure this was where he would find the King.

Before they had retired for the night, he had determined to approach the King again with a proposal to hasten the end of the siege. The novelty of the siege engines was already wearing thin; the next logical step, once the engines had inflicted enough damage, would be for Richard to make a full assault upon the walls—but before he could do that, Gisburne hoped he might turn the day's frustrations to his advantage and push for negotiation. That way, at least, someone from within might see the King face to face, and take the news back inside.

The arrival of de Puiset was a blow to the plan. The Bishop of Durham was, if anything, even more hawkish than his King.

Gisburne and de Rosseley arrived at the trebuchet to find him already holding forth. "This crime..." Gisburne heard. "This treachery..."

The King looked tired, and Gisburne guessed he had hardly slept. He did not wish to know whether it had anything to do with the upset in his bodily functions.

Several of Richard's most trusted knights eyed the pair of them as they approached—but none made any move to waylay them. Gisburne was one of them now.

De Puiset had his sheathed sword in his hand and was shaking it at Richard as he spoke. "Just give me the word, my lord, and I will—"

"Yes, yes, Bishop," said Richard irritably, as if de Puiset were stating the blindingly obvious. Of course, what the King said, de Puiset would do, except where the Pope's dictates went against them. Richard counted himself a pious man, but like his father, his relationship with men who served two masters could be strained.

"I say we go now, while they are still bleary-eyed from half a night of bombardment," said de Puiset. "Let me lead them. Nothing would give me greater pleasure than to teach that upstart Murdac a lesson."

This was the very last thing Gisburne wanted to hear—and the very last thing he wanted to happen was for de Puiset to come personally knocking on Mélisande's and Galfrid's door.

But then something occurred that he had not expected.

Richard—up to now, somewhat subdued and too weary to argue—said, "You're surprisingly keen for the fight, de Puiset, considering you paid to be released from your crusader vows."

De Puiset reddened—as much, Gisburne thought, from anger as from humiliation. "I judged matters in England to be the more pressing," he said.

Whether he had intended it or not, this was quite the worst thing to have said to the man who had left his kingdom at the mercy of his scheming brother.

"Just remember how you came by your titles, de Puiset," said Richard, darkly.

And there, Gisburne saw his moment.

"My lord," he said. "May I suggest an alternative strategy?"

"Please do," growled Richard.

De Puiset, who had not yet noticed the new arrivals, turned suddenly. If there were a point where horror, anger and contempt converged, it was writ across de Puiset's face at that moment. "Guy of Gisburne?" he said, as if the words were: "You slept with my mother?" He looked at the King and back again, incredulous. "What in the name of Jesus Christ and all the Apostles brings you here?"

Richard stared hard at the Bishop. "*I* do," he said. He looked back to Gisburne. "Out with it."

Gisburne took a deep breath; he would have but one chance. "The bombardment proceeds well. But there is a danger of it proceeding *too* well. You do not wish the prize to be destroyed by the taking of it." He knew better than to appeal to Richard's mercy, for he had none. But perhaps if he appealed to his greed...

De Puiset huffed at this impertinence. "It is hardly your place to tell the King what to—"

"It's not *anybody's* place to tell me what to do," spat Richard. "There's sense in what you're saying, Gisburne. Go on."

"You have shown your clear intent," he said. "But now you have a chance to take the castle before more damage is done. If you could only go to them now, to show yourself, to prove..."

"Show myself?" said Richard. "Prove? What need have *I* to do anything for their sakes? They are traitors and I am their King. I do not *go* to them. I do not have to *prove* to them... And before you try to persuade me further, know that Marshal came to me with the same suggestion. If I would not go for him, I certainly will not go for you."

"I understand," said Gisburne, biting his lip. "But if there were a way to convince..."

"*Convince?*"

Now de Rosseley intervened. "Perhaps if Gisburne could go to them," he said. "Approach the walls to negotiate. He is known as Prince John's man, and is well known to Murdac. If anyone can convince them, it is he."

Gisburne stared at de Rosseley, completely taken aback, but Richard did not dismiss it. He turned back to the King. "You cannot be seen to go to them, my lord, it is true. But I can." He looked Richard straight in the eye as he spoke, hoping he would hear in these words an echo of a rainy night in the paddock at Gisburne's manor house.

"Really, my lord..." said de Puiset. "You heard it from their own lips. He is *known as Prince John's man*, so can hardly be trusted to..."

"Do it, Gisburne," interrupted Richard. Then, turning to de Puiset, a look of disdain upon his face, said: "He is my man now."

Gisburne had to fight not to smirk. *Thank you, Bishop. I could not have done it without you.*

"But you know my terms," continued the King. "No concessions, no favours, no negotiation. Surrender must be total."

"My lord," began Gisburne, "I have friends in the city, lately involved in my mission, who—"

"Total," snapped Richard. "No favours." Gisburne knew that to push further risked losing the opportunity altogether. He bowed his head.

"Sir John will accompany you," added the King. "To ensure these conditions are met."

While de Puiset continued to bluster, going progressively redder in the face, de Rosseley also bowed to his King.

"Have my herald bring two white wands," called Richard. "And prepare their horses."

XLIX

It was on the morning of the third day of the siege that Will Cobbe called Sir Radulph Murdac to the battlement of the inner bailey's gatehouse. What the Constable did not know, however, was that the negotiation that was to change the course of the siege had already taken place.

It had been the sudden lull in the bombardment that had lured Galfrid up from the cellars. He had no reason to suppose that this one would last any longer than the others, but it was becoming close and airless down there and he had a sudden need for open air and daylight. Leaving Mélisande and Llewellyn to prepare a meal—if you could call barley porridge a 'meal'—he had crept up the stairs and out into the courtyard of the keep, every minute expecting the terrible battering to resume.

The courtyard was deserted but for the rats. Three stinking, mangled lumps of meat lay upon the rubble-strewn ground, seeping red-black fluid into the mud, each host to a cloud of flies, and the chief object of the rats' interest. Dead things, sent over in the last wave. *So much for fresh air,* thought Galfrid. He lifted his helm, pulled off his arming cap, put the helm back on his head and held the cap over his nose and mouth. At least that only stank of his own sweat.

Every minute the halt continued, his curiosity grew. Galfrid knew he could not really be alone up here. There were still guards on the battlements; that he couldn't see them did not mean they weren't there. When he did see movement, high on the gatehouse tower, he caught a fleeting glimpse of Murdac's head, then what might have been de Montbegon. They were, in all likelihood, scanning the besieging army, looking for signs of an assault.

Galfrid ran up the steps to the battlement on the keep's east wall and peered out. The besiegers appeared to be idle, the siege engines' crews sitting upon their machines as if they had simply lost interest. No shields were being prepared, no ladders, no troops massing. Nothing. He looked up to the gatehouse tower again, to see two guards peering out, wondering, just as he had been. But Murdac had retreated below again. Perhaps he had contented himself that no attack was imminent. But Galfrid wasn't content: something, he was certain, was coming.

He ran back down into the courtyard, where men with rags across their faces had emerged to clear the dead things. They'd likely be tossed over the south wall onto the rocks below. But Galfrid was already heading north, towards the gate of the keep.

It took some minutes to get the porter to attend him and let him through the wicket gate into the outer bailey, and as soon as he had, Galfrid ran to the great, heavily fortified outer gatehouse tower and raced up the steps. This was the main gate into the castle; when the attack came—*if* it came—this would likely be their focus. But it was also the closest Galfrid could get to the attackers.

"All right, Will?" he said. "What's going on?"

"Bugger all," said Will Cobbe, staring out at the sprawling army. "No idea why, though."

Cobbe was a decent sort. He had a good brain, too. Most of his peers simply breathed a sigh of relief at the end of the bombardment—but not him. Like Galfrid, he was growing more uneasy by the minute.

"So why have they stopped?" said Galfrid.

Cobbe shrugged. "Perhaps they've simply run out of things to throw at us."

"Then why not attack? Why wait?"

"Perhaps they're preparing to mine, to try to get into the tunnels."

"Or perhaps a delegation is coming. Look." Galfrid pointed, and there, in the thick of the army, towards the southern side, two horsemen were weaving their way forward. He watched in silence as the riders broke from the front line, and kept coming.

"Jesus..." said Cobbe. "I'd best send for Murdac." And he ran and shouted down the stair.

Galfrid, meanwhile, squinted at the approaching horsemen. It was too far to make out faces, and the morning light threw them into shadow, obscuring further detail—but the shape of the lead rider on the black horse was suddenly familiar.

When Cobbe returned to his side, he was chuckling to himself.

"What is it?" said Cobbe.

"Nothing, nothing," said Galfrid. "You know how it gets, being cooped up in here..."

"I do that," said Cobbe. A boy appeared at the top of the stairs, and Cobbe turned. "Go to the Constable. Tell him he must come—"

"Wait a minute," said Galfrid. "Let's not be hasty."

Cobbe looked at the riders, then at the boy, then at Galfrid again. "What?"

"We need to be sure first."

Cobbe's frown grew deeper. "Sure of what?"

"That they are what we think they are." As he spoke, he was hastily calculating how long it would take for the boy to find Murdac, and for Murdac to make his way from the keep to the outer bailey gate. Not long, but it should give him just long enough.

Cobbe looked out towards the horsemen again, now close enough to make out the sticks held aloft in each of their hands.

"They're carrying white wands," he said. "The sign of truce. What other reason can they have for coming than parley?" He turned to the stair doorway again. "Boy?"

The messenger jumped.

"Not so fast," said Galfrid, and held up his hand. The boy looked deeply confused—Cobbe hardly less so. "Let's hear what they have to say first."

Cobbe clearly thought this madness, but was either too polite or too bemused to say outright. "I'm not sure that is a good idea..."

Galfrid could make out the faces. The second rider had been harder to guess, but now there was no doubt. He smiled to himself.

"How far away are they now, would you say?" said Galfrid.

"What? A hundred yards or so," said Cobbe, bewildered. Then he could stand it no longer. "Look, this is ridiculous, they'll be here any moment." He signalled to the lad. "Go, now—and be quick about it!"

"Boy," called Galfrid, and the messenger stopped again. "I last saw him in the cellars. Look there first."

He nodded, and ran off. Should buy Galfrid a few more minutes.

Cobbe advanced to the edge of the parapet, gripping his crossbow, and called down: "Who goes there?"

"A delegation from Richard, King of England!" came the reply; de Rosseley's voice.

Cobbe was at a loss as to what to say next, but Galfrid came up beside him and leaned over the battlement. And there were Gisburne and de Rosseley, their horses stamping at the far the edge of the moat.

"All right?" said Galfrid.

"Jesus..." said Cobbe, and tried to pull Galfrid back. "Don't *talk* to them!"

"But I know them."

"Galfrid?" The voice was Gisburne's.

The squire leaned out again. "I know we had a falling out," he called, "but this is ridiculous."

Gisburne stared, open-mouthed, then laughed. "God, but you're a welcome sight..." His eyes hunted the rest of the battlement. "Mélisande?"

"Hale and hearty," said Galfrid. "Llewellyn driving us to drink, but definitely alive. Good to see you, too, by the way, Sir John."

"We are also fine, since you didn't ask, Squire Galfrid," said de Rosseley.

Galfrid laughed. "Well, that's good. But how on God's earth did you come to be..?"

"Long story," said de Rosseley.

"Then it had best keep. Murdac is summoned, so if you've anything to say, say it quick." He cast a glance at Cobbe, who now stood by with all the ease of a man who had been unwittingly drawn into a conspiracy.

"Listen to me," said Gisburne, "the King will not come and show himself. Not even the Marshal could persuade him, which means he won't come for anyone or anything."

"Why the Hell not?"

Gisburne shrugged. "Something about a grumpy scruffbag of a squire."

"Ha, ha," said Galfrid. "Well the news from my side is hardly any better. Murdac flatly refuses to believe the King himself is here. Doesn't *want* to believe it, I'd say."

Gisburne sighed. "If someone could only come from within— someone who knows him, who is trusted. If they could see him with their own eyes, and report it back..."

"Report what back? What is this?" The voice was Murdac's, and in the next moment his face appeared over the battlement, de Montbegon's lurking close behind. The Constable's eyes widened at what he saw. "Gisburne? What trick is this?"

"No trick, Sir Radulph. I come to tell you that King Richard is here and is intent on punishing this castle and all in it."

Galfrid saw poor Cobbe blanch.

"If you value your lives and those of your people," Gisburne continued, "you must yield without delay. Believe me, it is the only hope for clemency."

"Is that the entire message?" said Murdac, his voice devoid of expression.

"What more need be said?" replied Gisburne.

Murdac's eyes narrowed to slits. "You say there is no trick, Gisburne. And yet you, who served Prince John, now come to me as a representative of John's enemies. How am I to believe a single word you say?"

Gisburne held his gaze for a time, but the Constable was chillier than the north wind. "If you don't believe me, believe your own eyes. Or send someone you do believe..."

"No one will leave this castle," said Murdac. "Go back to your master, whoever he now is, and tell him that." He turned away.

"Cobbe?"

Will Cobbe snapped to attention.

"I wish you to count to ten," Murdac instructed, "and if these two have not left by the time you reach it, shoot Gisburne's horse."

And with a last scowl at Galfrid, the Constable turned and strode away.

L

Sir Fulcher de Grendon shook his head and peered cautiously about the courtyard. "This is folly, Master Bartholomew. Even now Sir Radulph is in his tower, planning his strategies. But does he think of the good people under his protection? Of *their* fates? " He shook his head again. "Great folly, I say."

The cellarer nodded and looked like he'd rather be talking about barrels.

"Sir Radulph does not understand," said de Grendon. "He has not been up close to the King. But I have. And many times, too. The King is a harsh man. Some might say a brutal man." He thought of the bodies that had lately been hurled over the battlements and shuddered. "But one thing is beyond doubt." De Grendon moved in closer. "King Richard has God on his side."

Bartholomew looked back at him, wide-eyed.

De Grendon nodded. "It's true. I know, for I have seen him. I have seen it in his eye, in his bearing. There is no doubt: God chose him for King, chose him for his holy crusade, and now has chosen him for this task. And you know what that means, Master Bartholomew?"

Bartholomew frowned. "Errr..."

"It means that by defying him, we are defying *God!*"

Bartholomew's mouth fell open, and De Grendon nodded slowly, pleased at this effect.

"Sir Radulph insists the King is not out there, but I feel it in my bones,

Master Bartholomew. I do. And I have said as much to the Constable. I told him: there's barely a man here who would not now surrender, and rightly so. But the Devil plugs his ears, and with this stubborn defiance he risks damning us all. Now tell me, Bartholomew—seeing no evidence of God, doubting his existence even, would you, nonetheless, pray?"

"Well, I..."

"Of course you would! Why? Because caution is the wisest course. What if your doubts proved wrong? What then? Well, it's too late then!" He shook his head yet again, and looked up at the greying sky as if the impending rain were God's judgement. "Folly, Master Bartholomew. Such folly!"

He looked hastily about him again, to reassure himself that no one with a serious opinion on the matter was listening.

But someone was.

"HIM?" WHISPERED MÉLISANDE, ducking back around the corner of the tower.

Galfrid nodded.

"It's the first time I've heard him speak more than two words together," said Mélisande. "You're certain he'll do it?"

"He'll do it," said Galfrid. "He'll have no choice."

"When?"

"As soon as we can. Richard's men have been gathering stones for the siege engines. I don't know whether Murdac noted that, but I certainly did."

"Well, I'd better go and play my part, then..." said Mélisande.

"The main gate—within the half-hour!" hissed Galfrid as she slipped away. Then he strode out of the shadowed nook by the tower and headed straight for de Grendon and the cellarer.

Bartholomew looked up and gave his friend a broad, toothy smile—but Galfrid ignored him entirely and sailed straight up to the young knight.

"Sir Fulcher," he said with a bow.

"Squire Galfrid."

"May we speak? In private."

Without waiting for a response from either, Galfrid steered Sir Fulcher across the open courtyard, and away from wagging ears.

"You are one of Sir Radulph's most trusted men," whispered Galfrid.

"Well, I wouldn't exactly say..."

"*Most* trusted. Would it surprise you to know that he is well aware of your views upon this siege?"

De Grendon's face suggested it probably would—that he might even bypass 'surprise' to 'abject terror'.

Galfrid placed an arm about his shoulder. "There is a task of utmost importance that is asked of you, upon which depends the very future of this citadel..."

"A TASK, YOU say?" said Henry Rousel with a frown. "Then why does Sir Radulph not come to me himself?" Rousel was terse. Mélisande would have to work on him.

"This comes directly from him Sir Henry," she said. "And must remain in confidence."

Rousel half frowned, half smiled. "Not *Sir* Henry, my lady," he said. "Just plain Henry—as I've said before."

"My apologies," said Mélisande, blushing a little and lowering her head. "It's your bearing. I forget."

Rousel evidently liked the mistake. "No need to apologise, my lady..."

"But there is," she insisted. "For that, and for my behaviour following our first meeting. I embarrassed you, and for that I am truly sorry."

Rousel looked to either side, then leaned in closer and lowered his voice. "My lady, you were come to warn us of the impending danger." He nodded his head towards the army beyond the battlements. "Had we but listened sooner—had *he* listened sooner—we may have been better prepared."

It was not an entirely accurate assessment of the situation, but Mélisande was more than happy to accept it. Rousel's terseness, she now realised, was not directed at her, but at his superior—and what she had taken to be wariness she now saw was a grudging respect. All this was good.

She closed in and lowered her voice. "You will have seen that I was not bound in chains or thrown in a dungeon after my escapade, deserving though I may have been. That I have, in fact, the freedom of the castle. You may take this as proof, if you will, that I have Sir Radulph's complete trust."

"I cannot doubt the evidence, ma'am," said Rousel.

"I know well that you too can be trusted above all others. And that is why I tell you what I tell you now. Regarding this siege... The Constable has had a change of heart."

Rousel's eyebrows rose, disappearing behind his helm.

"You will have heard that there was negotiation with emissaries of the King from battlement."

"I heard, but..."

She raised a finger to silence him. "Murdac is ready to yield. But first someone must go to the King's camp, to receive the King's word. Murdac wishes to go in person—to see the King with his own eyes. But he must do so in secret. And someone he trusts must accompany him."

"Tell me what needs to be done," said Rousel.

"Is THIS REALLY necessary?" said de Grendon, peering from beneath the hood of his cloak.

"*In confidence*, Sir Fulcher," said Galfrid, leading de Grendon through the gate of the keep and into the inner bailey, gripping the knight's arm. He had no intention of letting him get away. "It must be so."

"And you say the horses will be waiting at the gate?"

"They will be waiting. But keep quiet, will you? There's a good fellow."

Spots of rain pattered dismally against their hoods. Up ahead, in the shadows of the great gatehouse, Galfrid made out the slight figure of Mélisande accompanied by two horses, one bearing a hooded rider.

"Is that he?" said de Grendon.

"That is who you will accompany."

"But it doesn't look like... I mean, I don't remember him being quite so..."

Then the mounted figure—a good six inches taller in the saddle than Radulph Murdac—turned and looked at them.

"But that's not Sir Radulph..." said de Grendon.

"Isn't that Sir Fulcher de Grendon?" said Rousel.

"He goes in Sir Radulph's stead," said Mélisande. She spoke lightly, making it sound the most normal thing in the world.

"I thought you said..."

"The siege engines are being prepared. He could not in all conscience abandon the castle, even now. But he has every confidence in Sir Fulcher."

Rousel looked at her with sudden doubt, and she cursed to herself. No one could believe Murdac would have confidence in a man like de Grendon.

She drew closer and lowered her voice as Galfrid and de Grendon approached. "You are the one Sir Radulph has faith in," she said. "You are his eyes and ears. But he had to send a knight. Even a fool like Sir Fulcher will do."

Rousel's expression was hard, and for a moment she was convinced the cause was lost. But then he gave a curt nod, and turned his horse to face the gate.

Galfrid, meanwhile, had ushered the confused de Grendon to his waiting horse and was now speaking to him as if he were a child. "Up you go, Sir Fulcher. That's it. In the saddle. Now, don't you worry about a thing—Henry here is Sir Radulph's most trusted man..." But as he spoke, Galfrid glanced back nervously across the inner bailey. Mélisande looked and saw that two of the guards at the keep were watching them, conversing intently. Then one pointed in their direction, and called down to another.

"We need to hurry," she muttered to Galfrid.

The squire hauled a swathe of white material from his tunic and thrust it in de Grendon's hand. "You carry this, sire. Hold it up nice and high. Do you think you can do that?" De Grendon looked at the white flag with a mixture of bemusement and disgust. It looked suspiciously like one of Master Bartholomew's aprons.

At Rousel's command the great gate began to open.

It seemed to take an age. De Grendon's horse stamped. Mélisande glanced back across the inner bailey to the keep gatehouse, and saw sudden activity there.

Rousel turned back momentarily, and Mélisande saw a last, fleeting doubt upon his face. She prayed to God he would not see the commotion. Then a distant cheer went up from Richard's men as they registered the gate opening, and he turned back. In the face of what was now really happening, the look on Rousel's face turned to one of determination and he rode out towards the King's great army with Sir Fulcher de Grendon at his side.

LI

THE RAIN WAS beating an insistent rhythm on the canvas when Richard ordered the siege engines to resume.

This time, Gisburne's entreaties had fallen upon deaf ears. Either that, or Richard's impatience for battle had got the better of him. Now, Gisburne paced anxiously beside the trebuchet, his eyes fixed upon the great gate.

Richard, not feeling that his lodgings were quite close enough, had had a large, open-fronted tent set up, with a clear view to the castle and the gallows before it. A heavy, elaborate table had been dragged from one of the finer houses, and it was at this that the King took his meal, listening to the cranking of the siege engine winches and anticipating further destruction, when the cheer suddenly went up.

Gisburne ran forward at the sound of it. He had seen the gate move, but at first had not believed it. But it kept opening, and now two riders were approaching to parley.

He looked back at the trebuchet, loaded and ready, and then at the King. He could clearly see the riders, and could not miss their white flag, but showed no sign of revoking his earlier order.

"Hold!" called Gisburne, and ran right out in front of the great trebuchet, the rain coursing down his face. "Hold!"

Richard stood, frowned, and raised his hand. The order to hold was shouted again, then repeated down the line, echoing along the ranks of men.

The riders slowed to a walk. Men-at-arms hurried forward as they dismounted, herding them towards the King's tent in a tight protective circle. Both fell to their knees at the sight of him.

There was plenty of room in the tent, but they stood just beyond the reach of its awning, and there Richard, ensconced in the dry, let them stay. Gisburne hovered to one side, struggling to see past the men-at-arms.

Richard took a deep breath and snorted. "I don't know you," he said irritably. Then he stabbed a finger at de Grendon. "Who are you?"

"S-Sir Fulcher de Grendon, my lord." He bowed so low he might have been praying to Mecca.

"Never heard of you," said the King, and turned to the other. "You?"

"Henry Rousel, sire," said Rousel.

"Sir Henry?"

"Just plain Henry, sire."

Richard scowled. "So this is who Murdac sends to his King? Two nobodies?"

"This nobody," said Rousel, "had the honour of forming a guard for you when once before you visited this place."

Gisburne thought this one of the bravest acts he had seen in days.

Richard's expression softened, then he harrumphed and shifted in his seat. "Well, then. What message do you bring?"

Both kneeling men stared at him, then at each other.

"Do you surrender?" said Richard.

Rousel opened his mouth, but nothing emerged.

Richard shifted in his chair, the anger rising. "Well, have you been granted the power to negotiate on Murdac's behalf or not?"

Still nothing came.

"Is there anything you *can* do?" bellowed the King. He threw up his hands and stood suddenly, knocking the chair over. "Oh, this is pointless! Get those idiots out of my sight! Send them back where they came from." He barged past, almost knocking de Grendon sprawling in the mud, and strode out into the driving rain. "Tell the crews to ready the throwing engines. And have them hurl something burning at the bastards still cowering in my castle. They're Godless already; let's show them what Hell is going to be like!"

A knight who Gisburne did not recognise stepped forward. "But sire, the..."

"Something burning!" shouted Richard.

Rousel and de Grendon, meanwhile, were hauled to their feet, and—slithering in the fresh mud—were shoved back towards their horses and abandoned.

"Bayard?" barked the King. A serjeant in the King's own livery jumped to attention. "Tell your crossbowmen that if these two are still within range after a count of twenty they can use them for target practice." The serjeant bowed as the King turned, stopped, then looked back and added: "And if they don't know how to count to twenty, tell 'em they can start when they please..." And he stalked off.

With one last look at each other—the limp, drenched white rag still dangling from de Grendon's fist—the pair hurriedly mounted their horses. But before they could ride out, Gisburne rushed forward and grabbed Rousel's bridle. "You have seen the King with your own eyes," he hissed. "That is your message. Take it back there and make sure it is told!"

Rousel nodded, then with a last nervous look across the ranks of Richard's vast army, turned and rode away.

And as both men pounded away up the hill, Gisburne ran full tilt behind the lines to prepare Nyght for what was to come.

LII

GALFRID AND MÉLISANDE'S ruse had not remained secret for long. They stood now at sword and spear point, surrounded by the castle guard as Murdac, shaking with fury, strode before them.

"I see it was a grave error to have granted you the freedom of this castle," he spat. Behind Murdac, de Montbegon stood grave and silent, watching with a critical eye. He was flanked by a now bemused Philip of Worcester and a body of men-at-arms, and beyond them a rag-tag gathering of those now under the castle's protection.

"Have you all turned against us now, like your wretched master Gisburne?" Murdac turned, addressing the question not to the captives, but to all those now gathered. There was a murmur; several knew the name of Gisburne. It seemed to Galfrid that rather than stir them to a common cause, Murdac's words were merely sowing further doubt.

The outcry at the great gate had already attracted a crowd. Some had clearly taken it to mean invasion, and had rushed to the defence of the gate armed with whatever they could find. Most, however, seemed to have come thinking surrender was imminent—and, thought Galfrid, did not appear saddened by this prospect. A few even carried bundles of belongings, which they now sought to conceal from the withering eye of their Constable.

"We did it to save the lives of everyone here," protested Galfrid. The sword points wavered at his throat. "As even you will see, when your emissaries return to confirm the presence of the King!"

"*My* emissaries!" laughed Murdac. But the murmur had grown to a buzz. All here knew that if Richard stood at their gates, their cause was lost. Murdac raised his voice. "They'll be hanged from the gibbet just like all the others!"

"Even the Lionheart respects the white flag of truce!" cried Mélisande.

"They will be hanged precisely because the Lionheart is *not* there," roared Murdac. "And they"—he thrust a finger at the gate—"do not wish us to know it!"

"Riders approach!" called a watchman from above. The muttering broke into a din.

"Whose?" shouted de Montbegon. "Theirs?"

"They bear a white flag!"

"Load your crossbows," ordered Murdac, his eye on Mélisande. De Montbegon frowned at that, and looked to Worcester, but the Constable's brother remained mute.

"It is Serjeant Rousel," called a second voice; Galfrid recognised Will Cobbe. "And Sir Fulcher de Grendon."

Murdac glowered at the news, but Galfrid smiled back at him.

"It's a trick," said Murdac. "Ready your weapons."

"Christ's balls..." muttered de Montbegon, then stepped forward, addressing the guards directly. "Open the gate!"

Murdac turned on him. "I am Constable here!"

De Montbegon, fixing Murdac's wild look with his own, took another step towards him. "You dare defy me?" he rumbled, and Murdac faltered. De Montbegon was by no means a hothead, but he was baron of great estates across Lancashire, Yorkshire, Lincolnshire and Nottinghamshire, and one of Prince John's closest supporters. More significantly, the men wearing de Montbegon's livery outnumbered Murdac's by three to one.

"Your orders, my lord?" called the porter.

"Open the damned gate!" demanded de Montbegon. "They are our own men!"

The porter and guards looked to Murdac and back again. The Constable, finally realising that the mood had turned against him, simply bowed his head. The gatekeepers, who Galfrid knew held Rousel in high regard, chose to take this as confirmation; the great gate yawned open.

Rousel burst through and into the midst of the scattering crowd, with a panting de Grendon close behind, the gate already closing behind them.

"Tell them," called Galfrid, before Rousel even had time to dismount.

Rousel looked to the knight at his side—his superior—but de Grendon merely looked about him in confusion and terror, rain coursing down his face.

"Tell them!"

Rousel could no longer contain himself. "It is the King. It is the King himself! I know him of old, and I tell you, I saw him with my own eyes. Sir Fulcher, too."

De Grendon nodded. "T-true..." he stuttered, glancing nervously at Murdac and his mentor, Philip of Worcester.

The effect was instant. What had been mere willingness turned, in that moment, into action—and, like it or not, Sir Radulph Murdac, Constable of Nottingham Castle and Sheriff of Nottinghamshire and Derbyshire, had upon his hands complete and unconditional surrender.

People rushed about, clutching loved ones and belongings to them. Those guarding Galfrid and Mélisande—already reluctant—forgot this duty and abandoned them. The Constable himself stood alone, bereft of purpose, his authority now quite gone. The castle had stood fast, but Murdac's defences were utterly destroyed.

"He'll kill us if we give ourselves up," he protested weakly, to any still listening.

"He'll kill you if you don't," said Galfrid. "Surrender is at least a chance."

"Fetch white flags!" ordered de Montbegon.

And even the garrison now jumped to his command.

LIII

GISBURNE, SITTING NERVOUSLY upon his horse, did not even wait for the gate to be fully opened: he snatched a royal standard from an astonished herald, and without shield or helm rode out, spurring Nyght all the way. He was dimly aware of cries behind him—whether in protest or surprise, he could not tell. But he did not stop for anything. In the aftermath of this surrender, he could not trust Richard—or rather, Richard's overzealous men—to do what he was about to do.

As he neared, the wet banner flapping wildly, a crossbow bolt whirred past his head and sank into the earth behind. Still he pounded on, the besieged now spilling from the open gate ahead of him.

Then he saw them.

He threw off the stirrups, gripped the pommel of the saddle and swung off Nyght's back before the stallion had even come close to a halt. Skidding in the mud as he landed, almost falling, he broke into a run.

Of those who had emerged from the castle, several had already thrown themselves upon their knees and were begging forgiveness of their King. Others merely walked forward with their heads bowed, as if resigned to their fate. Among them, Gisburne recognised de Montbegon—and there, looking utterly defeated, was Murdac. But Gisburne pushed past them all until he came face to face with Galfrid and Mélisande.

He beamed at them. Mélisande threw her arms about him, and Galfrid, for once, allowed himself an unrestrained smile. As Mélisande stood back, Gisburne peered past her—both of them—hunting for another figure.

"Llewellyn?" he said.

Galfrid shook his head. "Refuses to leave."

Gisburne nodded, resignedly. There would be reprisals, of that he was sure. Perhaps that dungeon really was the safest place.

As if suddenly remembering his duty, he drew his sword and levelled its point at them both. "Would you be so kind as to make yourselves my prisoners?" he said.

"Happily," said Mélisande with a smile. Galfrid said nothing, but his expression said it all: *About bloody time.*

LIV

Nottingham
28 March, 1194

"Is IT MUCH further?" said Gisburne. The rain had abated, but the distance they were having to travel to the promised knights was beginning to irritate him.

"Not much further," said Bayard. There was no "my lord" or even "sire"; he apparently saw no need for such courtesies.

"Why so far outside the main camp?" said Mélisande.

This time, Bayard did not respond at all.

"Did you not hear, Serjeant?" said Gisburne. "Why so far from the main camp?"

"You'll see," said Bayard, steering his horse towards a grassy ridge.

The King had kept his word. Victory had evidently pleased him, for when he turned to Gisburne and his reassembled company, it had been with a broad smile. "You asked for fifty knights. I give you a hundred!"

And, thus bathed in the King's benevolence, armoured and with shields on their backs, they had ridden out to meet their army, with Bayard as their guide, the cries of Richard's less fortunate captives echoing behind them.

As Gisburne had ridden from Richard's encampment, he'd felt a great weight lifting. The siege was over, his friends were safe. He was no longer in the company of Richard. It was not just that the man was dangerous and unpredictable, nor even his lack of humanity which made Gisburne feel physically sick. It was because the more Gisburne was in the King's presence, the more he felt infected by those qualities. He saw it in those who were close to the King—who perhaps had once been good men, but were now so afflicted by the King's contagion that they had forgotten themselves. He had seen the beginnings of that disease in himself. And, thanks to that, he now took pleasure in imagining Irontongue's blade cleaving the King's skull.

But what of this army the King had promised? The army that he would, within the hour, be commanding in battle? That there was to be a battle was now beyond question. Even as they had stood before Richard, a small company of men-at-arms had ridden in from patrol, and reported a great number of men advancing on foot from the north. If this was indeed Hood's army, then they had travelled full circle about the town. Wasn't that what wolves did, Aldric had said—circled their prey?

Gisburne had them describe what they'd seen in detail, and by the end was in no doubt. They were singing and marching twenty or more abreast along the road, they said. Numbers had been hard to judge—they had not wished to get too close—but were in excess of one thousand men. Perhaps thirteen hundred. And they had glimpsed at the heart of the army a single figure being carried aloft, seated upon a crudely constructed bier. He was garlanded with new spring flowers, a twisted crown of holly and ivy upon his head like a king of the forest. And upon his face, a bright, perpetual smile.

Thirteen hundred men... Still the number grew, and had this army but one victory under its belt, he had no doubt that number would double, and keep on doubling. But now, perhaps, they finally had the chance to take off the wolf's head.

"Did you ever find out what that strange engine was?" said Galfrid, out of the blue.

Gisburne frowned, bewildered, thinking of the siege engines. Clearly the squire had been pursuing some long trail of thought.

"The one at Inis na Gloichenn," he added. "The one you had brought back."

Gisburne smiled and nodded. "No idea. Llewellyn studied it for weeks. I believe he still has it stowed somewhere—probably in the bowels of that very castle."

"And he could not divine its purpose? Not at all?"

"It seemed to serve no practical function, except to move inscribed arcane symbols in various complex patterns. Astronomical, perhaps. His best guess was that it was meant to read the future."

Galfrid raised his eyebrows. "He didn't get it working, then?"

"Would we all be here now if he had?"

"Here," said Bayard flatly. They drew their horses to a halt and Gisburne gazed down towards the dell. Within it, skirted by trees on its far side, was an orderly military camp—white tents, cooking fires, horses neatly secured along a makeshift rail, and in among them, various figures in white surcoats milling about. Above it all, a banner flew—a green cross upon a white ground. It suggested to Gisburne one of the holy orders of knights, but although it was familiar, he couldn't place it.

Without another word, Serjeant Bayard turned his horse and rode away, and for the first time in an age, Gisburne's company was both complete, and alone.

"Well, let's see what we have to play with..." said de Rosseley, and urged his horse forward. The rest followed.

But Gisburne stalled, assaulted by an unbidden thought.

Mélisande turned. "What is it?" The others halted ahead of him.

It was as if the past few days' events had finally sunk in. As he sat there, staring, contemplating the slaughter that was to come and of which he was the unwilling agent, a new realisation struck, piercing him through like a bodkin point.

Ahead of him, somewhere upon the road, was a smiling madman with no good in his heart, no care for human life and no aim beyond the headlong rush into conflict—one who would be stopped by no one's death but his own. Behind him, much the same. The only real difference was the latter had a real crown on his head. He had a sudden and overwhelming urge to leave them to their mutual destruction; to ride off, right now, go far, far away and to simply let Hood's army meet with Richard's. To leave Richard to dirty his hands. He deserved nothing less.

There were several possible outcomes.

The possibility of Hood bowing to Richard and serving him faithfully, Gisburne dismissed out of hand. And all other possibilities, as far as Gisburne could see, were to the good.

There was a chance, however unlikely, that Hood would prevail. If Richard attacked as brutally as Gisburne knew he would, and some of his army rebelled, if the forces from Nottingham joined against him, or if an arrow or crossbow bolt—of which there would be thousands raining down—were to pierce that light armour he had favoured since his Crusade... Well, stranger things had happened. Richard would be swept away. Those few who still wished to remember him fondly could do as they pleased—but at least no more would suffer at his hand.

And what of Hood? Gisburne did not know for sure. All he knew, with absolute certainty, was that Hood would ultimately destroy himself. What precise form his end would take, Gisburne could not guess—but it would be both astonishing and savage, bringing chaos in its wake.

Far more likely, of course, was that Richard would win the day, crushing Hood and slaughtering his army to the last man. Then Hood would be dead, and the result much the same: one less murdering bastard in the world. But also—and it was this, perhaps, that appealed to Gisburne the most—in victory Richard would be revealed for what he truly was. Perhaps the scales would fall from England's eyes, and rebellion gain new impetus, with the martyred Hood—already a cult among England's common folk—as its focus. In every one of Richard's continental domains, they had risen against him at some time or another. Why not here? Gisburne imagined the fall of Richard—pictured him fighting and dying a brutal, bloody death on some nameless field at the hands of wrathful Englishmen, butchery meted out to him as it had been meted out to Harold upon Senlac Hill. Richard's name as hated and disgraced as he had allowed the loyal and noble Gilbert de Gaillon to be hated and disgraced—and through him, Gisburne.

All they had to do was turn their backs on all of this.

But when he stood back from these fantasies—much as they pleased him—he saw beyond them an England plunged into chaos, a return to the grotesque anarchy that had taken Old King Henry his entire reign to put right. And who was there like him to save England now?

Richard would surely destroy himself, just like Hood. It would happen in some war in Aquitaine or Limousin, which Richard loved and which hated him, far from the England that loved him and which he hated.

But his legend remained. It was a lie, that legend, just as surely as Hood's was. But was it not all the better for being so? And if it could do no more than hold the kingdom together, was that not preferable to blood and madness?

"Gisburne?" said Mélisande. "Are you all right?"

Gisburne looked up and saw de Rosseley studying him intently.

"Fine," said Gisburne. "I'm fine." And he urged Nyght on down the hill.

LV

THE TRUTH ABOUT their army dawned slowly. As they drew closer to the camp, Gisburne saw that several of the knights had their faces covered. Some wore their helms, all of which had faceplates of some kind. There was nothing so strange in that. But others, he noted, had veils about their faces, as Gisburne had seen among the desert nomads in Syria. Several were swathed in bandages, which also covered their hands.

Some did *not* have their faces covered—and seeing them, Gisburne finally understood.

"Great God," said de Rosseley. "He's given us lepers..."

Gisburne remembered where he had seen the knights' banner before. The Holy Land.

"The Knights of St Lazarus," he said.

"I thought I knew the banner..." said Asif. "But I did not believe it."

"They fight as fiercely as any knights," said Gisburne. "Often more so. I imagine they must have fought well for Richard."

"And this is how he thanks them?" said de Rosseley, and shook his head. "You have to admire his strategy. The leper knights are separate from the rest, unseen. And who will miss them?"

"Neither we nor our mission exist," said Gisburne. "And rest assured this battle will not be recorded in history, no matter how great our victory. Richard will see to that."

Galfrid sighed. "If we die.... Who will miss any of us?"

Gisburne turned to Mélisande then, and caught her wiping a tear from her cheek.

"Are you all right?" he said.

"Of course."

Gisburne thought to pursue it further, but saw a delegation approaching, and dismounted to meet them. There were three figures—at the head a tall, broad-shouldered knight whose armour and bearing marked him as someone of importance. His face was uncovered and bore the unmistakable signs that Gisburne had seen so often in Jerusalem. Swollen in places, obscured in others by scaly bumps and ridges that had begun to overwhelm his features—that had, Gisburne knew, begun to overwhelm his entire body.

Mostly, in England, one saw this only in beggars. Most of them had not begun as beggars, but leprosy—though regarded by the superstitious as a manifestation of sin—cared nothing for class. Baldwin IV, the Leper King of Jerusalem, had been proof of that.

The knight halted before him and bowed. "I am Hugolin of Ascalon, head of this order," he said.

"And I am..."

"Sir Guy of Gisburne, I know." He gave a lop-sided smile. "His Grace the King sent word. We may be kept apart, but do not think we are kept in ignorance."

Hugolin looked from face to face. He appeared unfazed by Asif, even by the sight of a woman in armour, but on seeing Tancred—whose face was hidden behind his steel mask—he stopped, and something that might have been a frown distorted his features. Where no one else thought to look closer, Hugolin did. "Do you share my Brothers' affliction?" he said.

"No," said Gisburne. "His affliction is of a different kind."

Hugolin nodded slowly. "You have my welcome," he said. "All of you." And he extended a hand of bandaged and deformed fingers. Gisburne grasped it. Hugolin smiled and closed his fingers. There was still strength in them—enough to grip a sword. "My men are yours, Sir Guy. What is our task?"

"A rebel force is coming. They march upon Nottingham as we speak."

"How armed?"

"Bows, mainly. And staves and spears."

"They are on foot?"

Gisburne nodded.

Hugolin grunted in satisfaction. "How many?"

"A thousand, at least. Perhaps thirteen hundred."

Hugolin frowned. "A hundred against thirteen hundred..."

"I know those odds do not sound good..."

"Good enough," said Hugolin. "But we must hit them fast, on open ground, before they have a chance to set arrows upon their bows. Otherwise..."

"I understand. I will say one thing, Sir Hugolin: I am not the Lionheart. I have but one aim—to destroy their leader and his lieutenants. The fate of the others means nothing to me. I am not out to punish them."

Hugolin nodded slowly. "You wish for less killing."

"Most will be easily broken, though some among them will fight to the last, for they have nothing to lose."

"You may appreciate I know a little about that." Hugolin turned and gestured to the small encampment. "Many of these men are kept alive only by the hope that they may take part in one last charge. This siege did not require it, more's the pity. They will thank you for this opportunity, Guy of Gisburne. And they will not disappoint you. You will see."

At that, he turned and called out to his men. "Knights of the Risen Saint! Up off your beds! Prepare to ride!" All about them, the men began to rise.

"Where do we ride, my lord?" called one.

"To battle!" At this, the whole camp rattled with sudden activity. Horses snorted and stamped; swords, helms and shields were strapped in place; men hauled themselves into creaking saddles and, one by one, lances were raised, until five score of them pierced the air.

Gisburne glanced at de Rosseley. There was no doubt that this was an awesome fighting force. And when Hugolin himself mounted up, lance in one hand, helm in the other, his face had creased into a smile.

Gisburne checked the strap about the battered wooden cylinder still buckled behind his saddle, and as he turned back, a group of young squires rushed forward and thrust lances into each his company's hands. De Rosseley hefted the familiar weapon with satisfaction. Gisburne sat and stared at his.

"Nervous?" whispered Mélisande.

"Is it that obvious?"

"It's natural," she said, her own voice perfectly calm. "If you had no fear, that would mean you didn't care, and if you didn't care..."

Gisburne took the point. But right now, he'd pay a sack of silver not to care.

"I am no general," he said. "I do not lead armies."

"You led an army at Inis na Gloichenn," said Galfrid, suddenly at his right side. "And we won, didn't we?"

"They did not see us coming," said Gisburne. With his arm tucked about the lance he drew his mail coif over his head, took the black and yellow painted helm off his saddle and put it on, pulling the chin strap tight. He frowned—hidden, now, beneath the faceplate—and bit his lip. "If we just had a way to hide our approach. To be on them before they had their arrows on their bows..."

An image flashed into his mind of his reckless charge to safeguard Galfrid and Mélisande as the besieged had spilled out of the castle. And all at once, by some strange alchemy of the mind, it struck him.

He turned to Galfrid. "You must ride back to Richard's camp, as fast as you can."

Galfrid glared, suddenly suspicious.

"Don't worry," said Gisburne. "I'm not banishing you. You won't miss the fight. I just need you to steal something for me."

LVI

He had not expected it to happen that way, but at least now, it seemed, things were back on the proper course. Gisburne was doing what he was meant to be doing, *where* he was meant to be doing it.

For a time, things were uncertain. Gisburne and his friends had managed to disappear completely within the King's army. Had that been their plan? It didn't seem to be, but it had proven remarkably effective.

On the second day, when the bombardment by the siege engines had begun, curiosity had got the better of him, and he had entered Richard's camp. It was a risk, he supposed, but he gambled on the fact that no one in this vast army was going to pay him any attention. And they did not.

All day he'd wandered. No one spoke to him, no one challenged him. He passed among them, invisible. But Gisburne and his company were invisible too, it seemed. It was not until the day was drawing to a close that he found them, with the King himself.

He realised his actions here were futile. He could do nothing against them, could enact no part of the plan. All he could do was watch. So he withdrew from the camp, and watched.

Now that, too, had paid off—except that Gisburne had an army of his own in tow. And what would that mean?

Sacrifices would have to be made. But, in the end, it would be the forest where this was played out. The forest where Gisburne's company would inevitably be drawn. The forest where he would have his revenge.

And so he would wait, and watch, until it was all over. One way or another, that would be soon.

LVII

GISBURNE RODE OUT in front, watching and listening. This time, they would not evade him. This time, they would not escape.

He gripped the lance tighter and took a deep breath. It had been a long time since he had been among so many horses riding in formation, and even at a trot the sound of it gave him chills. There was nothing on Earth, short of a stone wall, that could stand against a massed charge of armoured knights. On the backs of those horses they were still just men, who loved and feared and doubted as much as any footsoldier, but that sound—a sound you felt as much as heard, in the pit of your stomach—it made you feel anything was possible.

"They must be close," said de Rosseley. Gisburne turned to his friend, who had come up beside him. "We could do with some prior warning. How will we know?"

"We'll know," said Gisburne. Along this stretch, for the next few miles at least, the trees stood far back from the road. The open fields would give Hood's army no cover, but it also meant they would see their attackers coming from some distance.

"The charge..." said de Rosseley. "When it happens—when we are fully committed, and they see it for what it is—that will be when we are most vulnerable. If, in that moment, they have time to get their bows..."

"I have a plan," said Gisburne.

"Is it like your last plan?"

Gisburne smiled. "A good deal better than that."

"Well, that's a mercy."

Both laughed—and knew what the laughter was masking. It was not sport this time; they won only by killing and surviving.

Gisburne looked behind him nervously. No sign of Galfrid, back from camp. He needed him; Galfrid was the plan. Gisburne looked ahead at the empty road once more, losing himself in the sound of the horses, and took another deep breath. There would be time. Galfrid would come.

"I'm sorry, Ross," he said after a moment

"For what? For dragging me into this? I thought we'd buried that back at Clippestone."

"No, that that. Not exactly. I mean up there on the hill. When I stopped. I don't know what I was thinking."

De Rosseley laughed. "*I* know what you were thinking. I was thinking it too."

"Don't tell the others."

"Not even the good lady?"

"Especially her."

"Of all people, she would understand."

"Even so."

They fell silent for a moment. "It is not like you, Guy," said de Rosseley. "Having these doubts."

"Times change. People, too."

"They do indeed. But for the better as well as for the worse." He stopped again, debating with himself, then carried on. "Just promise me one thing. When all this is over, follow your heart."

"My heart?"

"That voice in your head. Whatever you want to call it. Do as it tells you."

Gisburne was about to ask de Rosseley what he meant when something new caught his attention—something so subtle, he wasn't at all sure it was real.

It was a sound—distant at first, but coming and going, like the wind. Something like.... singing. For a moment he thought his overwrought mind had spun it out of the hundred other sounds around him.

Then there it was again. He looked at de Rosseley and saw that he could hear it too. Hundreds of voices, just as they had heard back in the forest—distinct enough now to identify the tune, and for Gisburne to make out the half-heard words:

Robin's in the green-a
Fa la-la la-la laa!
His bow is ever keen-a
Fa la-la la-la laa!
His merry men are seen-a
Fa la-la la-la laa!
Dancing in the green-a
Fa la-la la-la laa!

"Ready!" called Gisburne. All turned their shields from their backs and passed arms through straps. Helmets were tightened. Lances couched beneath arms. Gisburne looked back again, straining to see past the ranks of cavalry. Still no sign of the squire.

"Stay close," he ordered. "Follow my lead. We commit only when we see their faces. Even then, keep your lances aloft until the very last moment." He took Nyght to a canter, and a hundred knights followed.

He looked back again, his breathing suddenly loud beneath the faceplate. *God's teeth, Galfrid—where are you?*

He heard a pounding of hooves off to his left, and turned back to see Galfrid burst from the distant trees and gallop along an intersecting track. The squire thundered closer, pulling alongside and slowing to a canter.

"Got it?" asked Gisburne.

"Got it," said Galfrid.

Gisburne lowered his lance across the pommel of Galfrid's saddle. The squire pulled a crumpled red mass from his tunic and began tying it about the lance point.

And suddenly Gisburne could see them—stretching the full width of the road, voices raised to the heavens, half of them waving staffs in the air. Not staffs: bowstaves.

His heart leapt. *Their bows are not strung...* De Gaillon had once told him how King Harold had caught an invading Norse army unawares—almost none of the Norsemen had time to put their armour on, which had turned the battle. To string a bow took valuable seconds—seconds that would work in their favour. But there was another factor upon which he now relied.

Galfrid rapped on the lance to indicate the task was complete. Gisburne raised it high, and the banner flapped free—a great swathe of red bearing the three gold lions of the King.

"Christ, Guy," called de Rosseley. "This is the plan? To deceive them into thinking we ride in the name of the King?"

"I watched you deceive an opponent into thinking a mace was in your right hand when it was in your left," said Gisburne.

"That was not the same."

"But we *do* ride in the name of the King, Ross. The deception is Hood's, making his men believe the King welcomes them with open arms..."

Gisburne did not expect de Rosseley to approve, but it was all too late now. Up ahead, a great cheer had gone up. They had seen the Lionheart's banner, and were already celebrating.

At one hundred and fifty yards, he began to make out faces—all smiling.

He took Nyght to the gallop, and felt the thunder grow behind him. Another cheer rose up at the sight of the King's men racing to meet them.

Then, at a hundred yards, Gisburne began to see expressions change. Smiles disappeared, replaced by doubt.

Fifty yards.

He spurred Nyght hard and lowered his lance, the banner whipping wildly. He heard a hundred lances follow suit, and the knights fanned out either side of him.

Twenty yards.

In the space of a moment, realisation dawned, and the great host split apart like a wasp's nest struck by an arrow.

Then the pounding cavalry rode over them.

LVIII

GISBURNE BARELY KNEW what happened on the first pass. He had participated in cavalry charges before, and the intensity of that experience was unlike anything he had ever known. The shouting, the screaming, the ground shaking under hooves, the sudden jarring, ear-splitting impact of wood and steel and flesh—like a wave crashing upon a shore; like *being* the wave, and having the roar rise up all around you, *through* you.

But this... this was like striking at a dandelion with an axe.

That they were not an army, not used to battle, was immediately apparent. With nowhere to run, experienced men would have held their ground—you could possibly dodge a lance if you knew how, but only if you could see it coming. These men ran blindly in every direction. They went straight under the hooves of the knights' destriers, or were speared in the side or the back, or felled by the attackers' swords. Barely any had armour; not more than one in ten any kind of helmet.

In the mayhem, a few of the knights' horses stumbled, throwing or crushing their riders, but for the most part they trampled the enemy like grass.

Every one of them seemed to evade Gisburne's lance point. Partly it was the sheer chaos, but also his own reluctance; the few terrified men who did cross his path he simply could not bring himself to spear.

And then it was over, and he was on the far side of them. He wheeled about, a line of knights turning with him like a great scythe blade.

The second pass was different. Looking around for his fellows and seeing none, he spied a big, stocky man who had also spotted him, and who was not running. David of Doncaster, one of Hood's most dedicated men. Gisburne urged Nyght on, and levelled his lance.

Doncaster stood firm, sword in hand, a great roar in his throat. He meant to sidestep the point, Gisburne supposed, and slash at either Gisburne or his horse as they passed, using their own momentum against them.

And then it happened.

A lance point—wavering at the end of ten feet of ash—is not easily moved with accuracy when couched, and if you know its limits and are quick enough, you can dodge it. Clearly, Doncaster thought he'd done so. So, for that matter, did Gisburne. But in the closing moment he felt something slam into Nyght's left flank. One of Hood's men had apparently run headlong into his horse's side; whether he survived, Gisburne was never to know.

The stallion stayed true to his course, but for a instant the impact nudged him to the right. It can only have been inches, but in that moment, Doncaster's fate was sealed.

Gisburne felt his lance jolt and twist down, and as it met solid resistance it sheared, the mid-section spinning in the air. A moment later, all was far behind him.

Gisburne heard rather than saw the effect upon his target.

The point had hit Doncaster in the open mouth, bringing his great roar—and his life—to an abrupt, shuddering end. When Gisburne risked a look back, he saw the big man—surely dead but still somehow staggering—the tip of the broken lance stuck through the back of his head, the bunched up banner of the King rammed in his mouth. He tipped backwards, the protruding lance caught the ground, and as he fell it twisted his head with an audible *crack*.

Gisburne threw away the splintered length of ash and drew Irontongue.

Hood's men's bows had been unstrung, and nearly all of them still were—because nocking the string meant standing still, and that almost none of them were prepared to do. But a few had.

As Gisburne wheeled around for a third pass, he saw a half-dozen or so crouched in a tight formation, now loosing swift volleys of arrows—not random, but concentrating on specific targets. Three knights were felled as Gisburne watched; a fourth stayed in his saddle, his shield like a pin cushion—but they shifted their attention to his horse. It fell, the knight rolled clear—apparently unharmed by the fall—but then three of Hood's men were on him, stabbing and kicking.

One gripped the stricken knight's helm and tore free. That should have been the end of him—Gisburne was still a good thirty yards away—but the moment the helm was off, the three men recoiled in horror. One scrabbled backwards, straight under the hooves of a riderless horse, and the other two hesitated, still horrified, until the leper knight staggered back to his feet, drew his sword and thrust it straight through the taller man's chest. The last of the assailants turned to run, but metal flashed in the air and the man dropped like a stone, Asif's chakkar embedded in his face.

A cry of "*Lepers!*" went up among the scattering horde—and even those who were not already terrified gave it up as a lost cause. All looked to their own preservation now—and that was their undoing. The Knights of St Lazarus cut them down as they ran, exacting revenge for their fallen comrades.

Gisburne, meanwhile, turned his attention back to the group of archers, who were now starting to disperse. At their head, Gisburne saw, was Gilbert White Hand—second only to Hood as an archer, and without doubt the one who had been directing the volleys with such deadly effect. Gisburne caught up with the first of them, clouting him about the head with Irontongue's blade. The man fell with a cry like a stabbed pig, and White Hand turned.

The others were too intent on fleeing to put arrow to string, but not White Hand. He reached for an arrow shaft, and as he did so Gisburne leaped from his horse and snatched up the fallen man's bow. He was crucial seconds behind the enemy archer, but then

Tancred—his helmet gone, his skull face grinning like something out of Hell—rode from nowhere, sword whirling. White Hand, looking up in horror, wavered for an instant—and in that moment Gisburne's arrow sank into his chest from barely ten yards.

They were the last to stand their ground. The battle was over, at least for now. But there were faces Gisburne had not yet seen. He turned this way and that, scanning a field littered with outlaw dead, and then he saw them.

At the very edge of the trees, heading north-west at a run, was a small, tight-knit group: the monk Took, Scarlet, Arthur a Bland, Will of Stuteley and a half-dozen others—and with them, a head higher than the rest, was Hood. As Gisburne watched, he turned and looked right at him. As if unmoved by the slaughter of his men, he smiled and gave a cheerful wave.

Then he turned, and the group plunged back into the forest, back towards their village.

LIX

One by one, the company gathered—all alive, and miraculously uninjured.

"A good outcome," said Gisburne to Galfrid as they stood apart from the group.

Galfrid seemed unconvinced. "Could've been better," he said.

"We'll get Hood," said Gisburne. "We'll follow him and we'll get him."

"I didn't mean that," said Galfrid, and looked towards the Templar. "I was hoping Tancred would die."

Hugolin had lost a dozen men to Hood's arrows, but the Knights of St Lazarus had not been idle. For every one of their men who had fallen, a score of Hood's now lay dead—and many more injured. Bodies littered the field in every direction, and from every direction came the cries of the wounded and dying.

Gisburne was sickened at the sight of it, and angry that Hood had driven him to this. But he could not hesitate now. If anything, it only made him the more determined. The army was broken, dispersed; but Hood had mustered them once, and could do so again.

"Hugolin?" he called, patting Nyght on the head. "I have one last favour to ask."

"Name it," said the knight.

"May we leave our horses with you?" Nyght gave Gisburne a long and searching look, and he was forced to look away.

"I'll care for them as if they were my own," he said. Then he took a step towards Gisburne and took his hand in both his own. "Thank you," he said, and Gisburne frowned. "Thank you for this..." He released him, and turned away.

Gisburne looked towards the place where Hood had disappeared, then turned back to Nyght and whispered an apology.

"WHAT NOW?" SAID Mélisande.

"Now, we hunt," said Gisburne, "for wolf. Take only what you need, and leave the rest with the horses. We travel light."

He threw down his helm and shield and nocked the string on his own bow. As he did so, he winced, and put a hand to his shoulder.

"All right?" said Aldric.

"I'm fine. That hasty dismount..." Gisburne flexed his shoulder, then slung the bow across his back by its strap and lifted the wooden cylinder. The action made him wince again.

"Let me help," said Aldric. "My crossbow is easier to carry than your bow, and my quarrels smaller. Let me take it."

Gisburne nodded, and handed it to him.

"Just don't drop it," he said.

Aldric hefted it over his shoulder. It was not as heavy as he had expected, but was considerably heavier at one end than the other. There was no tell-tale rattle from inside, but when he settled it in place, he could have sworn he heard the sound of liquid.

A hand patted him on the arm. He looked around and saw Galfrid draw up beside him.

"You are indeed honoured," said Galfrid, and Aldric looked askance at him. "That's not a joke," said Galfrid. "It means he trusts you."

"So... What's in it?"

Galfrid chuckled. "Perhaps you should have found that out before you took it. I don't know. Honestly, I'd tell you if I did. But seriously... if he says don't drop it, don't drop it."

"Why?"

"I was once charged with a similar task," said Galfrid.

"And did you drop it?"

"No," says Galfrid. "Someone stole it. Then *they* dropped it."

"What happened to them?"

"Hard to say," said Galfrid. "There wasn't enough of them left to really tell." Then he patted Aldric on the shoulder again, and walked off.

IV

DEATH

LX

Sherwood Forest
28 March, 1194

"WELL?" SAID GISBURNE.

Galfrid, crouched, flicked at the leaf mould with his dagger point and sniffed. "Nothing."

For hours they had tracked their prey, back into the heart of Sherwood—back towards the hidden village. The outlaws moved fast, but they were on their scent. They had encountered two other members of Hood's army along the way: one had been dead from his wounds, collapsed over a log. The other glimpsed them and fled into the undergrowth like a deer. He had been left to his own devices.

Gisburne was surprised that they had not stumbled into more of the scattered men, but it told him something useful: if they were not coming this way, they can have been in no great hurry to return to Hood's service. It was as if the battle upon the north road had awoken them from a dream.

He cared little about the stragglers. All he was concerned with was the close grouping of prints heading north.

In the last few yards—in a tiny clearing in which a large oak had at some point fallen and been cleared away—the clearly marked trail had inexplicably vanished.

"They cannot simply disappear," said Gisburne.

Galfrid stood. "A dozen's a lot harder to track than five hundred," he said. "And this lot treads lightly. I believe they could disappear if they really set their minds to it."

De Rosseley frowned. "Did they only now discover that we were following them?"

"That," said Galfrid, "or they meant for us to follow this far."

"And then what?" muttered Gisburne, eyeing the surrounding trees warily. They were close; perhaps a little too close. He recalled Hood's jaunty wave from the edge of the forest. "We are exposed. We need to move, one way or the other."

"There is a path of sorts up ahead," said Mélisande. "Old. Winding away through the trees."

"It's supposed to be the village to which no roads lead," protested de Rosseley.

Aldric nodded in agreement. "And last time there was a path like that, Sir Tancred said it led to traps..."

"There will be traps," said Gisburne. "That much I can guarantee." Then he looked towards the silent Templar. "Tancred?"

Tancred shook his head. "I do not know this place."

He turned back to Galfrid. "Could they have taken the path?"

Galfrid sighed. "I can't say they didn't. But they were not far ahead of us. If we can just—"

Gisburne's raised hand silenced him. Across the clearing, at the edge of the trees, Asif stood, his back to them, utterly motionless. Listening.

Gisburne crept over to him.

"Someone watches us," whispered the Arab.

"Our friend the Norseman?" said Gisburne. "Could he have found us again?"

Before Asif could reply, there was the *thwack* of an arrow striking a tree inches from them. Birds flew up, twittering madly. Gisburne and Asif ran. Another arrow—closer this time—drove into the earth at their heels.

There was no time to argue. Either they took the path or died here. Asif at his shoulder, Gisburne plunged ahead into the forest, the others breaking into a run behind him. As they fled, two more arrows, in quick succession, struck the trees as they passed, sending splinters flying.

Gisburne was not certain how long they ran, but two things made him stop. One was the likelihood that, for now, they were out of range; the trees were more spread out here—it would be harder for their attacker to get close without being seen. The other was the fear of traps ahead.

They stood for a moment, catching their breath, bows at the ready. Aldric, panting heavily, slipped the cylinder off his shoulder and let it thump on the ground. He winced at the impact.

"He had us," said de Rosseley. "Had us cold. Why in God's name did the bowman not just kill us?"

Galfrid grunted. "I've no complaints on that score."

"Not bowman," said Aldric. "Crossbowman." All looked at him. "I heard the trigger. Believe me, I know that sound."

"But there were two in quick succession," said Gisburne. "Far faster than a crossbowman could reload."

"Then there must be two men," said Mélisande.

"One," Aldric said. "The sound... One bow. I am certain of it." He caught de Rosseley's sceptical look. "It's like a musical instrument. You get an ear for it."

Asif nodded. "I have heard of a device like this," he said. "A double crossbow, capable of firing two bolts without reloading."

"But such devices are rare as dragon eggs," said Aldric. "To make one and maintain it properly would require skilled hands. An enginer's hands."

"It hardly sounds like Hood," said Mélisande.

"No," said Gisburne. "It does not." But he had an idea what it *did* sound like.

"If he's such a bloody expert," continued de Rosseley, "then I am moved to repeat my question: why did this bowman"—he caught Aldric's eye—"*crossbowman* not manage to hit any of us? Even *I* could have done that."

But Gisburne understood. "He wasn't trying to kill us," he said. "He was herding us, making sure we took this path. The path the others clearly did not."

"May we guess why they did not take it?" said Aldric.

"Because they wished to stay alive," said Gisburne.

"Traps?"

"Traps. Conceived, if I am not mistaken, by the same mind as the extraordinary crossbow."

"So, we are to continue, then," said Mélisande with a frown, "into the traps?"

"We have two advantages," said Gisburne. "For one, the traps protect Hood's village, which means the village lies beyond. For the other, we know the traps are there."

The various members of the party exchanged glances. Mélisande merely raised her eyebrows. "What happened to doing the precise opposite of what your enemy wants?"

"A change of plan," said Gisburne. "They've come to expect that of me. They think that right now I will be resisting their attempts to divert us, and instead striking out after our prey in the hope of finding their trail again. We might do that, and we might even succeed. But there was another thing de Gaillon used to say— something, he once claimed, that took priority over every other rule: whatever your enemy does not expect, do that."

He looked around, and one by one they nodded in agreement.

"So, we move on," he said.

It no longer mattered to him that they were walking into danger. When were they ever not? They were where he wanted them to be. Where Hood wanted them. Back in the game.

LXI

THE TREES AHEAD were gnarled and old, and closed about them
as they advanced. They were strangled with ivy, in places itself
as thick as a tree. To some of the ancient, warped trunks great
shelves of dank fungus clung. The path seemed to take them
back into some lost time—a time before man, from whose
unknowable depths the ever watchful faces of the trees stared
back at them. Gisburne was in no doubt they were back in
Hood's realm.

All were vigilant. Progress was slow—the path now difficult
to see in the undulating, root-tangled floor. They had fallen into
complete silence, encouraged somehow by the strange deadness
of the air about them.

Quite suddenly, the tree cover broke and gave way to a tiny
glade—a small patch of hazy sky above, a fairy ring of toadstools
in the mossy floor below.

As Gisburne stepped into it, a crow flapped wildly out of a
nearby tree. Every one of them jumped at the burst of noise.
"Well," said de Rosseley, the bird's harsh cry ringing out across
the forest. "We might as well have sounded a fanfare."

Galfrid's gaze followed the black shape. "If only we could see
through his eyes," he sighed. "Perhaps we'd see where they are."

"Maybe we can," said Mélisande, swinging into the low boughs
of a huge oak, then up, away into the swaying top branches.

A moment later, she dropped down again. "There's a thin column of smoke to the northwest."

"What colour?" asked Gisburne.

"Black."

"They want us to see it. They know how to hide a fire." He laughed to himself. "It's Hattin. Herding us into a trap along a narrow path, and baffling us with smoke... Hood's idea of a joke."

"So what do we do?" asked Aldric.

"What he thinks we will not," said Gisburne. "We head towards the smoke. Clearly somebody was there."

But before they could head off, they were interrupted by sounds of movement from the forest behind them and to their right. The cracking of twigs and rustling of leaves—hurried, rough, and heading their way.

"Boar?" whispered de Rosseley.

"Boar with two legs..." muttered Galfrid.

They drew back to the clearing's edge with readied bows and drawn weapons.

Three men burst through the trees, red-faced and panicked. They were lean, their clothes ragged, the first with crusted blood about his mouth where teeth had recently been knocked out. Behind him, the tallest had a scabbardless sword shoved through his belt, and a rusted helm which wobbled above his thatch of thick hair and scrubby black beard. The third had lost a shoe, and now walked with what looked like an arming cap tied about his foot. All were grasping bows that were nocked and ready to shoot. They were Hood's men, fled from the battle.

Black Beard was first to see them. He stopped dead, saying simply: "Oh!" Bloody Mouth turned to him, then looked back— just in time to meet de Rosseley's mace. The blow felled him instantly.

The others turned, saw that Tancred was already behind them, and—terrified at the sight of him—bolted across the glade.

"Get them alive!" barked Gisburne.

Galfrid took off after One Shoe while Asif drew a chakkar from his belt and hurled it at Black Beard.

Black Beard collapsed in an ugly tangle of limbs, a fountain of blood gushing where the blade had almost taken his head clean off.

One Shoe crashed into the forest ahead—but there Galfrid skidded to a halt, instinctively stopping Tancred with a hand against his chest.

"What is it?" said Gisburne.

"Not sure," said Galfrid.

Beneath One Shoe's crashing, there was a low creak, then a loud *crack*. A sound like a great hand swatting the bushes flat, then a terrible scream. They gaped in horror as One Shoe came spinning, flailing through the clear sky above their heads, hurled a hundred yards into the forest and a good forty into the air. He sailed out of view, and there was a crash, a cracking of branches and a sickening thud.

The scream stopped.

Galfrid looked down and realised his hand was still on Tancred's chest. Only then did he realise he had saved the Templar's life. He withdrew his hand as if from a scorpion.

"So much for getting them alive," said Mélisande.

"I must apologise," said Asif. "I meant only to knock him down, but he put his neck in the way."

Gisburne advanced to the edge of the clearing and stood next to Galfrid, peering into the gloom where One Shoe had met his horrid end. "Aldric?" he called.

Aldric came up beside him. "Traps," he said.

Gisburne nodded and put his hand on the young enginer's shoulder. "You go first."

LXII

GISBURNE HAD ONCE had occasion to cross a moor which, he was told, had deadly sucking bogs that could pull a horse under and were indistinguishable from solid ground. Being young and reckless, he had laughed at the warning—until he stepped upon what was clearly a patch of solid, mossy ground and found it no more solid than milk-skin.

· That had been a long day.

Now, as they crept forward, eyeing everything about them with suspicion, Aldric prodding and testing gingerly as they went, he was reminded of that moor. Except that this time, the dangers weren't just on the ground, they were in the branches of the trees, lurking in the bushes on every side, in the very air. Within twenty yards of One Shoe's death trap, Aldric had ordered them to halt. He studied the trees for a good minute, then said: "We must go around. Walk where I walk. Nowhere else."

"Unless you get killed," said Galfrid.

"Yes. Unless that."

They picked their way slowly, placing footsteps as carefully as if stepping on thin ice. When they finally rejoined the path, Gisburne looked back and saw, up in the tree, cunningly concealed behind a low bough, a timber arm upon a pivot. At its far end, poised, ready to swing down when its catch was triggered, was a heavy lump of stone and a scythe blade. Gisburne shuddered and moved on.

There had been no more sign of the mysterious crossbowman, which made him wonder. He, surely, was familiar with the positions of these devices. Had they lost him? Was he watching even now?

"Hold!" said Aldric. All stopped dead.

Aldric knelt and gingerly lifted a dead, grey stem of bramble that snaked across the path. It looked like nothing—like a hundred other twigs—until Gisburne saw, tucked beneath it, a hempen string.

"Step back," Aldric said. "But only where you have already stepped!" The company did so—four, eight, twelve paces. "Enough. That should be enough."

"*Should* be...?" said Galfrid.

But Aldric simply crouched as low as possible, took a deep breath, and pulled hard on the string.

From either side of the path came a sudden, jarring chorus of sharp *thunks*—an array of crossbows shooting almost, but not quite, in unison. The branches shook; bolts zipped over Aldric's head, driving into trees or hissing unseen into bushes.

Aldric lay low for some time, and appeared to be listening. Finally, satisfied, he stood and motioned them forward.

"Steady," he said, looking up into the trees. "Step clear of the string. One did not shoot..." As they hurried past, Galfrid—the last in line—paused for a moment, patted him on the shoulder, and with something akin to contrition, muttered: "You're doing good, lad."

Aldric smiled, then worked his way once more to the head of the party.

Further traps followed—sometimes a hundred paces apart, sometimes mere yards—but so many that Gisburne lost count. At first, he had thought them focused solely around the path; but then, as they were passing one trap, they found the trap makers had anticipated their move and placed another—a set of ragged iron blades, ready to spring from beneath a holly bush.

Some threats were familiar enough: cords that whipped across the path to decapitate them; axes that swung down; rocks that fell. But every once in a while there was a flash of genius. A mass of innocent-looking brambles that when disturbed spun violently and flailed its thorns. Thin withies, stressed like catapults and bristling with needles—each tipped, Aldric was certain, with deadly poison. So subtle was the first of these that Aldric had not seen it, and it was only discovered when it whipped out and struck the top of his helm. Pure luck had saved him that time: he had stooped to look at the forest floor. The needles were meant for his face.

Some traps were so bizarre that Gisburne could not begin to divine their purpose. One that they bypassed consisted of a huge, loosely covered cauldron, ready to tip its contents upon those passing below. What was the nature of the liquid, Gisburne did not know, or wish to find out.

Another fact struck him during their slow advance. Some of these traps might have been set a week, a month, a year ago; but some, clearly, were not. He knew, just as Aldric knew, that a crossbow could not be left under full tension for long—not if it was to retain any kind of power or accuracy. The string would stretch, the bow would warp, the trigger bend or break. Someone was tending these traps, and with same the care Gisburne gave his horses.

"Does this take you back to the Forêt de Boulogne?" said Mélisande. She smiled weakly; they were all tired and drawn after the day's events. In the past hour a fine rain had begun to fall, and was now dripping off the edges of their hoods.

"Another of Hood's little jokes, I have no doubt," Gisburne replied.

It was in the Forêt de Boulogne that Gisburne had set his own traps against Tancred's men. They were crude efforts compared to these, though it occurred to him that, but for an order from a captain to stay with the horses, those traps would have killed Aldric Fitz Rolf—the very man upon whom his life now depended.

"You are speaking of your attack on my castle," came a voice, sudden and unexpected. Tancred spoke so rarely now—this was the first time that he had volunteered conversation in days. "It rained then, too."

Gisburne shuddered to his bones.

"You remember that?" said Galfrid, his voice hard.

"A fleeting image," came the reply.

"What else do you remember?" said the squire.

"Galfrid..." said Gisburne.

"The torture? The fires of Jerusalem? The day we came to that Godforsaken island of yours, intent on..."

"Galfrid!" Gisburne turned and glared at him.

Galfrid lowered his head, but the muttering continued. "How do we know what's going through that head? How do we know what—?"

It was Aldric who stopped him this time, halting so suddenly that Gisburne walked into his back, and Galfrid into Gisburne's.

"That branch," he said, blinking through the rain. "It does not belong to that tree."

"Are you sure?" said Asif, squinting at it.

"How often have you seen an oak tree sprout a beech branch?"

"These trees of yours are still a novelty to me," said Asif with a shrug.

"I don't trust going under *or* around. I'll have to trigger it."

"Do what you must," said Gisburne.

Aldric had them all stand back and crouch down. He threw a cord over a higher bough and, with the delicacy of a tailor threading a needle, tied one end around the rogue beech branch. With the other end held loosely in his hand, he crept back, crouched, lowered his head, and as they all braced themselves, pulled.

The branch made a loud *crack* and jolted upward. Something rattled, and Gisburne risked raising his head. There, some ten yards ahead, he saw a lump of stone, barely bigger than a child's head, descending on the end of a rope. For a moment he almost laughed; but then came another sound, utterly incongruous in this remote place: a bell sounding, over and over, growing louder and more insistent by the second. Gisburne covered his head, waiting for what was to come next.

Nothing did. The striking of the bell slowed and stopped. The stone thumped to wet earth. No blades, no arrows, no wires. They crouched there for several minutes, until the resonating of the bell had faded to nothing.

"Did I miss something?" muttered de Rosseley.

"I don't think so," said Gisburne.

"What was its purpose?" said Asif. "To scare?"

Aldric sighed. He was exhausted, Gisburne could tell; they all were. "A marker," said Aldric. "Announcing our progress. When Hood hears it, he knows someone is here. And when the noises stop, he knows we're dead."

"Or that we've made it through," says Gisburne.

But that, at this moment, seemed a vain hope. The rain was growing heavier, and now the light, too, was beginning to fail. Gisburne was too tired to care about a soaking, but he knew the deepening shadows would hamper Aldric's efforts, who was already drained...

They only needed to make one mistake.

Gisburne had them press on for another hundred yards—a safe distance from the bell trap—and there, in a small clearing around an outcrop of rock, he finally called a halt.

Aldric, dog-tired as he was, insisted on checking every inch of it. Then, with the rock declared safe, tired to their bones, they slumped against the lee side and prepared for another night in the wild.

LXIII

GISBURNE HAD BEEN against lighting a fire, but Mélisande overruled him. There was a way, she assured him, that would put them at no risk of discovery—and she was already setting about it before he could protest. He was beyond arguing.

She cleared a small pit beneath the overhang of the rock—which also shielded the fire completely from view to the north and west—and within minutes had a small blaze going. The heat was meagre, but the effect it had on the company was immediate. Huddling closer, they smiled and rubbed their hands and chattered in low voices about insignificant things—relieved, for the moment, that they did not have to regard every leaf and twig as a threat to life. Gisburne smiled and, as Mélisande caught his eye, bowed to her superior wisdom.

"Your skills are remarkable, my lady," said Asif. "How anyone encourages wood to burn in this damp place is beyond me."

"Necessity is a great teacher," said Mélisande.

"You also fight as well as any man here. That is surely not a necessity."

Mélisande had an odd expression—half smile, half frown. "I would perhaps argue that point..."

"Such a thing is quite unknown in my country."

"In ours, too," said Gisburne. "Do not think Lady Mélisande is in any way typical."

"Oh, I do not," Asif continued, chewing upon some dried fruit. "But the *way* you fight... Many claim to have the skills of the *hashashin*—and mostly it is a boast meant to strike fear into those who would challenge them. But in your case, I think not."

"You are most perceptive, Asif," she said, staring into the flames.

"You also have great knowledge of the Arab world. I am curious about your time spent in the Holy Land. You did spend time there, did you not?"

For a moment she said nothing. Then she fixed her eyes on him. "I was in Acre when it fell to Salah al-Din."

Asif stopped chewing, and Gisburne stared at her across the fire. This was a story he had never heard. She glanced back at him—almost apologetically, he thought—then, blushing, but as serious as he had ever seen her, looked back to the fire and took a deep breath.

"I was in the Holy Land with my father and brothers when the Christian army was destroyed at Hattin. Everything was in chaos. They had me stay in Acre, telling me I would be safer there. And there they left me. I was nineteen years old.

"Acre fell to Salah al-Din without a fight. Being the kind of girl I was, I tried to effect an escape to Tyre; but I was caught. The guards laughed at me—at the audacity of my plan. That it was a woman attempting it." She shook her head. "Anyway... My noble heritage was revealed, and I was ransomed. This was not an unusual state of affairs. It happens often, in every kingdom and duchy of Europe. All very civilised, very orderly.

"So I waited for ransom to come. I knew I wouldn't have to wait long—my father was rich as Croesus. The ransom was high, but after all, I was his daughter.

"After three months, when still no ransom had been received, I convinced myself that my father and brothers were bringing an army to rescue me. I worked out how I believed it would be done, where the weak points were, what I would do to help when I heard the alarm and knew they were coming.

"They never came. I was in captivity for fifteen months. I later learned that my father had simply refused the ransom, complaining that it was too high. I was not worth it. Nor had he or my brothers any intention of fighting. All those years training, day in, day out, in the use of the sword and the lance—and for what? What use was it? Where was it when I needed it?

"But life was not bad. I was lucky. My captors treated me with respect, for the most part. I learned their customs, and their language—partly so I might better understand what I overheard. I even learned to read some Arabic. That pleased them greatly. But there was one of them, an older man named Hassan... He was *fida'i* of the Nizari—what we call *hashashin*. He had been an acolyte of Rashid ad-Din Sinan—the Old Man of the Mountains, leader of the fanatical sect—but had come over to Saladin. He had simply awoken one morning, he said, and saw, as if a fog had lifted, that his life was madness. Just like that. So he rode away and never went back.

"To do so was death, and every night he expected it to come to him, on the tip of a poisoned blade. One might think that would make him morose, but the opposite was true: he lived each day as if it were his last.

"Strange as it may sound, we found a common bond. He told me things of the *hashashin* that I do not believe he would ever have divulged to others. I told him of my brother's training, and how I had bettered him with a sword. That gave him great amusement. I went on to suggest that the greatest *hashashin* of all would be a woman, for no one would believe a woman capable of such deeds. He laughed at this too—but I could tell he also saw something in it. And he could see in me the willingness to fight—the desire to be strong, while deceiving with apparent weakness.

"And so, bit by bit, I became not a prisoner, nor a guest, nor even a companion, but a pupil. It delighted him, I think, to know he was creating something quite new—something of which Sinan would never approve. That I would be his final legacy.

"One day, he announced he was leaving. I believed the long-expected threat was finally coming. Only later did I discover the truth: that he had begun to suffer the effects of leprosy, and so was taking himself far from me. To spare me.

"I was distraught, of course, but he just smiled. He said he had one final test, and if I passed, I would never need him again. When

I asked what it was, he said I must stop waiting. I must walk out of the door by myself, and go home.

"And so I did. That night, I passed by my captors unseen. Climbed across roofs and over walls. And those city guards who had laughed at me... They never laughed again."

She wiped a tear from her face and looked about, as if suddenly returned to the present. "And here I am."

And here she was. They sat in silence for a moment, Asif nodding gently. All the things that Gisburne knew of her now found their place. He did not know why she had chosen to tell them here, now, but it did not matter. Strange as it was to hear about her life before they had met—when it had so long been kept from him—it somehow only made him feel closer to her.

"We're almost there," said Tancred.

All turned and looked at the Templar. He sat motionless, staring—like a gargoyle.

"What?" said Gisburne.

"These trees," he hissed. "This rock. Almost there."

Galfrid stared hard at him—seemed about to speak—then another voice silenced him.

"He tells the truth."

The company were on their feet, knives in their hands, swords drawn as a tall figure stepped out from the dark trees.

The dim glow from the fire lit his face as he did so, but Gisburne—Irontongue in his fist—had already recognised him.

John Lyttel.

They spread swiftly, surrounding him, Mélisande at his back, her dagger point at his belly—he was too tall for her to rest her blade on his throat.

Lyttel did not resist. Galfrid, Asif and Aldric had bows and crossbow trained on the surrounding shadows.

But there was no other sound, no other sign.

"I am alone," Lyttel said. "On that you have my word."

"Your word?" said Gisburne, laughing.

"My life is in your hands, whether you believe my word or not," said Lyttel. "That must be worth something."

"We'll be the judges of that," muttered Galfrid.

Gisburne stared at him suspiciously. For days they had hunted Hood, and he had eluded them. Now, a member of the Wolf's Head had just walked right into their camp.

Gisburne drew closer, Irontongue's point hovering before Lyttel's face. "So *why* is your life in our hands, outlaw?"

"I can lead you there." He spoke in a low whisper, as if afraid the trees themselves would overhear him. "I can take you to Hood's camp."

"To ensure we walk into your trap?" said Mélisande, pressing the point at his belly. "To be captured and killed by your master?"

"Hood is not there," said Lyttel. Somehow, Gisburne knew he was telling the truth.

"He will be," said Gisburne. "And soon."

"And the army?" asked Lyttel. Gisburne suspected a trick, but he looked into Lyttel's face and saw genuine concern. Lyttel never was blessed with a great deal of guile.

"You don't know?" said Gisburne

"Would I ask if I did?" The big man laughed irritably.

To his surprise, Gisburne found himself answering the question. "Beaten, dispersed. But for how long, I don't know."

Lyttel nodded slowly. "Then you have an opportunity," he said. "The one you've been waiting for."

"And what opportunity would that be?"

"To kill him."

Gisburne stared into the big man's face, looking for a hint of deception, but there was none.

Without prompting, Lyttel spoke again, more confidently. "This route you take through the forest is the old way, but it became too easy to find. So we fixed it. Now, not even Hood risks it. He will take the longer route, all the way around, knowing you are stuck here for the night. But some of us know the way through, and if you come with me now, you will reach the village ahead of him."

"Hood knows we are here?"

"Hood knows everything," said Lyttel. "He meant for you to take this path, to spend the night in this forest. To be worn down by it.

This is *his* forest, remember. Not yours, not the King's, certainly not Prince John's." He took a deep breath. "He is counting on at least one of you making it through, though."

"Me?"

"You. Always you. But there is one thing Hood did not reckon on."

"And what is that?"

"Me."

Gisburne pushed his blade point at Lyttel's throat. "You betrayed your fellows, supported a murderer and thief, used your knowledge to prise him from the jaws of justice and bring death to the King's own palace—the Tower you were once sworn to protect. Tell me, John Lyttel, why should we trust you now?"

Lyttel fixed his eyes on Gisburne's. "Because I want what you want."

"And what is that?"

"An end. To this madness..."

Gisburne looked into the face of a man who had once guarded the Tower with almost unblemished record, who had served his King and fought with honour at Hattin. And in it he saw truth. He saw pleading. Advantage.

"Lead on."

"You are certain of this?" said Mélisande.

"As certain as I ever was of anything."

Then they kicked dirt over the fire and followed behind John Lyttel.

LXIV

LYTTEL MOVED SWIFTLY, smoothly—he was amazingly quiet for such a big man. The past months had made him a creature of the forest, and of the forest's night.

Away from the fire, their eyes grew accustomed to the gloom, but Gisburne found it was impossible to properly penetrate the shadows about their feet, which made the going uncertain.

For all but Lyttel. He seemed to move with such little regard for the terrain that Gisburne wondered if they had moved beyond the traps—if, indeed, they were already beyond them where they had camped. But then he looked back and glimpsed, in the thick darkness, a row of iron spikes high in the trees ready to swing down upon the unwary. Gisburne supposed Lyttel could make the journey blindfold.

They heard water before they saw it—the rush and babble of a stream flowing fast over a rocky bed. Lyttel dived through a gap in the trees—which seemed to lead nowhere—and there it was.

It was clear why Hood had chosen this spot. The river was clear and in plentiful supply; and though it was neither deep nor wide, the far bank was high and looked near-impossible to climb, giving the outlaws a natural moat. It was spanned by a log bridge some thirty feet to their right, which a brave horse might cross, but which even men could only traverse in single file. The bridge could be withdrawn or tumbled into the river to hinder attack, and there were thick ropes attached to it for this very purpose.

Further to their left, the land rose up to a low escarpment of rock—a good lookout point—and the river bent away around it.

But there was no lookout, and no guard upon the bridge. No one to haul it back to the opposite bank.

As they stood at the end of the log bridge, Gisburne glimpsed the flicker of flame ahead. The lights of Hood's village. The thought of it—of finally being here—sent a shiver through him.

Then there was the smell. It was one he was familiar with—not from places where people chose to live, but where they had died. It was the stink of the battlefield near Thessalonika two days after the battle; the reek of the barn in the Limousin where they had found an entire family—ten, at least—dead by their own hands. The stench of the infirmary ward in Jerusalem where those who would not recover lay—rotting while they yet lived, a hair's breadth from the mortuary.

Lyttel hesitated at the bridge, as if, after all he had done, he was suddenly reluctant. Then he turned to Gisburne. "Prepare yourself," he said, and he strode across.

Gisburne had often referred to it as a village, and it was certainly that. Beyond a line of trees on the opposite bank, their way suddenly opened out—so unexpectedly wide that they all stopped out of sheer surprise. The wood had been partly cleared, the earth trod hard, though the settlement was dotted with huge, ancient oaks that served as support for some of the larger structures.

There were huts—some high in the trees—and stalls for animals, a forge, butts for archery practice and, raised about a huge oak of unguessable age, a great wooden hall in the old Saxon or Norse style, like an overturned ship.

It seemed a thriving community—and one that had gone entirely its own way, with no need of barons, clergy and kings. Had it been bustling with Hood's people—or even entirely empty—it may yet have maintained the illusion. But the few signs of life told a grimmer story.

Dazzled by the torches after the dark of the forest, Gisburne did not see them at first: movement in the shadows, a slight figure. Then another. More of them—until finally he realised, just as one suddenly realises that the ground upon which one is standing is crawling with ants.

Gisburne advanced and shaded his eyes from the torches' glare. They were everywhere, in the dark—thin children in rags, old women, sick men. All those too weak or ill to fight. They sat, motionless, and stared blankly at the intruders, like pale ghosts. He was not even sure they were all alive. Doubtless, when they came here, they thought they had found protection, but it had become a grove of death.

Gisburne stepped further, feeling revulsion and rage rise in him. His fellows advanced slowly behind him, fanning out, each discovering their own horrors. From one tree hung an iron cage containing what was once a man. To the trunk of another were nailed human hands— grisly trophies from enemies, Gisburne assumed, or wrongdoers. Or just the unlucky.

The still air wafted, and the stink hit him again. He heard Asif exclaim under his breath. It had come from beyond a large rock at the far end of the village. Gisburne strode towards it.

Lyttel saw him go. "Do not go there..." he said, a note of pleading in his voice.

Gisburne, unperturbed, plucked a torch from a tree as he passed, stepped past the rock and then reeled at the smell. Things buzzed and flew up, and tiny clawed feet scampered into the dark. And suddenly he realised that what he had taken to be a tangle of thick, old tree roots was no such thing, but a mass of emaciated bodies, thrown into an open pit until they filled it, limbs twisted, dull eyes and empty sockets staring. He staggered back, and turned away.

This place was not just outside the law, but outside of all order, all humanity. All sanity.

Striding back—wishing to put as much distance between himself and that pit as possible—Gisburne caught Lyttel's eye and saw shame.

"I understand your desire to see this undone," said Gisburne, fighting to suppress his fury. "There is humanity in you yet, Lyttel. The remnant of a good man. You were that, once. But what I do not understand is how it came to this. What changed you so, to become complicit in *this*..."

Lyttel nodded slowly, head hanging low. "You know, I hated you, Gisburne. You are right. I was, I hope, a good man, trusted by all. And I repaid that trust. Then one night as I was guarding the Tower battlement, someone broke in, just to prove it could be done. No one was killed, nothing stolen, no harm done or meant. But the breach of the walls... That was surely down to someone's failing, and could not be permitted again. It might have been any one of my fellows on that battlement that night. But it happened to be me."

Gisburne bowed his head, knowing it was he who was the intruder.

"The Tower Constable was a fair man, but also hard. He had little choice. I had, at any rate, only been given the post as a favour to Geoffrey of Launceston, who sought good treatment where he could for those who had survived Hattin. I never even met the man, but it had felt like some compensation after the long road from Hattin, and capture."

"You were captured at Hattin?" said Mélisande.

"I was," said Lyttel. "And for a long time thought I would die. There was no one alive willing to pay ransom for this." With a wry smile, he indicated his own huge frame. "But I must not complain. Had I not been kept longer in the Holy Land, I would never have met my wife. She was—*is*—a Syriac Christian. She risked everything. Travelled back with me to England. Endured the name-calling, being spat at—far worse from those who had never left these shores than those who actually fought out there. They didn't stop to ask her religion, or wonder why such a man as I had loved her. They just saw a Saracen.

"When I lost my post at the Tower, I had not seen her for weeks. That was the one bright thing on the horizon—that I could finally go home. I was free. But when I got there, she had gone. No word, no hint as to why or where. I stayed a while, but found my neighbours had as little love for me as they'd had for her. Having no money, I had to give up the house, sell all I had. All her things, too. And I knew then that even were she alive, even if she thought to come looking for me, she would never find me again, nor I her. I realised I was not free. I was a prisoner—and this whole land was my prison. Mine and thousands like me, whose lives mattered not one bit, whose bodies did not even belong to them, and had no value to those that owned them.

"Then I heard of someone who proposed a different way. A way in which people might truly be free." He lifted his head. "And, that, Guy of Gisburne, is what so changed me."

Lyttel looked Gisburne in the eye, and it was Gisburne's turn, now, to feel shame.

"I say all this so you will understand why I acted as I did, but it does not excuse it. It does not excuse this..." He gesture towards the pit of the dead. "There is such a thing as too much freedom."

"I have had many names in my life, but the very worst of them— that which I hate the most—is John Lyttel. If I am ever again a free man, my only desire is to return to my father's mill in Isledon and once again become plain John Attemille."

"Then let us make that happen," said Gisburne. "And wipe this place off the face of the Earth."

LXV

THINGS MOVED SWIFTLY. Gisburne relieved Aldric of his burden and dispatched him to act as sentry. Then, as the rest of the company made preparations—watched by the empty, uncomprehending eyes of the thin ghosts in the shadows— Lyttel hastily explained the particulars of the camp. Gisburne strapped vambraces on his forearms and slung his quiver upon his belt as he listened.

There were two cabins high in each of the largest trees: the treasure store, containing all their spoils, and the armoury. Within the latter, amongst sundry weapons filched from the victims of their attacks, were another hundred bows and twenty barrels of arrows—enough to seed another rebellion.

Gisburne gazed up at them, knowing what must be done. "If there is anything about this camp that you value," he said to Lyttel, "take it now. Keep it about you."

Lyttel shook his head. "There's nothing."

As he spoke, Gisburne lowered his eyes and caught sight of a figure framed in the shadowed doorway of a thatched hut. It was tall and rangy, and leaning upon a staff. Gisburne thought it must be an old man—one of Hood's aged rejects, he supposed— until it stepped forward, revealing a lad of no more than fifteen.

Even after all this time, with him having so grown, Gisburne remembered him. The boy Micel—the one Hood called Much.

His face looked pale, and as he moved, it was clear he could not do so without the support of the quarterstaff. In the dim light of the torches, he caught sight of Gisburne, and his expression contorted into anger and hatred.

"Traitor!" he cried, his voice catching. It was, Gisburne realised, addressed to Lyttel. "You brought them here! Traitor!"

Lyttel stepped towards him, but the boy had drawn a knife.

"Get back inside," ordered Lyttel.

"You *poisoned* me!" said Much. There was more than anger in his voice. There was disbelief, despair, betrayal. "Gamewell said to watch you! You poisoned my food! Tried to *kill* me!" He raised the blade with a quaking hand.

"To save your life, boy!" said Lyttel. "So they would not take you with them!" He swatted the knife from Much's hand. The boy stumbled, sank to the ground and sobbed. Gisburne was about to talk to the boy—to comfort him—when another voice spoke out from behind him.

"Guy?" it said.

It was a voice he had heard for half his life—at one time, he had been as accustomed to it as his mother's or father's. Even now it was so familiar, so unchanged by time, that for a brief moment hearing it seemed in no way strange. As he began to turn, already half smiling, the strangeness—the wrongness of it in this terrible place—dawned on him like the slow waking from a dream.

Marian. It was Marian. She was alive. And she was here.

She shuffled out of the doorway of Hood's great hall into the torchlight—and all sense of familiarity disappeared.

He thought of how she had looked that time at Dover Castle—the evening seemed impossibly distant, though it was little more than two years ago: her beautiful lips always ready to laugh, her hazel eyes sparkling but also curiously sad, her gestures so disarmingly open, so honest.

It had been a wretched evening. He had been the reluctant guest of an even more reluctant host—the petulant weasel Matthew de Clere—and at dinner had been placed in a draughty position about as far from the fire and the food as possible, what Gisburne's father referred to as "one up from the dogs." As he had sat there, anticipating the morrow's grim sea voyage and dabbling in the dregs of the cold soup whilst de Clere's hounds were thrown choice cuts, Marian had been the one glimmer of light.

Her dress had been of blue-grey, her veil and wimple of white, topped with a simple circlet of silver. *Plain enough for a nun,* he had thought. But that had only thrown her beauty into greater relief; the curve of her breasts and hips, the curling wisps of auburn hair that escaped the veil, the natural, unaffected grace with which she bore herself. She had always been beautiful, and in later years had become beguiling, yet carried it with unselfconscious ease and a blissful ignorance of the effect it had on others. Yet another reason why Gisburne had lost his wits over her.

What stood before him now was like something broken. She looked at him with an odd, twisted smile, the stained dress hanging on her bones like a winding sheet upon a corpse. Her face was gaunt and skeletal, her eyes unfocused and underscored by deep shadows, her hair knotted and dirty. She was like the ghost of the woman he had loved—like something returned from the grave.

As she tottered towards him, he saw she was barefoot. Hood had taken her shoes—a precaution, he supposed, against her running away. But she did not seem about to run. He doubted there was the strength in those shaking limbs, or the awareness in her head of where to run or why.

"Guy..." she said again, her voice dreamy and distant. She stopped, looking up at him with something like love in her eyes. It both captivated and horrified him.

She stretched out filthy fingers to his cheek—then recoiled as they met solid flesh.

"But how can you be here?" she said.

"We're going to bring you back," he said. The words surprised even him. He turned and looked about, and saw that everyone now was watching. For an instant he caught Mélisande's eye— and she turned away. Marian was now surveying the assembled faces with a look of wonder. It gradually lapsed into a frown as her gaze came to rest upon Lyttel. "You betrayed us..." she said, barely louder than a whisper.

Lyttel's head drooped, then he, too, turned his back on her. She drifted towards him, and as she did so, almost as if in a dream, stooped and swiped her hand across the ground. Gisburne saw something flash in it, and realised she had Much's knife.

"No!"

Lyttel turned. The knife rose and fell. It was slow—almost languid. But it gave Lyttel no warning. Gisburne heard him cry out and saw the blade had connected, its point biting deep into his left shoulder.

Lyttel grabbed her thin wrist and shook the knife free. She became suddenly frenzied—screeching and uttering vile, blasphemous curses. Asif and de Rosseley leapt forward and dragged her off, features contorting with rage as she spat in the big man's face, then she too collapsed to the floor and dissolved into hysterical sobbing, yards from where Much still lay.

Mélisande rushed to Lyttel, but he waved her away irritably. "I'm fine," he said. "Look to yourselves."

And in that moment, Aldric came running full pelt from the forest. "Men are coming," he hissed. "From the southeast."

Gisburne looked around. They were not ready.

"I will hold them at the bridge," said Lyttel.

"No..." protested Gisburne.

"Don't worry about me," he said. "Do what you must, but do it fast. You have minutes, no more."

There was no time to argue. The big man threw a hood over his shoulders to cover the wound and, taking up Much's discarded quarterstaff, headed off.

The band ran for the trees. Gisburne—the last to go—snatched up the wooden cylinder, looked at Much and Marian sprawled upon the ground, and, realising he could do nothing about them, turned and ran into the shadows.

LXVI

ROBIN HOOD SET a single green boot upon the end of the foot-worn log and leaned upon his knee.

"Well, well!" he said with a broad grin, his teeth white as a wolf's in the light of the pale moon. "What do we have here?"

"Lyttel?" called Took. The monk's voice was stern, but Hood raised a hand to silence him. The others—Scarlet and a dozen or so more—peered around their master at the towering, motionless figure blocking the log bridge, a staff grasped in his hands.

"You told me to let no-one cross this bridge," said Lyttel, his voice slow and steady. "And that is what I am doing."

Hood stood dumbfounded for an instant, then threw back his head with a great guffaw. He turned to those behind him, gesturing towards Lyttel with his cocked thumb, and they all joined in the laughter—even the normally severe Took and the sour-faced Scarlet.

"Well..." Hood said, turning back to face his opponent. With one foot still upon the log, he pointed to the big man's staff. "Has Little John become a peasant now, that he fights with a stick?" Those behind him chuckled.

"I have no wish to *kill* you," said Lyttel.

That elicited an "*Oooh!*" from those gathered. Hood narrowed his cold eyes and smiled. "Well, if it's sport you want..."

Without a pause, he unhooked the string from his bow and, stepping up onto the log, wielded the bowstave like a quarterstaff.

"How's this?" he said. One of his men cheered him on.

He leapt forward, whipping the bowstave around—to be blocked by Lyttel.

"You are good, brother," said Hood with a grin. "But of course you are! You would not be among the chosen otherwise." Then he whirled the stave about, swiping at Lyttel with a flurry of blows. One, two, three: Lyttel's staff met each one.

Hood swung at him again. Staff met staff in sharp, clattering rhythm. Hood was nimble—far more than Lyttel—but the bigger man was able to anticipate his moves. Hood feigned a low strike, and swept the bowstave around and high in the air.

Almost caught out by the move, Lyttel thrust his staff upwards. He blocked the blow just short of his skull—but as it struck, with a resounding *crack* of wood upon wood, his left arm gave, and he cried out.

Hood laughed and got in two good jabs with the pointed nock of his bow. Lyttell winced, his feet slithering upon the log as he stepped back.

"Can't let you have it all your own way!" said Hood, twirling his bowstave around as if he were a jongleur. Then, as they squared up to each other for a second round, Hood saw a deepening dark stain upon Lyttel's shoulder, black in the moonlight.

"There's blood on you, brother," he said, his eyes narrowing. "Not of my making. What are you hiding?"

His demeanour shifted. There now seemed an air of malice, and he went for Lyttel once more, blows hard and vicious. Hood swept the bowstave about, back and forth, raining down blows, and Lyttel parried frantically, wood cracking against wood—but he was not as fast as his adversary, and one in every three strokes found an elbow, or a shin, or struck a glancing blow to the big man's brow.

He was forced back, his booted feet slipping, stumbling upon the wet, half-rotted wood—then the nock of Hood's bow jabbed into his thigh, and with a cry of pain, he doubled over.

Hood paused, grinning at his handiwork, ready to shove the panting giant into the gushing brook—when Lyttel's staff thrust forward into his stomach, then whirled about and cracked him across the temple. Hood's knees almost buckled beneath him, he tottered and swayed—then another blow sent him flying off the bridge and into the icy water with a great splash.

For a moment Lyttel stood in triumph, Hood's followers—now silent—looking on in bemusement. Then a crossbow bolt struck Lyttel full in the chest and sent him spinning.

HOOD ROSE FROM the dark water, shook his head like a dog and stood over John Lyttel, dripping wet, laughing. "I declare you the winner, John Lyttel!" he said. Then, with the point of his bow, he lifted the edge of the Lyttel's hood, revealing the bloody stab wound. "But you did not keep your word, did you? Others have come this way, have they not?" He gazed up into the trees, in the direction from which the bolt had flown. "Our mutual friend would seem to think so." Then he lifted his foot and placed it on the protruding quarrel.

Lyttel, still conscious—but barely—uttered a choking cry of agony. Hood withdrew the foot and stroked his wet beard. "Hmm," he said, shaking his head with dissatisfaction. "Too noisy..." Then he placed the same foot on the flat of Lyttel's chest, his smile now quite gone.

"You lied when you said you did not want to kill me," he said, and he pressed Lyttel beneath the water until the bubbles ceased.

LXVII

THEY CAME LIKE animals: dark shapes, crouched over, loping out of the shadows, their feet moving without sound upon the beaten earth floor.

Just one walked upright, unbowed by caution, untouched by fear; his face was in shadow, but Gisburne knew the shape of him by heart.

He stopped and stood for a moment—the others creeping around him, bows readied—and seemed to be sniffing the air. As he turned, his eyes and teeth glinted in the torchlight.

For a moment Gisburne was sure he looked right at him. But he didn't move, didn't flinch. He was certain he could not be seen in these shadows. But as the gaze lingered, he felt a shiver pass through him, nonetheless. Then Hood kept turning, looking for signs of them. The outlaw knew they were here. Somehow, something had alerted him. Had it been Lyttel?

Gisburne's stomach growled, reminding him that he had eaten nothing but dried scraps and stale bread for days. He looked about for the big soldier; even crouching, Lyttel would be taller than Hood, who was himself taller than most. But there was no sign, and Gisburne felt a creeping dread. Lyttel was not the sort of man to run; only one thing would have kept him away.

To his surprise, Gisburne found himself uttering a prayer—perhaps the second or third time he had done so in more than ten years.

He did not think the words would help Lyttel—he had never really believed that—but he wanted to say them anyway. He liked to think that if it were he lying dead or dying out there, someone would do the same for him.

Hood and his men had not moved from the forest's edge. Gisburne had an arrow already set, but still he did not dare move—not for fear of being seen, but of being heard. The place was eerily quiet, and only in the last few moments had he realised that the poor, half-dead wretches who'd haunted the edges of the village had disappeared. Even the half-dead, it seemed, feared death. Or perhaps, with Hood's return, they anticipated something worse even than that.

The silence was broken by a sudden movement: padding feet, the swish of cloth. From the great hall, Marian—pale as a ghost—was running. She ran not so much to Hood, as into him, yet she was now so slight that the dark figure gave not one inch. She threw her arms about him like a windblown rag wrapping about a post.

"Rose!" said Hood, and Gisburne saw the glint of teeth. Hood was not afraid to be heard, he never was. Then he took her by the shoulders and pushed her away. "You are a pathetic creature, aren't you?" he said. This was louder—meant for Gisburne to hear.

Gisburne gripped the bowstave tighter, and felt the resistance of the string against his fingers. He raised the arrow point, looking at the place on Hood's chest where he meant his arrow to go; where Hood's heart was meant to be.

There would be no honour in this, but he was past caring. This creature had to be put down.

Marian staggered as Hood gripped her upper arm, then he turned her roughly around. Holding her close again, he stepped forward, holding her against him. In his other hand Gisburne now saw the gleam of a knife.

The outlaw's eyes hunted about the shadows—looking for what must be there.

"Guy?"

It was so casual. So natural. As if he were calling to his friend from another room. He moved forward, further into Gisburne's sights, his men close behind.

"I know you're there, Guy. Come on out, old friend." He laughed this time, but there was irritation in it. Impatience. "I haven't got all night."

No, thought Gisburne, *you haven't...* He adjusted his aim to those cold eyes, those gleaming teeth.

"You know there's a crossbowman out there, Guy?" said Hood.

Gisburne hesitated, the arrow one-quarter drawn.

"You've encountered him before. In fact, he's been watching you all this time. And if you shoot, he shoots."

"Doesn't matter," said Gisburne. "You'll still be dead."

Hood whirled, his eyes fixing on the tree behind which Gisburne stood, and he broke into a wide grin. Gisburne looked him square in the eye, and drew his arrow back until the feather fletching touched the corner of his mouth.

"Oh, but he won't shoot *you,*" added Hood, matter-of-factly. Gisburne froze, the arrow fully drawn and ready to fly, its point aimed between Hood's darkly glinting eyes. "No. One of your friends."

Gisburne had not feared a crossbow bolt, but Hood's words were like a barbed point in his guts.

"I'll leave it to him which one," continued Hood. "He goes his own way, anyway. Doesn't need to pause to reload, either. Clever! But perhaps you've already worked that one out..."

"A lie," said Gisburne. His right hand began to shake with the effort, the string—in spite of his leather glove—cutting into his fingers.

"Lie?" said Hood, sounding put out. "Me?" Then he raised his hand and a crossbow bolt smacked into a tree—but not Gisburne's tree. It was the one behind which Mélisande now crouched.

Gisburne relaxed his arm slowly, releasing the tension from the bow, then stood.

"*No!*" hissed Mélisande, but there was no choice. Not one he wished to make, at least.

He stepped forward, into the clearing, the arrow still on his bow. Marian whimpered at the sight of him. The monk, Took, stepped forward, but Hood halted him with another gesture of the blade, and greeted Gisburne with one of his epic smiles.

"Glad you could make it. What do you think of the place?" Hood looked about impatiently. "Well, come on. All of you. I want all of you in the open..."

Before Gisburne could respond, Galfrid appeared at Hood's right.

"Master Galfrid!" said Hood cheerily.

Galfrid scowled. "That's *Squire* Galfrid..."

Mélisande emerged from the trees, expression proud. Hood bowed low. "Honoured, my lady!"

From the far left came Asif, then from the right, de Rosseley and Aldric. All had arrows ready on their bows.

At the sight of Asif, Hood frowned, squinted in disbelief, then threw his head back in a great laugh. "Well, well! This is turning into quite the reunion! You never disappoint me, Gisburne..." He bowed again. "Welcome to the Greenwood, Asif al-Din ibn Salah."

Asif said nothing. Still chuckling, Hood turned his attention to the others. "Now you two, I do not know..." He pointed the knife at de Rosseley and Aldric. "But I am sure that..."

There was an intake of breath from those gathered about Hood. Two took a step back. Hood himself, eyes wide, was staring at the vision now before him: Tancred, emerging from the shadows like a wraith. Took crossed himself, and for almost the only time in his life, Gisburne saw confusion upon Hood's face.

"Tancred de Mercheval?" said Hood incredulously. "Allied with *Guy of Gisburne?* How is this possible?"

"Tancred is changed."

"Changed? I heard he was *dead.*"

"He is," said Gisburne. "Asif, too. And I've died more times than I can count. But I've come back specially for you, Robert."

"To drag me to Hell!" chuckled Hood. "Is that why you led an army of the dead against me on the north road? That was unexpected, Guy, I must say."

"We are all dead in our various ways," said Mélisande with a cold expression. Hood shot an irritable glance at her.

"Except me," quipped de Rosseley. "I intend to live forever."

"I'm with him," said Aldric.

Hood looked de Rosseley in the eye, as if trying to see into his mind, and narrowed his eyes. "Well, you've come to the wrong place for that."

Gisburne took a step forward, and Hood's men tensed. Hood's blade tightened against Marian's throat and she whimpered again.

"Everybody dies, Robert," said Gisburne through gritted teeth. "Even you. I know you don't believe it, but we've come to convince you. To end this misery." The wind gusted, making the torch flames flicker, and the stench of corpses wafted through the courtyard.

"Misery?" said Hood, and looked around in bafflement at his fellows. "I thought we were having a good time." He looked suddenly hurt. "You could at least show a little gratitude."

Gisburne snorted. "Gratitude?"

"Tell me. What were your life's greatest moments, its defining points?"

Gisburne said nothing, but Hood—ever talkative Hood—seemed determined.

"Let me help you out," he said, and counted off on his fingers, tapping the knife blade against them, inches from Marian's throat. "You were knighted following capture by John—because of me. You destroyed Castel de Mercheval to bring the skull of the Baptist to England—for me. You made a dramatic capture of the kingdom's most notorious outlaw at the Clippestone tournament. Me again. And Inis na Gloichenn—I gave you that, too." He bowed his head towards Tancred. "All your greatest victories are because of me."

"The defeat of the Red Hand at the Tower was also your doing," said Gisburne. "Yet you missed it out. Why is that?" He spoke not to Hood, now, but to the dark trees. A fury briefly burned in Hood's eyes, and was extinguished. "What does any of it matter now?" said Gisburne. "What if I just kill you right here?" He felt his fingers tense against the bowstring.

Hood's broad grin returned. "Well, then, your everlasting infamy will also be down to me."

"Alan O'Doyle!" called Gisburne, and looked into the trees, from where the crossbow shot had come. Hood's smile fell. "I know it's you. I know your work. The work you did for your brother. This man you protect... You know he used your brother's death to get himself out of the Tower—that Niall died so Hood could live?"

There was no movement, no reply, but the seed of doubt might be enough. His eyes flicked around the shadows at the forest's edge. O'Doyle had shot one bolt. Gisburne was certain he would not have reloaded whilst they were in his sights. That meant he had one bolt ready—one only—and now they knew where he was.

Gisburne's company must know he meant to act; he had chosen them, trained them, for this moment. But Hood sensed it too: Gisburne saw his hand tense about the knife and bring it closer to Marian's exposed throat.

A sudden movement from one of the huts made Hood turn. A groggy Much staggered from the doorway, and Hood smiled.

And Gisburne drew his bow, loosed and ran.

Arrows hissed all around as his company scattered. His own shot flew wild, hampered by the need to protect Marian; it hissed past Hood's ear, and the outlaw almost dodged into its path.

A man's voice cried out in pain—he did not see who. From the trees he heard the *thunk* of a crossbow. Someone fell—heard rather than seen—and Gisburne threw himself into the doorway of a low hovel. The cylinder on his back thumped hard against the half-open door and made his stomach lurch, but as he turned he glimpsed Mélisande disappear behind a great heap of logs. She was alive, but two bodies now lay slumped in the courtyard.

An arrow zipped by him. He recoiled as it struck the doorpost, splintering wood. A presence behind him made him turn; an old woman—thin and bony, her face sagging—stared at him out of the dark with a vacant expression.

Gisburne peered out and saw Hood backing into the great hall, dragging Marian as a shield. He saw the fallen men, too, and felt immediate relief.

If any of his own had been hit, it had evidently not stopped them finding cover. They had been outnumbered, but had had the advantage, surrounding Hood's men in a wide, dispersed arc.

The outlaws, packed in a tight group, had got by far the worst of it. The two on the ground—one looked to be Will of Stutely—must have fallen immediately, and a third had taken an arrow in his thigh and was even now scrabbling desperately towards cover.

If O'Doyle's bolt had hit home, there was as yet no sign of it.

A dark shape moved behind the nearest hut—the one from which Much had emerged—and he saw Asif dodge out of the shadows and loose an arrow.

Gisburne whistled, and Asif turned and grinned at him. As best he could, Gisburne tried to convey—with gestures—what he meant to do, hoping to God Asif understood. The Arab nodded and drew six arrows from his quiver. One, he placed upon the bow; the others, he gripped between the fingers of his draw hand in a manner that Gisburne had only seen among Saracen archers—and only among the elite.

He nodded, then Gisburne drew Irontongue and launched himself from the doorway.

It was barely forty yards from his hiding place to the great hall, but it felt like four hundred.

Arrows flew—he heard the whistle of their feathered fletchings, one passing so close he felt its breath on his face. But almost all of them were flying at the enemy, Asif shooting so rapidly that he had loosed all six in the time it had taken Gisburne to run six paces.

He heard a cry far to his right; one of Hood's men. After that, for a moment—the moment Gisburne needed—no more arrows flew.

He hurtled into the hall's darkened doorway, the wooden cylinder at his back jumping and rattling. One last arrow drove into the hall's outer wall.

And for a moment he stood panting, sword in one hand, bow in the other, face to face with Hood, the hall's great tree spreading up behind him like some tentacled creature emerging from the earth.

Gisburne's arrival had caught him by surprise—he had the bow off his back, but no arrow in his hand and a stunned expression upon his face. Gisburne threw his bow down and went at him.

Hood barely had time to draw his own sword, parrying Gisburne's swing inches from his face in a jarring collision. A spark shot through the dark air.

Hood pushed him away, smiling and baring his teeth like a wild animal, and swung back at him. Gisburne jumped backwards, cursing the burden on his back. Reaching behind him, he drew his seax and parried a second crushing blow, then brought his sword about in a sweeping horizontal cut at Hood's exposed neck.

The outlaw saw it coming, dropped and rolled, throwing his sword away from him as he did so.

It was a crazy manoeuvre. No knight or man-at-arms would let go his key weapon—you'd have to cut it from his hand. But in this, as in everything, Hood was utterly unpredictable.

In an instant he had rolled to his feet and snatched up his sword again—but that instant was time enough for Gisburne cut the strap of the wooden cylinder.

He let it fall. His heart was in his mouth as he heard it strike the ground. But he was not dead. Not yet.

He attacked—but Hood, instead of defending, went at him again, grinning and grunting with every feverish swipe. He had not had a knight's years of training and was not so skilled a swordsman as Gisburne, but the blows were hard to predict—wild and unrestrained, with all of Hood's strength behind them. Gisburne retreated, parrying again and again, the relentless attack giving him no chance to counter. Then his heel stopped hard against something, and he stumbled. He felt himself fall.

Time slowed. Hood's distorted visage leered over him, eyes wide, spit flying from his mouth, sword passing a thumb's width above Gisburne's face.

Gisburne reflected, distantly, that it had been a lucky escape; less lucky was the blow then connecting with Irontongue, with enough force to send it spinning from Gisburne's hand.

He landed hard, the wind knocked out of him. By the time he knew what was happening, the seax had been knocked from his other hand. For a moment, it almost seemed funny: a moment ago, he'd been sneering at Hood for dropping his sword, and now here was Gisburne, himself weaponless.

Hood swung again—straight down, sword whistling through the air in a killing blow.

Gisburne raised his right arm instinctively—and Hood's blade stopped hard against it.

Hood looked stunned. The blade had struck the steel vambrace on Gisburne's forearm—one of Llewellyn's gifts—and stuck between the teeth along its lower edge. In another moment, Hood could withdraw, and strike again; but Gisburne did not hesitate, and twisted his arm with all the force he could muster.

Trapped, the sword blade unexpectedly snapped, the end ringing through the air and falling uselessly to the ground. Hood tottered back, staring at the broken hilt. Gisburne leapt to his feet and before his opponent could gather his wits, thrust the vambraced forearm at his face.

The teeth scythed across Hood's cheek. He roared, and staggered back towards the shadows, his face bloodied.

Irontongue, was Gisburne's next thought. But as he looked for the sword, something sharp rammed into his back, making him cry out. He turned and swatted the figure aside, his fist meeting little resistance, and saw it was Marian. She crumpled in a heap, Gisburne's seax tumbling from her grip. It had not penetrated his mail—he doubted it had even drawn blood—but when he turned back, Hood was gone.

He crouched over Marian, who was moaning feebly. She would be insensible for a little while, but she'd live.

Then he saw what must have tripped him: Llewellyn's cylindrical box. He glared at it. "Christ's boots, I hope you're worth this..." he muttered.

Hearing the sound of clashing blades from the courtyard, he retrieved his weapons, propped the box in the shadows by the door, and rushed back outside.

In the fierce fighting, arrows had been soon depleted, and bids to retrieve them had—inevitably—drawn the fight into the open.

A thin-faced man with a brush-like beard had broken cover at exactly the same moment as Asif. For a second they stood rooted to the spot at either end of the open courtyard, eye to eye, each with an empty quiver. The bearded man's eyes flicked to the floor, where an arrow lay just ten feet from him, then back to Asif. A second pair of eyes glinted behind him, and as Asif looked to them, the bearded man ran.

Asif's hand was already at his belt, and he swung with a grunt. Metal flashed and rang through the air in the dark forest glade. The disc bounced off the man and went spinning skyward as he lurched forward, and for an instant Asif was convinced he had inflicted no damage. But there came a choking cough, the man pitched forward onto his face, and red sprayed and frothed from him as he thrashed in the spreading pool.

The second man had already darted from the shadows, going for the same arrow. Asif gripped the second chakkar and let it fly—but the man had seen his comrade's fate and knew what was coming. Fast as a fox, he dropped and threw up his hand, apparently intent on hurling the weapon back at its owner. The disc sailed past and stuck in an ash tree at the forest's edge; without a pause, the man leapt forward, reaching for the fallen arrow.

It was only when attempting to grab the arrow shaft that the man realised what had happened. There were no fingers, just streams of blood pouring from the severed stumps which grubbed uselessly in the sticky, crimson mud about the arrow. He let out a howl of anguish as Asif drew his sword and ran at him.

MÉLISANDE HAD EMERGED a moment after Asif, with only a dim sense that others about her were doing the same

Her target was a man who had suddenly appeared from behind the great hall with a spear, and looked like he might give Asif trouble. Sword drawn, her bow in her left hand, she made a dash at him. He turned his spear on her, but she knocked its point out of her way and stepped on the point, and would have slashed him with the return stroke had he not had the presence of mind to drop the spear and run. He fled into a dark alley between huts, and she pursued him into the confined space—and almost crashed straight into him.

He was not weaponless. She hadn't noticed the mace at his belt, but his retreat had given him time to draw it, and he now stood, wild-eyed and defiant, feet planted wide apart, the crude, hammer-headed club raised and ready. There wasn't the space to swing her sword in the narrow lane.

"Well, well," said a voice behind her. She glanced back and saw the leering face of Will the Scarlet, revealing black teeth as thin as a rat's. "Here's a pretty one..." He took a step forward, his long knife glinting. Ahead of her, the other raised his mace.

Mélisande dropped her bow, wrapped her gauntleted hands about the blade of the sword and swung it like an axe. The upswing countered the mace; then she brought the sword's crosspiece down into her attacker's unprotected skull. He dropped like a felled ox, and she pulled the sword free and thrust the point of the blade behind her.

The point bit, and Scarlet howled in pain. She turned and battered the hilt across his chin, then cracked it against his knuckles as he staggered back. The knife dropped point-first in the mud. She plucked it up and went to finish him off.

But Scarlet was not as badly hurt as she might have hoped. Moaning like a tomcat in heat, he turned and ran—and this time, the retreat was no bluff.

Mélisande thrust the knife through her belt, took up her bow and ran back into the courtyard. Scarlet was running unevenly across the open space, zig-zagging between others in conflict. Looking around, she saw an arrow stuck in a support post to her left, its iron tip still visible. She sheathed her sword, pulled the arrow free, placed it on her bow, and put it through Will Scarlet's right leg.

He screeched like an animal. The arrow stuck halfway through his leg, just below the knee, and became embedded in the mud as he fell. He writhed there, unable to stand or crawl, pinned to the earth like an insect.

DE ROSSELEY SAW Hood's man aim and draw at Mélisande as she ran after the spearman.

Where and when he had got the arrow, de Rosseley had not seen, but he did not stop to think. He launched himself forward, his sword swinging through the air when he was still yards away. The bowman heard his heavy footfalls advancing and turned, his bow, at full draw, now on his attacker.

By then it was too late. De Rosseley's blade struck the bowstave and it exploded into splinters, sending the bowman flying flat in the mud. The arrow span up into the air; de Rosseley heard it clatter on the roof of a nearby hut as he advanced to finish the bowman off.

He was raising his sword again when there was an impact, and pain shot through his side. For a moment, he thought an arrow had hit him—then realised that if that were the case, he probably wouldn't be wondering anything. He turned and saw Much, swaying, pale-faced, dagger in his hand. De Rosseley just had time to register the anger and terror in his face before punching the pommel of his sword into the boy's nose.

He inspected the damage at his side. The dagger point had barely penetrated the mail, but had still managed to draw blood. He cursed under his breath, turned again to the now almost recovered bowman. Then a second pain seared through his calf. He looked down to see Much, his nose streaming blood, sprawled upon the floor, feebly withdrawing the knife he had stuck in the back of de Rosseley's lower leg all the way to the bone.

De Rosseley kicked the boy senseless, and winced in pain.

Then the bowman was up again, sword drawn, and going for de Rosseley as an easy kill.

ALDRIC HAD ALREADY felled two of Hood's men when Much left his mark upon de Rosseley. A third was stalking steadily towards him, seemingly oblivious to his spanned and loaded crossbow, when Aldric glanced again at de Rosseley and saw a sword raised and ready to strike the knight.

He did not hesitate.

The bolt struck the bowman just below the ear, emerging a full inch from the far side of his skull. De Rosseley started in shock and surprise, then turned to Aldric and gave him a smile and a nod of gratitude.

But Aldric's attention was now back on the man still coming for him, a crude spiked club in his hands.

Why the man did not come faster, Aldric did not know. Perhaps he thought he was safe from his crossbow. Aldric had been frugal with his bolts and now had one left, but he had to span the bow first. And somehow—perhaps to avoid hand-to-hand combat, which he had feared ever since his injury in the Forêt de Boulogne—he found himself doing just that.

His attacker was half-smiling, half-grimacing as he paced forward, watching Aldric crank the lever forward and back. In this man's world, crossbows could not be spanned with any speed, but he had not reckoned upon the ingenuity of the man he now faced—for already Aldric was placing bolt upon bow.

All at once the man charged. Aldric, panicked, fumbled the bolt and barely raised the bow as his attacker barged into him with his whole body.

The loaded crossbow fell to the ground, and Aldric was shoved backwards, falling and rolling over. Aldric rolled and staggered to his feet, drawing his sword before the attacker could make his next move. Seeing Aldric's crossbow still spanned and loaded by his feet, the man smiled, dropped the club, snatched up the bow, turned it on its maker and squeezed the trigger.

The bolt did not fly. Instead, the man gave a strange, sharp cry and let the weapon drop, then looked at his bloodied hand in a mix of disbelief and fury. He grasped the spiked club and took a step—and without warning his eyes rolled, his mouth foamed and he fell to his knees, clutching at his throat.

Somewhere from Aldric's right, de Rosseley charged past in great limping strides, and with a roar—of anger, of pain, of bloody-minded defiance—struck with all his strength. The head jumped clean off, rolling and leaving a bloody trail.

"Thank you," said de Rosseley, panting, as the gushing, headless body slumped forward.

"You're welcome," said Aldric. And then he thought about the other crossbowman somewhere out there.

GALFRID STOOD BEFORE Took, sword gripped in both hands. The monk—lean and wiry, his thin mouth framed by a grizzled beard—fixed him with a hard stare, and he raised his blade.

"Where's your master, squire?" he said.

"Killing yours, priest," said Galfrid.

Took gave a dismissive laugh. Galfrid imagined the man could be kindly to those he deemed worthy, but right now was about as genial as a bucket of cold piss emptied from an upper window.

"My master is God," he said, scornfully.

Galfrid nodded slowly. "Well, perhaps it's time you paid him a little visit," he said, and swung hard.

Took dodged then countered. Galfrid parried with the flat of his blade, knocking the monk's sword away. The priest was clearly a canny fighter. Took eyed him for a moment, then struck at him again.

The blows came hard and fast. Once, the monk's sword tip caught the nasal on Galfrid's helm, twisting it, and forcing the squire to step back.

The monk had no armour. This should have given Galfrid the clear advantage, but Took showed no fear, and he was not rushing. But this was fact: if Took struck Galfrid, his mail would likely stop the blade's edge, but if Galfrid struck Took, he would cut him deeply. And he was tiring of fighting at the monk's pace.

Galfrid drove at him with all the force he could muster, trying to force an error. The monk's blade parried everything he could throw at him—then countered with a blow that slid down Galfrid's blade, bounced off his crossguard and smacked against his neck. Galfrid reeled with the impact and the pain; but for his mail coif, he'd be dead. He turned, staggered—looked about to fall—then dropped the act and swung full circle, bringing his sword around in a great arc.

Took leapt back—but not far enough. Galfrid's sword point caught him across the forehead. He felt iron graze against bone, and the monk roared. Blood streamed down his face as he staggered back, half-blinding him. Galfrid stepped forward, raising his blade for the kill.

What happened next was a blur. Something struck the blade hard, knocking it from his hand, and he was hit in the side of the head and sent flying. The landing knocked the breath out of him, and for a moment he lay helpless, his ears ringing, his helm askew. He felt no pain, but was uncertain whether he had escaped injury or was already dead.

Sideways on, as if through a haze, he saw Tancred, fighting like a whirlwind. Even as Galfrid watched, he cut one man's throat and gutted another. A third—unwilling to take him on—dropped back, found an arrow, and had it on his bow before he, too, was shot; by Asif, Galfrid thought.

More than we expected... thought Galfrid in his strange, distracted state of mind. Then he saw muddy, booted feet moving close by him. Took's.

Move... thought Galfrid. *Get up...* But his body would not respond. As he awaited his death, Galfrid thought abstractly about what had just occurred. Took had not struck him. There was no one else nearby. A bowman, then? No, not that—a *crossbowman...*

There was a logic to it. Hood's archers would have aimed for his body—any regular archer would. But to have struck his sword like that and glance off his helm, it had to have been aimed at his face. There was nothing regular in that. It might simply have been a stray arrow, of course, but his money was on their crossbowman.

He chuckled to himself, staring at Took's feet as the monk drew up alongside him. Blood dripped on the ground. Took's sword point swung low past his face, and he wondered vaguely, for reasons that were beyond him, what became of Master Hubert's lost stone blocks back in Durham.

Then pain surged through his right wrist, and his neck, and on through his whole body. His limbs twitched. The fear returned. He raised his head, and saw another pair of feet approaching.

Tancred's.

* * *

TOOK TURNED AND saw Tancred de Mercheval screaming towards him.

Tancred, whose startling views had inspired him to travel so far from the stagnant waters of Christian orthodoxy.

Tancred, who he had enticed to this very place, and who had aided them in their action against Gisburne at the Tower.

Tancred, who Hood had betrayed in spite of Took's entreaties, and who perhaps now was to prove their undoing.

And as he thought these things, he saw his own end rushing towards him. He thought of how the first blow would come. How he would parry. With what he would counter.

But he did nothing.

Tancred's sword point pierced his stomach with all of the Templar's weight and momentum behind it. There was no pain. Just an impact, and a horrifying pressure that seemed to have no end. A pop inside, then a rush to the head. A jarring, shuddering sensation—which some part of him knew was the blade sliding past bone. The heat of his own blood.

And as he was run through, he gazed up at Tancred—literally staring into the face of death.

He clutched the blade in both hands. Nothing moved. His legs were water. He looked down and saw the scarlet cascade. Then the pain rose so great in him he wanted only for it to end.

And the world slid from him.

TANCRED STOOD OVER Galfrid as Took fell, the squire looking back up at him in blurred incomprehension.

Tancred had committed the ultimate sin of a knight; he had lost his sword. As Took had fallen, gripping the blade that spelled his doom, his collapsing weight had ripped the hilt from Tancred's hand.

He looked down at Galfrid, so vulnerable at his feet, and hissed in frustration. The sword was not easily recoverable from the curled body of the monk. He hunted around for another—and saw Galfrid's.

He snatched it up, gave Galfrid a last look, then swung the blade.

It connected with the crossguard of an attacker's sword—one of Hood's men, who had seen Tancred without a weapon. His expression changed when he saw Tancred was armed again—and fell further as the Templar advanced, raining down blows. Parrying desperately, the man fell back, and Tancred advanced.

Then a low cry made Tancred turn. A second man, a long knife in one hand and a rough, spiked mace in the other, was creeping up upon Galfrid, and the squire—still addled from the blow, but sensible enough to realise he was defenceless—was scrabbling backwards upon the ground, limbs flailing like an upturned beetle.

And Tancred had taken the squire's weapon.

He turned back to his adversary, sword crashing hard against hilt. He gave the man no opportunity to attack, but he was defending himself like the Devil. He needed to end it—so he feigned a high blow, then sank his boot into the man's unprotected groin.

The bandit doubled and fell, and Tancred, shrieking like a wraith, whirled about and flew at the other, whose face twisted in utter terror. He blocked wildly with his mace and caught Tancred's flying blade—but the force of the blow thrust the mace into his own forehead. He staggered back and let go the mace, but one of its spikes had pierced his face, and he tottered about with the club hanging from it, looking for all the world like some bizarre figure from a mummers' play.

Tancred turned again; the swordsman, already on his feet, was almost on him, sword up, ready to strike.

Tancred was caught off-guard. There was no defence.

Then a great roar rent the air, and as if by some dark magic, the swordsman's head was cleaved clean in two. Half of it flopped on his shoulder in a splintered, gory mess right before Tancred's eyes, and the man collapsed like a sack, blood welling from the opened head like a crimson spring.

He fell at Tancred's feet, blood soaking his boots, and behind him stood the towering figure of the Norseman, a bloodied axe in his hands.

"Gunnar!" exclaimed Tancred in delight, extending a hand in friendship and gratitude.

Then something whirred through the air. Tancred jolted where he stood, stumbled back a step, and looked down at the crossbow bolt protruding from his breastbone.

As he swayed and fell, the Norseman cried out—a terrible, broken cry of anguish. As the roar turned to rage, he turned and saw the reeling outlaw with the mace still nailed to his head, and vented all his anger upon him.

The blow would have felled a tree. The man's head bowled across the courtyard, his body collapsing like a puppet.

Galfrid righted himself, his head still buzzing. It was wet all around, although the water was black and warm. Only gradually did he realise it was blood. Not his.

He staggered to his feet, then went to Tancred's side, where the big Norseman was already kneeling.

The Templar was still breathing. No one in all Galfrid's experience had clung so fiercely to life. But it was feeble, fading—and Galfrid was sure that this time, at last, Tancred would fail. And yet this was the one time Galfrid wished for him to live.

Tancred had saved him. Died for him.

The skull face turned, its eyes on the squire. A hand reached up and gripped his tunic with bony fingers. "Did I fight well?" whispered Tancred.

Galfrid could only nod.

"Did I do *right*?"

"No one could have done better," said Galfrid, his voice breaking.

There was nothing more: no sound, no movement, no last gasp of breath. One moment the Templar was alive, and the next an emptied vessel. The Norseman bowed his head, and his hand went to the hammer pendant about his neck, and Galfrid pulled away the dead fingers that still clung to his coat.

MÉLISANDE WAS SCANNING the forest for signs of the crossbowman when Gisburne reappeared. He crouched by her, behind the log pile. She did not turn to look at him.

"Hood?" she said.

"Gone." He followed her gaze into the dark shadows. "Our crossbowman?"

"Gone to ground again. He got Tancred, almost got Galfrid. Tancred saved him." She looked at him then and smiled. "The rest of us are well, I think."

"One man down..."

"Not quite," she said, and nodded across the corpse-strewn courtyard. Gisburne hunted about the shadows, seeing Aldric crouched between two huts. And there was Asif tucked in the doorway of another. And there, in the far corner, amongst a sprawl of butchered corpses, he saw Galfrid, knelt over a body... and opposite him, the big Norseman.

"Good God..." he muttered.

"I believe they call him Woden," said Mélisande.

A long, slow whistle—like the cry of a wolf—came from the forest's edge. Hood. Even his whistle was like no one else's.

There were rustles, and the sound of footfalls. Gisburne spied subtle movement in the shadows—saw a low crouching figure dart for the trees.

"He's calling them back," said Gisburne.

"What's left of them..." muttered Mélisande.

He broke cover and hissed to Galfrid. The squire turned and came to him, the Norseman close behind. Then Asif. Then Aldric, running low to the ground.

"Ross?" said Gisburne looking about. "Where's Ross?"

Just then de Rosseley appeared, limping and dragging the still insensible Much along the ground by one foot.

Gisburne saw the bloody rag tied about his leg. "Ross? Are you all right?"

"I'll live," he said, and let Much's foot drop. "This little wasp stung me." He gave him a kick.

A rustle from one of the huts made them start, and one of Hood's men—a skinny sort, with a weedy, adolescent beard—darted out past them and made for the gap in the trees that led to the log bridge.

De Rosseley drew his sword and was all for charging after the wretch when Aldric caught his sleeve.

"I might have set a small trap that way," he said. "To pass the time when I was on watch."

They heard the man crash into the forest. There came a *thunk*, and a scream—which abruptly ceased.

"Just a small one."

"Another one down," said de Rosseley, with some satisfaction, and winced as he put his weight on his leg.

Gisburne's eye's flicked nervously about the shadowy edge of the village. "We must get under cover quickly. Salvage what arrows you can and get back to the great hall. Don't think this is over. Hood's men came out of the shadows for arrows; we must assume they got some."

"But at what cost?" said Aldric, looking about him at the hacked and bleeding bodies.

"We got off lightly, thank the Almighty," said Asif.

"Thank your armour," said Galfrid, rapping his knuckles upon his dented helm

"Hood believes himself invulnerable," said Gisburne. "But he won't that mistake twice. And nor must we. Get to the hall, quickly!"

De Rosseley and Galfrid dragged Much between them, Asif and Aldric following close behind.

Gisburne gave a last sweep of the forest's edge, and a wailing moan made him turn.

There, face-down in the mud, some distance away, was someone Gisburne had thought dead, but who was now raising himself up on his elbows. Gisburne recognised the rat-like features: Will Gamewell. The Scarlet.

Scarlet caught sight of them. "You bastards!" he cried out, his voice mocking. "You're all dead!"

"Bring him," said Gisburne.

"Gladly," said Mélisande. A fresh arrow whistled past, no doubt prompted by Scarlet's outburst.

She ducked low, and, gripping him by the scruff of the neck, dragged the rangy figure towards the hall, his skewered leg bumping along the ground so he howled every inch of the way.

LXVIII

GISBURNE LOOKED AT the meagre fistful of arrows—some bent, some bloody—and shoved them in the quiver at his side.

"Aldric? You have bolts?" he said.

"Two," said Aldric. It was not the greatest of arsenals. Gisburne looked to the cylindrical box by the door, then back again.

"How many of them do you think there are now?" said Asif.

"Not many," said Gisburne.

"Took is dead," said Galfrid. "I saw it happen."

"And we have Scarlet," said Mélisande, and gave him a kick. Scarlet was tied to a post, a rag stuffed in his mouth. He raged into it as Mélisande continued past. She had wanted to leave the arrow through his leg, but Gisburne, ever pragmatic, had pulled it right through to use again. Scarlet's cry as he'd done so was terrible indeed. Aldric had treated and bound both this and de Rosseley's wounds, though the former with considerably less care than the latter.

"O'Doyle is somewhere out there," said de Rosseley. "If it is him."

"It's him," said Gisburne. "I have never met him, but I recognise his work. It was he equipped his brother, the Red Hand."

"Then that is most of the Wolf's Head accounted for," said Mélisande.

"There's only one that matters now," said Gisburne.

393

"Where's John?" whined Much, now fully conscious. "Where's John Lyttel?" He cowered in a corner, grasping his knees; Marian slumped next to him, wide-eyed, lost in her own world. Asif kept a watchful eye on both, though Gisburne doubted they had any fight left in them. The Norseman—as downcast as Gisburne had seen anyone—sat silent and motionless away from the rest of them, seeming bereft of purpose.

No one seemed willing to volunteer an answer to Much's question—until Scarlet, for the third time, worked the rag free and blurted out, with graphic attention to detail, just how Hood had finished off John Lyttel. Much lurched forward, clawing at the bound man, only to be dragged back by Asif and de Rosseley while Mélisande again stuffed the offending hole. Much sat, utterly despondent, and sobbed—but secretly, Gisburne was pleased. There surely was no chance Much would fight for Hood now.

For an hour, voices had called out from the forest, goading them. Cackling laughter, weird taunts, cries like animals. After a while a heavy rain began to fall. Gisburne was glad of it: let them contemplate the deaths of all they knew in the cold and wet. But even a soaking seemed not to dampen their spirit.

There had been talk of lighting a fire in the hall's great hearth, but Gisburne had ruled against it. Better they stay in the dark, he'd said, and all had seen the sense.

From time to time, Gisburne had peered out of the windows, but seen nothing. Galfrid was crouched on watch by the great door. Though open only a crack, he had a clear view to what Lyttel had called "the armoury", high up in its tree, and the single ladder to its entrance. Barrel upon barrel of arrows waited up there.

Once or twice an arrow had hissed out of the shadows towards them—perhaps Hood's men had seen movement, perhaps simply to remind them that they were there—but they were token gestures. If Hood got his hands on those barrels, however, everything would change. So far, there had been nothing; they knew it was being watched, that anyone trying to make the climb would be stuck with arrows. Still, the possibility would be on their minds, as surely as it was on Gisburne's. There was one unknown.

Gisburne crouched in front of Scarlet and yanked out the rag.

"You've been desperate to talk since you got here," said Gisburne. "So talk."

"Drink," spat Scarlet. "Then talk."

Gisburne gestured to Mélisande, who reluctantly passed a flask half-filled with ale. Gisburne tipped it down Scarlet's gullet; he gulped noisily, half of it coursing down his front, then pulled his head back and flashed Gisburne a rat-toothed grin.

"So, what d'you want to talk about, eh?" he said with a sneer. "Hood's plans? What he's going to do to you? You really think I'm going to tell you?"

Gisburne shrugged. "If you've nothing to tell us, there's no reason for you to live."

Scarlet snorted. "I will tell you one thing. Hood's not going to kill *you*. Not ever. He's going to *hurt* you. Kill and defile all those around you." He nodded towards Asif. "They'll skewer the Saracen first. Then finish up with your precious squire. The woman, though—she'll be mine. I'll have her. Then cut her. Maybe leave her alive, after a fashion."

"You'll find that hard to do with your throat cut," said Mélisande.

Gisburne could see she was shaking—not with fear, but barely contained rage. He saw her grip her knife tighter.

"It's just talk," he said.

"Just talk?" whined Scarlet. "Of course it's just talk—that's what you wanted, isn't it?" He laughed—a horrid, hoarse, cawing laugh.

She glared at him in fury and disgust.

Scarlet's smile vanished suddenly. "It's going to happen, though. Do you know why? Because you didn't even have the balls to kill me, when you had the chance."

"Easily remedied," muttered de Rosseley.

Gisburne, undeterred, leaned forward. "O'Doyle," he said. "What about O'Doyle?"

"What about him?" said Scarlet—and immediately, Gisburne saw he had touched a nerve. "I hate that smug fucker. I don't care if you *do* kill him. Hood won't mind, neither."

"Why not?"

"Didn't like the way he was cosying up to his precious Rose." He nodded towards Marian. "That's why Hood wanted him on the outside." Then he looked Gisburne in the eye, and smiled. "Set him up with a special mission, he has."

Gisburne frowned. Scarlet chuckled again. "He has special orders if Hood dies."

"To kill me?"

"He'd like that, O'Doyle. And I'm not saying he won't, when he's off the leash. But this... This is much better..." He licked his bloody lips and leaned forward confidentially. "If Hood dies in this forest, O'Doyle's gonna kill the fucking King!"

Gisburne stared in disbelief as the outlaw's laughter rang out. As if in sympathy, voices from the rain-sodden forest joined him, howling like wolves.

Marian wailed and rocked back and forth at the sound. Much blocked his ears, unable to take any more. "Stop him!" he begged. "Stop him laughing!"

Asif strode over to Scarlet and pressed a foot on his wounded knee, and the outlaw's laugh turned to a cry. "Is this what your master did to John Lyttel?" said Asif, his eye burning. He applied greater pressure. "Do I have it right?"

Scarlet was screaming now, and Gisburne waved Asif away. Scarlet spat after him, his defiance seemingly limitless.

Asif stepped out of spitting range, his back to the window, and an arrow whistled in the darkness. The Arab jerked and staggered forward, his eyes bulging. He fell to his knees, an arrow in his upper back.

Scarlet whooped in triumph. Gisburne and Mélisande rushed to Asif's side, supporting him.

"Careful! Careful!" said Aldric as they leaned him back against a post. The Saracen's face was pale and ashen, his breathing rough.

"I told you!" cackled Scarlet with delight. "What did I tell you?"

Gisburne unbuckled Asif's coat of scale and let it fall. The arrow had skimmed the top of the scales, passed through the mail on Asif's left shoulder and driven down at an angle into his chest.

Gisburne could see the fletching on the arrow in the dim light. Green; one of Hood's own.

"Told you he'd hurt you!" whined Scarlet. "You won't stop him!"

"Someone shut him up!" bellowed Gisburne, and de Rosseley stepped forward and clouted the outlaw around the head.

Asif was alive and still conscious—but only just.

"If we can light a small fire I can cauterise and bind the wound," said Aldric. Gisburne nodded to Mélisande, who immediately set about finding tinder. "But for that, we must remove the arrow, which risks further damage."

"It has to be done," said Mélisande, scrabbling in her purse for steel and flint. She struck them together, the sparks bright in the gloom.

"No, wait..." said Gisburne, putting his hand before Aldric. "Hood's broadheads are fixed to the shafts with beeswax. If the shaft is drawn, the head will stay inside. We'll never get it out."

Mélisande was blowing on the tinder, breathing the fire into life and piling kindling onto it.

Gisburne felt the front of Asif's chest, then turned to face his friend.

"You all right, old friend?"

"I've had better days," whispered Asif. He coughed and winced with the pain.

"There's something I have to do," he said. "It will mean more pain..."

Asif merely nodded.

"Help me," said Gisburne to Aldric, unbuckling Asif's sword belt and lifting his mail coat up to his chin. Gisburne pierced a hole in Asif's shirt with his seax, then ripped the front open.

On the front of the Arab's chest was a purplish bulge in the skin. "The arrow point has almost passed through," he said. "It's not far below the surface. We must push it through."

He looked Asif in the eye again. Asif nodded.

"Heat the iron ready," he told Aldric. The enginer nodded and crouched over Mélisande's growing blaze as she heaped more upon it, playing his knife in the flame.

"Ross? I'm going to need your help here." De Rosseley nodded, expression grim. While Gisburne stripped the fletchings off the arrow shaft, he knelt down, wincing at his own injury, and placed a hand flat upon Asif's breastbone.

"Don't worry, old man," he said quietly. "We'll sort you out."

Then, at a nod from Gisburne, he pressed firmly against Asif's chest while Gisburne pushed the arrow.

At first, it resisted, and Asif gritted his teeth as Gisburne applied more pressure. He shook, and a sweat broke out on his face.

Suddenly the point broke free. De Rosseley grabbed the bloody arrow and whipped it out from the front.

The moment of triumph was short lived. As Aldric approached, the knife blade smoking, blood began to flow faster. Asif choked, his lips turning blue.

Gisburne tried to stop the blood, but he already knew it was hopeless. Asif coughed, his eyes bulging. He could not draw another breath. He tried to speak, and Gisburne drew in close, hoping to hear some last words. But none came. Asif's head fell back.

All stared in silence, the fire crackling.

Then something stirred behind them. "I told you!" hissed Scarlet. "Skewered!"

Mélisande stepped forward and without hesitation slashed her knife across his throat. His eyes bulged in disbelief as he watched his own gurgling blood cascade into his lap. "And I told *you*," she said.

De Rosseley stood, jaw clenched, sword in hand, and without a word turned for the door.

"No!" called Gisburne, leaping forward and grabbing de Rosseley by the shoulder.

The knight turned on him, sword raised, then checked himself. "He must be made to pay for this," he said.

"He will," said Gisburne. Then he glanced again at the wooden cylinder and knew it was time. "And I mean to do it."

"You're not going out there?" said Mélisande.

"They will try to get arrows from the armoury," Gisburne said. "First, that chance must be eliminated. Then Hood." As she watched, he took off his belt, threw off his gauntlets and his horsehide coat. Then the heavy mail coat came over his head and fell to the floor.

"Are you mad?" said Mélisande, wide-eyed.

Gisburne buckled his sword belt and quiver over his plain black tunic. "You heard what Scarlet said. He won't kill me."

"And you *believe* him?" she said, incredulous.

Gisburne said nothing, but took up his bow, then went and crouched over the long wooden box.

"Galfrid—stop him," she pleaded.

The squire turned from his post at the door, gave her a long look and said—for once, without a trace of irony—"He knows what he's doing. You have to trust him."

"But without your mailcoat..." she said, turning to him again.

"It's going to get hot," he said.

"At least wear this..." said de Rosseley, and he held out the tough, battered coat of horsehide. "I wouldn't know you without it, and they might not either."

"Keep it safe for me," said Gisburne. Then he prised open the wooden cylinder.

Aldric peered over his shoulder at the contents: a dozen arrows, nothing more. But instead of iron arrowheads, they were tipped with strange earthenware bulbs, each sealed with wax and little bigger than a plum.

"Llewellyn's parting gift," he said, and loaded them carefully, one by one, into his quiver.

"Tell me," he said to de Rosseley, "how Richard beat the impregnable stronghold at Taillebourg?"

De Rosseley frowned, and shrugged. "The Lionheart didn't attack it at all. He systematically destroyed everything around it— every village, every field—until the horrified garrison was drawn out into open battle."

"Destroy everything they hold dear..." said Gisburne. "That's been Hood's strategy. And now it's mine." He gazed at the bloody, featherless arrow that had killed Asif, lying on the ground. Stooping, he picked it up. Hood's arrow. "You all want vengeance.

Well, now you'll see it done. I will draw him out, and when he comes I will drive this into his rotten heart." He tucked the arrow into his belt. "Remember what you need to do," he added. "And keep water near."

Then he burst out of the door into the driving rain.

LXIX

THE SKY WAS already beginning to lighten as Gisburne emerged. But dawn was to come early that day.

The first arrow flew from Gisburne's bow and struck the treetop armoury, exploding into blinding flame. As the wave of heat hit him he set another on his bow, drew and shot. The second burst of Greek Fire would make sure of it.

He did not know whether they had seen him, but they surely knew he was there now. Hood's armoury—his arrows, his bows, his new revolution—were being consumed by flame in front of his eyes. That would hurt him. And there was something else that would hurt him even more.

Gisburne turned his attention to the tree beyond the hall—perched within its thick branches, a hut that was almost the mirror image of the armoury. The treasury.

He stalked closer, rain coursing down his face, then loosed another of Llewellyn's arrows. And another.

The treasury roared into flame. The village glowed golden. From the hall, he heard Marian's manic laughter as the fire spread.

Then the wolves came.

Gisburne stood at the end of the village, silhouetted against the pulpit stone, and let them come. Two. Three. Five. No more than five.

In the stark light, they looked lean and hungry. They wove through the village, arrows on their bows—and then they saw him.

"There!" One pointed.

But Gisburne's bow was already drawn. "Welcome to Hell!" he shouted. Flames burst to the left of them as a hut was engulfed. They recoiled in shock and terror—but then flames blossomed on their right, the heat pushing them back once more.

He shot again. And again. One by one, the huts burst into flame until the terrified bowmen, cowering as if from dark magic, were surrounded on all sides by the crackle and roar of consuming fire, herded into a tight group.

Then arrows flew from the hall, and they cried out as they fell.

They ran. But Gisburne's company was out of the hall now, cutting them down as they scattered. One turned on Gisburne, bow drawn—and Gisburne loosed the last of his fire arrows into the man's chest. He shrieked as he turned to a column of flame, his wildly loosed arrow—aflame from tip to nock—roaring through the air over Gisburne's head and shattering against the rock.

Gisburne moved forward, sending two regular arrows into the outlaws—one sinking into a man's back as he ran at de Rosseley and killing him outright, the other felling a great haystack of a man who was still running with three arrows in him.

Then, suddenly, no one was running.

They stood, looking about them, lit by flame, sweat on their faces, the crackle and hiss of the fire mingling with the moans of the dying.

Only now was it dawning on Gisburne's company that it might be over—that Hood's men were finished.

But as they turned over the bodies, what Gisburne already knew slowly became apparent:

Hood was not among them.

"Where is he?" said Mélisande, scanning the shadows beyond the trees, made darker than ever by the surrounding flames

"He'll come," said Gisburne.

Aldric, gazing about him with a stunned expression, drew closer to Gisburne. "I have never seen anything burn with such ferocity," he said.

"Courtesy of Llewellyn of Newport," said Gisburne.

"Best Greek Fire west of Byzantium," said Galfrid.

Aldric smiled, and forced cheer into his voice. "I should like to meet with him. Find out what's in it."

"Talk to him nicely and he'll give you the recipe," said Mélisande.

Aldric frowned, and sniffed the air. "That smell... Smells like..." Then he caught sight of the man Gisburne's last fire arrow had burned—or what remained of him—and Gisburne thought he paled a little, and swayed.

"It'll be over soon," said Gisburne.

Aldric turned to him. "I'm sorry, I—"

He never finished the sentence. The words turned to a cry, and he spun about and fell, a crossbow bolt in his right shoulder.

Mélisande pointed towards the trees: "There!"

With a growl, the Norseman ran forward—but a second bolt slammed into his collarbone and sent him reeling.

Two shots. This was their chance... "Get him!" says Gisburne. "Alive if you can!"

Ross and Galfrid plunged into the trees. The Norseman—still somehow on his feet, driven by pure vengeance—went crashing after them.

They hauled Aldric to the edge of the trees by the hall and propped him against an oak. "It's all right," he insisted. "I'm all right."

"It needs attention," said Mélisande.

"I know what it needs," said Aldric, then shuddered. "I've been here before, remember?" He gave Gisburne a weak smile. "Other shoulder this time. At least I'll be equally crippled on both sides."

Gisburne put his hand on Aldric's arm and was about to speak when a horrifying shriek split the air. Gisburne and Mélisande stood and turned. They silently placed arrows on their bows—and Marian burst from the hall and ran headlong for the trees, half-screaming, half-laughing, her ragged shift soaked by the rain. Gisburne went to pursue her as she fled, but then something made him turn back— back to what she had fled, what had made her scream.

And there, in the doorway of the hall about the great central oak, a figure loomed.

"She's quite mad, you know," said Hood, stepping forward, his face lit by the fire, his eyes glinting like a devil's. His bow was ready— one arrow upon it, one other in his bow hand.

Gisburne blinked away the rain and looked at Mélisande. It was a mistake, her being here. A terrible error. This was supposed to be between him and Hood.

"Go," he whispered.

She stared at him. "What?"

"Go," he said, louder. "Away from here. To safety. This is not your fight."

"*Now* you tell me this is not my fight?" she said. "You're dreaming, Gisburne. Here is where I stay."

"You see?" said Hood. "Women. Impossible." He sighed deeply and gazed after Marian. "Poor Rose. She was quite charming once, too. But one tires of them, don't you find?"

But Gisburne wasn't listening. He was thinking how fast Hood was at drawing his bow. He was wondering if he could match it—and he was thinking about Mélisande, who should not have been here.

"I have often wondered whether it would be you who killed me," said Hood, changing the subject. "Even as far back as Jerusalem."

Gisburne stood for a moment, listening to the patter of the rain blending with the crackle of the flames. "Because I discovered you were a murderer?" he said.

The words bounced off without leaving a mark. "There just seemed something *fitting* about the possibility. Poetic, almost. Don't you think so?"

"I think it sounds like the rambling of a madman."

Hood's face fell and his eyes hardened. Then it passed and his expression contorted into a child's pouting parody of sorrow.

"Do you really think you can kill me?"

"You know I can."

"True," said Hood, snapping back to his normal self—whatever that was. "It's one of the things I always liked about you. But then again..." He cast his eyes up, as if searching for words. "It's not... whether a man *can*, but whether he *will*."

The hairs stood up on Gisburne's neck at his choice of words. Thynghowe, nearly two months earlier. The ill-fated, nocturnal gathering of barons. "You were there..."

"I'm always there," said Hood with a smile. "I'm everywhere."

Gisburne saw Hood's fingers tighten against the string of his bow. He felt his own shoulders tense. Hood took a step sideways, and Gisburne matched him, stepping the opposite way.

"I was disappointed when you said no," said Hood. "I was looking forward to it."

"I know you were," said Gisburne. "That's why I said it."

"Hmm... It's like the way you persist in calling me 'Robert,' just because you know it irritates me. If I didn't know better, I'd say these were not the actions of a good friend."

"I? Your friend? I've come to kill you."

"Just because you want to kill someone, doesn't mean you don't love them."

"I heard the Lionheart utter the very same words not three days ago. You two really were made for each other."

"Precisely my point! When I learned that it was he who had sent you, I was in raptures! Well... we'll see who wins the game."

"You think you can win against *him*?"

"Why not? I've nothing better to do with my time."

"I heard about your little plan—with O'Doyle."

Hood's face fell a little. "Scarlet blabbed, did he? Well, he deserved what he got, then. Horrid little man."

"It's a suicide mission you've sent him on," said Gisburne.

"They're by far the most interesting, I find. Though there's always the chance he might actually *succeed*. How interesting *that* would be!" He chuckled, then sighed again. "The hardest part was keeping him from killing you. He really doesn't like you, you know. Another reason he had to go."

Gisburne laughed a grim laugh. "Gods... Whatever will people do for entertainment when you are gone?"

Hood chuckled. "Oh, this is where the *real* entertainment begins." He took a step forward. Gisburne and Mélisande tensed. "You think I care for the life in this body? No, no, no! When I die, *that* is when I am truly born."

"I never knew you were so pious, Robert."

"Heaven? God and the angels? Now those really *are* the ramblings of a madman. No, I mean to live forever—like your friend said, except that I really *will*, in the hearts and minds of men."

"You will be forgotten as surely as the grave worms will pass you into the soil," said Gisburne.

"You really think so... It's happening already, Guy. Songs, stories, rituals, superstitions. These are the building blocks of immortality—stronger by far than the stones of those dreary cathedrals your squire loves so much. And do you know why that is?"

Gisburne felt no desire to answer.

"Because a stone is just a stone, and in time, people forget why they were put there. They become no more than a bland enigma. But a story, a song... People never forget why *they* are there, why they need *them*." He grinned, and his eyes glinted. "You will be remembered too, you know. Oh, yes! Just... not so kindly." He shrugged. "But it's out of our hands, old boy. It no longer matters, now, what I am, or what I do. I am already their hero. And I will always be so, growing, changing, according to their needs. All it takes to live forever is to be freed from the tyranny of truth. Of fact. Of history. Throw off these chains, and what might we not become? No, it doesn't end here, least of all if we kill each other. It *begins*."

"Are you just going to talk all night?" said Mélisande.

Hood drew his bow so fast that Gisburne, who was looking right at him, did not even see it. All he saw was a flash of burning hatred in Hood's eyes, his teeth bared like a wolf, and a bow from which the arrow had already flown. Mélisande uttered one brief, sharp cry, and he saw her flying backwards, her feet rising clear of the forest floor, the bow and the one arrow she had not had time to draw falling uselessly into the mud. She stopped hard against a tree, then sank to the wet ground with Hood's arrow in her chest.

"She shouldn't have interrupted," sighed Hood.

Gisburne, his every sense overthrown by rage and horror, drew without thought. Some part of his rioting brain registered a second arrow upon Hood's bow, as Gisburne, the string drawn back past his ear, loosed wildly, hearing his own roar as he did so.

It was a savage shot, all instinct.

But the arrow flew true.

Hood was already close to full draw when it hit. Gisburne's arrow point struck the straining bowstave, glanced off and passed through Hood's left shoulder, leaving a string of blood in its wake. Hood's great warbow, bent almost to breaking point, exploded into a thousand shards of yew, its splintered parts spinning in every direction. But as it did so, his arrow also left the bow.

Gisburne heard a hiss, and a crack, and something struck his head with the force of a hammer. There was a searing pain; his knees buckled beneath him. Tasting blood, he put his left hand up to his face, realised that he could not see it, then felt the hot splash upon his palm. Then the hand met something solid—sharp—where it should not be, protruding from his left eye.

As the hand made contact, a white heat of pain tore through his head. He may have cried out—he wasn't sure. Lights flashed and crackled. A continuous, high-pitched note played, so loud it blocked out all else. With a weird detachment, he realised he could no longer distinguish between the pain he felt and what he saw or heard. Vision blurring in his remaining eye, he looked back up, across the fire-lit clearing. A cloud of dust still hung in the air where Hood's bow had been destroyed.

But there was no Hood.

Gisburne's head swam. He blinked hard to clear his one good eye—and the other burned as if stuck with a hot poker. He fell forward then, the darkness drawing itself over him, his last conscious vision that of Mélisande slumped against the tree, eyes staring, face deathly pale, a single tendril of sweat-soaked hair upon her brow, and an arrow in her heart.

LXX

Sherwood Forest
29 March, 1194

THE FIRST THING he saw was a bloody handprint.

His eyes could barely focus, but it was there, in the flickering half-light, stamped upon rock. He blinked, frowned at it. Where he was, he couldn't tell. But he knew he was shifting in and out of consciousness. The dream—the nightmare—had been a taste of Hell: it seemed a perpetual torment, something from which there would be no escape. In the dream, Mélisande had died. His heart still pounded at the memory of it—still half-believed in it. But now he knew that was not real, and this was.

Thank God.

Through the indistinct haze, he now saw that there were others like it—more handprints, some no bigger than a child's—all in faded colours. And around these, dancing in procession across the uneven surface of the rock, strange little stick figures: men, animals, other things he could only half-identify.

They swirled. The room—if room it was—began to spin.

And then he remembered. The Forêt de Boulogne. This was the Forêt de Boulogne. The cave in which Mélisande nursed him. He nearly died, because of Tancred. But... That couldn't be right.

Tancred died, in a different forest. He saw it. And that cave... It was more than two years ago. He remembered everything, now—all that followed: the battle at Castel Mercheval, the skull of St John the Baptist, capturing Hood, his escape from the Tower, the Red Hand, and Mélisande...

Then he realised. That wasn't the dream; this was.

His limbs flailed. He felt like a straw doll. Fighting to open his right eye, he found it stuck fast. It felt covered in tar. It tore open suddenly and he thought he saw flames licking. Blurred shadows moving.

He tried to lift his head, and all turned to black.

HE CRAWLED ON his belly, sticky, sweaty, blind. Half of him was hot, the other cold and wet. Leaves and mould, sticking to him. There was flame—he could hear the crackle, smell the smoke, feel the heat on his skin. But his eyes registered nothing. One was real, one not. But which?

The left side of his head felt like it was splitting. His hand went to it, unthinking; something sharp pierced his palm and pain and light exploded in his head. A single, incessant note scraped across the inside of his skull.

Fucking hurdy gurdy...

He crawled, with no idea where he was heading. The heat subsided, gave way to the cool and damp, and he staggered to his feet, hands held out before him, not knowing whether he was stumbling to safety or into a trap.

He saw Mélisande. Dead, an arrow in her. Not real. No, he did not want that to be real.

Shapes and colours began to swirl. Then suddenly the ground gave way. He fell. The shock of icy water.

And all went black once more.

LXXI

HE AWOKE SHIVERING under a black sky.

Water. He had been in water. He lifted his right hand and realised he still was, although only inches deep. His sight had returned—to one eye, at least. Lifting his head slowly, he tried to focus on the bright horizon beyond his feet, but his vision blurred. He blinked to clear it, and the pain shot through his head again.

He remembered.

He lay still for a moment, allowing time for his faculties to return, testing each limb with tentative movements. And, bit by bit, he began to make sense of his surroundings.

The water he was lying in was slimy and still—only a couple of inches deep by his head, but deeper towards his feet. He waggled them. Perhaps a foot deep or more.

Above him was rock. He smelled mud and mould and decayed animal. When he lifted his head, he could see that the bright horizon was a strip of daylight beneath a rock overhang—a ragged curtain of foliage in front of it, and the glimmer of running water beyond.

And before it, his face bobbing close to Gisburne's chest, was a dead man. The bearded visage was pale and bloated, the eyes bulging, but Gisburne recognised John Lyttel nonetheless—washed here by the current, his quarterstaff drifting in the still water by his side. To have survived, to be clinging to sight, and for this to be the first face he saw... It crushed what remained of his heart, made it something harder.

He understood now. He must be close to where they had crossed the log bridge. That was where Lyttel had gone to delay Hood; where he had died. And when Gisburne had staggered, blind, he had stepped right off the edge of the outcrop and into the stream. It was a miracle his brains hadn't been dashed out on a rock.

He had not escaped unscathed. He reached up and touched the flesh near where the arrow shaft was embedded in his left eye, and felt the fresh, warm ooze of blood.

There was a part of his mind that seemed somehow separate from his body, and able to apply cold logic to his situation. Had Hood's arrow hit him, he'd be dead. He also seemed to remember the sound of the impact *before* he was blinded. He concluded that the arrow must have struck a nearby tree and shattered, sending part of the shaft into his eye. That meant the barbed arrowhead was not in him.

Ignoring the flashes of pain and light that the slightest touch produced, he gripped the bloody, slippery shaft—all the while imagining the consequences if he were wrong.

The length of ash wood clicked against bone as he slowly drew it free, teeth clenched, knowing he must not cry out. The last of it slid out all at once. His head span. He thought he might vomit. Something thick dribbled down his left cheek, and he fumbled for something with which to bandage it, cursing himself for not having prepared it first. He pulled roughly at the edge of his tunic, but it was having none of it, so he gripped the protruding neck of his undershirt and yanked at that. A ragged piece barely the length of his hand tore off. He threw it down, and then—taking deep breaths to slow the pounding in his chest—drew his eating knife, found the bottom hem of the shirt, and cut away a long, even strip.

This, he wrapped about one half of his head. It was tight—too tight—but somehow this more familiar discomfort was reassuring.

His thoughts turned to what he must do next. It was impossible to know who or what was still out there. Perhaps Hood was dead—he saw his arrow strike him—but perhaps not.

He sheathed his eating knife and ran a quick audit. His sword was gone, the wood-lined scabbard snapped and twisted beneath his legs. But the seax remained in its sheath at his back. There was his eating knife, of course, and, tucked into the same belt, he still had the bloody arrow that had killed Asif. And Lyttel's quarterstaff bobbed nearby.

It was not much of an arsenal. He wasn't even sure how effective he *could* be in a stand-up fight. He flexed his shoulders and felt he could probably draw a bow—if only he had one.

Then he heard it. A familiar voice, singsong.

"*Gu-uy... Gu-uy...*"

Hood, calling him as one calls a cat or a dog. And he was getting closer.

Gisburne had hit him, he was certain of it. But the outlaw was not done yet. If Hood were to find him here, and could still draw a bow, Gisburne would be shot like a rat in a barrel.

He tried to prop himself up, but his head swam again. He knew he was weak from loss of blood. Hearing the crunch of footsteps above him, he lay, barely breathing, waiting—hoping—for Hood to pass. Perhaps he would not think to look here. Perhaps he did not even know this place existed.

"Where are you, Guy?"

Only then did it occur to Gisburne that he must have left a trail of blood. Hood would find him.

Gisburne drew out his seax, fingers tight around the wrapped cord grip. It was the one substantial weapon left him—but it was only useful if his enemy was close. He thought of Asif—poor, dead Asif—and his talk of throwing weapons. A stone, a disc. A knife.

He hefted the old seax and felt its weight, but the heavy blade would not serve. It would simply be throwing his most valued weapon away. Reaching out, he caught Lyttel's staff with the tips of his fingers and eased it towards him. It was the final parting gift from their brave ally. But what use was it in this low space? Gisburne cursed his stupid luck—a knife he could not throw, a staff he could not wield and an arrow he could not shoot.

His mind raced. The thought of tying the eating knife to the staff struck him; a spear would improve his chances, at least. But as he took up the seax again and began to unravel the cord wrapping, some other words of Asif's came to him: *A stick of wood and a string...*

He looked at the staff, and the seax. He had a stick. He had a string. And... He clutched at his belt. He had an arrow...

He raised his right knee and pulled the staff against it. It was no bowstave, but it had some flex in it. He went back to the seax's cord wrapping and unwound it as fast as he could, hoping to God it would long enough ...

It was—just. Whether it would hold was another matter—there would be no test, no second try. Just one shot, by which he would live or die.

With the seax, he chopped a notch near each end of the staff, then tied the cord in a bowyer's hitch about each end, tucking one loop into one of the grooves.

Then there was the arrow. He stared for a moment at the shaft, bereft of its feather fletchings. It needed something—something to catch the air, to make it fly straight. He hunted around for the discarded scrap of undershirt torn from his collar, found it floating in the water, squeezed it out, and with shaking hands tied it around the nocked end of the arrow. It would have to do.

He stopped for a moment, listening intently, suddenly aware that he could no longer hear Hood's footfalls.

"Guy?"

The voice was unbearably close—and now Gisburne fancied he could hear someone wading through the water.

He turned the staff sideways across the low cave, jammed the nocked end against the rock, pulled the other end towards him and pushed it hard against its belly. It bowed—reluctantly. He edged the remaining loop towards the groove, the whole bow quivering, suddenly fearful that he had tied it too short, that he would run out of time. The end of the staff slid against the rock. He gave one last shove—and the loop slid into place.

The sounds of displaced water drew steadily nearer.

He prayed that it would be enough. That the cord would not snap. That the staff would not break.

The wading stopped, and Gisburne held his breath. Then it began again.

He lifted his feet clear of the water, hooked the bow over them and drew back on the string. The he nocked the arrow, resting its shaft between his feet.

And he waited.

It had gone quiet again. He thought back to that time by the road, bow at the ready, waiting for Hood—who never came. It would not happen again. He wanted it over with. This time, live or die, it was to be on his terms.

He let out an audible groan, as of a dying man. Then he lay back, feet braced against the bow, squinting the length of the arrow. His head was pounding, and he struggled to judge the distance with his one eye.

And then a shadow loomed in the opening.

Gisburne drew back the cord, willing the bow to hold together. It cut into his fingers. He shook with the effort, but kept going, until the terror of the staff cracking became unbearable.

"*Gu-uy...*"

Gisburne released. The bow leapt forward, the string slapping his booted toes hard enough to numb them. He heard his arrow clatter against rock on the far side of the river, and his heart sank.

But the figure staggered backwards.

Then a little more.

It uttered a strange sound—like a sigh.

Gisburne realised the arrow had passed straight through him.

It was the last clear thought Gisburne had, before time slipped away from him again.

LXXII

HE DID NOT know whether moments or hours had passed when he emerged from the stinking hollow.

A fine rain was falling. He stood unsteadily and looked up at it, blinking in the daylight. Pain seared him as he blinked, but it was a different pain. The scoured, empty socket throbbed darkly, and he could feel the tattered lids pull at the improvised bandage.

Of Hood there was no sign.

He had hit him, that was certain. The outlaw should be dead.

He glanced up to the black crest of the escarpment, then along its ragged edge. No sign of life. He waded backwards a few paces, and the tarry reek of burned wood and blackened earth hit his nostrils. He saw a great pall of dark smoke rising from the direction of the village.

He stepped further back, and a dark shape to his left caught his eye: a crouched figure. He reached for his sword, but found he had only the empty, broken scabbard. The man did not move, and looked to be deep in prayer. Gisburne's left hand had reached for his seax and found that gone too—then he realised the man was dead.

He was one of Hood's; which one, he could not tell. It might have been Arthur a Bland. An arrow stuck out of his neck where it met his collarbone, but evidently it hadn't killed him outright. He had staggered the two hundred yards from Hood's camp before collapsing into a tangle of blackened briars, from which he now hung like a puppet. As Gisburne approached, he realised the man had also been on fire.

He waded out further, feeling the water's resistance, searching along the opposite bank. There: the arrow that had killed Asif. That was blackened with his blood – that was still sticky with Hood's, and now partly encrusted with grit.

It cannot have been long ago. He tossed the arrow in the water and watched it float away. It had served its purpose. Hood was dying.

He had to find him—to see it with his own eyes.

He turned and waded back to the hollow to retrieve his seax, shivering in the cold water.

And there, as he crawled under, he saw John Lyttel again. He sheathed his seax, caught hold of the big man's foot and hauled him out of that dank hole. It did not seem a fitting resting place. He didn't exactly know what would, but then an idea struck him and he floated the body out into the middle of the stream.

"Goodbye, John Attemille..." he said. Then he gave the body a shove, and let it be carried away by the swift water.

As he stepped back, his heel touched something and he heard the ring of metal. There, on the rounded stones in the clear water, lay Irontongue. He plunged his arm in and drew it into the air again, holding it briefly in his hand before feeding it into the bent, broken scabbard.

Hauling himself up the bank, he headed back towards the flames, one thought keeping him moving.

One terrible thought.

IF THE VILLAGE had been bad before, now it was a vision from Hell. The air was a pall of choking smoke, lit orange by the still-burning fires, stinking of pitch and burnt flesh. The ground was littered with the corpses of Hood's men—so many that in places the mud was puddled with red. The flames had spread to Hood's great hall and the ancient oak burned at its heart, with a heat as unbearable as the parched plain of Hattin. And amidst all this, passing strange, stood the smoking tree that had housed the treasury. It had burned with such fierce heat that the molten riches had cascaded in rivulets down the gnarled trunk, transforming it into a tree of silver and gold.

He found Mélisande still propped against the tree, her face pale as the drowned John Attemille's, Hood's arrow still in her.

He fell to his knees and wished to go back to the river—to be carried below its surface and sink into the oblivion of ever deeper waters.

He grasped her hand. It was warm, warmer than his. It must only have been minutes ago that he left here. Precious, lost minutes.

He bowed his head and listened to the flames.

She stirred. He started violently, thinking he had imagined it. Then he heard her halting breaths, and her eyes flicked open and looked right at him. He stared, dumbfounded. "You're alive..." she croaked. He almost laughed at that. Then she reached up and took his face in her hands.

He realised he probably looked worse than she did.

"I am sorry," he said.

She shook her head, smiling. "Don't be," she said. "Is it done?"

"Yes... I mean... I think so." He let his head drop. "I should not have brought you here. Dragged you into this."

"Dragged? You did not drag, you *invited*. I came of my own free will."

"If it weren't for me, you might now be fit and well in some castle somewhere..."

She smiled. "If it weren't for you, Gisburne, I'd be dead."

He frowned and shook his head; what she was saying made no sense. Then, to his astonishment, she sat up, unbuckled her belt, and pulled aside her surcoat, revealing the gleam of metal; the breastplate he had given her, Hood's arrow embedded in it. He helped her unbuckled the straps and then, shaking with the pain, she cast it and the arrow off.

"Broken rib, I think," she said. "Whatever you do, don't make me laugh..."

And then, laughing to himself with tears in his eyes, he held her to him. She winced and sucked in air.

"Sorry—does that hurt?"

"Yes," she said. "But don't stop." And she held him tighter.

A cough broke the spell. Gisburne stood and looked to the next tree, and there was Aldric. He had removed the bolt himself, and his arm was bloody and limp. But he was alive. "Don't mind me," he said. Then he dug his heels into the earth and slid himself up onto his feet against the wet tree trunk.

Gisburne laughed in relief. He helped Mélisande to her feet, then turned and looked across the fire-ringed courtyard of blood and bodies just as Galfrid and the Norseman—the crossbow bolt still in his shoulder—approached, dragging a battered and bloody Alan O'Doyle between them. They threw him on his face in the mud, and Galfrid tossed his fancy crossbow down next to him.

"Don't ever say I don't do anything for you," said the squire.

"I should like to study that..." said Aldric, pointing tentatively at the crossbow.

"It's yours," said Gisburne. Then he looked at Galfrid. "But how did you—?"

He was stopped by the next arrival, dressed in a black horsehide coat that had clearly seen better days. Only his limp gave him away.

"Ross?" said Gisburne.

De Rosseley threw back the hood. "You told me to look after the coat," he said. "But I thought I might as well make use of it. I knew O'Doyle would kill me on sight—but not you. So I became you. And as I led him a merry dance, these two"—he gestured to Galfrid and the Norseman—"circled around and finally got the bastard." He sighed. "Took them a bloody age, mind you."

O'Doyle had struggled onto his knees—something told Gisburne that his treatment at the hands of the Norseman had warned him against going further. Gisburne indicated he could rise to his feet, and he did. But still he looked at his captor with defiance.

"You know you're the last of them," said Gisburne. He cast an eye across the field of bodies. "The last one still alive, at any rate."

"Not quite the last," said O'Doyle. His glanced around furtively, as if he were uncertain whether to say more. But he was past caution now. "Hood's alive."

"You've seen him?"

"Walking out of the forest. Heading north."

"Injured?"

O'Doyle nodded.

"Badly?"

"Bad enough. But he won't stop; not until he's dead. And that's why I'm telling you this, Gisburne. So you know you have not yet won."

"He isn't dead yet," said Gisburne. "Which means you don't get to shoot at the King."

"It's not him I most want to kill," said O'Doyle.

Gisburne narrowed his eyes. "My quarrel is not with you, Alan O'Doyle."

"But mine is with you."

"What if I were to let you go?"

The Norseman growled darkly at the suggestion.

"Your father destroyed our family," said O'Doyle. "And you killed my brother. Don't pretend compassion now just to salve your conscience."

"It's not pretence," protested Mélisande. Gisburne looked at her in surprise. "At the end, on the Tower battlement, after the most bitter fight, Gisburne tried to save him." Her gaze went to Gisburne then darted away. "He did not know I saw it. Doubtless his mercy embarrasses him."

Gisburne stared at the ground. "He was my brother," he said. "Just as he was yours."

At this, O'Doyle's hard expression altered. He stood in silence for a moment, then took a step towards Gisburne.

The Norseman's axe felled him before he could take another. He collapsed, his head split in two.

The Norseman, his work done, vengeance taken, swayed and blinked as if only now affected by the bolt in his collarbone, then turned and walked away.

They watched as he picked his way across the courtyard to Tancred's lifeless body, lifted it, then turned again and walked in silence straight into the blazing inferno of Hood's great hall in a great whirl of sparks.

ACROSS THE BLACKENED, apocalyptic ruin of the grove, another figure staggered through the smoke.

Much. They watched as he walked by, seemingly oblivious to their presence, as if he would just keep going until he dropped.

"Much?" called Gisburne. The boy did not respond. "Much?"

The second time, he stopped.

"Micel," he said. "My name is Micel."

Gisburne nodded, then asked the question he feared the most. "What of Marian?"

"Dead," he said grim-faced. "And that was a mercy."

All Gisburne could feel now was relief. One less thing to carry.

"How?"

"She ran screaming from the escarpment. I heard the noise as she fell. Then I saw her carried away by the river, her head surrounded by weed, her dead eyes wide open." He bowed his head, his shoulders shaking.

"Leave this place, Micel," said Gisburne. "Run from it. As far as you can. But remember all that it has taught you."

And with no further word, Micel turned and ran.

"WHAT NOW FOR us?" said Mélisande.

"We bury Asif," said Galfrid.

Gisburne nodded.

"And after that?"

"For you, Aldric Fitz Rolf, nothing."

"That's it? You're abandoning me in the woods with a crossbow wound yet again?"

"Last time I told you to find a new master. A better master," said Gisburne. "This time, I mean to provide something more tangible.

When we reach our horses, go straight back to Nottingham Castle and find Llewellyn of Newport. They will say he is not there—may even deny he exists—but persist. Tell him I sent you. There is no better physician. But the man is also old and in need of an apprentice. This is the future I promised you."

"And you?" said Aldric.

"Hood is still out there."

"You must rest," protested Mélisande. "You're injured. Half-dead."

"I won't rest until I've seen him in his grave," said Gisburne. "Keep your bows ready and on your backs. Gather what arrows you can."

"Where will he go?" asked de Rosseley. "Where *can* he go?"

But Gisburne already knew the answer.

LXXIII

Kyrklees Priory
30 March, 1194

BRIGA WAS IN the herb garden when the bell rang. It was not the steady, ordered bell of Prime or Sext. They were hours from either—this was the urgent clamour of alarm.

She squinted up at the Priory building. There were no cries, no suspicious plumes of smoke. Nothing to indicate trouble, but for the wild tolling of the bell. She cursed her poor old knees and hoped it would be worth the effort of getting to her feet.

Then a shrouded figure flew from the doorway, and was sure that it was.

The past few weeks had been troubled. Her relationship with Prioress Magdalena had become strained, and in the past day that tension had only been increased by the new arrivals.

The injured men had claimed to be survivors of some battle, and certainly they showed signs of having been in combat. They were roughly clad and underfed, but well muscled—from using the bow, Briga thought.

Yet Briga had heard of no such battle, thought they looked more like labourers and poachers than soldiers, and suspected they had made the journey on stolen horses. It worried her who they might be harbouring, but Magdalena had welcomed them with open arms.

It was the journey that most troubled her. Most were tight-lipped about the battle itself, but one or two had mentioned Nottingham.

And that, in itself, was a puzzle. It was a good sixty miles to Nottingham. Two days' ride, at a fair pace; one, at a considerable push—a push some of them had clearly made. But there were any number of abbeys, priories and houses of healing within a few miles of Nottingham. So why had these men come here?

Briga suspected it had some connection with their mysterious benefactor—the one who, in recent months, had taken to leaving treasure at their gate, and which Magdalena accepted without question. "Gifts from God," she called them. The wages of righteousness. Though none dared speak the name, most knew from whom they came; and while many idolised him, Briga begged to differ. She had heard other tales—of threats, of torture, and worse. If these men had *him* as master, then having them here was only inviting trouble—and aiding villainy.

The men were tight-lipped about this, too, and when asked directly—Briga had a tendency towards directness—had looked about as if they were being watched or heard, and said nothing. Briga had only ever seen its like in those who feared offending God.

Briga's directness had added fuel to her problems with the Prioress, though they were not the cause. The mysterious gifts at the gate seemed to have brought about a schism within the Priory; certain nuns fell out of favour with the Prioress. There were whispers of victimisation—by the Prioress herself and the other nuns. And the cruelty had not limited itself to verbal abuse or unfair treatment.

It had come to light when a young nun of high promise—Sister Matilda—had come to her for advice on a scriptural matter. The girl had always been bright, passionate and pious—a rare combinations in Briga's experience—but of late had been strangely subdued. Briga had questioned her, hoping to help if there were problems the girl was having. She had laughed it all off, but when Briga had taken her hand and seen the angry burns upon her forearm, she had recoiled as if in pain. Briga asked if she had suffered them in the kitchens, and when the girl had failed to answer, pressed harder. Finally—quite unexpectedly—she had broken down, and the wild stories came out. In public, Prioress Magdalena was all kindness and civility; but in private, she hated the girl. She called her sinful, and worse things that Matilda would not repeat. She had had other nuns hold her down and had applied hot irons—to drive out the badness in her, she'd said. And she made her swear before God not to tell.

That she had now broken that vow told Briga that this was no wild fantasy. And wild fantasies do not burn flesh.

Briga's world had turned upside down. She'd tentatively addressed the issue with Magdalena, who had, of course, dismissed it. But then Matilda became ever more withdrawn, even avoiding Briga. Then the old nun knew what perhaps she had long known, but refused to believe: that it was all true. That Matilda was now suffering even worse treatment, and felt she could not even trust Briga. And why should she, when it was Briga herself who had brought this upon her?

In her halting confession, Sister Matilda had spoken of cuts, scalds, scourging and much worse. Things she would not name. Briga now began to suspect that beneath the ordered surface of the priory a deeper darkness lurked, that there had been others who had suffered similar indignities, perhaps over years, but were too afraid to speak out, or else accepted them gladly. There were a few, she was now sure, who colluded in Magdalena's secret punishments for their own warped pleasure.

Over the weeks, after the scales had fallen from Briga's eyes, another matter came into focus, one that had always troubled her. The death of Magdalena's predecessor, Elizabeth of Staynton.

Her sudden illness and death had taken all by surprise, and none had taken it harder than Magdalena. She spent hours in prayer, until she collapsed from exhaustion. She wailed in grief. She flagellated herself for her failings. All thought it the greatest demonstration of her devotion to Elizabeth. Only Briga was troubled by it.

In death, Elizabeth had suffered delirium and hallucinations. Magdalena called her "blessed," and said she had been granted ecstatic visions on her path to holy bliss. But Briga, who had tended her to her last breath, knew they were far from ecstatic. Her visions were nightmares, and wracked the Prioress's body with pain. Symptoms that in their suddenness could be ascribed to belladonna.

She had dismissed the suspicion as incredible, but now she began to feel differently about them. In recent days, she'd sensed that her own usefulness had come to an end, and that Magdalena resented the part the old nun had played in her rise to power. In the past two weeks, as the troubles with Sister Matilda had brewed, Briga had even become wary about her food and drink.

"What is it, Sister?" she said to the nun. It was Sister Agertha— one of the few of Magdalena's faithful who was also still friendly to her.

"A man..." panted Sister Agertha, sounding more excited by the prospect than Briga felt a nun had the right to. "No, not just a man..." Her face beamed, as if she had just laid eyes on Christ himself.

"You're not making sense, girl. Calm down and tell me plainly."

"Come and see!" she said, and turned and dashed away.

Briga struggled to her feet and hobbled after, coaxing her old legs back to life to take her to this new wonder.

From the small herb garden that Briga herself had established over thirty years ago, there were two doorways back into the Priory: one led to the cloister, past the kitchens and refectory, and the other— considerably smaller—led directly into Magdalena's cell.

Except at night, the door to the cloister was always open. Magdalena's door was always closed.

What now served as Magdalena's cell had once been a communal parlour, its small adjoining room serving as the Priory's library. On becoming prioress five years before, Magdalena had declared the library would soon outgrow this cramped space, and relocated it above the western range, reorganising the space around it to serve as a new parlour. Most of the nuns were thrilled at the change— it was a sign that Kyrklees was advancing, expanding its fund of knowledge and securing its place in the world. Briga alone, it seemed, watched as Magdalena took both the old library and the parlour for her own, and wondered at it.

She had had too many occasions to wonder of late, but back then, she had put her doubts aside. She had helped Magdalena into this position, after all—had been per protector and mentor all these years, ever since she had come to the Priory, a lost wretch of a thing, barely seventeen. One might even say Magdalena had been her life's work. Some people tried to change the whole world—an ambition that was both futile and vain in Briga's view, even for kings. Far better, it seemed to her, to cultivate one's own garden with proper care—to change just one life for the better.

She had never had children—her vocation had called long before that was ever a possibility. Perhaps, in this, she was fulfilling that instinct. If that was selfish, well, at least it also helped. And did the Church not idolise motherhood?

Magdalena *had* been a mother. None talked about that now—few even knew of it—but the instincts and drives she now indulged were of quite a different kind.

Magdalena herself was just arriving when Briga got to the cloister. A body of nuns—almost the whole priory—were gathered about something upon the stone floor, just yards from the main door. They parted as Magdalena approached, casting their eyes low to avoid her gaze, and Briga saw the man.

He was clad in green, in the manner of a forester, yet more outlandish. He was large, too—muscled like the others, but much more so. If he was an archer, as Briga supposed, he had been one all his life. His face, though cut and bloody, was handsome—impossibly so—his hair and beard neatly trimmed. He was also bleeding. And he was smiling.

Taken individually, none of these things were of any great note. Yet there was about him—in his face, his bearing, his clothes—that which inspired a sense of awe, even in Briga. And she understood at once why Agertha had been so stirred.

Magdalena stopped, and stared in wonder.

Wounded though he was, none had dared even to touch him.

"Is it really he?" she said, haltingly. She had many voices: the stern matron, the no-nonsense organiser, the loving angel at the bedsides of the sick. But now, she sounded like a girl again.

One of the nuns nodded eagerly.

"You're sure, girl?" said Briga, coming up alongside the Prioress.

"I saw him once before," the young nun whispered. "When I was little more than a child. At the tournament at Clippestone. There is no doubt."

Magdalena gave a great sigh and clutched at her breast, then crossed herself. And Briga heard her mutter, under her breath: "The Lord of the Forest..."

"What do we do?" said one of the older nuns. Briga could not see her, but recognised the voice: Sister Constance—ever one of the more practical ones. "Every baron in the north wants his head."

"We give him our care," said Briga. "Without judgement. Just like the others." Then she looked to Magdalena, suddenly aware she had answered in her stead.

But by some miracle, Magdalena's face showed no trace of anger. Instead, she seemed herself to be in a kind of ecstasy—transported by the sight of the figure at her feet.

"This one requires special care," she said. "Take him in there."

And she gestured across the cloister, towards the door of her own cell.

LXXIV

GISBURNE KNEW THE moment they arrived at Kyrklees that his instincts had been right.

Outside the priory's gate a horse was abandoned and wandering loose. Not just a horse, but a destrier, a knight's horse—worth more than a house, or five years of a labourer's life. The livery was familiar; it had belonged to one of the Knights of St Lazarus, and must have strayed after the battle. Even in dying, Hood was lucky.

The horse was streaked with foamy sweat and its legs were shaking; it was so thirsty that it was trying to drink from puddles whipped almost dry by the wind. Gisburne knew of no one who would abandon such a horse, or leave it in such a condition. No one except Hood.

Galfrid went straight to it, tipping water from his leather flask into his cupped hand for it to drink and speaking gentle words whilst Gisburne hammered upon the heavy wooden door.

His head reeled. He had lost blood, had barely slept. He felt ragged—wrung out. But he would see this through.

The rain had kept off, and the ride had been swift. They had said their goodbyes to Aldric at Nottingham and retrieved their horses from Hugolin, already making preparations to leave. Gisburne was glad to see Nyght—glad too, he looked well and rested. On the whole, the horses looked far better than their masters did.

All had been shattered by the death of Asif. De Rosseley, in particular, took it hard; he had known the Arab only a matter of days, but despite his jibes and jokes, Gisburne could see he had developed a great respect for him. If anything, that had made de Rosseley more determined to pursue the task. When Gisburne had suggested he stay at Nottingham with Aldric to have his leg properly treated, he had looked as if this were the grossest of insults. Gisburne had not pursued it after that.

Galfrid had been quiet, but it was a different kind of quiet from before. When he spoke, the hostility was gone. Gisburne felt that, at last, they were on an even footing, and of that he could not be more glad. When this was over, he would mend things properly with the squire. With his friend.

The door of the priory swung open with a clatter, and the face of a young nun peered out.

"Hood," said Gisburne. "Is he here?"

"I don't know what you—" she began, but Gisburne barge past.

"You do not push your way into God's house," said a firm voice ahead of him. There stood an old nun—seventy if she was a day— her face harder than a seasoned soldier.

Gisburne stopped and bowed. "I am sorry," he said. "I am forgetting myself. But our need is urgent." His head was throbbing, and his command of his battered body felt tenuous at best.

She looked them up and down. "You are in need of assistance?"

He realised they must look a rough crew—muddy, ragged, bloodstained. "We seek one called Hood," said Gisburne.

"First things first. Who are you?"

"Gisburne," he said. "Guy of Gisburne."

"And what is your interest in this Hood, Guy of Gisburne?"

"He is dangerous," said Gisburne, almost pleading. "To you, to everyone. We mean only to stop him."

She regarded him for an age. "You may find he has stopped without you," she said. "He was close to death when last I saw him." She stood to one side and gestured towards a door across the cloister.

He bowed again in thanks, and gestured for her to lead the way.

*　　*　　*

THE DOOR TO the Prioress's chamber was not fully closed. Gisburne pushed it with a finger and, as it creaked open, peered inside.

The chamber was empty. He crept in, uncertain quite why he felt the urge to remain silent, but going with the instinct. It was neat and orderly—sparse, as a nun's or monk's cell ought to be, but more spacious than most—and with its own fireplace. There was a small desk with a candle and quills for reading and writing, a simple pallet, a jug and bowl for water and a chamber pot. At either end of the pallet was a door: one, facing them, opened into gardens, just visible through the cloudy glass; the other, to their right, presumably opened into to another room. Both were closed.

The pallet was stained with blood; the floor was smeared with it, as if something had been dragged through the room to the right-hand door.

"What's in there?" asked Gisburne.

"That is the Prioress's personal library," said the nun. "No one is permitted in there."

Gisburne looked at Mélisande, then back at the old nun.

"There are manuscripts that only those of the strongest faith are permitted to see," she added—but sounded as if she did not believe it herself.

"Is there any other way out?"

"No."

"Locked?"

"Always."

"Then we'll kick it in," said de Rosseley, apparently forgetting the state of his leg.

The old nun looked momentarily alarmed, but then, after a moment of decision, reached into a crevice in the fireplace, produced an iron key and placed it on Gisburne's palm.

"I have never used it," she explained, "but I have always known."

"Clearly your self-control is greater than mine," muttered Mélisande.

There was a sound from beyond the door, a ringing clatter of metal striking the floor. Gisburne knew from the sound exactly what it was.

"Do you normally use knives in a library?" he whispered—but the old nun just stared back at him, bemused.

They positioned themselves about the door as Gisburne drew his sword, turned the key in the lock and shouldered the door open.

None could have been prepared for what they saw.

A nun—the Prioress, Gisburne was sure—leapt back in shock, something falling from her hands to clatter on the stone flags with a splash of red. She stared from one to the other, and whimpered.

Upon a table before her, Hood lay spread out, dressed only in a white linen shirt, his arms stretched out like the Christ. The veins in both wrists had been opened, and as Gisburne stepped forward he saw that his blood was draining into cups on the floor: one brimming full, one—as yet—half empty.

A third cup lay where the Prioress had let it fall. Her quivering mouth was ringed in dripping red.

The old nun crossed herself.

Gisburne stepped forward, feeling the gorge rise in his throat. The Prioress whimpered again, shook her head and backed away, Hood's blood glistening upon her hands and face. Then, as he looked about the gloomy chamber, he saw its shelves filled with horrors: mummified body parts, pieces of skin—possibly human, aborted foetuses in jars, scored bones. Weird fetishes fashioned from dead animals. If this was a religion, it was not any that Gisburne knew.

"It is his power," she whined, as if it explained everything. "The Lord of the Forest... We must drink of it... It raises us up... Makes him part of us!"

"Do you not see, woman?" barked Gisburne. She jumped back at his words. "Do you not *know?*"

She frowned, and whimpered, and moved her bloody hands about.

"Upon his neck," said Gisburne. "Look there!"

She leaned over, poking at the slender band about his neck with a crimson finger, speaking in a pathetic voice. "But... there is nothing but a thong of leather..."

"Look again!" roared Gisburne, and stepped forward. The woman flinched. He reached around the back of Hood's neck and dragged the copper disc on the thong to the front.

"See?" he said, turning it towards her. For a moment, her face was blank; then realisation dawned, and she took a step back. Behind him, the old nun uttered a cry.

"Do you know it?" he said. She shook her head—put bloody hands to her ears. "Do you recognise it? You should! He's part of you already, woman. Your own *son!*"

Her head still shaking, she gave a wail which seemed like it would dissolve into tears, but which instead just grew and grew into a horrifying scream, and she burst past them, habit flying, out through the cell and into the cloister, screaming and screaming like some crazed animal.

The company ran in pursuit and were just in time to see her stop within the courtyard—suddenly still, suddenly silent. It appeared she had run into the embrace of a young nun, whose presence had miraculously quelled her madness. Then she slithered to the ground, her own blood pooling about her, and the cause of the miracle became plain. The young nun, whose haunted face showed no emotion, was gripping a knife, now wet with her Prioress's blood.

The old nun, hobbling behind them, looked on in horror. "Oh, God! Sister Matilda!" she said, her voice quaking. "Oh, God!"

Another cry went up—from Mélisande, this time. "Gisburne!"

He turned; she was still by the cell door.

"It's Hood..."

He ran back, his body feeling heavier than it had ever felt in his life, a new, indefinable dread growing in him.

Hood's body was gone from the table in the demonic chamber. The door to the gardens was now open, a spattered trail of blood leading through it.

He followed. Up ahead, Hood staggered drunkenly through the graveyard, powered by some impossible reserve, as if somehow blessed with ten times the life of a normal man.

Gisburne sheathed his sword, unslung his bow, and drew an arrow from his quiver. But as he placed it on the bow, watching the white figure reel into the meadow, a great tiredness came over him. His shoulders slumped. What was the point? What reason did he have now?

And, exhausted, he walked on through the graveyard, towards the spot where Hood, his strength gone, finally collapsed.

They stood over him as he lay, his breathing laboured, the bloody saviour of the greenwood.

"Please..." he whispered, his voice husky. "A bow..."

It was so absurd that even now Gisburne laughed. "Are you mad?"

"*Please...*" said Hood. There was genuine pleading in his voice. It was the first time Gisburne had ever heard it in him. He tried to raise himself up, but slumped back. His breathing was coming fast now, his face paler than his shirt. "One... last... shot," he said. "I lived... by the bow. Let the bow... now decide... where I will be buried." He gestured towards the graveyard. "Not over there!"

"No," said Gisburne. "Do you think me a fool?"

Hood looked pained. "Guy... *Please...*"

In frustration, Galfrid stepped forward. "Give him the damned bow!" he said, snatching it from Gisburne and thrusting it and a single arrow into Hood's hands.

At the feel of them, the outlaw looked suddenly content, at peace. With feeble hands he placed the arrow upon the string. "Where this arrow lands," he said, "there shall I lie..." Then, with a sudden show of strength that made the hairs on Gisburne's arms stand on end, he drew the bow all the way to his ear—then turned towards them and loosed the arrow.

It smacked full force into Galfrid's chest. Eyes wide, the squire staggered backwards and fell. Gisburne cried out. Mélisande and de Rosseley rushed to him as Hood's laughter rang out across the quiet meadow.

"That's where I shall lie," he chuckled, pointing a feeble finger. "In the heart of an Englishman!"

They were the last words he ever uttered. With a howl of anguish, Gisburne drew his eating knife and plunged its slender blade deep into Hood's heart. He slumped to his knees, staring into Hood's shocked, but still smiling face.

Gisburne's heart thumped, and his breaths came hard and fast. He looked at Galfrid. His face, though in every detail familiar, looked strange and waxy—not like his old squire at all. In the strange, numb silence, Mélisande and de Rosseley seemed to be trying to help; to remove the arrow, to treat the hurt. He wanted to go to him, to speak with him, to hear some last words.

But there would be none. For Gisburne knew that Galfrid was already dead.

His mind reeled. He leaned over Hood, drew close to his face. Was there still life there? He placed both hands on the end of the knife and, with clenched teeth and a growl of rage, pushed it deeper still, until the black bog-oak handle all but disappeared into the welling, bloody wound.

A last hiss of air sounded in Hood's throat, and the cold light in his eyes was gone.

It was then that Gisburne saw it. The copper token—the worthless disc that had been Hood's only link with his origins—lay upon the outlaw's blood-drenched shirt. He had seen it a thousand times as he lived and fought at Hood's side—in Sicily, in Thessalonika, through the Holy Land. But the crude design he had seen so often made sense to him only now. For there, in rough pointillé work, was the image of a flower.

Rose... Hood's horse. The whore in Jerusalem. The name he gave to every woman he ever grew close to. The secret to the enigma had been right there, under his nose, the whole time. From the very first moment he had met him in Syracuse, at the inn under the sign of the blue boar.

Staggering to his feet, Gisburne began to laugh. Mélisande turned to him. She may even have said something, but he was only dimly aware of it. He could see only the disc clearly. Everything around it—around him—was blurring. He gripped it and yanked it free, chuckling like a fool, rubbing his thumb—wet with Hood's blood—over the dirty, corroded surface and turning to the light as if there were somehow more to be drawn from it, some magic yet to be unleashed.

If there was, it was of the darkest kind.

For as he looked at the curious little flower, he saw that it was no rose at all. Though it bore a superficial resemblance, some of the petals were tucked and turned, stylised to fit within a circle.

Hood had even distorted that truth. Ten thousand cursory glances had confirmed and reconfirmed what one close examination would have revealed to be false. He had seen what he wished to see, coining a legend—one told by him to him, and him alone, and all of it a mistake. A lie.

Gisburne laughed all the harder—he wondered if he would ever stop.

He turned the little disc between his blood-sticky fingers, and in his mind, the awkward little design started to unfurl, the petals returning to their proper shape. It began to look like something he had seen before.

Planta genista. Common broom.

Gisburne flung it wildly from him, as if it had burned his flesh—as if it were noxious poison. It flew, spinning in the air, the broken thong trailing behind, landing with a *plop* in the still water of the pond.

He stood for a moment, swaying, staring after the cursed token—Hood's final joke. The joke of which even Hood himself was not aware.

He saw Galfrid's dead body laid out upon the grass like a crude effigy. Mélisande's hand reaching out to him. Her face was clear for an instant—her mouth moving slowly. She was talking to him, but he could not hear what she was saying.

Then the world rocked and span and slipped off its axis. And the black fell about him once more.

LXXV

GISBURNE WOKE FROM a vivid dream on a pallet of straw, a sliver of sunlight glancing through the tiny window.

The feelings from the dream were still with him—fresh and vital as the day—and for a moment he lay gazing at the mote-speckled air, not daring to move for fear of dissipating them.

Galfrid had been alive, and was helping him fill the stone horse trough in the top paddock. It was sunny—he could smell summer in the air—and Galfrid was telling him a rambling, nonsensical story, which Gisburne—for reasons he could not unravel—had found absurdly funny. At some point—the passing of time was indistinct—he felt a hand on his back, and he knew it was Mélisande. Her cool fingers pressed the sun-warmed linen against his skin, and though he could not see her, he knew, with the same certainty that he knew his own name, that she was smiling.

It was not like most dreams. There was nothing strange or disjointed about it, nothing outlandish. It had all been quite normal, quite real. But it had another quality which, in his experience of dreams, was rare indeed. For he had felt utter contentment—complete, all-encompassing joy.

It had been real, for as long as it had lasted. He had believed it.

Never had he felt so reluctant to wake. He yearned to return, knowing it was impossible. And now, as he savoured its lingering impressions, he was losing even those. He was returning to the hard world, unwillingly accepting that what had just passed was all illusion.

He blinked in the light. He was in the Priory at Kyrklees. Blind in one eye. Galfrid was dead, and Asif. And Hood and Tancred too. But he—he was alive. It made little sense to him. He did not even want to try to make sense of it.

He had no idea what day it was or who was here with him; sleep— or perhaps the dream—had made his last waking memories seem impossibly distant. He was not entirely sorry about that.

Ross and Mélisande had been alive, last he remembered. He felt a sudden need to see them—but he had no idea whether they were in the next room or a hundred miles away. Part of him actually hoped for the latter; at least, then, he could inflict no further suffering on them.

He dragged himself up, his body heavy, his balance uncertain. His clothes, some close to rags, were folded and in a neat pile upon a stool, his sword stood without its scabbard in the corner, and his scrip bag hung upon a plain iron hook on the back of the low door. All his battered goods had been treated with care but for his mail coat, which sat in a pile on the rush-covered floor as if those here had not had the first idea what to do with it. He stood and pissed in the pot at the end of the bed, judging the distance badly. Then, with unsteady steps, his blind eye disorientating him, threw on his clothes—all but his sword and abandoned mail—and wandered outside.

Beyond the herb garden, in a small graveyard, an old nun stood by a new grave. He remembered her: the old nun who had welcomed them. As he approached, she turned; old she may have been, but her hearing was sharp as a cat's.

"You're awake," she said with a smile.

"So it would seem."

"My name is Briga. We met before, if briefly. It would seem I am now the Prioress. For the time being, anyway; we'll see what is decided when the dust has settled."

"Have I been asleep for long?" he said. He felt somehow foolish asking it.

"Two days. Do you feel well? Rested? No signs of fever?"

But Gisburne's gaze was on the mound of newly dug earth. There were fresh flowers placed there—primroses, wood anemones and the first wild daffodils of spring. Briga turned her attention back to it.

"Your squire," she said. And with those words, the reality of it—the awful finality—suddenly hit him.

"Yes," he said, though to what purpose, he did not know.

"We buried him in sight of the chapel." Briga's tone was neither severe nor sentimental, but had a simplicity and directness that Gisburne found immediately reassuring. "Lady Mélisande told us he would have liked that."

He thought to ask if she was here, but his attention was caught by two more mounds of earth some distance away—a deliberate distance, it seemed to him. Two more graves; mother and son. On these, there were no flowers.

"And them?" he said.

Briga glanced at them with distaste. "Those I shall not be visiting so often. But I suppose everyone deserves their plot."

Gisburne gazed beyond the edge of the graveyard, to the meadow where both Hood and Galfrid had died. In the spring sunshine, with insects buzzing, it seemed too idyllic to have played host to such horrors. He caught sight of the reeds by the pond, and remembered: the token, the flower. He shuddered, and pushed the memory down deep.

The little woman reached up and felt his forehead, then touched the bandage. "Your eye is healing well. You're lucky."

Gisburne snorted. "Lucky?"

"I've seen plenty of men die from lesser wounds."

"I'm not allowed to die."

Briga chuckled. "You think God has a purpose for you?"

"I don't flatter myself by thinking that."

The old woman's smile vanished. "It's not flattery. God has a purpose for us all. The trick is working out what it is." She stared off past the jumble of crooked stones to the fresh graves.

"Mine was to be tested by her. Yours was to be tested by him." She looked up into his face. "Your friends told me all about it, Sir Guy. Though I had heard your name before. In stories."

Gisburne shuddered again—at the thought of being the subject of stories, at what nonsense they might contain.

Reading his expression, she waved her hand dismissively. "I took those with a pinch of salt," she said. "And I was right to. I already suspected *he* wasn't what everyone said he was."

"I fear we brought disaster upon this place."

She shook her head in dismay. "Disaster was already here," she said. Then she turned to him, her face open and candid. "Do you know what makes me most angry? Not that she did evil; not that alone. It is that she persuaded people to believe in her. That she persuaded *me*. In all my years, this is the thing of which I am most ashamed. It was I who championed her, in spite of everything. I was so proud when she became Prioress. Sister Elizabeth—the Prioress before her—was never convinced. She said she was, but in truth she sensed something wrong, from the very start. And I—through naivety or vanity—refused to see it. For thirty years..." She shook her head again. "God, what have I done? How many have suffered at her hand, while my back was turned?"

"You cannot blame yourself for the sins of others."

"Can I not? It was I brought her here, Sir Guy, all those years ago. *I*. And it was faith made me do it. Do you know Vézelay?"

"I do."

She nodded. "I was returning from there—from pilgrimage—full of all the things such a place inspires. You know the Magdalene's relics reside there?" She sighed. "I had always loved the Magdalene... Then, passing through the Vexin, en route to the coast, I wandered into chaos. Soldiers everywhere. The land scoured. The place was on the brink of war."

"Old King Henry," said Gisburne distantly. "The King of France and the Count of Blois were pointing their lances at Normandy, but the Old King was having none of it. My father gave me chapter and verse."

"Well, I took refuge in a wood. A curious idyll, in the midst of it all. And there was this girl, barely more than sixteen. Barefoot, standing, staring. No bag or purse. No sign of how she came to be there. Just as if she had dropped out of the sky." She chuckled, once.

"She had been used by men, I did not doubt. But when I spoke to her, she answered in English. Perhaps she had been among the camp followers. I never did know. I'm not sure she did. But then she said her name was Mary. And I... I saw it as a sign. I had come from the shrine to Mary Magdalene, and here was this ragged, lost girl... She said she couldn't remember where she was from. So she came back with me. And that wood, I learned, was called *Le Bois d'Espeir*—the 'wood of hope'—after the fresh water spring that rises there. That fuelled my faith further still. And, for want of anything better, she became Mary of Hoppewood. I took her in, protected her. She must have had the babe growing in her belly even then."

Gisburne thought of the copper token. The flower that Hood— impatient, oblivious Hood—had always taken to be a rose. The secret at which it hinted was hidden now in but two places on Earth: sunk at the bottom of a pond, and in Gisburne's heart. And there it would stay.

"It's not your fault that you were deceived," he said. "That your trust was abused."

She looked him square in the face, her grey, sad eyes as bright as a child's. "It will always feel so. The nun who stabbed Magdalena... Sister Matilda. She was one of the purest souls I have ever met. And yet look what she was driven to. What other terrible things must have passed under this roof?" Her mouth quivered and she turned away, no longer able to hold his gaze. "The girl will do her penance, but she will have a chance to be redeemed. We owe her that much, at least. Christ teaches forgiveness. I, in turn, will try to forgive Magdalena. I will. But for now, I say *good riddance*." And, then shaking with rage, she actually spat at the Prioress's grave.

Briga wiped her mouth with the back of a wrinkled hand, then gave a humourless laugh. "See how her poison continues to infect? To spread hate?" She sighed heavily, as if trying to expel all her woes with one breath. "Faith is everything to me. It is my life. To think that it was misplaced for so long..." She shook her head, unable even to finish the sentence. "There are many sins, many crimes. But none more bitter than betrayal."

Gisburne looked at Hood's grave. "That man buried yonder—I cannot begin to reckon the evils for which he is responsible. Yet once, even I believed in him. Perhaps now he can finally do some good."

This last comment he had intended to be dismissive—to suggest that now, his blood and bones might at least enrich the soil—that though none would place flowers upon that grave, it may yet nourish new growth of its own. But even as he said it, the wider possibility occurred to him. What if Hood's wild boasts about his legend were true? What if, months or years from now, its distorted story inspired others to acts of genuine worth? Of valour, fairness, justice?

Would this not be the best possible revenge upon Hood—not for him to be lost to posterity, but to become its servant, and an agent for all the good things that he never once believed?

Suddenly, his thoughts went to the Christ—an earthly life ended in humiliation and torture, from which, nonetheless, the noblest of ideals sprang. Perhaps, even in Magdalena's crazed idolatry, there existed a grain of truth.

"*Doing*," said Briga, breaking in upon Gisburne's thoughts. "That is how I deal with things. Not sitting and brooding on what cannot be done, but by concentrating on what can."

She was speaking as much to herself as to Gisburne.

"That is a philosophy I wholeheartedly endorse," he said.

She nodded to herself. "I will personally scrub Magdalena's library clean of its filth. That will be my task, and my penance."

"Let the other nuns see it first," said Gisburne. "In fact, make sure they do."

Briga gave a weak smile and nodded.

Gisburne gestured towards the infirmary. "You tend to the poor and sick of Sherwood here?"

"We do," said Briga, happy to switch to this topic. "I never understood what compelled them to come all this way. Until now."

"More will be coming, out of the forest. The survivors of Hood's ministry. Give them food and shelter, and set them upon the right path. Show them what compassion is—empty though their bellies may be, that is the thing of which they have been most starved." He dug into his scrip bag and hauled out a thick leather purse, which he held out to her. "Here..."

"Our coffers are already full," protested Briga, her hand raised. "Hood's ill-gotten gains—though I am hardly comfortable that we have profited from his crimes."

"Keep it. Keep it all. Turn it to the good. And the purse, too. Please."

He pushed it closer, and reluctantly she took it. Her hand dipped at its unexpected weight, then with shaking, crooked fingers, she pulled apart the cords and peered in. The contents made her gasp. Not silver; gold. "Why, there is enough here to feed the five thousand..."

"Build a new chapel. Somewhere in sight of Galfrid's grave. And dedicate it to the Magdalene. The real one."

Briga smiled, bowed her head, and clutched the purse to her breast. Gisburne was happy to do without the rigmarole of a token argument. He had only known this woman these few minutes, but he liked her already.

"He might be alive now, were it not for me," he said. He did not know where the words came from—they seemed to emerge all on their own.

"You don't know that," said Briga. "He was his own man. Perhaps you helped him to truly live."

Gisburne nodded, numbly. But a sudden, desperate emptiness came upon him—one so profound, so overwhelming, that had another grave been lying open before him he would have let himself fall into it.

One of Briga's crooked hands shot out, and grasped his fingers. Her eyes were fixed on his with a fierce intensity. "You will think an old nun knows nothing of life and love," she said. "But listen to me: I was born the very same year as Queen Eleanor, may God bless and protect her." She crossed herself. "We are in our seventy-second year, she and I—both graced with long lives, and the challenges those bring. But none of us knows when we shall be called. So make the most of life. Cherish every second. Once wasted, years cannot be got back, and hollow regret makes a poor bedfellow..."

Gisburne stared down at her, dumbfounded. She gripped his hand tighter, and shook it in time with each of her words.

"Lady Mélisande... She loves you. Love *her*. Protect her."

He should have been taken aback, but there was something in her manner—an honesty—that made the sudden intimacy seem the most natural thing in the world.

"I don't think she needs my protection," said Gisburne, wondering, somewhere in the back of his reeling head, what exactly had passed between the two women.

Briga chuckled. "No, she does not *need* it. But that is not quite what I meant..." She cocked her head to one side, peering past his arm, back towards the Priory, and her face lit up. "Ah!"

Gisburne turned, and there, emerging from the herb garden, was Mélisande de Champagne, smiling as she approached; Sir John de Rosseley—bandaged, limping, but ever unbowed—following close behind.

And in that moment, he was decided.

LXXVI

Cliftone
April, 1194

"I HEAR RICHARD has spoken in praise of Gilbert de Gaillon," said de Rosseley. He sipped his cup of ale and looked across at the swaying trees. It was a beautiful day. A proper spring day, thought Mélisande. "Plans are also afoot to take his bones for reburial at Rouen—and his old lands are to be restored to his nephew."

Gisburne nodded. "That is good news indeed." He almost managed a smile. "I had never thought such a thing possible."

"What would any of us have done, if we'd stopped to think if it were possible?" said Mélisande. She smiled at Gisburne, but it seemed wasted on him. He looked like a man done with life.

"There's much I would not have done," conceded Gisburne, staring into the depths of his cup.

The three of them were sat around a table outside an inn. The sun shone; the spring air was fresh and charged with new possibilities. But Gisburne was like the last chill wind of winter.

"Well..." said de Rosseley after a moment. "It would seem all your goals are achieved. Tancred is redeemed. You are released from Prince John's service and have a generous gift from the King. And Hood is finally gone."

"Gone..." said Gisburne, with a grim laugh. "Are you sure?"

De Rosseley smiled. "I should be. I put him in the damned ground myself. Believe me, I stamped that earth down *hard*."

"That's not him in the ground," said Gisburne with a shake of his head. De Rosseley gave Mélisande a look somewhere between concern and bemusement. "In the heart of an Englishman," continued Gisburne, "that is where Hood lies..." He laughed bitterly. "Did you note that word? *Lies*... Lies are Hood's legacy."

"But the *man* is dead," said Mélisande. "And you are alive. And I am glad of it."

Gisburne put his hand to his eye, seemed momentarily surprised to find a bandage there, then scratched, gingerly, at its lower edge. Mélisande noticed a slight tremor to his hand. "There is one more duty yet to perform," he said. "I must tell Sir Robert Fitzwalter of the fate of his daughter." He said this as if he dreaded it more than all the bloody confrontations of past days put together.

Mélisande cast her eyes down. "What will you tell him?"

Gisburne turned his cup around on the table top. "Lies," he said. Then he looked her in the eye. "Well, wouldn't you? I always thought there was greater value in truth, but now... Sometimes lies are better."

"It's over now," she said.

"But at such a cost." He let his head drop, staring at the table top. "There was a time I could have taken it in my stride. But now..." He sighed heavily. "People talk of victory and defeat as if they are as separate things—as distinct as night and day. But I have never known one without the other. And this victory... It is more bitter than any defeat I have ever known."

De Rosseley gazed into his ale for a moment, then raised his cup. "Here's to Galfrid," he said, and they all drank in silence.

"What of you, Sir John?" asked Mélisande after a moment. The jollity sounded forced, and it was, but she'd rather that than silence.

De Rosseley took a deep breath, then let it out slowly. "Time to settle. Rest these battered bones. Become a damned farmer."

Mélisande laughed. "You think being a farmer is restful...?"

"Well, time to settle, anyway," he said. "And..."

"And?"

"There is a woman. Back home."

Mélisande's eyes widened. "This is a revelation. How did you keep *that* so quiet?" She looked to Gisburne, but he seemed so locked in his private world that not even this could coax him out.

"A revelation to me, too," de Rosseley said. "It is someone I have cared about all my life, and I never even knew it. For years I've been searching for a suitable match—a high-born lady—but the real answer was under my nose all that time. I have learned to pay attention to such things of late."

"I take it she is *not* high-born?"

"Far from it."

"That will not make you popular."

"I've been popular all my life, my lady," said de Rosseley with a smile. "Time to try something different."

Mélisande smiled. "Assuming she'll have you, of course..."

De Rosseley chuckled, and blushed. "Yes. Assuming that. But I have a good feeling about it. About everything, actually. Spring is upon us, the rains have abated. It is time for things to go right. Don't you agree, Gisburne?"

Gisburne snapped out of his reverie, but appeared entirely unaware of what had been said.

"Time for things to go right," de Rosseley said. Then, when no answer was forthcoming, he added: "So, what will you do, Guy?"

But he just shook his head. "I'm done, Ross."

Gisburne spoke little after that. Mélisande watched him sink back into a world of his own—distant, inaccessible. Back behind the walls of his fortress.

LITTLE WAS SAID as they mounted their horses. Mélisande saw de Rosseley studying the pair of them, his gaze flicking back and forth, clearly expecting something, uncertain whether he should stay or go.

So distracted was she by it that she did not even see Gisburne come up beside her.

She jumped at his sudden presence—then saw that he was holding out a small package to her. It was little bigger than a pear, wrapped in green silk and tied with a fine yellow ribbon. For a moment, she thought that was what it was. She thought of Llewellyn and that drink of his.

"What's this?" she said.

"A gift," he said.

She took it.

And there was nothing more after that. He did not say goodbye. He did not speak another word. He merely gave a nod to each of them, turned his horse toward the north, and rode away up the hill. The pounding of the hooves felt like blows.

There was disbelief upon de Rosseley's face as they watched him go. He looked at her, then after Gisburne, then back again.

"Somehow, I thought..."

Mélisande nodded. De Rosseley did not need to finish the sentence—anyway, she did not wish to hear it. Somehow, to utter the words would only make it more real.

He shook his head in dismay. "I don't understand."

She shrugged. It seemed a woefully inadequate gesture. "He is hurting," she said, "and needs to heal."

"He's damned lucky to be alive."

"I don't mean his wounds, Sir John."

De Rosseley frowned, then nodded.

"You said he had achieved all his goals," said Mélisande. "But in doing so he has lost everything."

"Surely not everything. In one respect, at least, I thought he had gained."

She gave a weak smile. "Gisburne asks nothing of me. He never has. Never questioned who or what I was, never asked about my past or where my loyalties lay. To him, I was just as he found me. What I said, what I did... I have never encountered anyone like that before. The one time he did ask something of me was on the battlement of Dover Castle. I almost died as a result. It was my choice to follow him, and mine alone; but he blames himself. And for Galfrid. For Asif."

De Rosseley pondered her words for a moment. "There was something he said to the King. Something about Asif. He said the man came of his own free will, and that he merely extended an invitation."

"It was true of us all," said Mélisande.

De Rosseley bowed his head, nodding slowly. "But Gisburne cannot allow himself to fully believe it."

"He wants to, but... He is not as separate from the world as he would have everyone think."

De Rosseley sighed. "I always thought that Gisburne didn't really need other people, but now I see it's just habit. He has simply spent too long on his own, relying on no one but himself."

"Haven't you done just the same?"

"Me?" De Rosseley drew himself up in his saddle and affected indignation. "I *relish* company, my lady. The good cheer, the camaraderie. We are not alike, he and I. I actively seek out the company of others."

"And then beat them senseless them with an array of weapons..."

"I dispute 'array.' I'm gregarious, but not ostentatious."

"You are different, it's true; in some ways, at least. Perhaps that's why you get along so well. But I think you're wrong about Gisburne. He needs people as much as any of us. Perhaps more."

"He will realise, one day," said de Rosseley, suddenly serious. "I am sure of it. How could he not? And this..." He gestured vaguely in Gisburne's direction. "Do not take it to heart."

But it was already far too late for that.

She smiled once more, though there was little joy in it. "He will never again ask anything of me. Of that I am sure."

GISBURNE STOPPED UPON the brow of the hill and looked back towards the inn. The two mounted figures—so familiar, even with their faces obscured by distance—were still there. He was glad of a last glimpse.

The parting had been painful. Pain upon pain. Many times he had asked himself if it was really necessary, if there were not some other way. But, hard as it was, he knew this was how it had to be. He was not her master; he did not want to be. As he had turned to leave, at a loss for words, he had tried not to look upon Mélisande's face. But of course, he had. And he had seen her pain too.

It would pass. Mélisande would understand. He had to believe that was true. And then everything would be different.

For now, though, it felt like the pain would never end.

Unable to look any longer, he wheeled Nyght about, touched his spurs to the stallion's flanks, and was gone.

DE ROSSELEY GAZED after Gisburne's departing shadow in silence.

Mélisande tried not to, but failed—and when she looked up and saw the hilltop empty, it seemed all meaning was gone from the world.

Talos snorted, and Mélisande suddenly remembered the gift, still clutched in her hand.

The last of him.

She had no desire to wait. She craved this last vestige, this last evidence of his existence. Not fragile memory, but something she could touch. Something *real*.

Holding the silk-wrapped package in her left palm, she tugged away the thin yellow ribbon.

"So, what *will* he do?" said de Rosseley, still staring northward to the vacant, darkening hill.

"Enjoy his rewards," she said distantly. "Live life."

As she spoke, she pulled on the wrapping, the gift jumping and spinning on her palm as the green silk unravelled, until finally the last of the gossamer thin material whipped away, and into her hand fell a short, heavy iron key, its bow heart-shaped.

She smiled at it. *An invitation...*

"But what good are such rewards if you're alone?" said de Rosseley.

Mélisande closed her hand about the key. "He's not alone," she said. "He never was."

Then, heart pounding, she turned her horse and spurred it towards the north.

EPILOGUE

The Tower of London
August 1204

THE JUG EXPLODED against the wall, spraying those nearest with wine.

"I know what the *problems* are!" screamed King John. "Do you think I don't?"

Richard de Percy—spattered from head to foot—wiped his eye and looked to Roger de Montbegon, who seemed about to speak, then thought better of it.

The King looked for something to hurl after it and turned on them again, his eyes wild.

"Problems, problems, *problems!*" he howled, flinging his cup, his fury so fierce that the surrounding barons, even armoured as there were, took a step back. "All you ever bring to my door are *problems!*" With the final word he turned over the table, the few remaining objects upon it—a platter, fruit, a knife—clattering and bouncing across the floor. "Well, let me tell you—I have no shortage of those. I am *rich* with those. What of *answers?* Who will bring me them? Does not one among you have the brains for it?" He paused for a moment, his eyes sweeping about the room. "Or is it the *will* you lack?"

Then he picked up a chair, and with a roar swung full circle and let it fly. The barons broke apart as it smashed against the council chamber wall, sending splinters of wood high into the air.

The problems that year had been many.

In March, Philip, the French king, had taken Château Gaillard. The key to the defence of Normandy and the Lionheart's pride and joy, it had been deemed impregnable by Richard. He once said he could defend it were its walls made of butter.

In April, John's mother, Eleanor of Aquitaine, had died. The last of her generation, an anchor during all the storms, she was the power behind three English thrones—and one French one.

In May, the city of Caen—burial place of the Conqueror—had surrendered to the French without a fight. Caen was one of the two cities upon which control of the region rested; Rouen was the other.

In June, Rouen—lacking the will to fight for John—had followed suit.

By August, the whole of Normandy—the once insignificant duchy which had conquered England and Sicily and given John's father his claim to the English throne—had slipped through John's fingers.

And they laughed at him. *Lackland*, they called him. Softsword.

Even now, Philip was striking into the very heart of Angevin territory, and was poised not only to take Poitou, but Anjou itself. The mighty empire that had been his father Henry's lifelong labour was unravelling before John's eyes, and it seemed there was nothing he could do to stop it.

It should have been possible. He had the forces, he had the will. But everywhere he was betrayed.

After the siege at Nottingham and the final reconciliation with Richard, he had served his brother loyally, right to the end. And while he was never the great military genius that his adored brother had been—his interests were too diverse, his tastes too broad—he had demonstrated he knew well enough how to deploy men, and how to lead them, too. He had shown it at Évreux, and at Gamaches. He'd shown it when he'd brought the English army within striking distance of Paris, and returned with the captured Bishop of Beauvais as a prize. He had shocked them all.

But how many of those now around him remembered?

Not one. It suited them to forget. In the relentless quest to demean him and his predecessor—to make the brilliant day of the dead king the brighter by extinguishing all light in the dark night that followed—even these achievements were now ascribed to Saint Richard the Lionheart.

John turned slowly around the chamber in the awkward silence, his eyes focused on nothing. "Get out," he muttered.

De Percy took a step forward. "My lord, if we—"

John turned on him like a wild dog.

"*GET—OOOOOUT!*" He held on to the last syllable until his breath was spent, his mouth dripping venom, his face so red it looked fit to burst. Half the company had quit the room before the roar ended.

He stood, then, in the emptied chamber, gradually recovering his breath. *The Angevin temper...* It was known, even celebrated. Richard had it; his father Henry had it. Quite clearly, he had it too. It was the result, so it was said, of the Angevin dynasty being descended from the Devil. Old King Henry had liked that story. That being the case, how could anyone blame John for these histrionics? They were his inheritance.

He chuckled to himself. Spying a flask of wine that had escaped the mayhem by the fire, he hunted around for a cup—booting a pomegranate across the floor as he did so—found one, filled it, and gulped it down. That eased things a little. He filled it again. No, they couldn't blame him; but they would anyway.

A sound made him stop, the cup at his mouth.

No servant would enter so soon after his outburst—they knew better. For a moment he thought it must be that bastard de Percy coming creeping back. If anyone would it was he, with some new argument, some new complication, some new problem. But de Percy, like the others, had left by the southwest stair. The sound—a footstep, he was sure of it—had come from the northern end of the chamber.

John squinted through the arches that joined this chamber to the next, trying to penetrate the shadows there. He could see nothing; hear nothing. And then one of the shadows stirred and began to approach.

It was black from head to foot, and immediately familiar.

"Welcome back to the White Tower, Sir Guy," he said with a

smile. Gisburne stopped and stood before him, his head slightly bowed. John looked about him at the broken, scattered objects. "Sorry about the mess," he said.

The knight was dressed in the familiar, black horsehide coat, although this one looked brand new. A leather patch covered his lost left eye. He seemed hardly to have aged.

John chuckled to himself. "Well, I know better than to ask how you got in..."

"Do not let anyone blame the guards on duty," said Gisburne.

"I'll make certain of it. It's my castle now, I can do as I like."

Gisburne walked over to the table, righted it, then placed a heavy gold ring upon its top. John stepped forward to investigate.

"God's teeth," he said. "This is my personal seal. Where did you get it?"

"You gave it to me."

"Did I?" John raised his eyebrows, struggling to recall. If he had, it must have been years ago. A decade, at least. "You could have been issuing writs and edicts in my name all this time..." Then he laughed to himself. "But you never would, of course. Truth be told, it was probably safer in your hands than mine."

He gave a mirthless laugh, then gestured to the chaos of destruction about the chamber—which only now struck him as a symbol of the realm as a whole. "You're not quite catching me at my best." He gave a deep, shuddering sigh. "Normandy has decided they prefer to bend over for the French King than to fight for me, my barons openly snipe and criticise and not even my mother is around to quell them."

"It's worse than that," said Gisburne flatly.

He smiled. "Well, it's good to see you, too." Turning the ring idly in his fingers, he stared for a moment at the knight's face, half in shadow. A thousand questions jostled in his mind—but just one fought its way to the front.

"I said I would never call upon your services," said John, "and I never have. Not in all these years. And in all that time you have never come to me. Why now?"

Gisburne lifted his head. "Because you're going to need me," he said.

ACKNOWLEDGEMENTS

A great many remarkable people have contributed in some way
the Hunter of Sherwood trilogy—from historians and novelists to
re-enactors and makers of bits of medieval kit. There are some—
chance encounters at one event or another—whose names I never
knew, and others who never realised they were contributing (a lucky
escape for them; plausible deniability and all that). All are due my
gratitude, nonetheless. So, accepting the near inevitability that some
will be missed, I would like to thank:

Stuart Orme, Chris Carr, Dominic Sewell, Ian Flint, David S.
Baker, Dara Hellman, Dan Melia, Gillian Pollack, Allen W. Wright,
Robert Fortunaso, James L. Matterer, Alison Weir, Tom Asbridge,
W. L. Warren, Bernard Cornwell, Imad ad-Din al-Isfahani, William
FitzStephen, Bridget Clifford at Royal Armouries, Emily Fildes
at Historic Royal Palaces, English Heritage, John and Anita Van
Hassel of Windrose Armoury, Nev Wilson and everyone at Avalon
Archers, Nick Winter at Arbalist Armoury, The Longbow Shop,
Kristoff Mussolini of Irondale Longbows, Dave Greenhalgh (Dave
the Moneyer), Peter Crossman of Crossman Crafts, the legendary
Tod of Tod's stuff—maker of Gisburne's eating knife—and most of
all my long-suffering family, my equally long-suffering editor David
Moore, and Jason Kingsley, for horse sense and for first having the
idea to make Gisburne the hero.

ABOUT THE AUTHOR

Toby Venables is a novelist, screenwriter and journalist who also lectures in Cambridge, England. He inhabits various time periods and occasionally writes about zombies. A descendant of the Counts of Blois and Champagne, he numbers the slayer of the Moston dragon among his ancestors, but despite being given a longbow at the age of twelve has so far managed not to kill anyone. In 2001 he won the Keats-Shelley Memorial Prize, and squandered the proceeds. Hood is his fourth novel.

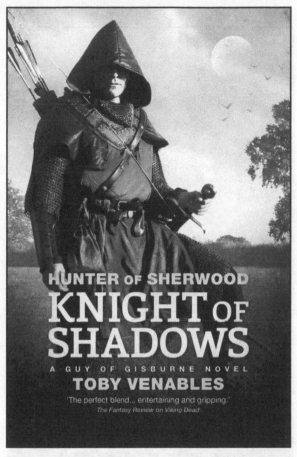

HUNTER OF SHERWOOD
KNIGHT OF SHADOWS
A GUY OF GISBURNE NOVEL
TOBY VENABLES
'The perfect blend... entertaining and gripping.'
The Fantasy Review on *Viking Dead*

England, 1191. Richard Lionheart has left the realm bankrupt and leaderless in his quest for glory. Only Prince John seems willing to fight back the tide of chaos threatening England – embodied by the traitorous 'Hood.'

But John has a secret weapon: Guy of Gisburne, outcast, mercenary, and now knight. His first mission: to intercept the jewel-encrusted skull of John the Baptist, sent by the Templars to Philip, King of France. Gisburne's quest takes him, his world-weary squire Galfrid in tow, from the Tower of London to the hectic crusader port of Marseilles – and into increasingly bloody encounters with 'The White Devil': the fanatical Templar de Mercheval.

Relentlessly pursued back to England, and aided by the beautiful and secretive Mélisande, Gisburne battles his way with sword, lance and bow to a bitter confrontation at the Castel de Mercheval. But beyond it – if he survives – lies an even more unpredictable adversary.

Also by Toby Venables

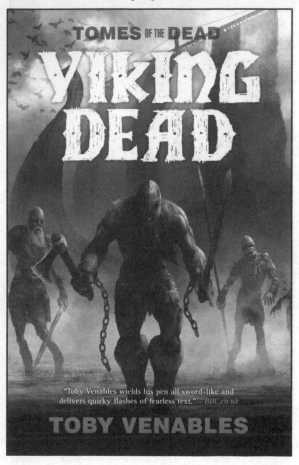

UK ISBN: 978 1 907519 68 0 • US ISBN: 978 1 907519 69 7 • £7.99/$9.99

Northern Europe, 976 AD. Bjólf and the viking crew of the ship *Hrafn* flee up an unknown river after a bitter battle, only to find themselves in a bleak land of pestilence. The dead don't lie down, but become draugr – the undead – returning to feed on the flesh of their kin. Terrible stories are told of a dark castle in a hidden fjord, and of black ships that come raiding with invincible draugr berserkers. And no sooner has Bjólf resolved to leave, than the black ships appear...

Now stranded, his men cursed by the contagion of walking death, Bjólf has one choice: fight his way through a forest teeming with zombies, invade the castle and find the secret of the horrific condition – or submit to an eternity of shambling, soulless undeath!